WAKE THE NEIGHBORS

WAKE THE NEIGHBORS

RICHARD ADAMSON

www.blackrosewriting.com

Black Rose Writing | Texas

ISBN: 978-1-68513-112-8
PUBLISHED BY BLACK ROSE WRITING
www.blackrosewriting.com

Printed in the United States of America
Suggested Retail Price (SRP) $22.95

Wake the Neighbors is printed in Calluna

To Helene.

To Helene.

CHAPTER ONE

He didn't want to look. But of course he had to. That's one of the first rules of driving a car — look where you're pointing the thing. And so he did. And what he saw angered him. Just as he'd expected it would. Frightened him a smidge, too. That was a surprise.

The flock blanketed his front lawn like a giant feather eiderdown, each bird facing this way, glaring straight at him. Mocking. Taunting. Snickering.

Phil stomped on the pedal — not the brake, the gas. He didn't want to kill the birds, just scare them a little. The same way they scared him. But of course, that's impossible. These birds don't scare. Ever.

As Phil's snazzy sports car buzzed past the flock, the birds remained motionless. Like gravestones. Not a single feather twitched. Perched on their skinny rod legs, crammed in tight, beak-to-beak, wing-to-wing, ass-to-ass, the ridiculous waterfowl had transformed Phil's elegant emerald lawn into a silly sea of pink. How many birds had gathered to mock him? Phil didn't bother to count heads — he knew exactly how many. Fifty birds. One plastic flamingo for every year of Phil's life.

He had asked her not to do this. Birthday parties are for young men — men with something to celebrate — not for middle-aged saps struggling to stay relevant in a youth-centric industry where thirty is up the hill, forty is on top of the hill, and fifty is over the hill. Yes, it all comes down to prepositions. And dirt. *Up*, *on*, *over*, and eventually *under*.

Carol had promised not to make any fuss over his big day, but he knew she had something up her sleeve. Why else would she have insisted he keep his golf date despite those thunderstorms in the forecast. *A shame about poor Phil getting struck by lightning on the third hole. That's a very painful place to get struck. And on his birthday, too. But hey, at least none of the flamingos was hit.*

Phil's golfing partner was Kevin, Carol's brother. Kevin claimed he had never seen the weather forecast, which was probably true considering the guy spends all his time on the internet posting conspiracy theories. Phil didn't know which threw off his golf swing more today — trying to ignore those distant thunder claps or trying to ignore his brother-in-law's latest claim that the Chinese government was putting listening devices in breast implants.

Phil slowed his car and looked up at the house. He wondered if his sexy sister-in-law will be at the party. If so, he'd better watch what he says around her new boobs.

The street seemed fairly quiet — the guests must have parked their cars around the corner so they can surprise him. Well, if it's a surprise they want, it's a surprise they'll get.

Phil did not turn into his driveway. He thumbed his nose at the birds, planted his foot firmly on the gas pedal, and gunned his Corvette. He'll turn back soon, of course — he doesn't want to be a jerk about this — but before he tackles those hilarious gag gifts and rip-snorting birthday cards he's got to psyche himself into the proper mood. And he knows just how and where to do it.

Phil shifted down to first and pulled a sharp left at the end of his block. It's time to go visit some real birds. Live birds. No, not strippers. Actual birds. If he's going to pull himself out of this funk, he's got to go confer with his favorite team of spiritual advisors. Ducks can listen and nod knowingly as well as any psychiatrist can, and very few shrinks will work for popcorn.

Phil turned onto the Lakeshore Expressway and five minutes later was at the park, slowly extricating himself from his car. The vintage 'Vette had been a gift from his darling wife for his forty-eighth-birthday — two whole flamingos ago. She had meant well, and he loves her dearly for it, but he does not love the car. In winter, the thing skims too low to plow through the drifts to the ski hills. And in summer it offers no room for his golf clubs. Not a full set, at least. And forget strapping his kayak on top. But size isn't the worst thing about this car. What Phil hates most is the way the vehicle constantly reminds him that his knees aren't what they used to be. Every time he climbs out of the thing he feels like an old man struggling to get out of the bathtub.

Before walking down to the waterfront, Phil stopped by the refreshment stand and bought a bag of popcorn. The smell of the buttery treat stirred his appetite. Geez, he was feeling better already. The sky had cleared and the soft evening breeze blew sweet birthday kisses from across Lake Michigan. The park's beach front bustled with the tender lilt of children laughing and lovers not laughing. In the shallow waters a gaggle of ducks paddled aimlessly, waiting for handouts as payment for their charming company like bar girls in a western saloon. And the best part — not a single flamingo in the flock.

Phil has always liked ducks. When he used to walk Scout here, he would never let the pooch bother the l'il quackers. And whenever Phil and Carol dine at the Chinese joint, Phil never orders Peking Duck. Hell, it would be like eating a dog. Carol, on the other hand, has no trouble ripping into a juicy mallard or whatever model waterfowl the Asian cooks prefer to boil up for her. Heck, she'll eat just about anything. She's very practical that way. Every other way, too. Birthdays don't faze her. But then, why should they — she's four years younger than Phil and she works in residential real estate, a pursuit where middle-aged women thrive. Home buyers trust an older woman. Makes them feel like they're buying a house from their mother. It's not like that in the public relations and advertising racket. Especially for a man. Few millennials will trust their father with the marketing of their latest hot new, totally awesome ginseng energy drink or ginseng shower gel or ginseng small engine oil. Seems the only campaigns Phil scores these days are for prescription medicines. Mostly boner pills. Many with ginseng.

Phil planted his fifty-year-old butt on the worn wooden slats of his favorite bench and flicked a piece of popcorn into the water. A couple of ducks scrambled for the prize. Phil tossed out another piece. The winner this time was the same duck who'd snatched up the first piece. So Phil cocked his arm well back and aimed his next morsel squarely at the loser duck. The slower duck. The older duck. The duck with the enlarged prostate. Phil flung the puffed kernel hard and fast to make sure the buttery treat hit its mark close to the elderly bird's arthritic, weak-sighted, iridescent, balding head.

"What ya tryin' to do — kill him?"

Phil was surprised to hear the man speak. He'd assumed the old fellow sitting at the far end of the bench with his eyes shut was asleep.

"Just trying to make sure every duck gets his piece," Phil explained.

"You sound like a girl I used to date."

Phil laughed. He held out his bag of popcorn to the man.

"Don't mind if I do." The old guy stuck his long skinny fingers into the paper bag and pulled out a big greasy handful of buttered corn. "Thank you, kind sir."

The first thing Phil had noticed about the man was his full head of silver hair. More and more nowadays, Phil finds himself envying old guys with thick hair. Phil's hair was thinning. It was also turning gray. He had tried dying it, but the darkened strands just drew attention to the large areas of pink sub-flooring showing through. Hey, maybe that's why Phil didn't like those pink flamingos — they reminded him of his pink bald spot. Looks like this session with the ducks is already starting to pay dividends in self-awareness.

Phil offered the old fellow another handful of popcorn which the man eagerly accepted. Slim, fit, and clean-shaven, the guy was no park bum — his designer jeans didn't shout out any cheap big-box label that Phil was familiar with, and the beige sports jacket worn over an untucked black t-shirt whispered top-quality linen, not rayon or polyester. All-in-all, quite a hip look for a man in his late sixties, early seventies. But there was one thing wrong with the picture.

The fellow's clothes didn't fit. They were too small. The legs of his jeans and the sleeves of his sports jacket didn't finish their full journey to where they ought to be, thereby leaving the impression of a growing boy wearing last year's wardrobe. Or more likely, a father who has raided his son's closet.

The man stuck his hand once again into Phil's bag of popcorn, this time announcing as an excuse for his enthusiastic appetite, "My birthday."

"You're kidding!" Phil turned more fully toward the old man and cocked one knee up onto the bench. "Mine, too."

"Uh, huh..." The old guy seemed highly unimpressed by the temporal coincidence. He just nodded toward the ducks and said, "So every year you celebrate by trying to put a waterfowl's eye out."

Phil turned back toward the lake and lobbed another piece of popcorn to the birds. "The big five-oh."

"Congrats," mumbled the man between chews.

"Yeah, sure, thanks. Same to you."

The man reached over and dug out another mittful of popcorn. He truly seemed hungry. "Fifty, huh. You don't seem any too thrilled about it."

"Who'd be thrilled about turning fifty?"

"For starters, anybody who'd got hit by a buffalo stampede at forty-nine." The old man tossed a piece to the ducks. "You know, there are worse things than turning fifty."

Phil understood the man's point. "Yeah, I suppose to you fifty must look pretty young."

"To *me*?" The man straightened up in defiance. "You're assuming quite a lot, aren't you, pal?"

"I… I'm sorry, but I—"

"I'm just yankin' your chain. Yeah, I suppose I've got a few years on you." The man reached over and snatched still another handful of popcorn. He probably thought Phil owed him for the insult. "Fifty, huh? So tell me, sonny, you got your driver's license yet?"

"Driver's license?" Phil didn't understand. "Of course, why wouldn't I—"

"Just yankin' it again. Geez, man, lighten up."

"Sorry. You got me at a bad time." Phil smiled and extended his hand out for the man to shake, "Phil. Excuse the butter."

The man grasped Phil's greasy hand. "Zachariah. Excuse the hydrogenated corn oil and petroleum derivative that looks a lot more like butter than it tastes."

"Pleased to meet you, Zachariah."

"Call me Zack. All my younger friends do."

"Yeah? What do your older friends call you?"

"Brenda. Their eyesight ain't too good."

Phil laughed. He liked this guy. "Live around here, Zack?"

"Just passing through. Haven't seen Chicago for…" The man looked to the sky and started to calculate the exact number of years on his fingers but soon waved the effort away and just said, "for a long, long time."

"Guess there's been some changes since you were here last."

The man huffed and shook his head. "You don't know the half of it. Yes, quite a few changes."

"I don't like change." Phil waited for a reaction. He expected the old guy to heartily agree with this simple comment. But Phil was wrong.

"You don't like change?" the old man said with obvious disapproval. "Why that's just stupid. That's like saying you don't like life itself."

"You think change is good?"

"You ever been to a nineteenth-century dentist?"

"Happily, no."

"Believe me, change can be good." The man licked his fingers. "Except for what they've done to butter." The man took out a clean white handkerchief and wiped his fingers with it. "It's nice to get out and see some change. Some of us are hungry for change. Some of us find change satisfying, refreshing."

"Gotcha." Phil had it now. He understood where this guy was coming from. Literally, coming from. "A fugitive from a rest home, huh?"

Zack thought this one over for a moment before answering, "You know, Phil, you're absolutely right. A rest home. That's exactly what I'm running away from."

"I guess those places can get pretty dull."

"You can say that agai—" Zachariah suddenly started coughing. Or maybe choking.

Phil patted him on the back. Gently. "Popcorn go down the wrong way?"

"Not really, but I'll take that as an excuse if you'd like to buy me a drink."

"Of course." Phil glanced back toward the concession stand where he'd bought the popcorn. "What can I get you, Zack? Juice? Soft drink? A bottle of water?"

"Don't suppose they sell beer?"

"'Fraid not, but..." Phil suddenly got an idea. He turned to the old man. "Zack, how are your teeth?"

"Fine, thank you. How are your balls?"

"All present and accounted for, thank you. Tell me, when was the last time you sank your chompers into a good solid steak. I don't mean that machine-tenderized leather they dish out at the nursing home. I'm talking a two-inch-thick char-broiled sirloin."

"A two-inch sirloin?" The man thought this one over. "Geez, let's see... musta been eighteen-and-forty-three. Delmonico's in Abilene. Before they put in that swishy salad bar."

"Eighteen-forty-three?" Phil laughed. "You must be a little older than you look."

"You got that right." The man said.

"Zack, my friend," Phil sprang to his feet and clapped his hands. "How would you like to be guest of honor at a party? A birthday party."

"Tonight?"

"Tonight."

"Will there be beer?"

"Imported and domestic."

"Dancing?"

"Jitterbug, rock, and boogaloo." Phil added, "Although none of the ladies will be quite your vintage."

Zack smiled. "I'm in."

CHAPTER TWO

Carol Hodworth tucked the blanket up under the old fellow's chin and asked, "You sure there's nobody I can call?"

"I'll be fine, Carol." Zachariah Mossip slipped his arms out from under the plush blanket and adjusted his pillow. "You'd think at my age I'd know enough not to mix beer with champagne. I'm truly sorry."

"You, my friend, have nothing to apologize for. My husband, on the other hand..." Carol looked across the room at Phil who was passed out in the leather recliner chair, feet up, head back, eyes closed, snoring and snorting like an asthmatic bull. "He should know better."

"Don't be too hard on Phil," Zachariah said. "He's going through a rough time. He'll soon—" Zachariah started coughing again but managed to finish his sentence, "He'll soon adjust. We all do."

Carol sat down on the edge of the thin mattress of the pull-out bed that had, moments ago, been a sofa. The springs creaked as she handed the elderly fellow his glass of water from the end table. Zachariah propped himself up on one elbow so he could take a sip.

When he finished, Carol took the glass from his frail hand and slowly eased him back down on his back again.

She was worried about the poor guy, the way his health had deteriorated so quickly. When Phil first brought him in to the party, Zachariah had looked to be in his late sixties, but somehow during the past few hours he seemed to have aged ten years. Carol patted the thin, hard mattress and said, "You should let me give you a proper bed. Nate won't mind."

"No, no. I'm not putting an eight-year-old out of his bunk. This will do just fine, Carol. Much softer than the cot at the hostel. I'm sure I'll sleep like a baby." He patted Carol's hand. "Just don't you let me sleep late, okay? My bus leaves at nine-forty."

"If you say so." Carol didn't like the idea of this elderly gentleman taking a long bus trip. Not with his cough. Once again, she told him, "You're welcome to stay here with us for a few days. It's the least I can do. I really do owe you one." Carol looked over again at her unconscious husband. "Without you, Sleeping Beauty would have wimped out, maybe missed his party altogether. Phil doesn't like birthday parties, especially his own."

"He would have missed a good one," Zachariah said. "You're a heck of a dancer, Carol."

"I had a good partner." Carol tenderly patted his knee, and then she stood up. She was anxious to get upstairs and load the dishwasher. "Don't you worry, we'll get you on that bus in time. Although, I don't see why a grown man with no children is in such a hurry to go all the way to Disney World when there are so many other nice places to—" Carol stopped herself. She'd suddenly remembered what particular group of men without kids went to Disney World. She looked down at the man, her face frozen in poorly concealed realization. "Oh, I'm sorry."

He laughed. The sparkle in his eye affirmed he wasn't offended. Still, Carol had to finish her point. "You're gay?" she asked.

Zachariah nodded... "as a truckload of confetti."

Carol gave his blanketed toes a squeeze. "No wonder you dance so well."

Zachariah started to chuckle, but his laughter dissolved into another coughing fit. Carol handed him the glass of water again.

She watched him closely as he sipped. She didn't know if it was the bad light in here or what, but the old dear's skin actually seemed to be turning a sickly shade of gray as if the blood were literally draining from his face as he drank. She asked him once more: "You must have somebody I can call. Somebody in... what was the name of that town you said you were from?"

"Perpetuity... Perpetuity, Wyoming."

"Odd name."

"Odd town."

Carol wanted to keep Zack talking. She needed reassurance that she was right in not calling for medical help. So she sat down on the bed again. "I've always wanted to live in a small town," she said.

"You have?" Zack seemed surprised.

"I don't like the city."

"Have you ever lived in a small town?"

"No."

"Take it from me, small towns aren't all they're cracked up to be. There's nothing wrong with the city."

"You ever try to raise kids in the city?"

"Can't say as I have."

"It's not easy. But I'm afraid I'm stuck here." Carol looked over to her husband who was snoring away, his mouth hanging open like he was waiting for the dentist to check on his insurance. She said, "Drooling banjos over there says small towns are for people who've given up on life. He claims that he *requires* the city. He *feeds off the energy. The vibes keep him young.*"

"He may have a point. I'm sure the action helps."

"Bullshit, if you'll excuse my French. What keeps a person young isn't what's outside — it's what's inside. Look at you. You were dancing up a storm tonight. Now, I don't know which particular birthday you were celebrating today, but—"

"My one hundred and eighty-seventh."

Carol laughed at his little joke. "And I must say you don't look a day over a hundred and eighty. And why? Because you think young. It's not *where* you live, it's *how* you live."

"Geez, Carol, I don't know…"

"Besides, what's wrong with getting old?"

"I have no idea," Zack said. "Although I'm learning rather quickly."

"You're not old. You're mature. Well-aged. Like good cheese."

"That would explain the smell."

Carol gave him a playful slap on the knee and stood up. He seemed all right. And she was anxious to load that dishwasher. "Now, is there anything else I can get you before I leave?"

"Matter of fact, there is one thing."

"What?"

"Would you happen to have a pen and paper?"

Carol pulled open a drawer in the end table and took out a ballpoint and a scratch pad. "It's Nate's," she said, handing him the pen. "He likes to make notes when he watches the Weather Channel." Carol glanced at the top page of the pad. "I see tomorrow's going to be partly sunny and sixty-two. Barometer rising. Nate wants to be a meteorologist."

Zack examined the page. "That's very good writing for an eight-year-old. He even spelled Fahrenheit correctly. He's a bright boy. But I'm not surprised."

"Well, I am. Could have gone either way." On that cue, Carol looked over at her sleeping husband who was now barking like a circus seal expecting more fish. "I guess I'd better give Zippy a poke. You certainly can't sleep with that going on."

"Leave him alone. I'll be fine."

"But it's like sleeping next to a leaf blower."

"My dear, last night I slept in a room with five men, each of them sawing wood louder than the next. Next to that, this room is like a library."

"Well, if you're sure."

"I'm sure. And on behalf of both Zippy the seal and myself, let me say thank you. It was a lovely party. A perfect way to end another year."

"And start a new one." Carol wanted to end this on a positive note, so she announced, "Next stop, Disney World." She started to reach for his bedside lamp. But he stopped her.

"If you don't mind, leave that light on. I have a few notes to make."

"Of course." Then she thought of something. "If you want to write a letter home, maybe I can text or email someone?"

"No, thanks. This is just a memo for myself."

"Then I'll see you at breakfast. On our way to the bus station we'll stop by the hostel for your bags."

"No need. I told you, I can grab a cab."

"Won't hear of it," she insisted. And lastly, as she left the room, Carol gave him a big happy thumbs up. "Next stop, Magic Kingdom."

Zachariah Mossip returned her optimism with a big thumbs up of his own. But if Carol had to be honest, the way that skinny old thumb was shaking she feared the only magic kingdom this nice elderly fellow was likely to be seeing anytime soon was not in Florida. And it didn't boast any cartoon mice.

And certainly no spinning tea cups.

CHAPTER THREE

Phil Hodworth woke up facing several mysteries.

First, how long had he been sleeping in this recliner chair? This was an easy question to answer. One look at the pale sunlight filtering through the basement windows told him he had slept late but not so late that the kids were up, because if they were up, he'd know it.

Second mystery: What was that bed doing here? There's no bed in this room. *Oh, right, yeah, the sofa converts. We've never subjected any guests to sleeping in the thing after Carol's brother threatened to sue for his bad back. But it converts.*

Good. Two mysteries down. One more to go. Namely, who is that person lying in the sofa bed? And does he have a good lawyer?

Phil couldn't see the occupant's face. But it must one of the party guests. Someone who drinks too much and is too cheap to order a cab. But who? This is a tough one. The description fits so many of Phil's friends.

"Good morning, sir."

Phil turned to see eight-year-old Nate step into the doorway.

"We're out of fuckin' milk."

"Quiet, son." Phil pointed to the sleeping house guest. "You'll wake him. Or her."

"Sorry," Nate whispered. The kid was foul-mouthed but kind.

Still wearing his flannel Chicago Blackhawks pajamas, the tousle-headed little scamp tip-toed over to his father's leather chair and whispered respectfully, "Sir, we're out of fucking milk."

Phil whispered back, "I told you not to use that word."

"What's wrong with saying *milk*?" Nate smiled. Unlike his father, the kid could never make a wisecrack without smiling.

"You know what I mean."

Nate didn't give up. "But we're alone. Just us men."

Phil had nobody to blame for this but himself. He had told the boy that hockey players do sometimes swear but only when they were alone with other hockey players. Never around women. The topic had come up a couple of months ago when Phil took Nate to a Blackhawks game and made the mistake of sitting near the bench.

"Be quiet," Phil said, indicating the bed. "He's sleeping."

"I don't fuckin' think so."

Phil had had enough. "Okay, young man, I don't ever want to hear that word from you again. Never ever. Do you understand?"

"But, sir—"

Phil kept his voice low. "And stop calling me *sir*. It won't help. I don't care that Aiden's parents are shipping him off. You're too young to go away to military school." Phil sat up and slipped his shoes on.

"Aiden says they have an awesome electronics lab."

"That'll be for the older boys."

"And a stable. With horses."

"They'll be for the girls."

"There are no girls."

Phil hadn't thought of this. "No girls? Geez, Nate, why would you want to go to a school with no girls?" Phil knew that his son liked girls. He liked them very much. Sometimes too much, according to his teacher.

Phil hefted himself out of the big easy chair and walked to the sofa-bed so he could get a better look at his sleeping guest.

Nate said, "No girls means I won't have to watch my language. I can say any words I want."

Phil carefully pulled back the covers and took a look at the man's face. "Holy shit."

"Like that one," Nate said.

Phil could hardly believe his eyes. He barely recognized the man. The poor fellow certainly didn't look this bad last night. Could it be that the cool, hard light of morning has carved out all these jagged lines and wrinkles? Could the bright white sunlight be bleaching out the pink skin and leaving behind this sickly grey pallor? Last night, under the soft yellow lamplight the old guy looked to be in his early seventies. Now he looked to be in his early hundreds.

"Who is he?" Nate asked.

"Shhh! We don't want to wake him."

"I wouldn't worry about that," Nate said.

The boy had a point. Phil called softly to his guest, "Zack? Oh, Zack?" Phil kept his voice low, afraid that speaking too forcefully might blow the delicate old fellow into dust, like puffing on a dandelion ball. "You okay, old fella?" he asked.

Phil might as well have been talking to the plastic flamingoes. The man didn't stir. Phil tried once more. A little louder this time. "Morning, Zachariah. How you doing, pal? Have a nice sleep?"

Still nothing. Phil knew he should touch the old guy, give him a little nudge, feel for a pulse, but Phil was a coward when it came to death. At his own mother's funeral he refused to go near the open casket. Carol, on the other hand, had no problem with it. Always a practical sort, she had gently taken Mom's cold hand and slipped the wedding ring from Mom's stiff finger because Mom had said she wanted the ring to go some day to Nate's bride. Phil wished Carol were down here now.

Phil said, "We better call an ambulance."

"Good. Maybe *they* can get my pen back." Nate reached out to touch the old man's right hand.

"No, Nate." Phil swept his boy's hand away. That's when he noticed the ballpoint pen clutched in the old man's thin, boney fingers.

Nate said with over-exaggerated frustration, "But I gotta write down this morning's temperature, humidity, barometric pressure."

Phil screwed up his courage and touched the old man's wrist. Yup, ice cold. He felt for a pulse. Nothing. Phil sighed, "Aw, hell."

Nate placed his hand on his father's arm and urged it away from the old man's hand. "That's okay, sir. I can use a pencil."

Nate always was a sympathetic boy.

• • •

Phil and Carol stood on the porch and watched the paramedics carry the stretcher down the front steps. The two attendants had an easy lift — by Phil's estimation their skinny burden, now covered head-to-toe in a white cotton blanket, couldn't have weighed more than a hundred and twenty pounds.

The county medical examiner had come and gone. So had the officer from the sheriff's department who would be the man responsible for locating the next of kin.

As the two ambulance attendants weaved their grim way across the front lawn, Phil called out, "Careful. Don't trip over the flamingos."

Along the street, half the neighborhood had trickled out of their doorways to settle themselves into small clumps along the sidewalk like clots of cholesterol along a hardened artery. In this old, quiet neighborhood the appearance of an ambulance or a fire truck always attracts special attention. So does a police car, although that particular attention is usually confined to the parting of drapes.

Phil called down to his son, "Out of the way, Nate." The curious boy had his head stuck inside the open rear doors of the ambulance.

At this point, Phil and Carol's seventeen-year-old daughter, Taylor, stepped out of the house. Her head was bowed but not with respect to her Mom and Dad's recently departed house guest. She was just looking at her smart phone. "So, like, how do you spell it?" she asked.

"Spell what?"

"The dead guy's name. Zachariah-what's-its."

"What are you doing?" Carol asked.

"Posting about Dad's party. I want to show how some of our guests prefer to leave feet-first."

Carol now realized Taylor was using her phone to shoot a video. She grabbed the instrument from her daughter's hands. "Show some respect."

Phil decided this was a good time to go back into the house. He'd promised to fold the sofa bed away and clean up the rec room.

He went down stairs and started to gingerly peel the sheets off the mattress that covered the fold-away bed. He rolled them into a ball, being extra careful not to shake anything out onto the rug. He wondered, should he put the sheets in the laundry or burn them? He didn't see any crabs or bed bugs or anything, but that didn't mean their eggs weren't here. Sure, the old guy looked clean enough, but he confessed he had been living in hostels. Who knows what vermin the poor man might have brought along with him.

Phil inspected the bare mattress. Don't dead guys usually soil themselves? Not this one. Everything looked clean. Phil lifted the iron frame up and pushed the whole awkward contraption back into the couch. When he finally had the thing folded away, he looked around for the three cushions that finished off the conversion. And that's when he saw it.

A sheet of paper. Note paper. It was lying on the carpet. Under where the bed had just been.

At first, Phil assumed it was just Nate's usual weather notes — stats the budding meteorologist liked to jot down every morning and then mark on graphs and post on his cork bulletin board. But no.

This wasn't Nate's handwriting. This was written by an adult. A shaky adult, but an adult. Phil took the piece of paper over to the table at the end of the sofa so he could turn on the reading lamp. Lately, Phil's fifty-year-old eyes have been needing extra light.

Phil now noticed that there were actually two pages. It was some sort of letter. But wait. No letter starts with the words, *Being of sound mind and body.* This is a will. A last will and testament. Handwritten. Signed by Zachariah Gideon Mossip.

Phil sat down on the edge of the sofa. Without the cushions the sofa's springs were hard on his ass. But Phil soon forgot about his ass.

Forgot about the crabs and bedbugs too.

CHAPTER FOUR

The history of just about every small town in American includes what locals always refer to as The Great Fire. The town of Perpetuity, Wyoming, suffered its Great Fire in 1877. The first building to be rebuilt of brick rather than of wood was the saloon. The second was the church. Then the bank. Then the post office. And finally a schoolhouse. By 1879, with all necessary needs taken care of, folks decided it was time to turn their attention to artistic and cultural constructs. So they built themselves a bigger saloon. And finally an opera house.

Referred to locally as *The Op*, the Town of Perpetuity Opera House is the sort of sparkling architectural jewel most communities would flash at every opportunity. They would proudly morph its iconic image into an official town logo and print it's silhouette on Chamber of Commerce letterhead and weave it into welcome mats to be hawked in local tourist traps. But the town of Perpetuity, Wyoming, has no Chamber of Commerce. And no tourist traps. And most definitely, no welcome mats. So the beautiful Perpetuity Opera House sits in shy anonymity just off the main drag where it modestly avoids eye contact like the prettiest gal at the dance who is convinced she's chosen a gown that is far too revealing for the party.

Viewed from the street, this lovely classical building reveals a *décolletage* of French Renaissance and English vernacular styles. To view the Gothic bits, one must step inside and peek up the petticoats, high into the vaulted ceiling where great timber beams support wooden cathedral arches. From these sturdy beams hang two mammoth cast iron chandeliers, originally oil flamed but later convinced to accept, first, coal gas jets, and finally electric bulbs. Now LED's of course.

Like most buildings in Perpetuity, the Opera House has been kept in excellent repair. Its theater seats have been reupholstered many times over, and a few years ago the town cultural committee installed a state-of-the-art, multi-channel Dolby sound system. This last upgrade was hardly necessary, seeing as how the acoustics of the hall are perfect, but Mayor Sam Beckwith insists on keeping up with the times. It's a matter of optics. And in Perpetuity, optics are survival.

Mayor Sam Beckwith is an expert in survival. That's why the citizens originally hired him as their wagon master and why today, every four years or so, they appoint him their mayor. Survival, in fact, is why Sam Beckwith has called this meeting here at the Op tonight.

Sam stepped up to the lectern and tapped the microphone with two calloused fingers, "Testing, testing, one, two, thr—" The powerful Dolby audio system protested his silly words with an ear-piercing squeal of feedback.

"Jesus, Sam," Jesse Black called out from the back of the room. "Would ya turn that damn thang off before ya deafen ol' Lorelei even more."

Lorelei shouted back, "Who you callin' a whore?"

Sam switched off the mike and looked out at the audience. As always, the house lights were up so he could see the entire crowd, if such a meager turnout could be called a *crowd*. Barely one hundred of the theater's three hundred and twenty-four seats were occupied.

So sad. Meetings nowadays, even important ones like this one, rarely pull in more than a handful of the valley's twelve hundred and eighty-eight residents.

Sam cleared his throat and projected his husky voice to the back of the room just as he used to do as wagon master out on the trail when he addressed these exact same people from the back of his horse. Sam looked at nobody in particular as he bellowed, "Well, friends, looks like we've lost another one."

A few groans. A curse word or two. Especially from Clay Dawson. "Shit, Sammy. Who the hell now?"

"Zachariah Mossip," Rupert Thatcher answered from the other side of the theater.

"Zack's gone?" remarked Leonard Stahlmeyer in surprise. "I was wondering why the Gardens was closed."

"Shame," Frieda Bjorquist offered. "Saw the sign on the front door. Figured Zack's fridge had busted again."

"Didn't Bob Gilchrist put a new compressor in that thing last October?" Clay asked.

"Thermostat, not a compressor," said Bob Gilchrist. "And it was early September. Runs good."

"Yeah, sure, I know, I know." Leonard said impatiently. "But after you installed the new thermostat the compressor went. Took a week and a half to get a new one. I remember 'cause I let Zack stash his chicken balls in my icebox."

"It ain't an *icebox* — it's a fridge," said Clay. "Geez, dude, ya sound like you're two hundred years old."

"Shows what you know, Clay. We didn't have no iceboxes two hundred years ago."

"Yes we did."

"How would you know?"

"My ma told me about 'em."

"Yeah? Well, she oughta know."

"Hey! That a crack about Ma's age?"

"No. It's a crack about her weight."

"Oh, right." Clay settled down. "Ma does tend to yo-yo a tad."

"People, people..." Sam raised his outstretched arms to try and funnel the spilled conversation back into the bottle. "Like I was saying, Zack seems to have walked. We've checked with everyone in the valley. Been no sign of him for nine days now."

"Well, I for one am not surprised." said Mildred Spivak. "It was only a matter of time."

Nathanial Burkett nodded his agreement. "Young fool always was the curious one."

Roy Frith added, "Poor little guy was just lonely, ya ask me."

"Who asked ya?" someone said.

"Now see?" Roy said. "This is why I don't come to these things no more."

Mayor Sam Beckwith could only shake his head. Seems he's lost control of another meeting again. He wandered to the edge of the proscenium stage and sat down, letting his legs hang over the lip. He had learned over the years to let them talk things out.

"Nine days..." Little Eunice Cartwright shook her wee, pig-tailed head in sadness. "Silly goof probably didn't last a week."

"They never do. Not anymore."

A cold, heavy silence settled over the room like a wet shroud. Mayor Sam Beckwith decided this was a good time to finish making his announcement. He spoke quietly from his seated position, "Pastor Gorely has scheduled a memorial service this coming Sunday. The service will be *in absentia*, of course. The guest of honor will not be attending."

A few heads bowed, but not enough, Sam thought. There was a time when folks cared about losing a friend and neighbor. But not anymore. Nowadays, folks walked away from the valley far too often for anyone to work up much real grief over the loss. Willy Havelock walked last year. And just five years prior to that, Anthea Thorpe walked. And fourteen years before that, Hilliard LePage. It was getting to be a steady parade, a parade that no longer turned heads.

"Any idea where Zack was aimed for?"

Mayor Sam could have answered, but Bob Gilchrist beat him to it. "Where d'you think?"

"Oh, yeah."

"Poor guy. I hope he got far enough to shake hands with Mickey."

"We'll never know, will we, Sam," said someone in back.

"Probably not." Sam understood why the question was directed at him. He and his son usually took care of these things. "Isaac and I searched his apartment. Everything of any import was there. By all indications, it's safe to say Zack had no form of identification on him."

"Thank heavens for small miracles," said Violet Snelling.

"So who's gonna take over the restaurant?"

"We'll miss Zack," somebody said, "The kid was a hell of a cook."

"Mixed a damn fine mojito, too."

Sam got to his feet. Time to look official. "The floor is open to suggestions."

"How about Rebecca? She knows her way around a stir-fry."

"Thank you, Jed," Rebecca answered. "But I must warn you — Daddy raised me strict Baptist. There'll be no strong drink."

That was all Nathanial Burkett needed to hear. "Any other nominations?"

"How about Olive Gorely. She's got no objection to serving hootch."

"Yeah, that's the problem. She won't leave any for the rest of us."

At one time the room would have heard an immediate objection from Olive to this insult, but nowadays Olive rarely came out to meetings. Or out anywhere else.

"How about Doc Milburn? Isn't it about time we gave him something to do?" That suggestion came from Angus Murphy, and it was a darn fine idea. Except for one thing.

"True, Doc has a lot of time on his hands." Roy Frith carefully looked over the crowd to make sure Doc Milburn wasn't in attendance. Satisfied that he was not, Roy continued, "But y'all know what a butterfingers the Doc is. The man'll spill more than he serves."

Sam checked the clock on his smart phone. He was anxious to close this meeting and get back to home, watch that Hollywood dance contest show he likes. Sam slipped his phone into his pocket and wound things up with, "As you all know, Zachariah had no kinfolk, therefore, hence, and to wit, his real property shall revert to the town. During this time of probate may I remind you all to remain especially circumspect in light of—"

"Circum-who?"

"Geez, Sam," Hadley Pefferlaw said. "Would you toss that Thesaurus into your hay bailer and get back to plain English?"

Sam has taken a lot of flak for his efforts to improve himself over the years. So he just finished with, "Just watch your step, okay? And I'll see you all at the memorial service. Meanwhile, spread the word that we're looking for a new owner/operator for Shangri-La Gardens. As usual, land and business transfer will be undocumented and limited to valley residents only. The kitchen is in pretty good shape. Electrics have been upgraded to 200 amp. Somebody will want the place, I'm sure." This was a fib, of course. Sam wasn't sure of anything anymore. The valley was changing. Its people were changing. And Sam found it all quite unsettling. He didn't like change. Nobody in town liked change. Well, almost nobody.

Seems poor Zachariah Mossip was dying for it.

CHAPTER FIVE

Valerie Kohler finished reading the note and removed her wire-rimmed eyeglasses. Phil thought she would look better in darker, bolder frames, but hey, he wasn't here to give fashion advice. He was here to avoid a trip to Wyoming.

"So what's the verdict?" he asked. "No dice, right?"

"Shangri-La Gardens," she muttered to herself as she settled back in her high-backed chair and assumed a standard, lawyerly summation attitude, fingers tented as if she were praying for a more lucrative assignment. "Business plus the associated chattel. Might include the building. Might not. We won't know until we search title. State registry. Wyoming, huh?"

"Perpetuity, Wyoming," Carol said. "Ever heard of it?"

Valerie shook her head, *nope*, adding, "Western towns can have some odd names."

"I'm sure it's a lovely place," Phil said, adding, "if you're a buffalo."

Phil knew he was being a dick about this, but he felt like a fool wasting Valerie's time. This handwritten document Zachariah had left behind couldn't possibly be valid. And even if it was, the old gentleman's estate couldn't be worth the fee Valerie will charge for probating it. After all, the poor man was travelling by bus and staying in men's hostels.

"I Googled it," Carol said to Valerie. "The town seems to be nestled in a little valley in the heart of the Rockies. Looks like a very pretty spot, but small. The town has no website."

"Probably no broadband either," Phil said. "Just dial-up Pony Express."

Carol explained her husband's sour attitude, "Phil is afraid I'm going to ask him to pack up and move."

"Honey, you're free to go anytime. I told you, I'll come visit you for a month or two every summer." Phil turned to the lawyer and added, "I'm only kidding, of course. There's no way I'm spending a whole month in Wyoming."

Valerie stretched out her long thin arm and lifted the note off her desk for another look. She was a long woman — long arms, long neck, long face. This time she didn't bother with her reading glasses. "Hasn't been notarized. No witnesses. And no executor has been designated. But that said..." She waved the piece of paper like it was a white flag and she was surrendering. "If there's nothing better lying around, and nobody contests this, sure, this thing could hold water." Valerie squinted at the note's signature. "You say Mr. Mossip has no family?"

"That's what he told me," Carol said. "Apparently, he's always lived alone."

"Gay," Phil offered. "Although you wouldn't know it to look at him." Phil realized how this sounded and quickly added, "Nice fellow, though. A lot of fun. Liked his beer. Real good dancer." Phil hoped he'd saved himself. He'd never been sure about Valerie's sexual leanings. He knew she played tennis. And golf. She's never referred to a husband or a boyfriend. A photo frame sat on her desk, but it was facing away from Phil.

The attorney picked up a second document from her desk. "Death certificate says he died of pneumonia."

"He had a bit of a cough," Carol said. "But to tell the truth, it didn't sound bad. Not at first, anyway."

"Any idea what age Mr. Mossip was?" Valerie asked.

"Funny thing…" Phil leaned forward and rested his elbows on the attorney's black enameled desk. The slab of modern furniture was cold as a coffin. "That day in the park, the evening when I first met him, he looked pretty good. Not very old. Seventy, seventy-five, tops. But next morning when we found his, uh, his body and all, holy shit. Older than Job. His face was all wrinkled up like one of those ugly Chinese dogs. You know those, uh…" Phil fished for the name of the breed.

"Shar Pei?" the lawyer prompted.

Phil snapped his fingers. "That's it. Shar Pei. Overnight, from a sweet, soft spaniel to a wrinkled up, ugly-assed Asian pooch."

"Like this one?" the lawyer turned her mystery picture frame around so Phil could get a good look at the photo of her posing proudly with her fat, wrinkled, weird-looking Chinese dog.

"Right." Phil paused ever so slightly before saving himself, "I hear they're very intelligent." Phil smiled. Still, he couldn't help adding, "Not the best drivers, though." Phil chuckled at his slightly racist remark, but he was alone. Tough room.

Valerie Kohler put her wire-rimmed glasses back on again to re-examine the handwritten document. "Mr. Mossip's hand looks steady. And he claims to be of sound mind and body. He also seems to know he is dying." Valerie read the letter aloud: *Dear Phil and Carol. Thanks for making my last moments of mortal dalliance so warm and enjoyable. As a small gesture of gratitude, please accept this token of my appreciation. It's not much, but it's all I have. Don't worry about anyone contesting this document. The last thing they'll want is public attention.*

Carol said, "I thought that was rather odd."

"Indeed," said the lawyer. "And it gets odder." Valerie continued reading. *"Your presence in my home town will not be welcomed. But don't let them chase you out — not until you've discovered the secret for yourselves. I would tell you what that secret is, but Phil already*

thinks I'm a nutloaf. Many happy returns, if you so choose —
Zachariah Gideon Mossip."

Carol turned to her husband. "That true? You called him a nutloaf?"

"No. Well, maybe. But he knew I was joking."

"Nobody ever knows you're joking."

Valerie put the papers down on her desk and removed her glasses again. Too bad about those wire frames. She could look so good in dark ones. Like a hot librarian. Or a dungeon mistress. On cue with Phil's thoughts, Valerie slapped the papers into submission, saying, "This will be tied up in court for quite a while. Probating a thing like this could take years."

Phil could see the billable-hour dollar signs flipping in the lawyer's eyes like fruit symbols spinning on a slot machine, so before she had a chance to hit the jackpot he told her, "We can't afford to get involved with something like this. Why don't you just hand this thing over to whichever government agency takes care of this sort of stuff while Carol and I get on with our lives secure in the knowledge that we made a nice old fellow's last hours warm and comfortable. That's plenty good enough for us. Right, honey?" He turned and gave his wife a smile.

"Of course," said Carol. But then she added, "Although, it would be nice to talk to Zachariah's friends. Let them know how he spent his last hours."

"Good idea." Phil wanted to end this meeting on an upbeat, positive note. So he said as he stood up, "We'll search the net some more. Get Taylor to help us on her social media sites. I'm sure we'll find someone out there who knows Mr. Mossip."

But Carol stayed seated. "That isn't quite what I had in mind, Phil."

Of course it wasn't. Phil knew that.

He sat his sorry ass back down. After all, he might as well get used to sitting. Something told him he was going for a long drive.

• • •

Phil Hodworth checked his speedometer once more. Shit, he was cruising at almost eighty, and yet the local cowboys in rusty pickup trucks were passing him like he was standing still. Even the tourists in RV's and camper vans were flying by, which seemed pretty crazy considering the strong, gusty crosswinds that were blasting their broad, square asses from across the open grasslands.

The suggested speed limit on this deserted Wyoming stretch of interstate was seventy-five, but Phil concluded that such a number must not mean much when there are so few police officers around to point it out to you. The main impediments to any Wyoming driver's swift progress are the pedestrian wildlife — the wild turkeys, the deer, bison, antelope, elk, and moose. Too bad Phil hadn't driven his 'Vette here. A car like that rides so low a driver could slide right under a moose without knocking off his cowboy hat. The driver's cowboy hat, that is, not the moose's. Oh, well, at least this Toyota of Carol's is easy to get into and climb out of. And it's quiet. Maybe too quiet.

Phil checked his rear-view. Yup, Nate and Taylor were still back there — he hadn't left them at the last rest stop. Thanks to today's digital devices, the noise level of a Hodworth family road trip has decreased substantially. For eight-year-old Nate, game apps have replaced *I Spy*. And for seventeen-year-old Taylor, social media has replaced actual verbal communication with fellow passengers. As a result, this drive across four states has so far been blessedly quiet. But Phil knows such digitally induced tranquility can't last forever. It will soon end when the tall peaks of the Big Horn Mountains start playing peek-a-boo with the phone signals.

Sure enough, after an hour or so, the digital signals suffered a quick death, and Nate and Taylor were left with nothing to get on but each other's nerves. Happily, this leg of the trip should be short. According to the nice lady locked inside the Toyota's GPS, the town of Perpetuity was just a couple of hours ahead, tucked away deep within the rocky cleavage of the Wyoming mountains.

As the Toyota climbed higher, everyone noted their ears popping. Phil was surprised at how fast the mountains seemed to jump up out of nowhere. Topography is like that in Wyoming. No foothills to warn you. Just miles and miles of flat prairie grasslands that will occasionally roll up and wrinkle like a loose rug on a hardwood floor. Then all of a sudden the sub-flooring tilts skywards and Mother Nature lays down a mountainside she has shag-carpeted with pine trees. Round the next bend the fickle gal decides to redecorate, replacing the thick green forest with brown patches of alpine meadow sprinkled with beautiful bright, yellow wildflowers. And then, before your son's allergic nose has a chance to sneeze, you're back in grasslands again. Flat, windswept, totally unpopulated grasslands.

During one such lonely stretch, the Toyota's sexy GPS lady gently urged Phil off the four-lane interstate and onto an even lonelier two-lane county road. A half-hour later she suggested a sharp turn onto a rough, narrow paved cow path that slithered over sagebrush-littered steppe and zig-zagged down a switchback into a river valley. The river was presently disguised as more of a creek, but it might have been a river a few months earlier. Down here things started to green-up again, and the road, which was now paved with some sort of red rock aggregate, funneled its way into a canyon, the sort of place where outlaws of the old west might hide out. As Phil threaded his way through one particularly steep-sided gorge, the lady inside his GPS reluctantly confessed that she had lost all contact with her heavenly guidance: *Re-calculating, re-calculating. I have no idea where the hell you are. Good luck, handsome — you are now on your own.*

Abandoned in the virtual isolation of a pine-forested mountain pass, Phil's thoughts turned to the Donner party — that infamous wagon train of brave pioneers that got stuck somewhere out here one cold winter back in the nineteenth century. Didn't they resort to cannibalism after their GPS gave out? Phil thought about the motel he was headed for. He hopes it has a well-stocked mini-fridge.

This trip, needless to say, was not Phil's idea. Spending five days in Elk Scrotum, Wyoming, or whatever this place is called, was not Phil's idea of a summer vacation. But Carol wants to see this restaurant that old Zachariah has bequeathed her, and Phil owes her one. She doesn't know Phil owes her one. But he owes her one. Or more correctly he will when she finds out. And Carol always finds out.

It happened last February when Phil was assigned to entertain a couple of visiting V.I.P. clients for a weekend. The two Asian men, owners of a Korean shoe company whose ginseng-infused orthopedic inner soles Phil was hoping to tout, had never been ice fishing, and they wanted to see how they liked it. Turns out, they didn't. The fishing stunk. The weather stunk. And the local Northern Michigan craft beer stunk. So the two Korean boys got a ginseng-infused brain wave. They decided that, since they were this close to the Canadian border, why not take advantage of the low Canadian dollar and go visit the casino, the one they could see out the frosty window of their unheated fishing hut across the lake. At least the beer should be better.

Of course, while up in Canada Phil's Asian pals insisted on checking out some local Canadian culture which turned out to be a darn good idea because, with those great foreign dollar exchange rates, the breakfast buffet at that strip club was an absolute steal.

Phil wanted to tell Carol all about this slight change in plans, but his Korean buddies made him swear to keep his big American-apple-pie-hole shut. According to them, Korean wives are not as understanding as Yankee wives are.

So Phil never did tell Carol about the detour. Nor did he mention the Canadian dollars he'd lost at the blackjack table. But sooner or later she's going to find out. She always finds out. And when she does, it will be nice to have one in the bank. And that's why Phil Hodworth is now chauffeuring his sweet, understanding Yankee wife off for a week of dusty fun and giggles in East Buffalo Turd, Wyoming. Or whatever.

"Here it is, kids," Carol announced, indicating a road sign ahead. "*Perpetuity. Population 1288.*"

Phil commented, "Funny... don't most towns usually round-off their population numbers? You know, like 1280 or 1290."

From the back seat, Taylor said, "Judging by the age of that peeling paint, it's been 1288 for a long time."

"Will they be changing it now?" Nate asked.

"Changing it?"

"You know, to 1287."

It took Phil a beat, but he finally got it. "Oh, you mean since Zachariah died. I don't know, Nate. Maybe."

Carol added, "If we moved here, they'd have to change it to 1291. Down one, up four."

Taylor didn't like this arithmetic. She corrected her mother, "Up *three*. I am *so* not leaving Chicago."

This prompted Carol to muse aloud, "I wonder if they have any universities around here?"

"This is Wyoming," Phil said, "You want higher education you climb a mountain."

Nate laughed. "Good one, Dad."

Phil was happy Nate had gone back to calling him *Dad* again. That *Sir* nonsense had stemmed from a misguided effort by Nate to show how he would fit in with military culture should his father allow him to attend boarding school with his friend Aiden. Now if Carol will only ease off on this ridiculous idea of moving out here. Sure, the nice old man's bequest includes a business, but come on, a Chinese restaurant? Carol is normally the practical one in the family. But lately...

"Stop here." Carol pointed to a service station up ahead. "I need to take something for this headache."

"Headache?" Phil jumped on this like a duck on a kernel of popcorn. "Get used to it, honey. I warned you. We're over a mile high. Your brain swells."

"That's not true," Carol said.

"No? Then how come this morning I had trouble getting my hat on?"

"Is Dad joking?" Nate asked.

Carol opened the glove compartment to get to her bottle of pain pills. "Nobody ever knows, Nate."

Actually, Phil was more than happy to pull into the station. He didn't want to scare everybody, but he had been getting a little worried about the gas situation. The needle has been cuddling up dangerously close to empty for some time now. Seems the citizens of Wyoming don't like to clutter their lovely highways with silly things like gas stations.

While Carol and the kids went inside to get soft drinks Phil grabbed the handle of the gas pump and prepared to fill his tank, but before he had the gas cap unscrewed a teenage boy in overalls popped out of nowhere and grabbed the nozzle from Phil's hand. "I'll take care of that, sir."

"Oh, sure. Okay. Fine." Phil was a little taken aback. He hadn't had anybody pump his gas in twenty or thirty years.

While the kid pumped, Phil tried to make small talk. But the boy wasn't terribly chatty. What teenage boys are?

When the kid finished filling the tank, the boy checked the oil, examined the radiator coolant level, and topped up the washer fluid. All with a big shit-eating grin pasted on his fresh, organically raised face. The kid finished off the job by cleaning the windows, not just the windshield but all windows, side and back. And the headlights. Phil hadn't seen service like this since... well, ever. So when he handed the boy his credit card Phil included a couple of bucks cash tip.

"Why, thank you, mister."

"You're welcome. Tell me, is it far to the Shamrock Motor Court?"

"Far? Heck, nothin's far in Perpetuity. You just follow this road about a mile and a half to the first light."

"The *first* light?"

"The *only* light. We say *first* for a joke."

"Oh, right. Funny."

"At the light, you turn your wagons left. Don't bother waiting for the light to change — it never has. Another two miles, and you're on Main Street. The motel is on your left. Three blocks. Can't miss it. But if ya come to Betty Jane Hepplewhite's beauty parlor and taxidermy shop, you whip them ponies a sharp one-eighty on account of you gone one block too far."

"Got it. And the Chinese restaurant? That along the way?"

"Shangri-La Gardens?"

"Main street, right?"

"'Fraid she's closed. We got a nice Italian place, though. Jasper's Trattoria. And there's Stahlmeyer's Deli. Great ice cream. Hey, your young 'uns might get a kick outa the Shamrock pub. Best bison burger in town."

"Thanks. We'll check it out. But first I want to have a look at the Chinese place."

"A *look*?" The kid's warm smile cooled slightly. It didn't freeze hard enough to break off — it just sort of turned to icy slush despite the warm afternoon. "Now, why would you want to just look? I tol' you, it's closed."

"I'm sort of a friend of the owner."

"Young Zack?" The smile was definitely gone now. And Phil didn't like the suspicious look that had replaced it. "Mister, you from Chicago?"

Phil was starting to understand now. No secrets in these little places. "Yes. Just got in."

The kid's eyes narrowed slightly as he asked, "Name Hodworth?"

Phil chuckled and stretched his hand out to the boy, "Phil."

But the kid didn't accept the offer of neighborly greeting. In fact, he completely ignored Phil's hand. Just left it hanging there. Frozen in mid-air. Like Phil was showing him how to hold a tennis racquet.

The kid turned his attention to the two dollar bills that Phil had given him. Then he squinted back at Phil's face again. The boy seemed to be considering giving the money back. But he didn't. Instead, he clutched the bills tight along with Phil's credit card and hurried off to the station. When the kid got to the door of the building, Carol and the kids were just coming out, but the boy didn't stop to hold the door for them. He just sort of stepped aside, out of their way, as if they were carrying some terrible disease. Kind of rude, Phil thought. Then the kid went inside.

When Carol got to the car, Phil had to ask her, "Everything go all right in there?"

"You want this?" Carol handed him a can of cola. It wasn't his usual brand.

Phil took the soda pop from her. He felt the can, "This is warm."

His daughter, Taylor, rolled her eyes, "Lady says the fridge is tired."

Nate held up a folded brochure he'd carried out from the station's store. "Dad, can we go here?"

"Where?" Phil asked.

"A water park," Carol took the brochure from her son's hand to show Phil. "Looks like fun."

"I guess so, if you want." Phil was hardly listening. His attention was still on the doorway of the gas station. He asked Carol, "By any chance, they seem to know who you were?"

"They? Who? In there?"

"Yeah."

"Why? Were they supposed to?"

Phil didn't bother to answer — the young attendant was returning with his credit card.

The kid handed, or more accurately pushed, Phil's credit card back to him. "Cash only," the kid announced.

"Cash? But... So why'd you take my credit card?"

"I, uh... I forgot."

"Forgot? How the hell do you—?"

Carol jumped in. "Pay him the cash, honey. It's okay. We'll stop at a bank machine." She turned to the young attendant, "There a bank machine in town?"

The kid silently nodded in the affirmative. Phil fished some bills out of his pocket, extracted enough to over-pay for the gasoline, and told the kid to keep the change. The kid said nothing.

As he drove away, Phil watched the weird attendant shrink away in the rear view mirror. The teenage boy was standing perfectly still. A statue. Expressionless. No smile. No frown. No nothing. Just standing. And watching. Like those fifty damn flamingos that once stood on Phil's front lawn. And like those skinny plastic birds, this skinny plastic kid gave Phil the creeps. Phil actually shivered. His finger went to the electric button that rolled up his side window.

Seeing him closing his window, Carol automatically reached forward to adjust the AC controls. Phil stopped her. "No, don't."

"You don't want the air conditioner? Then why'd you roll up your window?"

"I felt a chill."

"A chill?"

From the back seat, Taylor said, "It's only, like, ninety degrees in here."

Carol asked him, "Are you okay"?

"Dad's joking," Nate said.

"Yeah, right, Nate." Phil felt an icy drip of sweat trickle down his spine. "I'm joking."

Carol asked tentatively, "So I can turn on the air conditioner?"

"Go ahead." He was feeling better now. He gave her knee a squeeze to let her know he was okay.

Carol looked out at the passing scenery. "Looks like good land for farming."

And she was right. Unlike much of the landscape they had been driving through since leaving Nebraska, this section of Wyoming looked like it was well cultivated. Neatly plowed rows of dark, rich soil running perpendicular to this road were waiting for something to pop up. And freshly painted wooden fencing embraced some fine, handsome horses.

"Do you think they'll have riding stables?" Taylor asked, showing some rare enthusiasm for something that doesn't have to be charged by USB cable.

"We'll ask," Carol said.

"They call it the Cowboy State," Nate said. "Not the Cow*girl* State."

"Lots of cows," Phil said, pointing to some far-off green grassy slopes.

"I think those are sheep, honey," Carol said. "Did you make that appointment with Dr. Holman yet?"

"My eyes are fine. That weird kid back there smudged the windshield."

As per instructions, Phil pulled his ponies left at the non-functioning traffic light, and a few minutes later he was hauling his wagonload of happy Hodworths down the paved, surprisingly wide main drag of beautiful downtown Perpetuity.

"There it is," Carol said, pointing to a small restaurant sitting halfway along the second block.

Phil slowed to a crawl but didn't bother to park. Carol had made an appointment to inspect Shangri-La Gardens tomorrow with a local real estate agent. So, for now, he'll just double-park here for a quick look-see. It's not like he's going to block any traffic. Not in this town. Nor anywhere else in this state.

Full-length, vertical blinds choked off any hopes for a glimpse through the restaurant's front window. Across the top of the facade, a cheap, yellow plastic sign barfed up garish, red letters announcing *Shangri-La Gardens, Chinese and American Food*. In the bottom corner of that sign, a faded phone number whispered that, if you're lucky, delivery might be available, but don't count on it. Bookending these humble promises were raised, decorative green silhouettes of what looked to be marijuana plants but were probably supposed to be bamboo trees or palm fronds or something equally unnatural to the arid climate of Wyoming. Beneath one corner of this string of lies, a single aluminum-framed door cowered in a recessed entranceway. Suction-cupped to the inside of that door, a small plastic card with a clock face announced, *Back at...* But the return time will always be a mystery — the clock had no hands on it.

All in all, this was one depressing picture. But not to the eyes of Phil's eternally optimistic real estate agent wife.

"Good location," she said. "Lots of parking. And it certainly has character."

"Think they'll have fortune cookies?" Nate asked.

"Nothing that will include me," Taylor answered. She shared her father's enthusiasm for small towns.

Phil slid his foot off the brake and allowed the car to start rolling again. Up ahead he could see the sign for The Shamrock Motor Court. Within a minute he was pulling into the parking lot.

The single-story structure comprised thirty units which were splayed out in a V-shape of two slim legs. A grassy courtyard and a small swimming pool sat nestled in the crotch. At the foot of one of those legs, a two-story big toe boasted a home, an office, and a family-style restaurant called The Shamrock Pub.

"Kid at the station says the burgers are supposed to be good." Phil omitted the part about these particular burgers, and possibly the kid, being made from game meat.

Carol pointed out a sign in the pub window, "Looks like they brew their own beer."

"I like the place already." Phil gave Carol an approving smile and wondered now why he'd let that kid spook him like that. So the kid knows who he is. Big deal. Why shouldn't he? For the past several weeks, Carol has been corresponding with some newspaper reporter here in town. The teenager at the gas station probably read the reporter's story about Zachariah's death and the family who has inherited his restaurant. Doesn't mean the weird kid is going to wish Phil into the corn field or something. Geez, man, get a grip. Phil left the engine running so Carol and the kids could enjoy the air-conditioning while he went inside the office to check in.

The wooden screen door bounced shut behind him with a satisfying *clunk*. Phil stepped up to the counter just as a man stepped out from an inner office. Phil started to identify himself, but he didn't get far. As with the kid at the gas station, this desk clerk already knew who Phil Hodworth was and what the purpose was for Phil and Carol's visit here to East Lower Skunk Scrotum, Wyoming. But then, why shouldn't the guy know? Phil had made a reservation, and a place like this can't get that many people checking in on a Wednesday afternoon in early June.

The desk clerk — a nice-looking man with an Irish accent and a matching head full of curly dark Irish hair — gave Phil four electronic room keys for two rooms. Phil thanked him and went back to the car.

Once into their rooms, a quick security check assured the kids that they had all the necessary amenities for survival — wireless internet, wide-screen televisions, mini fridges, microwaves, and free popcorn. Phil and Nate hit the pool for a quick dip and then walked the girls across the parking lot for dinner.

Turns out that kid at the gas station had told the truth — the burgers in the Shamrock Restaurant were indeed excellent. Phil got adventurous and tried an elk burger which the waitress assured him was low in fat and high in omega-3. It tasted pretty good too, although, truth be known, Phil would have tried anything this waitress recommended. She was an attractive redhead with a lush Irish accent, lush red hair, and lush freckled cleavage which, like the eyes of an old master's oil painting, always seemed to be aimed straight at the viewer. At the end of the meal Phil was tempted to ask her if she would be serving breakfast, but he didn't want to be that obvious — Carol, Taylor, and Nate would only kid him about it. As it turned out, his question was unnecessary. As Phil was over-tipping her, the waitress flashed him a big juicy smile and said she looked forward to serving him in the morn and that he should be sure and try the johnnycakes with chokeberry jam, whatever the hell that is. He thought she winked at him, too, but Carol disagreed. She said the wink had been aimed squarely at young Nate — Phil had just gotten in the line of fire. Nate happily agreed.

All in all, the meal was a big success except for one thing: Throughout the meal a crying baby at a nearby table was working at full volume. At first Phil felt sorry for the infant's mother who was dining alone and had nobody to assist her in muffling the child. But it soon became apparent that the woman wasn't the least bit concerned about the welfare of the infant. Nor was she embarrassed about the discomfort the noise was inflicting on the diners.

When the Hodworth's had finished their burgers, Phil suggested they find a quieter place to eat dessert. He asked the Irish waitress to recommend a spot and she suggested a deli down the street that made its own ice cream. *Very tasty*, she promised him, licking her lush lips as if those lips, not the ice cream, contained the candy sprinkles. She even topped off her recommendation with a whipped-cream-drenched wink. This time Phil was sure the sexy server's sweet-tipped arrows were aimed straight at him and him alone. Even Carol could see the woman was coming on to him, although Carol didn't seem particularly worried about it.

Phil had always admired Carol for her confidence around flirty women like this. She knows Phil looks but he would never stray. And that's nice. Trust is good. Or maybe she just thinks these women aren't serious about their offers. Especially now that his waist is getting a little thick and his hair is getting a little thin.

Phil decided to skip dessert.

• • • •

When Carol switched off her bedside lamp, Taylor was still sitting cross-legged on top of her bedspread, hunched over her smart phone like a Buddhist monk praying to the goddess of social media. During this trip the girls were sharing one room while the boys bunked in the other. This was okay with Carol — she saw it as a good opportunity to do some bonding with her daughter, maybe indulge in a little chick talk. But so far there's been little talk. This is their first night in Wyoming but their second night rooming together on the road, and Mom still can't seem to compete with the internet.

Carol rolled away from the light, toward the wall, and bid her daughter a quick, "Nighty, night, Tay."

Taylor chuckled but at something that had absolutely nothing to do with her mother's presence. So Carol closed her eyes and hoped for a power outage.

A little later — Carol wasn't sure exactly how much later as she was adrift in that gray, not-quite-awake-not-quite-asleep netherworld — she heard Taylor's voice mumble, "Mom?"

It could have been a dream. Carol tested the reality with, "You say something?"

No response. Yes, must have been a dream.

Then Carol heard a softly muttered, "Nothing."

Carol rolled over to face her daughter's lamp light. "What is it?"

Taylor was lying on her back, phoneless, staring up at the ceiling. She didn't look at her mother as she said, "I think I know why you want to move out here."

"You do?"

"Dad."

"Your father doesn't want to move here."

"You think things will be different."

"They would, I guess. But—"

"Like, he won't have to work late anymore."

"No. Not at the office, anyway. But running a restaurant isn't a nine-to-five thing. We'd both have to—"

"And he won't have to travel so much.'

"No, not if he left his job in the city. But I seriously doubt he'd do that."

"You and Dad would be together more." Taylor turned and looked at her mother. "You'd like that, wouldn't you?"

"Of course I would, but—"

"So you should move here then." And with that said, Taylor rolled over and switched off her bedside lamp. In the darkness, her disembodied, ghostly voice continued, "I'll be living on campus, anyway. So, you know, like, why not?"

"Your father would never go for it."

"He will if you push."

"Push? Your dad? That's not how we do things."

"Well, maybe for once you should."

Carol overlooked her daughter's slightly insulting tone. "You think I should nudge him along, huh."

"Why should he always be the boss? Pushing won't hurt. It won't hurt a bit."

"But I don't know if I want to move out here. I don't know if I want to leave my own job."

"Well, if you do, you should go ahead and do it. Marriage is supposed to be an equal partnership."

"Ours is equal."

"You think so, huh?"

Carol had hoped for some bonding, but this wasn't quite the bonding she'd had in mind.

Taylor concluded with, "Just saying is all. Night, Mom."

"Sweet dreams, Tay."

That was enough chick talk for one night. Probably, enough for the week.

CHAPTER SIX

"You asleep, Dad?"

Through his closed eyelids Phil could see morning had arrived, but he had no idea how much morning was waiting out there, so he kept those eyelids shut tight. After all, this was supposed to be a vacation.

"'Cause if you're not asleep, you might want to see this."

Phil opened one eyelid. And to his surprise Nate was staring into it. Just inches away.

Nate continued, "I just went down to the pool..."

"I told you not to go in the pool. Not by yourself."

"I didn't go in the water."

Phil tried to show some anger, but he was too groggy to work up much of a froth. "Doesn't matter. I told you not to go near the pool unless I or your mother or your sister was—"

"Have you seen it?"

"Seen what? The pool?"

"The car."

Phil opened the other eyelid. The tone of his son's voice chilled him awake like a splash of ice water. "Car? Whose car?"

"Our car."

"What are you talking about?"

Nate answered in a sing-song voice that mimicked his mother's usual method of delivering bad news, "I'd be happy to tell you, but I don't think you're going to be very happy to hear it."

In one fluid movement Phil threw the covers off, rolled his legs out of bed, and asked, "What happened? Somebody hit it?" The feel of a shag rug on his toes reminded Phil he was in a cheap motel. He shuffled his bare feet across the silly carpeting and hurried to the curtained window.

"Dad, the door's open."

Phil looked to the room's front door. "No it isn't."

"Not that door. *That* door." Nate pointed to the fly of Phil's pajamas.

Nate was right. Phil tucked himself in and pulled his t-shirt down for extra caution. Then he safely slid open the window drapes.

The Toyota was parked directly in front of his room. Phil ran his eyes over the vehicle. "Looks all right to me."

"The wheels...?"

Looking head-on like this, Phil couldn't really see the car's wheels, but now that the boy mentioned it, the vehicle did look huddled low and close to the ground.

Nate said, "I think somebody's buggered them."

Phil hurried toward the door, saying as he walked, "Who the hell taught you that word? I don't even use that word."

"You will now."

But Nate was wrong. When Phil opened the door and saw the whole picture, he said, "Aw, shit."

Both tires on this side were flat. Not just low but dead flat to the rims. Phil stepped farther outside.

The gritty, cold concrete stung his bare feet as he tip-toed around to get a look at the far side of the vehicle. Sure enough, the tires on that side were flat too.

An elderly man was sitting on a lawn chair in front of the room next door. He looked over at Phil and said, "Somebody's buggered your tires good."

At least now Phil knew where Nate had picked up the new word.

· · · ·

The logo on the door of the squad car boasted, *Perpetuity Police Department — To Swerve and Protect.* Phil pointed to the misspelled word, "Shouldn't that be, *Serve* and Protect?"

Officer Dagleish, a handsome rock of a man in his early fifties who looked like he just stepped off a 1950's cigarette billboard thumbed his blue-gray Stetson back from his tanned forehead so he could more clearly see the idiot who was asking such a dumb question about his department's motto. "Well, you see, it's like this. These here mountain roads, all twisty and zig-zag-like, are filled with tourists, their eyes on their cell phones instead of on the road. Believe me, in the course of my workday, I gotta do more'n my share of swervin'."

"I see," said Phil.

The cop looked to Carol, his hard, rugged face slowly softening into a sly grin. "He always that easy?"

Carol patted her husband's shoulder. "He hasn't had his coffee yet."

The police officer turned back to Phil. "It's what we in law enforcement call a typo. Town can't afford a repaint. 'Sides, the way I see it, it's a nice ice breaker. Takes people's minds off unpleasantness like this here." The cop kicked at one of Phil's vandalized tires.

The morning was sunny and already warm. Nate and Taylor, were inside their rooms, getting dressed and, one of them at least, washing herself up for breakfast at the motel's pub.

The cop kneeled down beside Phil's car. He looked up and said, "Looks like we've got a big ol' ten-oh-four on our hands."

"What's a ten-oh-four?"

"Buggered tires. Four of them. You see, a ten-oh-three would be—"

This time Phil jumped in with the punch line. "*Three* buggered tires." Phil laughed to show the officer he got the joke.

The cop's face turned to stone. "Ten-oh-three's a sexual interference. 'Round here we don't joke 'bout something like that."

Phil's smile immediately dropped. "No, of course you don't. I just—"

The cop flashed that sly smile at Carol once more. "He is easy, ain't he." The cop straightened himself up. "A ten-oh-four is vandalism to personal property under five thousand. I don't know what a ten-oh-three would be. Never had one."

Phil was starting to recognize this man's distinct and mildly annoying sense of humor. He'd seen it that day in the park. He asked the officer, "You aren't any relation to Zack Mossip, are you?"

"Not directly. But you might say we grew up together."

"I thought so. You see, I'm—

"Phil Hodworth. Chicago. Last known contact of the deceased's." The cop walked around the car and examined the vehicle as he spoke. "I'll miss young Zack. We all will."

"*Young* Zack?" Phil commented with a smile. He figured the cop was being ironic. Joking again.

The cop picked up something from under the car, examined it, and dropped it into Phil's hand. Phil recognized the tiny length of rubber tubing with the plastic cap as a valve stem.

"Sliced clean," Officer Dagleish pointed out. "Some kid's idea of fun."

Phil looked around at the other vehicles sitting in the motel's lot. They all looked fine. None of them had flat tires. But every one of them had out-of-state plates. Phil offered a conclusion of the situation to the cop. "Tourist brats — they must make your job a lot more difficult at this time of year."

But the cop saw things differently. "Oh, I doubt this is the work of a tourist. This sort of mischief is usually local. We get it all year 'round."

"Local?" Phil was surprised by the cop's disparaging confession about his own home turf.

Carol was surprised too, "But it seems like such a nice quiet little town."

"Oh, she's quiet, all right. That's the problem. Youngsters 'round here are bored stiff. Mindless vandalism adds a little excitement to an otherwise dull day." Officer Dagleish reached into his breast pocket and took out his note pad and pen. "But hey, at least it gets the little assholes outdoors and off their screens and devices."

"You joking again?" Phil asked.

"Okay." The officer spoke as he wrote. "We'll say I'm joking."

Phil noticed something odd about the cop's uniform. The man's holster held a huge six shooter revolver that looked to be straight out of an old John Wayne civil war cavalry flick. Phil pointed to the giant gun. "That thing looks like quite an antique."

Chief Dagleish just smiled and said, "Sentimental value." Then he handed the piece of notepaper to Phil. "Rupert should be on his way. He'll fix you up. If he's not here soon call that number, tell him The Chief says to move his lazy butt."

"Thanks." Phil looked at the name and number on the paper. "His rates good?"

"Rates? When you're the only mechanic in town, you can charge anything you damn-well please." The cop smiled, tipped his hat, and said with sarcasm, "Welcome to Perpetuity, folks." Then he got into his squad car.

Phil turned to Carol, "Not even the locals like this town."

As they stood watching the police car drive past the motel's restaurant, Phil's thoughts turned to those johnnycakes that had been recommended by the waitress last night. The Irish waitress. The waitress with the big sexy hair. And the big sexy—

"Hungry?" Carol asked.

"Yeah," Phil answered. "Now that you mention it…"

• • •

Angus Murphy, owner of The Shamrock Motor Court and Restaurant, stood at the front window of his office and watched the police car drive across the parking lot, out toward the exit. As the car passed by the motel's office, Police Chief Enoch Dagleish stuck his big muscular arm out the vehicle's window and waved a big muscular howdy. Angus returned the wave even though he knew darn well the Chief's gesture had been aimed, not at him, but at the beautiful gal in the waitress uniform who was standing behind Angus. Sure, men around town will often give Angus a nod in passing. But they wave at Colleen. And then they smile.

Still looking out the window, Angus next turned his attention to the sad sight across the parking lot. The Hodworth's vandalized Toyota squatted low on its four crumpled tires like a newborn fawn. "It is just nay necessary," Angus said in his thick Irish brogue. "There's nay excuse for such hooliganism, I tell ya. The valley has naught to worry about. The gentleman has a grand career going for his bonnie self back in Chicago. A bigshot marketing exec doesn't suddenly pack up and haul kin and kith over a thousand miles to the highlands. Not on a wee whim. What truck would a fellow like that have with running a cheap li'l chinky restaurant? I tell ya, there's nothin' here to get ourselves worked up about. Certainly nothing that would justify our acting like common hoodlums. The lad has nay plans to move here, I'd bet the motel on it."

Getting no reaction to his words, Angus looked around to make sure his wife was still behind him. Turns out she was there in body if not in spirit. The stunning thirty-seven-year-old lass, with skin so translucent she seemed to be lighted from within, was going through her usual hair-volumizing exercise, a ritual she performed every morning before entering the restaurant to serve breakfast. She had bent herself over forwards and was now placing her hands behind her long slender neck to make sure gravity was doing its part. Then she quickly flicked her head back and gave her auburn locks a final shake to ensure that the long waves cascaded fully and magnificently across her wide white shoulders like a wild brush fire spreading over snow. Then she turned toward the mirrored wall behind the cash register and pouted her lips to make sure that the new color of lip gloss Angus had bought her from off the internet did indeed go with her gingham waitress frock.

"It's a bonnie match," Angus assured her proudly.

Satisfied with her appearance from the neck up, Colleen now turned her attention to the low-cut bodice of her peasant-style dress. She shifted and jostled until she'd boosted up just the correct orbit of cleavage, making sure that both heavenly planets rose above the cotton horizon in equal proportions. In Angus's opinion this was all a pointless exercise. For a woman blessed as generously as Colleen, there was plenty of room for error.

Colleen hoisted her left breast another quarter inch and commented, "I think it's wrong too, dear."

Angus guessed she was talking about the Hodworth's damaged car, not about her left tit.

She continued, "Why discourage them at all? Personally, I would welcome the Hodworths with open arms. He's a fine-looking gent. And she's quite a pretty girl-next-door sort, if you like that type — and I know you do." Colleen winked at Angus.

Angus had to smile. His wife had dropped her Irish accent, saving it instead for her customers in the restaurant. She had also, long ago, dropped any pretentions of sexual marital fidelity. And Angus was fine with that, too. A hundred years of marriage will do that. To make a ride last this long, jealousy and suspicion and other signs of a fragile ego have to be tossed off your wagon and abandoned on the side of the trail. Otherwise, the excess weight will just bog your wheels down in the mud. Angus Murphy was proud of his luscious lass, so why not share and share alike. Most couples in town have open marriages. Faith and begorrah, it's the only means of coping with the boredom.

"Here comes Rupert," Angus announced as he watched the flatbed truck bounce into the parking lot. "Sweet deal that lad has got. Slicing 'em up one day — patching 'em up the next."

Colleen draped a loving hand over her husband's shoulder and squinted out into the brilliant morning sunshine. Rupert Thatcher, the driver of the flatbed, saw her and waved. She returned the greeting then said to Angus, "Rupe told me he toyed with the notion of scratchin' it up a bit — you know, taking a key to the door panels. But I told him that would be overkill. No need to be any meaner than we absolutely must, right?"

Angus gave his girl a kiss on the cheek. "A heart as big as your knockers, darlin'." He followed the kiss with a playful swat to her bum. "Now go flash them in some lucky lad's face. And for once try not to spill any omelets into his lap." Sure, Colleen was clumsy, but what she cost in dry-cleaning bills, she more than made up for in tips.

As usual, Colleen gave her hubby's butt a loving tap as she left. And again as usual, Angus watched her walk away. Old habits die hard. And most habits in this valley are very, very old. And like most other things here, they rarely die.

• • •

The baby in the highchair cried and puked it's way through another meal, but somehow Phil enjoyed his breakfast despite the noise — the food was that good. He poured another dollop of maple syrup on his golden stack of johnnycakes and glanced up at the shamrock-shaped clock hanging over the bar. Ten o'clock. The guy with the tow truck had estimated Phil's car wouldn't be ready until at least mid-afternoon. Looks like the Hodworth family will be doing some walking.

When Phil asked if the service station might have a courtesy vehicle to lend out, the tow truck driver looked at him as if this here crazy city feller had just requested the loan of a Lear jet. *Courtesy car? Where do you think you are, fella — Cheyenne?* So Phil and Carol will have to take care of their business this morning by foot. Phil won't mind the exercise. All this traveling by car was playing havoc with his fitness regimen. According to the app on his phone yesterday he was barely fourteen steps from being classified as bed-ridden.

But before he starts hiking anywhere, he has to first change his pants. During breakfast the Irish waitress spilled maple syrup on his lap. She claimed it was an accident, of course, but there was something about her furtive glances as she gently dabbed the gunk off his thigh that made Phil think how psychologists say there are no accidents. Just sticky shorts.

Phil and Carol's first job this morning will be to go downtown and meet with a lady real estate agent. The agent's job will be to show them their recent inheritance, Zachariah's Chinese restaurant.

Phil's job will be to make sure Carol doesn't fall in love with the place.

• • •

The concrete slab set into the brick above the door of the old building read: *Perpetuity Banner, founded 1889.* A plastic sign beside the door said the newspaper's offices were on the second floor.

Phil paused to get his breath before tackling the climb. At his own dumb suggestion he and Carol had jogged here to work off some of that syrupy breakfast. Phil checked his fitness app. Yup, his pulse rate was a lot higher than it should be. "This mountain air leaves a lot to be desired," he gasped, "like oxygen." Phil coughed. "Could use a little moisture, too." Phil's throat felt dry as sawdust.

Carol hadn't heard his whining — she was already halfway up the stairs. The maddening thing is, she never goes to the gym. Granted, she is almost five years younger than he is.

Phil grabbed hold of the old worn bannister and attacked the steps two at a time just to show he could do it. When he reached the top, Carol was waiting, holding the door open for her poor old breathless hubby.

The second floor office was just one large open space. It housed three unoccupied steel desks and a bunch of file cabinets that sat on dark, well-worn, plank flooring. Two of the desks held computer monitors. The room's lone occupant — a slim woman with short grey hair — must have heard Phil's footsteps on the stairs because she was already out of her chair, walking this way. Or maybe she had just heard Phil's lungs gasping for air.

Violet Snelling, who looked to be about seventy years old but fit, had been communicating with Carol by voice, text, and email for the past two months. Her social media sources said that Violet split her time equally between her jobs as newspaper reporter and as real estate agent. Today, she seemed dressed for hocking real estate. Her tailored lavender linen blazer worn over a matching silk lavender top seemed to invite an offer just above market value. Her white cotton slacks that ended mid-calf seemed to suggest there might be problems with the plumbing. The building's plumbing, that is, not Violet's. The abbreviated slacks looked ready for high water.

She started to drag a couple of solid oak chairs up to her desk for her visitors, but Phil quickly jumped in to lend a hand. He found the chairs surprisingly heavy, so he didn't wait for an invitation to sit his tired ass down in one of them. Carol sat in the other chair. Violet remained standing.

"Heard you folks had some trouble with your car."

Carol treated this simple statement of fact as though it were an apology from this lady on behalf of the whole town. "Oh, it was nothing, I'm sure. Just some kids with too much time on their hands."

"You got that right," Violet said. She took a seat on the corner edge of her desk. Now she looked more like a newspaper woman. "Too much free time and sweet-fuck-all to do with it. Big problem round here."

Phil was tempted to reinforce her comment and say that growing up in a small town must be particularly dull for a teenager, but he held his tongue. He didn't want to offend this gal's home turf.

Violet asked, "You guys don't want any coffee, do you?"

Phil thought that was a strange way of putting it. "No, thanks," he said. "Just had breakfast."

"The Shamrock?" Violet asked.

"Yup."

"Colleen serve you?"

"Yes," Carol said. "You know her?"

The real estate lady stood up, squinted at Phil's crotch, then sat back down again. "Must've changed your shorts already."

Phil had to laugh. "You must be a good reporter."

"Might be if there was ever anything to report around here." Violet glanced at a steno pad that was lying open on her desk. "So, tell me again about how you met young Zachariah."

"Young?" Carol commented.

"Yeah, uh..." Violet jotted down something on her pad, although frankly, Phil felt it was really just a delaying tactic to give herself time to think. "It's just a figure of speech. You know, like the way you might call a bald man, Curly. Or a tall guy, Shorty."

Phil added, "Or any politician, Honest."

Violet stabbed her pen toward Phil like she was nailing a gold star to his forehead. "You're fast. I like that. You would fit in real nice around here." Then the smile dropped from her face. "Too bad." Her voice dropped off.

"Too bad?" Carol asked.

Violet flipped to a second page of notes previously scribbled on her steno pad. "You met Zachariah in the park."

"Shared a bag of popcorn with him."

"You say he was on his way to Florida."

"Disney World."

"Figures." Violet recalled sadly, "It was always a dream of Zack's to see *The Happiest Place On Earth*."

Carol nodded. "He seemed to be a kid at heart."

Violet added, "A special kind of kid. In fact, the only one of his kind in town."

Phil understood. "Must be tough to be gay in a little place like this."

Violet agreed, "Folks out here don't take quick to new ideas, alternative lifestyles."

Seeing the possibility of a helpful ally in this woman, Phil jumped on her remark, "Yeah. Small towns, eh?"

"You don't know the half of it." Violet slowly shook her head in sadness.

This prompted Carol to ask her, "You don't like living in Perpetuity?"

Violet answered simply with, "Have you seen it?"

Phil laughed. Looks like he has an ally in this woman.

Carol answered, "We haven't seen much. Not yet. Just these few blocks from the motel."

"Then you've seen it. And what's more, you'll get a second delightful look on your walk back. By that time you should have 'er pretty well memorized."

Carol was obviously taken aback by the woman's attitude, so she jumped to the small community's defense. "It seems like quite a charming little place to me."

"Well, I won't argue with you." Violet opened her desk drawer. "Wouldn't be right. As president of the Perpetuity Chamber of Commerce, it's my job to make you folk feel welcome." Violet lifted a small set of keys out of the drawer. "So shall we go take a gander at this charming little business Zachariah has bequeathed to you?"

"No, no." Phil wanted to quickly set everyone straight on this, "It isn't our property. Not yet. The will is still in probate. Somebody might contest it."

"I wouldn't worry about that." Violet went over and lifted her handbag from off a coat rack. "Zachariah had no family to lay claim to his estate. And even if he did — take my word for it — folks aren't lining up around the block to run *any* sort of business in this burg, especially a Chinese restaurant."

Phil laughed at the irony. "And you say you're *president* of the Chamber of Commerce?"

"Yes. And in the interest of full disclosure, I must warn you — not everybody around here has my enthusiasm for this shit hole." With that said, the news reporter/real estate agent/town promoter led the way to the stairway.

Carol, still somewhat stunned by Violet's harsh words, seemed hesitant to follow her. Phil, on the other hand, was plenty eager. Like a puppy, he jumped out of his chair and happily trailed the snarky seventy-year-old gal down the steps. Two at a time, of course. He had found talking with this woman to be invigorating.

CHAPTER
SEVEN

Taylor wasn't sure precisely when she lost sight of her little brother, but she knew it was somewhere between Jewel and Joel.

She had been working her way through her address book — texting her friends and asking if any of them still went on vacations with their families, and if so, how did they survive the mind-numbing boredom.

At one point, in the middle of the J's, Taylor paused to look up and check on Nate. Mom had instructed the little goof to stay here in the motel's playground area, safely away from the pool enclosure. Last time Taylor had looked, Nate was indeed obeying orders, goofing around on the swing set. But now the swings were totally goof-free and there was no sign of the little doink on any of the other equipment.

"Nate," she called out, her eyes scanning the surrounding bushes and searching up into the branches of a particularly tempting tree. Her squirrely brother wasn't in it. The only people she saw out here were a couple of motel guests lounging by the pool, inside the fenced-off area. She slipped her phone into her pocket and got up off her chaise lounge to go have a look. If Nate had somehow sneaked past her and slipped into that swimming pool, she'd kill him. She wouldn't rat on him, of course. That would only get her in deep shit. Mom would say Taylor shouldn't have been messing around with her phone. But what else was a seventeen-year-old supposed to do in this little town? There were no other teenagers around the motel. Any kids Taylor's age would surely have started their summer jobs by now and not be wasting time beside a swimming pool drowning their little brother.

Taylor was now close enough to the pool to see that her brother was not in it. Not unless he was lying on the bottom.

Taylor opened the gate and stepped inside the enclosure. Nope. No sign of Nate in the water, just a couple of little girls paddling around with pool noodles. Taylor stepped closer to the edge. The two little girls were about Nate's age. On the far side their father was sitting in a lounge chair. He looked at Taylor and smiled. Probably a perv. Taylor was wearing shorts and a baby doll camisole that showed a bit of belly button, but nothing sexy. That doesn't matter with these old guys, though.

The father had a newspaper on his lap, probably to cover the boner Taylor was giving him. Geez, shouldn't the old perv be keeping his eyes on his two little daughters splashing around in the deep end instead of ogling a hot young woman?

"You looking for your son?" the father called out to her.

Son? That was gross in so many gross ways. "Brother," Taylor yelled back.

One of the little girls looked up. "He said you were his mother."

Taylor rolled her eyes. Nate pulls shit like this all the time. "Have you seen him?" Taylor asked.

One little girl just stared up from the water silently, her mouth open like a frightened trout while the other little girl said, "He asked us to come into his room with him."

Taylor could do nothing but shake her head at this news bulletin. She knew her little brother wasn't really a sex maniac. But the curious idiot sure could sound like one sometimes.

The little frightened trout joined the conversation, "There's a low pressure system moving down from Canada and we might get thunderstorms, so he said we should come into his room with him."

The father laughed. "Your brother is quite the little meteorologist."

"That's *one* word for it." Taylor left the pool area to continue her search. Nate must have gone back into the motel.

As she crossed the parking lot, she looked up at the sky. The clouds were indeed getting dark.

• • • • •

Nate was scared. But he nudged the door open anyway.

He looked into the darkness. He knew he wasn't supposed to be here. The sign said so. And he would never have come this far if he hadn't seen the little girl go in first. She was quite pretty.

The large building appeared to be a garage — no windows, just three wide doors across the front and one small door in the side. That side door had a white sign on it with red letters that said, *Danger. Keep Out. No...* and then a big word which Nate didn't have the patience nor the time to sound out aloud. He didn't want to lose track of the little girl. She was his age. Maybe a bit older. Eight or nine. Nate has always liked older girls.

This side door was now open a crack. He pulled it open wider. Not far. Just enough to peek. He couldn't see inside very well — his eyes were still in outdoor mode. His pupils needed to adjust. *Dilate* was the scientific word.

Slowly and carefully, he stepped inside. He was still blind, but he could hear a radio playing. Funny how your ears don't have to dilate, just your eyes.

He could now see an electric light bulb glowing at the far end of the garage. He closed the door gently behind him and shuffled farther into the darkness. His eyes were getting better now. Shadows were coming into focus and...

And there she was. Across the room. By the bare light bulb. Sitting on a stool at a work bench. And she was... Holy shit.

Nate couldn't believe his ever-widening pupils. The little girl was smoking a cigarette. Nate had never seen a girl his age smoke before. Boys, yes. But not a girl. He, himself, had tried smoking once at the beach when he and his friend Aiden had found an especially large butt in the sand. But a girl? Never. Oddly, she somehow looked even better to him now. Prettier.

This was clearly not her first time. She knew what she was doing with that thing. She took long, deep puffs, and when she finally blew the smoke out from between her pouty lips, the blue cloud seemed to just keep coming and coming like it was never going to stop. At one point she even blew rings. Nate had never seen that before, not from anyone, kid or adult. This girl was incredible. Absolutely in-freakin'-credible. Nate felt a warm front moving in from his head to his toes.

He kept watching her. After a couple more puffs she stopped smoking long enough to take a drink. Not from a glass, from a bottle. Nate couldn't see what the bottle was, but it definitely wasn't a water bottle. This bottle was brown. And she was enjoying it. A lot. Nobody closes their eyes and smacks their lips after a long swig of friggin' water.

Nate couldn't take it any longer. He stepped closer and said, in his best, nicest clear voice, "Hello."

The girl almost choked. She spit out her mouthful. Coughed. Sputtered. Finally, she managed a, "Jesus H. Fucking Christ."

Nate stepped farther into the light. "I scare you?"

"Damn straight you scared me." She brushed the spilled liquid off her lap. "Look what you made me do."

"Sorry."

"What're you doing here?" The girl stayed on the stool as she whisked away at her dress.

"I saw you this morning. When I was eating breakfast. You were in back."

"The kitchen," she explained. "I help Angus with dishes and stuff."

"My name's Nate."

"Good for you." She took another puff of her cigarette.

"And yours?" he asked.

"None of your business, that's what it is. You shouldn't be in here, little boy." She took another swallow from her bottle. Then, "But I suppose it's not your fault. You probably couldn't read the No Trespassing sign."

"I could so."

"A big word like that? Don't fib."

"Can you read it?" Nate asked.

"Sure, I can. But I'm—" The girl stopped herself, then muttered, "I'm kind of advanced."

Big deal, Nate thought. According to his teacher, Nate was advanced. But he didn't go around bragging to everybody about it. He looked at the bottle she was holding and recognized the label as the same drink his father had ordered last night in the restaurant. A local beer. She took another swig. Then she burped. In-fucking-credible.

The girl carefully rested her cigarette down in a tin ashtray and stood up. "You gotta get out of here, kid."

"You want to go over to the playground?"

"Thanks but no thanks," she said. "I'm a little bored with the swings."

"Me too. You want to wrestle?"

"What?"

"Wrestle. It's fun. You'll like it."

The girl laughed. "You coming on to me?"

"I don't know what that means."

"Bullshit."

"I know what *that* means."

Nate was puzzled. Something wasn't right about this girl. Sure, her voice sounds like a kid's voice, and her face looks like a little girl's face, especially with those long pale eyelashes and those dimples in her cheeks. But the way she moves... and the way she holds that cigarette...

Finally, Nate had it figured out. "You a midget?"

The girl laughed. "No. Are you?"

"I'll be eight in August."

"Nate... Nate..." She seemed to be testing the name on her tongue as if she was trying a new flavor of ice cream and seeing if she wanted more. Finally, she made her decision. "That's good. I like that. Parents are getting better with names nowadays. Your full name Nathanial?"

"Just Nate."

"Jewish?"

"No."

"We don't have any Jews here. They're allowed now, we just don't have any."

"Oh." Nate didn't know what to say, but that was okay. He was happy to just watch. She looked so pretty with those eyelashes and dimples and that little upturned nose. And except for the skunky beer and cigarette smoke she smelled good too. She must be wearing her mother's perfume.

The girl took another puff from her cigarette. She talked as she blew out the smoke. "Tell me, Nate, can you keep a secret?"

"Sometimes." Nate was remembering the time he walked into the laundry room and caught his sister, Taylor, letting Gary Sontag put his hand up her sweater. Nate told everybody about that. He just had to — the look on Gary Sontag's face was so funny.

The little girl said, "Can you keep a special secret just for me?"

"Maybe."

"Can you keep it a secret that you saw me smoking?"

"I guess so."

"And that you saw me drinking?" She finished off the last swallow of her bottle of beer.

"Maybe."

"Just *maybe*?" The little girl pouted her bottom lip out like she was getting all fired up to cry. But Nate could tell she wasn't going to. He knew when a girl was serious and when she was bluffing.

The little girl started bargaining, "Will you keep our secret if I let you kiss me?"

Nate smiled. It was like she had read his mind.

CHAPTER EIGHT

The moment Carol Hodworth walked into the Shangri-La Gardens restaurant she knew two things: First, she knew she loved the place — it took her back to the Chinese restaurants of her childhood. And second, she knew there was no way in hell Phil was going to agree to keep it. Who in their right mind would? It was a museum of red, black, and gold Chinese kitsch. *Kitsch* being a kind word for *junk*.

Paper globe lanterns hung from the embossed tin ceiling like stalactites with goiters. Faded paper Oriental fans spread their boney fingertips across one of the room's walls like they were clinging for their very lives while frayed silk wall hangings lay pinned onto another wall like dead moths that some near-sighted collector had mistaken for butterflies. The back wall of the restaurant was forested with potted bamboo trees that tried their best to add a third dimension to a stained wallpaper mural picturing some Far-Eastern mountain, a scene which Carol sort of recognized but didn't know by name.

Across the front window of the restaurant, vertical blinds hung by their scrawny necks as if the phone call from the Governor had failed to come through. The floor-to-ceiling slats were embossed with a cheesy bamboo leaf motif that cast shadows of bigger, cheesier bamboo leaves across the wooden floor, a surface whose worn and sagging planks supported, obviously against their will, a dozen ceramic-topped tables and four times that many black-enameled chairs, each foursome huddling in a tight group to whisper unkind rumors about the cruddy chairs at the next table.

Yes, this place was a cheap Chinese dump all right, and yet Carol loved every MSG-laden square inch of it. Why? Because this was exactly how a Chinese restaurant should look — not like the New Age places filled with sparkling chrome that she and Phil go to in the city. In almost every detail, The Shangri-La Gardens Restaurant looked exactly like the places Carol had enjoyed as a child with her mom and dad. It was a perfect replica except for one thing.

Carol screwed up her nose. "We should be smelling garlic, oyster sauce, and rancid peanut oil." She sniffed again. "Not Christmas trees."

"Oh, that," Violet, the real estate lady, dismissed Carol's worry offhandedly. "That's just the roach spray."

This announcement sent Carol's eyes scurrying to the restaurant's baseboards in search of any sign of movement.

Violet continued, "Zachariah always preferred the pine-scented stuff. Said it went nicely with the lilac-scented rat cakes."

Phil smiled and patted Carol sympathetically on her shoulder. She could tell he was enjoying this. But he kept his mouth shut. Smart guy.

Carol was desperate for a positive spin. She wanted to see the tea cup as half full so she changed the subject to a more specific tea cup. "Tell me, Vi, did Zack serve Cantonese or Szechuan? And how about dim sum? I do love a good bau or shaomi."

Violet stepped over to the front counter and slipped a menu out from beside the cash register. "I'm afraid Shangri-La Gardens is Chinese in name and décor only." To prove her point she presented the cracked leatherette folder for Carol's perusal.

Meanwhile, Phil wandered to the back of the room to have a closer look at the wallpaper mural. After a quick examination he turned his back to it and announced, "Somebody should have told Zachariah that Mount Fuji is in Japan not China."

"Might as well be in the Rockies," Carol said as she ran her finger down the menu. "Steak, burgers, fries... Not a noodle or eggroll on the list." She handed the menu to Phil for his examination.

He studied the grease-splattered bill of fare, chuckling as he read. Meanwhile, Violet decided this was a good time for a quick history lesson: "When Lee Wong first opened this place, he pushed his chow meins and chop sueys, but it was a tough sell. Stage passengers, cowpokes, and fence riders just want their meat and potatoes."

"Stage passengers?" Phil said. "How old is this place?"

Violet had to think about this one. "I'd say a good hundred-fifty, hundred-sixty years, give or take a decade. This was the first formal eatery in town. And by *formal* I mean the cutlery didn't do double duty as weapons. Lee Wong figured the rowdy miners and ranch hands couldn't do much damage with a chop stick. He was wrong, of course. Just ask One-eyed Lamont."

"Ask him?" Carol laughed, going along with the joke. "I presume One-eyed Lamont has long-since passed on."

"Oh, yeah, right, of course. Long gone." Violet chuckled. Sort of.

Phil waved his hand to indicate the décor. "If it was such a failure, why did they continue with the Chinese theme?"

"That was Zack's idea. Such a sweet boy. When he took it over, he didn't want Lee Wong to feel bad. As you may have found out for yourself, Zack's a very tender-hearted kid."

There she goes again, Carol thought, referring to Zachariah as a *kid*. Must be some sort of regional, small-town habit. Like calling elderly women, *the girls*.

Meanwhile, Phil seemed to have his own problem with Violet's words. "Zack didn't want Lee Wong to feel bad? But you just said Lee Wong ran this place a hundred and sixty years ago."

"Yes, he did." Violet clasped her two hands under her chin as if to pray. "And *in sprit* Lee Wong will always be here. That's how Zachariah sees it."

"Very respectful," Carol said.

Phil gave up and turned away. "Maybe we should have a look at the kitchen." He walked towards a set of swinging double doors in back.

"I wouldn't look *too* close," Violet warned.

"Bugs?" Carol asked.

"You folks know anything about electrical codes?"

Carol looked to Phil. He answered for both of them, "Nope."

"Neither did the guy who wired this joint," Violet pulled a cell phone out from her purse. "You two go poke your noses around. I have to make a quick call." And with that said she walked to the front of the restaurant leaving Carol and Phil to continue on through the swinging kitchen doors at their own risk.

To Carol's pleasant surprise, the kitchen sparkled. Lots of stainless steel, polished aluminum, and gleaming white tiles. Although the equipment wasn't exactly state-of-the-art, the appliances seemed reasonably modern. She didn't know the proper names for all the commercial apparatus, but she recognized a large griddle, a range with two big ovens, a deep fryer with digital controls, a couple of microwaves, and a large dishwasher. Carol opened a refrigerator. No light came on. It must be unplugged. Same for the vertical freezer beside it. Both were clean and empty. Carol took a closer look at the range. "Electric," she announced to Phil. "I thought most restaurants use gas."

"Town like this probably doesn't have a natural gas line." Phil said. He slowly opened the cupboard doors under the sink, and Carol instinctively stepped back, ready to run. But she didn't have to worry. Nothing scurried. Nothing crawled. Nothing slithered.

"Wow." Phil exclaimed as he bent down for a closer look. "I wish our pipes looked this good. All copper. Even the cold. And clean as a hospital. Just look. Not a roach. Not a silverfish. Not even an ant."

Phil stuck his head even farther under the sink. "I don't see any roach traps. No mouse bait either." He pulled his head out. "What the hell was she talking about?"

Now emboldened, Carol opened a long broom cupboard beside the fridge. To her relief, this too had no wildlife.

She looked to Phil who was now examining an electrical outlet that one of the microwave ovens was plugged into. "Wiring looks up to code — three prongs and polarized."

Carol lowered her voice and spoke quietly, "She implied it's never been updated. She called it 'turn-of-the-century.'"

Phil opened a fuse panel. "I'm no electrician, but I know they weren't using 200 amps at the turn of the century."

Carol kept her voice low in case Violet was standing outside the door. "So why would she say the wiring was so bad?"

"Same reason she told us the place is full of rats and roaches when it's actually cleaner than a mermaid's twat. The old gal doesn't want us here."

"Shhh!" Carol wished her husband would moderate his language, but she had to admit he had a point.

"Look at it this way," Phil threw out his arms in dramatic presentation sending an enameled stock pot crashing to the floor. He picked it up as he went on talking. "It's a small town. They resent newcomers. They see us as interlopers. Gatecrashers. Carpetbaggers. Of course, there could be another reason."

"What?"

"She could have another buyer lined up. A friend. A local. Or maybe she wants it for herself, and she's priming us to sell it at a bargain price."

Carol didn't argue. What Phil was saying made sense. Ever since Carol had started communicating with Violet, first by email and then by telephone, Carol had felt that something wasn't quite right about the woman. There was a wall that Carol couldn't break through. Not by long-distance, at least. Carol had hoped that once she met Violet in person, the real estate lady might let down her guard, show some sincerity. But no. To put it simply, Carol just couldn't warm to her.

Phil continued with his diatribe against rural life, "You know what these small-town hicks resent most of all? Change. Just look at that dining room out there. The décor hasn't been touched since the Chinaman built it a hundred and fifty years ago. Never mind that it hasn't served a bowl of rice since General Custer was a corporal."

"Chinese *person*," said a woman's voice. Carol and Phil turned to see Violet standing in the doorway still holding her cell phone. "Lee Wong doesn't like the word *Chinaman*. Says it's derogatory."

Carol wondered how much of her and Phil's conversation Violet had heard. But Phil wasn't worried. He seemed to have another concern on his mind.

"Lee Wong?" he said. "But isn't he long-since...?"

"Lee Wong number three. Honorable great grandson. We call him Lee *Light*. Lives here in town. Lee is our token Chink." Violet winced at her own flub. "I mean Oriental. No, I mean Asian person. You want to go upstairs see the apartment? We've cleaned out most of Zack's stuff."

"Maybe some other time," Phil said. He signaled for Carol to follow him out of the kitchen. "We left the kids alone. They've probably murdered each other by now."

As Carol, Phil, and the real estate lady walked through the restaurant to the front door, a colorful item on the wall by the cash register caught Carol's eye. It was a Chinese abacus. Gingerly, Carol picked the antique beaded mathematical calculator off its hook for a closer look.

Too bad she didn't know how to use the thing, she thought. Because something in here certainly did not add up.

Taylor was half out of her mind with worry. Well, maybe a quarter out of her mind. After all, this was just Nate.

At least thirty minutes had slithered by since she'd first noticed he was gone and still no sign of the little reptile. What if she never finds him? Or worse, what if she does find him but he's, like, dead. Lying in a ditch. Or in a dumpster. Nate likes playing in dumpsters. The little idiot even got stuck in one once. He'd climbed up on some garbage pails to get into it, but the dumpster was empty so he couldn't get himself back out. Geez, if he's pulled that trick again Mom and Dad would go beyond mental, and Taylor will never get that car Dad has promised to pay half of if she graduated with honors which she indeed had done but that won't matter anymore because Taylor was the irresponsible zookeeper who had left the cage door open and lost Mom and Dad's favorite pet monkey.

Taylor looked around for the nearest dumpster. She'd seen one recently. Where was it? Oh, yeah, behind the motel. She hurried round to the back of the kitchen.

Yup, there it is. The green metal box sat amongst smaller garbage pails just like last time. Should she look inside the thing? *Could* she look inside the thing? Did she have the nerve? Of course, she didn't really actually believe that her brother's lifeless body was in there, but something sure smelled bad.

Taylor stepped closer to the bin. "Nate? You in there?"

No answer. It wasn't a large dumpster, just about four feet high, but it was certainly large enough to hold a body. Especially a child's body. And geez, it smelled putrid. A human body wouldn't start rotting that fast, would it? Nate's probably would.

The dumpster's hinged top was closed, so Taylor had no choice. She grasped hold of the metal lid. It was filthy. Greasy. Totally gross. She wondered — did small towns have rats like in the city? They certainly have raccoons. She'd seen one last night. That's probably why the lid was closed. Keep the raccoons out.

The lid was heavy. But she managed to get it cracked a few inches. Enough to peer into the stinky blackness and...

"Don't move."

It was a male voice. Not close. Several feet away. She didn't move. She just held the lid open a few inches and turned her eyes toward the voice.

The man was standing in the open back door of the restaurant. And he wore a white apron. And a hair net. He looked Asian. In his right hand he held a knife. A very big knife. The kind of knife chefs use. Or psychotic sex maniacs.

Or child killers.

"Stay perfectly still. He doesn't see you yet."

He? Taylor moved her eyes but not her head.

"Bears have poor eyesight," the Asian man said.

"Bears?" she said. "Are you serious?" Now she moved her head. "I don't see anything."

He pointed the knife. "Over there. See? Coming out of the trees?"

Taylor lowered the lid and raised herself on tip-toes so she could look across the top of the dumpster. Sure enough, she saw the animal. A bear. Big. Black. Close. Like about twenty feet away. He started walking toward her. Slowly.

The bear stopped to raise his head and sniff the air. Taylor looked back to the man at the restaurant. That back door was about twice as far from her as the bear was. Should she make a dash for it?

The Asian man had been holding his palm flat at her like a cop directing a motorist to stop. But now he curled his fingers and beckoned. "Walk this way," he whispered. "Slow. Don't run. You try to race him you lose."

With her eyes glued on the bear, Taylor started walking. Backwards at first. Then sideways. Slowly. But picking up speed as she neared the building.

"You're doing fine," the man encouraged. "He's more interested in the garbage than in you."

Finally, Taylor reached the stairs. And in four steps she was inside the building. The Asian man closed the screen door behind her. Then he closed the solid main door.

Taylor was shaking like a leaf. The Asian man noticed her discomfort and cleared off a high wooden stool for her to sit on. "Damn bears," he said. "We used to just shoot them. But nowadays guests get all bent out of shape: *Oh, no. Don't kill Yogi. Don't cap Pooh. He might have a family.*"

And now Taylor remembered what she had come here for. "My... my brother." she stuttered. "He's out there somewhere. Maybe in the garbage. With the bear!"

"Bear? What bear?"

Taylor recognized the voice. She turned and saw Nate walking in from the dining room.

"You little toad." Taylor jumped to her feet. "I told you not to go anywhere. You could've been killed. By a perv. Or that bear."

"Where?" Nate's eyes went to the door. "Out there?" He ran over to have a look.

The cook opened the inner door so Nate could peek out through the screen. The cook narrated, "About three hundred pounds, I'd say. Black, not a grizz. Male. Out of hibernation for about two months, still skinny, so it's hard to tell how old. He's a hungry boy. Visited us before. Loves my johnnycakes."

Nate smiled up at the cook. "I don't blame him."

The cook tousled Nate's hair. "You like Lee Wong's cooking, huh? You know, I used to have my own place. You would have loved it. Shangri-La Gardens. You like Chinese?"

"Sure."

Taylor didn't understand. What was this man trying to pull? She challenged the man with, "I thought Mr. Mossip owned Shangri-La Gardens. Mr. Zachariah Mossip."

"And I should never have sold it to him. Big mistake. When I ran the joint, the menu was strictly Chinese. Best egg drop soup west of the Mississippi. Sold it to Zachariah back in eighteen and—" The Asian cook cut himself off so suddenly it was like he'd bitten down on something hard and chipped a tooth. He turned away and looked out the window at the bear again. "There he goes. Back into the woods. Bye, bye, Yogi. I'm sorry you're out of season."

Taylor now noticed a little girl wander in from the dining room. She was pretty, about Nate's age, but she had a manner about her that seemed older. Almost sophisticated. But smarmy. Snotty. Like she knew something nobody else knew.

The cook noticed the little girl too. And he didn't seem to like her any more than Taylor did. He barked at her, "Where you been?"

"Nowhere. Just taking my break. Just out fooling around." On the phrase *fooling around* the little girl's pretty blue eyes went straight to Nate. She didn't quite smile, but that didn't matter — Nate was smiling enough for both of them.

Taylor got off her stool and grabbed her little brother's hand. She asked the cook, "You think it's okay for us to go out front yet? To the sidewalk?"

"No problem." Lee Wong answered. "The bear's busy with the garbage."

The pretty little girl added, "But do be careful. There's all sorts of wild animals out there." She turned to Nate. "A little boy can get into all sorts of trouble — trouble he best keep to himself." Then the weird kid winked at Nate, which was beyond creepy. Taylor had never seen a girl that age wink before. No wonder Nate was smiling like a ninny. The girl offered Nate her outstretched hand, "Come. I'll show you the way out."

But the cook had other ideas. He grabbed the girl's outstretched hand. "You stay here, Eunice." He pointed to a bushel basket full of potatoes. "Those things aren't going to peel themselves."

This was odd, thought Taylor. The cook spoke to the little girl as if she were an employee. An eight-year-old employee. Very strange. Like spooky strange.

This town just gets weirder and weirder.

CHAPTER NINE

It was a good thing Sam Beckwith was lying under his truck and couldn't reach his son's head with his crescent wrench. Otherwise he'd have used the cast iron tool to tap some sense into the kid's big hard noggin.

"Forget it," Sam said as he adjusted the wrench to fit the nut — the one on the fuel line, not the one he was talking to. "No fires."

"But gee whiz, Pop."

"And stop calling me *Pop*. You sound like *Dobie Gillis*." Since getting streaming TV, Sam's son has fallen in love with black and white television. Again.

From his position lying on his back under the engine, Sam could see his son's size twelves shifting back and forth, kicking the dirt like a batter getting ready for the next pitch.

"It doesn't have to be a *big* fire. I'll keep it contained." The boy's idiotic words tumbled down through the rusty engine compartment like marbles clattering through a peg board. "I'll keep the flames restricted to the kitchen."

"I said forget it."

But Isaac was on a roll. "I'll make sure Rance and the boys are standing by with their hoses. Worst that'll happen — a little water damage."

"That whole block is nothing but heritage structures."

"But now they're brick."

"Doesn't matter. They're framed with timber, old lumber that's been doin' nothing but sitting around drying out for a hundred and fifty years. The newest wood is in the roof of the savings and loan, and even that's been there since nineteen forty-five. Remember? War was done with, but everything was still rationed. We had a hell of a time scrounging those asphalt shingles."

"All I remember 'bout those years was tryin' to explain to tourists why I wasn't off fighting for my country."

Sam Beckwith wiggled himself out from under his truck and extended his hand. Isaac grabbed it and helped his dad get to his feet. Isaac was a good boy —just a little impetuous. Sam brushed dirt off his overalls. "It was hard for all of us, son. Just like with the first war. And the Spanish American."

"Luckily the government had no record of me. Otherwise, I'da had me some tricky dancin' to do."

"Like Tyler Jenkins," Sam said.

"That was Ty's own fault. The boy was just achin' to go kill himself some *Krauts*. Twenty-three years old, full of piss 'n' vinegar. By the time he reached the city he musta looked a hundred. I'll bet the recruiting officer laughed himself silly at the old coot come to join up."

Sam pulled a rag out of his denim overalls and wiped the grease off the worm screw of his wrench. "And now we've lost young Zachariah."

"I don't get it," Isaac said. "What makes a kid like Zack suddenly up and walk when he had a perfectly good life going for him here in the valley? Good business. Good friends. And yet off he goes."

Sam now used his rag to wipe the grease off his hands. "Some folks just have a hankering to experience what's on the other side of the mountain. See it with their own eyes. Smell it with their own nose. A person can hold back for only so long, and then..." Sam looked down at his own two feet and wondered how long it would be until he finally gave in and let them carry him off exploring. Nobody can take a life sentence forever. Especially when life is this long.

Isaac must have seen the dark shadow drifting across his father's face. The boy forced a smile and grabbed the greasy rag from his father's hand. "You don't have to worry about me, Pops. I'm perfectly happy. No place I'd rather be than right here at home with you."

Sam studied his boy's face. "Son, you are one amazing fella."

"Thank you."

"Happy as a clam."

Isaac corrected his father, "A clam with Wi-Fi."

"Not a spark of curiosity in you."

"Well, now, you see, that's not quite true. I'm plenty curious, but I don't need to leave home to satisfy that curiosity. Heck, none of us does. Not anymore. Not since satellite TV. And now the internet. Geez, why risk going to the outside world when the outside world can come to us. All we gotta do is click and swipe."

"And that's good enough for you."

"Sure. The way I see it, boredom is just the sign of a limited imagination."

"That's pretty good. Where'd you hear that?"

"Nowhere. Just made it up."

Sam had to laugh. He put his arm around his son's shoulders and walked him back to the barn. "I'm glad for you, son. You're easily the most contented soul in this crazy valley, and I'm glad for you."

"Thanks. I probably am. That's why I want to keep things as they are. *Exactly* as they are. No changes to the *status quo*."

"Well, you don't have to worry about the Hodworths changing anything," Sam said. "They won't be sticking around long enough. Not with the unpleasantness we've been tossing at them."

"Unpleasantness..." Isaac stopped walking. "Between you and me, Pop, I don't think *unpleasant* is gonna cut it. Not this time. These people own property here. Actual property. That's never happened to us before. Rudeness, bawling babies, punctured tires... that's kids' stuff. We gotta make these people hate this town. We gotta make them *fear* this town. And you know what inspires fear more than just 'bout anything?"

Sam was losing his patience. "Fire... that's your answer to everything. Always was. Always will be. I'm beginning to think you're a, uh... a..."

"Pyromaniac?"

"I was gonna say idiot."

Just then, Sam's cell phone started playing *Hail To The Chief.* Isaac had installed the ringtone as a joke, seeing as how his father was the mayor and all. Sam checked the caller I.D. When he saw the name, he eagerly pushed *answer* and asked, "So, how'd it go?"

"Well, Sammy..." The caller took a long, deep breath. This was clearly not going to be good news. "Tried my damndest," Violet Snelling, the town's pretend real estate broker said. "Made like the joint was overridden with rats and roaches. Told them the electrics had been installed by Thomas Edison after eating some bad pork balls. Told 'em about how, being a heritage building and all, the fire insurance rates would be sky high. I even said how the liquor license has lapsed and that there will likely be problems getting it renewed which will be a major drawback in a mountain town where the alcohol intake is higher than the oxygen intake."

Sam nodded in agreement even though Violet couldn't see him. "And you don't think you got through to them?"

"Him, yes. Her, no way. Sam, that woman loves the place. Says it reminds her of her childhood. You shoulda seen her. Personally, I think she's going to move in whether hubby okays the idea or not. Sammy, I think the chick is Mayberry Blind."

Mayberry Blind was a term used to describe city folk who have romanticized rural life so much they can't see the obvious limitations inherent in living in an actual small town. Sam sighed, "Well, thanks, Vi. At least you tried."

"We're all trying, Sam. But this time I don't think it's going to be good enough." Then Violet's voice rose to a higher, more upbeat register. "But you know Sam, I've been thinking. Maybe it's time."

"Time?" Sam suspected what was coming next.

"Time we finally welcomed some new faces. You never know. Might work."

"You really think so?"

"Maybe we're selling these people short. Maybe these ones can keep a secret."

"Can you guarantee that?"

Sam waited for a response. Violet's continued silence was all the answer he needed. He thanked her again for her trouble, then he hung up.

With his cell phone now lowered pointlessly at his side, Sam Beckwith stood looking out across the barn yard at the south field — sixty-four acres of good bottom land, or as good as bottom land can get in an arid climate like Wyoming's. The hilly field had been tilled and weeded and fertilized and planted and otherwise preened and was now patiently awaiting action from its spring seeds. Last year Sam had planted sugar beets but had lost thirty percent of the crop to Fusarium wilt, so this year he's planted barley. And next, maybe corn. Seems the dirt in this valley is the only thing that ever sees any change.

Sam turned to his son. "The Hodworths got a teenage daughter. She's 'bout your age." Sam clarified this with, "Your *frozen* age."

"Nineteen?"

"Might be more like seventeen, but that's even better. Nothin' scares a modern-day father more than having his daughter show interest in an older boy, especially the *wrong* older boy. And son, I think, with very little effort, you could fit that description."

"You want me to court this gal?"

Sam was losing his patience. "There you go again. Nobody *courts a gal* anymore. What I want you to do is hit on this chick."

"I dunno. Is she a comely gal? I mean, hot chick?"

"From what I hear, she's a stone fox." Sam stepped back and took a good look at his son. By modern standards the boy wasn't half-bad looking. Tall. Had most of his teeth. Real fine haircut, although that flaw can be modernized with a little gel and garden shears. The boy was a little thicker through the middle than when his wagon first got here, but judging by the tourist kids Sam sees at the town's water park these days, today's teenage girls don't seem to mind a bit of flab on their boyfriends. Or on themselves.

Sam slipped his cell phone out of his overalls pocket and scrolled to the number for Angus Murphy at the Shamrock Motor Court. When the Irishman answered, Sam made the usual small talk then said, "Listen, Angus, I want you to do me a favor."

"Sorry, Sam, not tonight. Colleen's already spoken for. We're swapping with the Stahlmeyers, and frankly, I'm kinda looking forward to it. Lately, Gerta's been staying away from her potato salad and it's starting to show."

"That's good news for all of us, Angus. But that's not the kind of favor I'm callin' about. I'm sending my boy out to you. Want you to give the lad a job."

Angus reverted to his Irish accent. He always does when he gets excited. "Faith and begorrah. A job? For Isaac? Holy mother of God, Sam, I don't know."

"Don't worry, he'll stay clear of the kitchen. Any chance the Hodworths will be having supper at The Shamrock tonight?"

"Fella's already made a reservation. Has the hots for Colleen."

"We all have, Angus, we all have. Here's what I want you to do with Isaac." Sam took a moment's pause to consider how this plan, if it is to work, will involve good judgement and a heavy dose of masculine charm. He glanced over at his son who was currently busy wiping the grease off the crescent wrench with the cotton waistband of his underpants.

Isaac smiled back at his dad and held the clean wrench up with pride to show its gleaming sparkle.

Sam continued on the phone call, "Like I say, he'll stay clear of the kitchen."

• • •

After inspecting their Chinese eatery Phil and Carol said goodbye to the real estate lady and walked back to their motel. Upon their arrival, Phil was thrilled to find his car fixed up with four new tires. He was not so thrilled, however, to find his two kids sitting in their rooms, hunched over their devices. On a beautiful morning like this they should be outside enjoying the noon-hour sunshine. Well, Phil will put a stop to that.

He slapped Nate on his backside and announced he was taking him and his sister for lunch at Stahlmeyer's Bakery, the German place where they'd had the delicious ice cream last night. Nate liked this idea. Taylor... well, with a teenage girl who can tell?

Once again, the bakery did not disappoint. Phil's pastrami sandwich, his German potato salad, and his beet salad were excellent. And since he'd already shot his diet all to hell at breakfast Phil joined the rest of the family in having ice cream, a local flavor called Huckleberry. It was delicious. All in all, the whole lunch would have been perfect if not for one small glitch. It started when the family was trooping out past the cash register. Carol tried to compliment the German lady on serving such wonderful food, but Carol's kind words were not accepted graciously.

"Ya, ya, I know," nodded the short and sturdy woman, totally unimpressed. "Best Bratwurst vat you ever taste. Mmm-mmm, lip-schmeckin' *gut*. Never had nothing like dat before. And for this I should be flattered."

"Well, I just—"

"What do you people know about good food anymore. All your taste buds have been burned off by nitrates, monosodium glutamate, hydrolyzed plant protein. I'm surprised you could taste the difference between homemade knackwurst and the factory *scheisse* you've been feeding this little one." The woman now addressed her bitterness to Nate. "You like my potato salad, too, little poisoned one?"

Nate answered, "What does *scheisse* mean?"

"Never you mind what *scheisse* means," the German lady snapped back. "*Kinder* should speak only when spoken to."

"But you just spoke to me," Nate answered.

The woman looked up at Carol. "This is how modern mothers teach their kinder to be? Talk-backers?"

Carol's eyes widened as she loaded a bullet into her verbal chamber, "I was just trying to compliment your food, but if you can't—"

Phil stepped in between the ladies, saying to the German woman, "It was very nice. Thank you." He nudged Carol and the two kids to the front door, out onto the sidewalk.

As they proceeded to the car, Carol said, "I don't care how good the damn ice cream is, we're not eating in that place again."

Phil said, "I warned you, honey. Small towns. People in these little places are a breed apart. They just don't cotton to—" He suddenly realized something was missing. He patted his shirt pocket. Nope, not there. "My sunglasses... I must've left them on the table. I'll catch up to you." He then turned and hurried back to the restaurant.

The spring on the screen door creaked as he opened it and stepped inside. He was prepared to explain to the rude woman why he'd returned, but he didn't have to — the front dining area was empty. The German lady must be in the kitchen slapping the cook around. No problem, Phil could see the sunglasses sitting on the table where he'd left them. He quickly grabbed them and was just turning to leave when he heard the German woman's voice leak out the closed kitchen door.

"I'm never doing nothing like that again. Never ever." Yes, it was definitely the German woman, but she sounded different. The hard, sharp edge that had sliced a piece off poor Carol had been softened, dulled down to a butter knife. In fact, if Phil was hearing correctly, the woman sounded as though she might possibly be sobbing.

"Never again. I don't care what Sam Beckwith wants," the woman said to someone. "Never am I doing nothing like that again." Phil recognized the name Sam Beckwith as the mayor of Perpetuity.

"But Gerta," said a man in a similar German accent. "This we must do. It's best. Best for us. Best for the town. Best for the valley."

"Then let Sam do it," the woman said. "Not me. Did you see that poor woman? Did you see the look on her face when I snapped at her? The look on her little boy's face? Such lovely people. Let Sam Beckwith play the Devil. Let Rupert Thatcher vandalize these poor people. Not me. I can't. This is not what we came to America to do. Not what we came out west to do."

Rupert Thatcher... that was the name of the auto mechanic who fixed Phil's tires. Had he also flattened them? Phil stood still. He didn't have a clue what these people were talking about. But he had to hear more.

Just then the screen door slammed. Phil turned to see a scruffy-looking teenage boy walk in. The kid was wearing ear buds with a connecting wire that disappeared into the knee pocket of his cargo pants. The music leaking out of his ears sounded like hip-hop. The kid looked at Phil but did not react. Standard procedure for a teenager in any town.

Phil started to leave, but just as he reached the door the German woman emerged from the back room. Her eyes opened wide when she saw him. Phil held up his sunglasses to explain. "Forgot 'em."

The woman asked, "You... you have been here long?"

Rather than lie, Phil turned to the kid and said, "You're deafening yourself with those, you know."

The kid flashed his middle finger at Phil. Also standard procedure. Phil bid goodbye to the lady and hurried out to the street.

Carol was waiting for him. "You get your sunglasses?"

He showed her his glasses and cocked a thumb toward the deli. "That German woman... I think she was being rude on purpose."

"That's nice," Carol said with her usual sarcasm. "Good to see it wasn't an accident." She walked to the car.

"No, I mean, it was like some sort of edict or something."

"Edict?"

"I overheard her. She said she felt lousy about it."

"She apologized?."

"She didn't know I was there. She said she was only following orders."

Carol laughed. "The German lady said she was *only following orders?*"

"Sounds silly, I know."

By now they had reached the car. At first, Phil didn't notice anything wrong. But once again, his sharp son did. "Holy *scheisse*," Nate said, "Here we go again."

Phil's eyes immediately darted to the tires. No. They seem fine. No flats.

"Oh... my... God," cried Taylor. She was standing behind the vehicle.

Three quick steps and Phil saw what the problem was. The rear window. Shattered. Not quite broken all the way through, but totally spider-webbed to the point of being opaque.

Phil immediately spun around and searched the street for any sign of the jerk who'd done this. A range of mountains bordered the north end, flatter grasslands to the south. No vandals running into either postcard picture. Could the asshole still be hanging around? Maybe. Don't they like to admire their work?

Phil could see a few people farther down the sidewalk, but none of them looked suspicious. None of them was running. Nor carrying a baseball bat. A half a block the other way a young couple was pushing a baby stroller. Across the street, in front of the bank, a woman was bent down tying her dog's leash to a lamp post. On that same side of the street, an elderly man was sitting on a bench. He seemed to be facing this way. Phil hurried over to him.

"You see him?" Phil called out as he stepped off the asphalt road and onto the sidewalk.

"See who?"

Phil pointed back to his car. "The jerk who did that?"

The man squinted at the broken window. "Oh, my. Isn't that a shame."

"You see the guy?"

"Can't say's I have."

Phil had a damn good idea who the guilty party was. It had to be that kid with the ear buds who had walked into the deli. But unless somebody had seen the little twerp do it, there was nothing Phil could do.

"Shit," Phil said to the old man. "I was parked for just a few minutes."

"Doesn't take long. Not in this town."

"Huh? What d'ya mean?"

"Kids around here..." The man spat onto the sidewalk. Something brown. Probably tobacco juice. "Nobody can drive a nice car in Perpetuity no more. Not a shiny new one like yours. Outa-state plates. New tires. Geez, fella, you're just askin' for it."

Phil couldn't believe his ears. This hayseed was blaming him for the crime. Blaming the victim for owning a nice car.

"Just a friendly tip," the idiot hick offered. "Next time you come visit our lovely burg, bring a shitbox. And most important — don't tell your insurance company you're comin'."

"The insurance companies know about this?"

The man spat again. "Why do you think our insurance rates are the highest in the state."

"You're kidding."

"Don't matter much, though. Nobody carries any."

"Nobody insures their cars? That's crazy. Besides being dangerous, isn't it slightly illegal?"

"So's bashing in car windows, but it doesn't seem to stop anyone."

Phil couldn't believe what he was hearing. "You got a police department. Can't they do something?"

"Suppose they could if they wanted to."

"*If they wanted to?*"

The man winked. "Marshal's brother-in-law owns the town garage."

"*Marshal?*"

"Chief. I mean *Chief.* Chief of Police."

"The guy that fixed my tires was that cop's brother-in-law?"

"Very close family. Shared a wagon on their way here." The man shook his head. "I mean, truck. A *truck.* I think it was a panel van."

Phil gave up on this guy and walked back to his car. When he reached Carol and the kids, he had just two words for them, "Get in."

Carol protested, "You can't it drive like this."

"Watch me."

Now it was Taylor's turn, "I'll die."

"Fine. Then walk. You know where the motel is."

Nate tugged at his Dad's t-shirt, "Are we still going to the water slides?"

Phil opened his car door for the boy to get in. "We'll see, Nate."

But Taylor still balked. "What if somebody sees me in this."

"Then they'll know you've visited beautiful downtown Perpetuity." Phil got into the car and waited. Finally Taylor and her mother reluctantly joined him.

As they drove down the main drag, Carol was examining the line of vehicles parked along the curb. "Funny..." she muttered.

"A riot." Phil answered.

"Funny how our car is the only one that was hit."

Phil took a look for himself at the parked cars he was passing. Carol was right — not a one of them had a broken window nor a flat tire.

Carol continued with her thought, "Same this morning at the motel — a whole parking lot full of cars, many of them out-of-state, yet ours was the only one that had its tires slashed."

"Yeah, I noticed that too," Phil said. "I'd have brought it up, but I figured you'd call me paranoid." Now Phil noticed something else about the vehicles he was passing. All the cars were fairly new, not old shitboxes. Granted, some of these nice vehicles could belong to out-of-towners. But not all of them. So, why did the old man lie about the locals all driving old wrecks?

And why was that German lady at the delicatessen instructed to be rude to Phil and his family?

And why was the real estate woman so discouraging about their Chinese restaurant? It wasn't that bad a place. And that brings up another odd thing.

That real estate agent, Violet Snelling, is the only agent in town. Carol had checked. Nobody else sold property here. Sure, the town is small. But just one real estate broker? And she's part-time?

The answer to all these questions, of course, was simple — these folks don't want strangers moving into their precious little town. No new neighbors, thank you, we have enough. Well, this is fine with Phil. He has no intention of spending another day in Perpetuity, Wyoming. Tomorrow morning the Hodworths are leaving these mountains and driving back to civilization as fast as their sad, abused little car can take them.

But first... Phil had promised his kids some wet and wild fun at the local water park and that's what they're going to get. Phil rarely breaks a promise to his kids, and these high-altitude hayseeds aren't going to make him break one now. But one thing is for sure — when Daddy gets to that waterpark, Daddy is going to be very careful where he parks his car.

CHAPTER TEN

The attendant in the ticket booth stuck his head out for a closer look. This was obviously a sight he'd never seen before.

"Four, please," said Phil with a smile.

The puzzled attendant at the Perpetuity Mountain Ski Club and Water Park asked the four people who were standing in the middle of the roadway, "Where's your car?"

"That's a secret," Nate answered.

Phil kept smiling as he presented his happy self plus the other three members of his happy family, each one decked out in happy, colorful shorts, sandals, and light shirts, and each carrying a tote stuffed with beach towels and bathing suits. The Hodworth troupe was intent on having some fun in this town even if it kills them.

The ticket taker pulled his head back into his booth, but it wasn't easy. Well into his fifties, he was no light-weight and neither was his head. Phil guessed they'd built the ticket booth around him.

Carol said with a chuckle, "I guess nobody's ever arrived here without a car before, huh?"

"Oh, we gits all sorts vehicles here besides cars. We git bicycles, motorbikes, scooters, R.V.'s. Heck, in winter, ol' Jed Eberhardt even drives his horse-drawn cutter through here. But to my recollection, nobody's never come by foot 'afore."

"Call us pioneers." Phil joked. "We're a hardy bunch." In truth, the family hadn't walked far. Phil had tucked the Toyota away in a grove of cedars just down the road where, hopefully, no local vandals will find it.

Phil handed the man a couple of fifties. "Two adults and two—" He stopped himself and corrected his order. "*Three* adults and *one* child." Phil knew darn well that, when his daughter changes into her swimsuit, nobody is going to mistake her for a child.

The attendant gave Phil four tickets and change, thereby allowing the Hodworths to shuffle and flip-flop their way into the park.

Located at the base and up the western slope of Perpetuity Mountain, the water park seemed rather small compared to the ones back East. But on the plus side, this park wasn't nearly as crowded as those attractions usually are. The parking lot was barely a quarter full, and from what Phil could see of the main water slide which ran down the ski hill parallel to the chair lift, business was slack.

The main slide emptied into a large wading pool at the bottom which was almost vacant of swimmers. This was seen as good news by Carol, Taylor, and Nate, but to Phil the static picture was rather unsettling. This dry, hot weather couldn't be more conducive to cool, wet fun — so where is everybody? Is this water park in some sort of trouble? Had there been a health scare? Had somebody discovered some new strain of antibiotic-resistant water-born bug in this thing? Surely, even here in Buffalo Barf, Wyoming, the amusement parks must have inspectors and health codes, right?

Phil looked up at the giant slide and thought how he'd like to tackle the thing and show the kids how it's done, but he was afraid of wrenching his back again. Last March, on the ski slopes in Wilmott, he had taken quite a tumble. He shouldn't have attempted that black diamond run, but he couldn't resist showing off for his brother-in-law's new wife. Actually, she looked a lot like that Irish waitress who'd spilled breakfast on him this morning, except the Irish woman's boobs weren't store-bought. Phil wondered if that waitress would be serving dinner tonight. She really did seem to be flirting with him. Man, if Phil were still single...

"Honey," Carol said.

"Uh huh?"

"I know what you're thinking."

"You, uh... You do?"

"And don't worry. You have my full approval."

"I do?"

"After all, there's nothing I can do to stop you."

Phil suspected they were talking at cross purposes, but he went along with the flow anyway. "That's very open-minded of you, sweet heart."

"Just don't come running to me if you can't walk in the morning. You'll have only yourself to blame."

"True..."

"I know how much you enjoy these slides."

"Oh, right," Phil patted his son on the head. "No, I think this time Nate can handle the rides alone. Right, buddy?"

Nate answered by running off ahead to the change rooms. The rest of the family followed, and moments later they were all in their suits and ready for some splashes and giggles.

The fun started at the big wave pool. And that's also where it ended. Nate was the first to stick his toe into the water. He was also the first to give editorial comment: "Well, that just sucks."

Phil followed his son into the thigh-deep water. "Geez, he's right."

Carol stepped into the pool. "What in the...?"

Taylor was last in but first to sum up the situation in specifics. "My breakfast tea was cooler than this."

Phil walked over to the closest bathers — two rather thick, middle-aged women who were standing motionless about twenty feet away. He skipped any introduction and just asked, "They heat this water?"

"No need," one woman said.

Her friend added with a proud smile, "It's natural."

Now Phil got it. "Hot springs?"

The ladies nodded in animatronic unison as if to say, *Got any other dumb questions, Einstein?* Phil had heard that Wyoming was dotted with hot springs, but he never dreamed anyone would use one to irrigate a water park. Not in summer, at least. Who wants to sit in hot water when it's ninety degrees out? On the plus side, Phil now understood why, despite the usual splash-time toys — fountains, spray rings, and water cannons — the few youngsters who were in attendance were standing like bored statues, wondering where the fun had floated off to.

Nate announced to all within hearing distance, "When I pee, it actually cools this down."

"Follow me," Phil called as he waved everyone out of the soup. "The slide should still be fun."

Trying his best to remain cheerful and save this day, Phil led his disappointed kids over to the boarding platform of the ski chair lift which, in turn, would transport them up the mountain to the entrance of the big water slide up top.

The ride up the ski hill, suspended high above the rocks and pine trees, turned out to be fun for everyone — everyone, that is, except Carol. Afraid of heights, the poor gal kept her eyes shut tight until she got to the top. Once safely deposited on top of the mountain Nate and Taylor ran off to the raised boarding platform from which they promptly launched themselves down the big fiberglass water chute that zig-zagged its way down the ski slopes like a soggy game of snakes and ladders. Meanwhile, Carol and Phil strolled around the grassy parkland that covered the domed mountaintop and took in the gorgeous panorama.

From up here Phil had his first good look at Perpetuity Valley and the surrounding hills and mountains, some of which were taller than this one. The immediate valley below had a smallish river running through it that obviously kept the lowlands and surrounding plateau green, although not as green as the pine-tree-jammed mountain sides. Phil could see just one decent paved highway running through the area — the one he'd taken to get here. The rest of the roads were dirt or gravel. Lots of white fences defined small farms and ranches. One brown bare patch at the base of a far hill looked like it might be an open-pit mine of some sort. Phil had read that lots of coal mines operated in this state. Or at least, they did before America's power stations saw the error of their ways.

While Nate and Taylor wore out the back sides of their bathing suits on the slide and chair lift, Phil and Carol explored the mountaintop and the shoreline of a small pond that had the audacity to call itself a lake.

Perpetuity Lake is the size of about two football fields. According to the woman who had helped the family board the chair lift, this small mountaintop lake is fed by hot springs and is the source of the warm water that flows down the slide and into that ridiculous splash pool. She said the lake is also the main source of the Perpetuity River. When Phil mentioned that this seems like a lot of work for such a little pond, the woman informed him that the lake is bottomless. Phil knew this had to be horseshit, but he played along with her just the same. After all, he's on vacation.

The lady at the chair lift went on to explain that, while the naturally heated lake is not terribly popular in summer, it is a big hit in winter. That's when the local townsfolk use it as an outdoor hot tub and excuse not to go curling. The winter fun-seekers run out through the snow from the chalet-style clubhouse, frolic in the water for a bit, and then scamper back indoors to their warm towels and hot toddies. Unfortunately, the clubhouse is closed in summer which Phil thought was a damn shame — he was dying for a cold beer.

Carol managed to find a soda vending machine outside the side entrance of the ski club's chalet, but the only drink on tap was some locally brewed poison called sarsaparilla. Phil and Carol tried a bottle and agreed that the syrupy sweet concoction was not drinkable by anyone over the age of twelve.

Meanwhile, Nate and Taylor took about three runs down the slide before reporting that they were bored and ready to go home. The two kids could have taken one last slide down the mountain and met Mom and Dad at the bottom, but Taylor said the chair lift was more fun and a lot cooler, so she and her brother hopped onto one of the two-person bench seats with Phil and Carol following in a seat behind them. As with the trip up, Carol closed her eyes once she was seated. She'd been a heck of a good sport. She could have just stayed at the bottom for the afternoon, but she didn't want to be a party pooper.

So that was that, Phil mused as he patted Carol's white knuckles and watched the mountainside fall away beneath him. Another beautiful summer day shot to hell in Coyote Cramps, Wyoming. Well, just one more night of this nonsense and he'll be watching this crummy little town disappear in his rear-view mirror. No, that's not quite true. Unless he gets the broken rear window replaced, he'll have to watch it disappear in his side-view mirror. Doesn't much matter exactly how he sees this town disappear, just as long as he sees it all disappear real soon. Well, maybe not that Irish waitress. He's not anxious to see the last of her. But that's silly. He's happily married. Deliriously happily married to the greatest girl in the world. Of course, if anything should ever happen to Carol, like if she accidentally fell out of a chair lift or something...

"Stop that!" Carol snapped.

"Huh? What was I—?""

"Please, don't do that." Carol dug her fingernails into his forearm with one hand while keeping her other hand tight over her eyes. "Sit still. Don't rock."

Phil wrapped his arm around his scared little girl. "Don't worry, honey, we're not very high."

"No? Would it hurt if we fell off?"

Phil looked down at the hungry jagged rocks waiting three stories below. Then he cast his gaze ahead to Taylor and Nate who were busy swatting each other in their bench seat fifty feet farther down grade. He patted Carol's hand and said, "Nobody's falling off anything." He knocked his knuckles against the corroded iron post that connected the rickety old wooden bench seat to the rusty cable a few feet above. "These things are perfectly safe," he lied. "Sure, this one is a bit of an antique, but I'm sure it's inspected regularly. Hell, the thing has been running for long, long time, I'm sure it will keep running a little while long—"

And with those words serving as an ironic cue, the sagging, old rusty cable and its arthritic iron mechanism shuddered to a slow, agonizing, and completely dead stop.

• • •

The huge bullwheel drive which hauled the cable and its passengers up and down the mountain at the speed of six hundred feet per minute sat housed in a cinder block building at the bottom of the mountain, and Bob Gilchrist knew that this was not really the best place for it. The electric motor would operate much more efficiently had it been placed at the top of the lift, but that would have meant burying heavy gauge electrical power cable all the way up the mountain, which would have been an expensive proposition with all this rock to drill through. So Bob Gilchrist decided to construct it this way. And so far, he's had no regrets. With very few upgrades to the original equipment, the machinery has run for twelve months of the year, week in, week out, for over fifty years with nary a glitch. And today was no exception, which was why it had hurt Bob so much to do this terrible, needless thing.

Bob Gilchrist took his hand off the double pole, single-throw switch that had just shut off five hundred and fifty kilowatts worth of electrical juice to the four-hundred horsepower DC motor. He looked up to the spring-activated ratchet brake to make sure it had engaged the bullwheel automatically as it was supposed to. And it had. "There you go, Sammy," he grumbled. "You happy now?"

"I know how difficult this must be for you, Bob." Sam Beckwith clasped his old friend's shoulder. "But it has to be done."

The silence inside the concrete hut broke Bob Gilchrist's heart. Normally, he would now be hearing the three-hundred-horse diesel auxiliary engine kick in and take over for the dead electrical motor, but not today. Today, the little room was quiet as a whorehouse on Christmas morning.

"You really think it's worth it?" Bob asked.

"You want to save this valley, don't you?"

Bob had to think this one over. "Suppose so."

"You don't sound too sure."

No, Bob was not sure.

· · ·

When Carol felt the chairlift stutter to a stop, she immediately asked, even though she knew it couldn't possibly be true, "We there already?"

"Something's wrong."

She squeezed her grip on Phil's arm even tighter. He didn't complain.

"Don't worry," Phil assured her. "I'm sure they'll have it running again in no time."

Carol loosened her grip on his arm but kept her other hand tight over her eyes. She wasn't really all that scared about falling — she just had vertigo. Looking down makes her dizzy, so she kept her eyes shut as she asked, "The kids okay?"

Phil called out, "You guys okay down there?"

Carol heard Taylor and Nate answer in the affirmative, more or less, but mixed in with their chorus of whines and grumbles came another voice. An unfamiliar voice. A man's voice.

"I'm cool," the man said. "Thanks for asking." The gentleman's voice came from Carol's left side, not very far away. "How about your own bad selves?" the man asked.

Phil answered him in a projected, but not a shouted, voice. ""We're good. This happen a lot around here?"

"Wouldn't know. I'm new to this, uh, this area."

Still chicken to spread her fingers and peek, Carol assumed that the man was seated in a passing chair, stuck while travelling up the hill parallel to hers on its way down.

The man continued, "Lovely afternoon, huh? A little too bright for some, I see. But I dig it. Your sun gets quite high at this time of day."

Our sun? What the—? Carol didn't understand.

The man continued, "Would your squeeze like to borrow my sunglasses? I can toss them over to you."

Squeeze? Oh, *wife*. "No, no," Carol said with eyes covered, "I'm okay, thank you."

Phil patted Carol's knee and explained to the man, "Afraid of heights."

"Not really." Carol spoke up loudly so the man could hear, "Just makes me a little queasy, is all."

"Stop it!" This was Taylor's voice coming from down below. "Mom, would you please tell this little turd to stop rocking."

Carol yelled, "Don't rock, Nate."

Phil added. "Sit still, son. Don't scare your sister."

"Your offspring?" the man asked.

"Presently," said Phil. "But we're open to offers."

Carol expected to hear the man laugh at Phil's quip, but the man didn't. Instead, he seemed to play along with Phil's joke, "I'm sure you'll get a fair price. Even for the little turd."

Phil chuckled, then got back to the subject at hand, the stalled chair lift. "I believe these things are electric. Must have some backup power, though, right?" Carol could hear the concern in her husband's voice.

"I imagine they do," said the man. "Probably nuclear."

"Pardon me?" Phil obviously didn't understand.

The man corrected himself. "No, that wouldn't make sense. Not yet. You've still got some carbon fuels left. Like I say, I'm new here." The man had a slight accent which Carol couldn't identify. Maybe Canadian.

Carol heard Taylor yell out, "Ewwww!"

"What's wrong now?" Carol yelled to the kids.

Taylor called back. "Would you please tell your son to stop farting."

"I didn't fart."

"Yes, you did," said Taylor. "I can smell it."

"That might be me," said the stranger in the chair next door. "Must've gobbled down the French onion soup a might too fast last night by the ol' campfire."

"Oh, great," Phil whispered under his breath for only Carol's ears. "A whole mountainside, and we get stuck next to a French Canadian gasbag."

Carol elbowed him. "Shhh!"

The possibly Canadian gentleman said, "Certainly is lovely part of the planet."

"Yeah, lovely," Phil answered, but with little conviction.

"Must say, though, it's changed a tad since I last crashed here."

"A tad or two." Now Phil was mocking the Canadian man. Carol wished he wouldn't do that.

"And when was that?" Carol asked, trying to make up for her husband's rude manners.

"Oh, geez. Let's see. On your solar calendar...?" The man sounded like he was counting on his fingers. "Hard to say exactly. I've sort of been asleep."

Phil said nothing. And neither did Carol. What the hell was this guy talking about? *Your* sun? *Your solar calendar? Asleep?* Carol had to see this guy for herself.

Slowly, she parted her fingers. Not far, just enough to make a slit as if she were peering through a mail slot. She took special care not to look down.

Turns out the man was seated barely twenty feet away. He was dressed in 1970s hippie garb, which, while surprising, was no big deal to Carol who tended to like retro herself. What did surprise Carol, though, was the color of the man's skin. Because of his Canadian accent, she had expected to see a white man. But this fellow was African-American. Or African-Canadian. He was younger than she'd expected, too — late teens, early twenties. Carol always had difficulty guessing ages of black people. And of Asians. She was not proud of this.

The man's retro outfit included bell-bottom jeans, a fringed buckskin vest, and a blousy, paisley polyester shirt. Apart from this rather bold costume, the young man was quite handsome, When he flashed Carol a big smile, he reminded her of that young black comedian whose name she could never remember. She'd probably remember the name if he were white, though.

The black man continued talking, but Carol now had trouble listening. The sight of all the empty air between her feet and the ground was making her dizzy. She closed her eyes and leaned against Phil's soft cotton-knit golf-shirt. Phil got the message and wrapped his arm tight around her. As always, it helped.

Phil interrupted the hippie, "Please, excuse us. My wife doesn't feel well."

"Of course. Peace, bro." The gentleman said no more. Not with his mouth, that is.

This time Carol heard it.

"Sorry 'bout that," muttered the handsome young African-Canadian as he farted again. And then again. And then again. "This planet... too much gluten."

Planet?

CHAPTER ELEVEN

Phil was pissed. And somewhat relieved. But mostly pissed.

An hour and forty-three minutes stuck with his ass plus the asses of his family dangling in mid-air high over the rocky slopes of Perpetuity Mountain, and not a single word of apology from the park's management. No refunds. No free passes. Not even a free bottle of sarsaparilla. Just some idiot in a ten gallon hat and a twenty gallon moustache helping Carol out of her chairlift seat saying, "'Lectrical power ain't too reliable in these parts, ma'am."

Phil asked the half-baked cowpoke, "Doesn't this contraption have some sort of emergency power? A standby generator or something?"

The cowpoke poked a long skinny finger into Phil's chest and said. "That's a darn fine idea you got there, slim. A standby generator. I'll table that suggestion at our next roundup."

Huh? Phil didn't get it. What's going on here? Are these rubes really as dumb as they appear? Is there a problem here with inbreeding? Are these folk the end result of too many indiscriminate Butch Cassidy-type leaps into the shallow end of the gene pool? Could be. This valley is isolated by ice and snow for four months of the year, so by the time February is finished, that chubby cousin with the extra molars and the missing nipple must start to look pretty darn hot. But there's one hitch to this theory: If these people are really as dumb as they appear, how come their little town is so prosperous?

Carol had been the first to notice it. While driving through the valley she'd noted that the locals seemed to be doing quite well for themselves. Their houses were generally well-kept, and most of the garages housed late-model cars and shiny new trucks. Phil had further commented that such affluence didn't seem to jibe with the valley's apparent lack of industry. So, how do these people pay for their new cars, nice homes, digital satellite dishes, and state-of-the-art electronic devices?

Phil was pondering this mystery, standing with Nate outside the change rooms, when he heard flip-flops flapping up behind him. It was Carol and Taylor running out from the washroom. They seemed to be worked up about something.

Carol was almost too breathless to speak. "You'll never guess what we just overheard in there."

Phil didn't have time for gossip. He just took his darling wife's hand and started walking. It was almost six o'clock, and he was anxious to get back to his car before dusk. And before it gets vandalized. Or stolen. Or set ablaze.

Carol dug her heels in and forced him to stop. "Listen. A couple of women. They came into the ladies' room. They didn't know we were there."

Nate asked, "You were on the crapper?"

"In the stalls."

Taylor was also excited, which is rare for Taylor. She took over for her mother, "They were talking about the poor family that was stuck in the chair lift all afternoon."

"Us," Carol explained needlessly.

Taylor continued, "One of the women asked the other, 'How long was Bob planning on leaving them up there?'"

"Bob?" Phil asked.

Carol said, "Must be the park superintendent or chief engineer or something."

Taylor now ran with the ball, "One of the women wondered why it took Bob so long to throw the switch when, and I quote, *just a half-hour would have done the trick.*"

"'Done the trick?" Phil asked.

"Those were her exact words," Taylor said.

Carol summed things up, "Phil, the whole thing was planned. They stuck up there on purpose. I heard it all."

"You shouldn't have flushed," Taylor told her mother. "You should've waited. Heard what more they had to say."

"I know, but I thought maybe they were waiting to go. There were only the two stalls."

"You're too nice."

Carol adjusted her beach bag on her shoulder. "You should have seen the look on their faces when they saw me step out of that stall. They absolutely froze."

Taylor added, "They'd been caught, and they knew it."

It was clear as fresh mountain spring water to Phil now. These mountain morons want the city folk to leave. To skedaddle. Get outa town. Do not pass Go, do not collect two hundred cow pies. But this... risking the lives of Phil and his family with this chairlift stunt. This was too much.

He looked around the park for someone to confront. An official ear to scream into. A nose to punch. A cowpoke to poke. Phil wondered where this park superintendent named Bob might be.

Carol, as usual, knew what was brewing in her husband's head. She placed her hand gently on his forearm and said. "Honey, there's nothing you can do."

"Nothing?" he snapped. Now he was transferring his anger to his wife. He knew it, but he couldn't help it. "Two fucking hours they left us hanging there. My whole family. Forty feet in the air! Somebody could have gotten hurt. Even killed. Look at you — you were scared shitless. *Nothing?* I don't think so."

"I understand," Carol soothed. "But let's give it some time. Think things over. Have some dinner." She turned to the kids. "Who's hungry?"

"Me," Nate said. "I could eat the south end of a north-bound goat."

Great, thought Phil. Now Nate was starting to talk like these hillbillies.

Carol turned to Phil, "Let's go honey. These people..." she waved her arm towards nobody in particular. "It sounds like they were all just following orders."

"Orders from the mayor. That's what the German lady said."

"Right," Carol agreed. "First thing tomorrow we'll go visit City Hall. You'll get to the bottom of this. You always do."

Phil hated it when Carol patronized him. He continued, "There's something going on here. Something big. Bigger than just *the locals not cottonin' to the new folk.*"

Surprisingly, Carol didn't dismiss his words as hyperbole. Instead, she went with the flow and quoted old Zachariah's note. She spoke the words as if they held biblical importance, "*Your presence in my home town will not be welcomed.*"

Phil continued the quote, "*Don't let them force you out.*"

And Taylor finished with, "*...not until you've discovered the secret for yourselves.*"

They paused and let the silence blossom.

Finally, Nate piped up, "I know a secret."

Carol returned to her patronizing mode, "I'm sure you do, sweetie."

"Wanna know what?" Nate goaded.

Taylor tried to turn her little brother off. "A secret isn't a secret if you tell it. Wipe your nose."

"The gravestones are phony." Nate wiped his nose on his beach towel.

"Gravestones?" Phil asked. "What gravestones?"

"Yesterday. In the cemetery. Eunice put out her cigarette on a gravestone, and I said—"

"Eunice?" Carol interrupted. "That little girl smokes?"

"I told her she shouldn't do it like that. Not on a gravestone. It was disrespectful to the dead guy."

Taylor said, "She's only, like, eight."

Nate continued with his story, "She said it was okay 'cause all the gravestones are phony."

Phil exchanged looks with his wife. *Fake gravestones?*

Nate finished his tale, "She said I shouldn't tell anyone. It will be our little secret. I like her. She's fun. She has a lot of secrets."

"That's it!" Carol barked. "You are not playing with that little girl anymore."

"Aww, but geez," Nate whined. "She's trying to quit."

Carol looked to her husband for some support on this one. But he had other things on his mind.

A fake graveyard?

• • •

The only table available for dinner at the Shamrock Pub that night was right next to the same screaming baby that had bawled all the way through Phil's last two meals here. He suggested trying another restaurant, but Carol and the kids were too hungry and too tired to move on. Oh, well, at least he'll have that Irish waitress to flirt with.

Wrong again.

A young man came to take their orders. He was about Taylor's age. Maybe a year or two older. Probably a summer student. He was a nice looking Nordic-type blonde with blue-eyes. His clean-shaven face had sprouted a small crop of pimples, but it was under moderate control. Trim and muscular, he was probably a college athlete.

The kid turned out to be quite charming, which was a damn good thing considering what a lousy waiter he proved to be. Poor guy couldn't remember the simplest order without writing it down. And he knew none of the basic waiter moves. Like serve on the left, take from the right, and don't ask your customer how to spell *bruschetta*. Phil had a feeling this was the kid's first night on the job, so he went easy on him and tried not to order any dishes that were difficult to spell.

After a few minutes Phil noticed that the boy never served any other tables other than the Hodworth's. But what really pissed off Phil was that all the other tables, including the one with the crying baby, were being served by the Irish waitress. So why wasn't she serving Phil's table? Had her boss noticed what was going on between her and Phil? Had he taken her off Mr. Hodworth's table for fear of offending Mrs. Hodworth? Or worse, had Carol secretly requested the switch. No, that was crazy. Carol was used to Phil's roving eye, and as long as he didn't actually act on his carnal instincts, she was fine with them. Well, maybe *fine* isn't quite the right word.

Throughout the meal the young man showed a keen interest in Taylor, which was no surprise — she was an attractive girl. Finally, at the end of the meal, Phil's suspicions about the kid's horniness were confirmed when the little hustler presented Taylor with a single red rose and said, "I finish work in a few minutes. I wonder if I might take you out for dessert. There's a fine ice cream parlor down the street."

"*All* of us?" Nate asked.

Carol hushed her son, "No, Nate. We'll have something here."

The young horndog finished his pitch by turning to Phil and adding, "If it's all right with you, sir."

Holy shit. Phil had to chuckle at the kid's transparent attempt at impressing the old man. Phil wasn't buying it, but what the hell. "It's fine with us. You kids take off."

Carol, too, wanted to show her encouragement. She picked up the rose that had already dropped from her daughter's hand and sniffed it. "It is a nice evening for a walk."

The ball was now in Taylor's court, and she batted it right back. Hard. She gave the boy a patronizing half-smile and said, quite off-handedly, "Thanks, but I don't eat dessert."

Phil's heart went out to the poor boy. Smarmy hustler or not, it's tough to hit on a girl in front of her whole family like this and then to get shot down.

Carol stepped in and said to her daughter, "You don't have to have ice cream. I'm sure they have other dishes."

"Oh, indeed they do," the boy said. "There's frozen yogurt."

"Thanks," Taylor said. "But I'm kinda tired. It's been a long day."

"Yeah," Nate said. "She's been sitting in a ski lift for two hours."

"Yes, I heard about that," the young waiter said. "You must have been terrible frightened."

"Not really."

Phil took the opportunity to ask the kid, "That sort of thing happen a lot around here?"

"No, I've never—" The kid suddenly caught himself and pulled a one-eighty. "Yes, now that you mention it, it does. Electrical power isn't very reliable in this valley. Always cutting out when you need it most. Refrigerators go down. Stoves go out. Dinners get ruined. And computers... forget it. You gotta backup constantly." The young waiter turned back to Taylor and said in pathetic summation, "So, uh, that's a pass on the date for ice cream, I take it?"

Phil, who was a little cheesed off with his daughter's attitude, decided to put an end to the young man's suffering. "We gotta get an early start tomorrow. I think we'll all just order our dessert here for now."

The poor kid got the message and rhymed off the restaurant's choices of desserts simply by reading the menu. After they'd ordered and he had left, the Hodworth family sat in awkward silence waiting for Taylor to explain herself. The only vocal sounds, however, were those blasted from that crying baby in the high chair. Finally, Carol forced the issue. "I thought he was quite nice."

"Well spoken," Phil added. "I liked how he almost never used the word *like*. Sort of a throwback to another generation."

"Throwback is right," Taylor said. "He's weird."

Phil didn't argue with his daughter because, in truth, she was absolutely right. There was something unsettling about the kid. A vibe that Phil had picked up from other young people in town. A bright adult openness where dark teenage angst should be.

The Hodworths waited, but the college boy never came back with dessert. Probably too embarrassed. On the plus side, the kid's replacement server turned out to be the Irish waitress. Carol inquired as to what had happened to the young man who had been taking care of them.

"Isaac?" said the waitress, whose name was Colleen. "I'm afraid he had to, uh, take a phone call." Colleen then served their desserts. As usual, she dropped a spoon. Picked it up. Adjusted her boobs, smiled at Phil, and said, "Enjoy."

He did.

• • •

Isaac Beckwith had never been so humiliated in all his born days. And in public, too. Turned down by a teenage girl who was young enough to be his great, great, great granddaughter. But of course, she didn't know that. The Hodworth girl thought Isaac was just a pimple-faced teenager. Well, she was half right. Isaac did have pimples. He has had them for over a century and a half, which adds up to a sizeable lot of squeezing and popping. But Isaac is no teenager. Nor is he a waiter. He is, in fact, an officer of the law — deputized a hundred and forty-odd years ago by Marshal Dagleish himself. The Marshal, of course, is now called Police Chief Dagleish on account of nobody uses the term Marshal anymore. Not unless they're leading a parade.

Apparently, this young Taylor gal is seventeen. Isaac's frozen age is nineteen, and because of his nice haircut he looks more like twenty-one. Curious how the gal's parents didn't seem to have a problem with the age difference. But no, they were totally cool with it. It was their snotty daughter who had the objection. Well, there's only one thing to do now. Onward to plan B — the plan Isaac had favored from the start.

Isaac slipped out of the silly brocade waiter's vest that Angus Murphy had loaned him and slid back into into his own black denim bomber jacket that matched his black jeans. He tucked the silly bow tie into the pocket of the vest and placed the garment on the counter by the kitchen's back entrance. He noticed a silver liquor hip flask lying on the counter. Probably belonged to little Eunice, the cook's helper. She likes a tipple now and again. Isaac unscrewed the cap and took a good pull. Yup, it was Eunice's all right. She always preferred Cal Thwaite's high-test brew over the store-bought swill. Isaac took another, longer swig, screwed the cap back on, and slipped the flask into the inside breast pocket of his bomber jacket. He noticed a butane lighter lying beside an empty chafing dish. It was one of those long-necked lighters people use to start barbecues. Isaac smiled. This was obviously a sign from God that Plan B was indeed the righteous course to follow.

Isaac pocketed the lighter and slipped out the back door. He skipped down the steps. Yes, literally skipped. That's how happy he was about finding the lighter. And God.

When you hitch up your team for a dangerous mission, it's always good to have the good Lord riding shotgun.

CHAPTER ELEVEN

In one graceful, easy swing, Emma Langtree lifted little Ezra out of the highchair and guided his chubby little legs into the twin openings of his stroller. She moved with the smooth grace that only a mother who's danced this ballet a thousand-thousand times could pull off. It was easier now that she had the muscles for it. Didn't used to, but after a hundred and sixty-six years of cradling her infant in the crook of her arm for countless hours of breast feeding, Emma's biceps were stronger than her husband's. And he used to be a blacksmith. Folks 'round town joke about Emma. They call her *Popeye*. They think it's funny. Or at least they used to. That right arm packs a hell of a punch now.

Her baby now secure in his seat, Emma weaved little Ezra's stroller through the tables and chairs to the front of the restaurant. When Angus Murphy saw her coming, he rushed from behind the cash counter to hold the door open for her. "Thanks again, Em, darlin'," he said.

"Breakfast?"

Angus nodded, "One more visit oughta clinch it."

"See you at eight then." She didn't mind, really. It was her civic duty. Plus, these meals were free.

Emma eased the stroller out the door and wheeled it across the motel's parking lot to the sidewalk. She could have driven her car here, but the restaurant is just a few blocks from her house. Besides, the baby has never gotten used to cars. He was always okay with the old wagons and buckboards, but there's something about the vibration of internal combustion engines. As soon as Emma puts the vehicle into gear, the baby upchucks. He isn't that way in the Sunday buggy, but Mayor Beckwith doesn't like for valley folk to use horse-drawn vehicles anymore. It's all part of keeping the biggest secret in the history of mankind, he says. Easy for him — he's not a mother.

Emma has always taken pride in how she's never let anything slip even though she's known the secret longer than just about anybody else in town. It could be said that she was the first to discover the whole deal. At first, she'd thought there was something horribly wrong with the baby. Everybody did. The Beckwith wagons had wintered over for a full six months and spring was blooming, but little Ezra was not. Emma was worried how, during those first five months, her baby hadn't put on any weight. He'd eaten fine throughout the harsh winter, thanks to the generosity of her fellow pilgrims and some very kind Arapahos camped nearby. Yet whenever she put Ezra on Jasper Carmichael's mineral assay scales the baby hadn't gained one solitary ounce of weight. No length either.

At first, folks thought the child was malnourished. Or maybe he was going to turn out to be a midget like in those pictures she'd seen on the circus posters back in St. Louis. But pretty soon other parents in the wagon train started noticing how their young ones weren't developing proper either. Little Charlotte Wallace wasn't getting her permanent teeth. Young Eunice Cartwright was stuck at four-foot, four inches with hands still too small to play her mother's pump organ. And poor twelve-year-old Willy Fortier, who'd been here for eight years and should be nearing twenty, was still singing soprano at church service.

All in all, it took quite a few years before folks finally figured out what was happening to their offspring. Or *not* happening. And even then, most couldn't quite believe it. Who would? When your son's testicles don't drop, you don't assume he's stopped aging — you just abandon any hopes of being called Grandma.

Emma stopped pushing the pram. She opened her backpack, fished out a sweatshirt, and slipped it over her t-shirt. No matter how hot the days might get, night breezes in Wyoming almost always carry a chill. Emma started walking again. She gently eased the stroller off the curb and continued to the corner across the street. As she wheeled Ezra over the tarmac, she noticed the baby had quietened down just as he always did. Needless to say, this was Emma's favorite time of day. The cool June evening breeze never fails to settle Ezra down.

As she hefted the stroller up onto the sidewalk, she noticed a man headed this way. He was oddly dressed. A soft, newsboy cap shaded his dark face. A suede vest with fringes tried its best to subdue a loud paisley print shirt that screamed for attention. All in all, the man seemed to be looking for the next bus back to the nineteen-sixties. When he got close, Emma noticed he was a negro. A darkie. No, that was wrong. Colored. Nope. Black. That's better. But Afro-American is probably best.

As he passed, he tipped his cap to her. "Evenin' ma'am."

Emma averted her eyes. Old habits die hard, especially for a woman who was born in the Old South.

"Coolin' off a tad," he said.

"Always does," Emma said, quickening her steps. Her acceleration wasn't racially motivated — at night like this she just doesn't like to encourage strangers of any color.

"Supposed to be another warm one tomorrow," he said, but now from behind her.

"So's I hear." Emma said without looking around.

"Nice to see Ezra feeling better."

Emma stopped. Had she heard right? Had the stranger called her baby by name? She turned and asked, "Do I know—?"

"Last time I saw him he had the colic."

Oh, right. Of course. Now she understood. This man must have been in The Shamrock and heard Angus call the baby by name. So she asked the man, "You were in the restaurant?"

"Just headed that way. Any good?" He started crossing the street.

"Uh, yes, very nice." Now that she took a good look at the fellow, he seemed vaguely familiar. She asked him, "You know my baby?"

"Hey, who could forget something like that? Cute little tyke. A bit noisy, though. Loud. Sounds like a leaf blower. But cute. Real cute." The man pointed up at The Shamrock. "I hope they have johnnycake. I do dig the johnnycake. With chokeberry syrup. Remember?"

"Remember? No. No, I'm afraid I..."

"That last night? By the campfire? You folks were kind enough to share your grub with me. Gotta tell you, I've missed that johnnycake. Haven't missed the pork and beans. But I've missed that johnnycake." Finally, the man tipped his cap once more to her, "Have a nice evening. Great to see Ezra doing so well."

"But I don't—"

Just then, a panel truck rumbled by. It blocked Emma's view of the stranger. By the time the truck had clattered past, the young Afro-American man was too far away for Emma to speak to without yelling. She didn't want to do that. She might wake Ezra.

And she certainly did not want to do that.

• • •

Isaac Beckwith was no idiot.

He knew he was supposed to alert the volunteer fire boys first, before striking the match. But if he alerted them too soon Chief McNeice would call Isaac's father to check that Isaac has council's permission for this burn. And that would only delay the inevitable.

The council tended to over-think and under-do. A lot of folks in Perpetuity are like that nowadays. The walking dead, Isaac calls them. All thought and no action. But not Isaac. He still has some gumption. Some pioneer spirit. He's still willing to take the bull by the tail and look the problem straight in the eye.

Isaac eased his truck down the narrow alleyway until he reached the back door of the Shangri-La restaurant. Then he stopped, turned off the engine, and pulled the whiskey flask from his pocket. One last swallow to fend off the cold night chills.

Isaac grabbed his flashlight — not the dinky LED one, the big, old D cell monster from his tool box. He shone the light on his wristwatch. Just past eleven. Perfect. Too late for tourists to be roaming about, but not so late he'd be dragging the volunteer boys out of their warm beds. Or out of their neighbor's warm beds.

He stepped out of his truck and, using the big flashlight as a hammer, busted through the back window of the restaurant. Of course, he could have simply borrowed the key to the building from Violet Snelling at the newspaper, but that would have given his game away, and Violet doesn't always approve of Isaac's propensity for sparking quick, bright solutions to dark problems.

Right after busting the window, but before entering the building, Isaac took out his cell phone. He swiped the pre-programmed number for town emergency calls. While waiting for the ring to be answered, he slipped the whiskey flask out from his pocket and took one more last pull.

"Hey, Isaac," Jenny McNeice answered. "Whaz up?"

"Hey, Jenn. Sorry to bother you during your dance show."

"No prob, I got a PVR. Everything cool at the farm?"

"I'm not at the farm. Uh, listen, I want to report a fire."

"Emerge or scheduled?"

"Emerge. Almost."

"Where?"

"Main Street. Shangri-La Gardens."

"The Gardens? Aw, gee, that's too bad. Hold on, I'll get Pete. He's on the hopper."

"No, no. Don't bother him. Let him finish up. There's no hurry. Just tell the fellas to come down to Shangri-La Gardens. But like I say, don't rush. Give me at least ten minutes."

"Ten? I thought you said this was emergency."

"I said *almost*. Better make it fifteen. It'll look bad if the pumper arrives too soon. The Hodworths will get suspicious."

"Hodworths? Who they?"

"You weren't at the meeting?"

"What meeting?"

"About the new folks. Week ago Wednesday."

"Wednesday? No way. That's the night my singin' show's on."

"You said you have a PVR."

"You like watching a football game after you know who's won?"

Isaac checked his watch. "Just tell Pete to be here in exactly fifteen minutes."

"Isaac, you got permission for this? 'Cause I haven't heard anything about no—"

"Fifteen minutes. The Gardens." And with that, Isaac hung up.

He lifted the two gallon gasoline can from the back of his truck and placed it on the sill of the broken window. But before climbing through he paused to take one more last pull of whiskey and to put on his safety glasses. Working on a farm teaches a man a thing or two about the importance of wearing proper safety equipment.

And Isaac was no idiot.

• • •

It had been a long day and Phil Hodworth was tired as an old dog. Trouble is, he was as horny as a young dog. Motel rooms had that effect on him. Sometimes, just walking down a hallway with a magnetic room key in his hand could inspire Phil's carnal cravings. Some sort of Pavlovian reaction. Maybe it was the smell of the pine-scented cleaning solvents that set him off. Who knows. Whatever the trigger was, hotels meant sex. Honeymoon sex. Vacation sex. Pay-per-view sex. And here he was — lying in a cheap motel room in Receding Gums, Wyoming, with a hot babe in bed beside him and he couldn't touch her. She wouldn't let him. She had a sunburn.

It was just a mild one, but Carol says it's distracting. *Thank you, Perpetuity Mountain Chair Lift And Rotisserie Cooker.* Of course, that wasn't the only impediment to Phil's hopes for connubial shenanigans. Phil and Carol are not presently lying alone in the bed. Taylor is sitting beside them so she can share their popcorn.

This was Taylor and her mom's room. Phil had transferred here because Nate is asleep in the boys' room. The sausage room, as Nate calls it. Tonight's movie is ladies' choice. That means a *rom-com* with accent on the *rom* not the *com*.

Phil swung his legs off the bed and announced to anyone who cared, "Going for some night air."

"Sorry, honey," Carol grabbed a handful of popcorn. "But we watched your end-of-the-world movie last night."

"Your *dumb* end-of-the-world movie," Taylor added.

Phil stood up, fastened the top button of his jeans, and grabbed his wallet off the dresser. "Might stop for a drink." He grabbed the room's key card and added, "If there's anything open in this burg that serves something stronger than sarsaparilla."

The ladies laughed. Not at his joke — at some line in the movie.

Phil opened the door and took a big lungful of night air. "Don't wait up. I might get lucky."

The girls laughed again. At the movie, of course.

A few steps across the parking lot and the night air felt a little cooler than Phil had expected. Must be the altitude. Should he go back inside and put on his sweater? No. That birthday cardigan made him look like his father. Besides, he was just going across the lot to the pub. During dinner he had noticed a big-screen television over the bar.

Phil took a moment to look up at the night sky. He'd heard that the dark skies out here were pretty spectacular, but if the stars were out tonight he couldn't tell — his retinas were still burned from that TV screen. He'd noticed lately that, as he grew older, his eyes took longer and longer to adjust to night mode.

The Shamrock pub looked closed, but he tried the door anyway. Yup, locked. So much for any hopes of watching ESPN. Same for any hopes of watching that hot Irish waitress. Not that he had aspirations for anything more, of course. He just thought it might be fun to flirt a bit, that's all. One day Phil will be too old to flirt. His innocent teasings will be misinterpreted as lecherous. That's the trouble with getting older. The line between scamp and pervert gets thinner and thinner until, before you know it, you're on a list of senior citizens who aren't allowed to hang near the dance academy.

Phil searched the street for any signs of life. He couldn't really tell if anything down there was open or not. He'll have to walk down for a closer look. He should first go back to the room and get his cardigan, but that thing really does make him look like he's hosting a puppet show. So he shivered a bit and continued down the street.

When Taylor had given him the sweater, she had told him that cardigans were back in style, which might very well be true if you're seventeen years old. But a guy Phil's age has to watch contemporary styles. They can backfire. Like that Sinatra-style fedora he'd bought a couple years ago. Sure, if you're twenty a hat like that looks retro. But if you're fifty there's no such thing as retro. There's just stuff you forgot was in the back of the closet.

Phil kept walking. He should definitely have worn socks. His feet were getting cold. So were his fingers. Phil shoved his hands into the side pockets of his jeans. No front pockets anymore. Not for Phil. Front pockets are on *Boot Cut*. Or *Classic Fit*. These jeans are *Relaxed* fit. Like his Sinatra hat.

To get his blood flowing, Phil stretched out into longer, faster strides. And after a couple of blocks he found he was indeed warming up. But more surprising, he realized his bad knee wasn't giving him any grief. In fact it hadn't caused him any pain at all today. Could the dry mountain air actually be good for his joints like Carol had suggested? Who knows? But normally a day like today, a day spent trying to keep up with the kids and climbing around a mountain, would have left him stiff as a hand-washed sweatshirt. But not tonight. Tonight Phil felt pretty darn loose and limber.

He hopped off the curb, crossed the street, and entered the main retail section of town where the street lights were brighter. As he bounced up onto the next curb, he couldn't help but notice his reflection in the window of a drug store. Who was that old fart? Look at how round-shouldered he is. Phil used to be ramrod straight. He adjusted his posture in the window, but it didn't seem to help. And whatever happened to Phil's ass? Must be these *Relaxed* jeans.

The drug store windows made Phil think of his prescription meds. He had two. One for blood pressure. Another for cholesterol. He hasn't started using boner pills yet, but he's sure he will someday. It's only a matter of time. Granted, Carol says he's still up to the task. But that's Carol. Such a sweetheart. Always rolls with the punches no matter how soft those punches might become.

Phil pulled his mind out of his pants long enough to realize he was now standing across the street from his own restaurant, the Shangri-La Gardens. So sad. Did Carol really expect a city dude like Phil to move out here to Toe Suck Corners and run a diner? It would certainly make her happy. So why not do it? Would it kill Phil to leave Chicago? Is Phil being an asshole about this? He probably is. Phil would do most anything for Carol. But this is asking quite a lot.

He crossed the road for a closer look at the pathetic little place. Poor old Zachariah meant well when he bequeathed this business to Phil and Carol, but did he really expect Phil to drop everything and come run it? The old fellow seemed smart enough — did he not realize what strife and marital heat such a gift might spark?

Phil stepped up to the window. No lights shone from inside the dining room, but a few reflected rays from the lamps out here on the street managed to sneak their way in despite their lack of reservations. Phil cupped his eyes to the glass for a better look.

It was like staring into a Chinese crypt. The little reception desk stood by the front door like it was waiting for mourners to arrive. Vague shadows spoke eulogies over the shabby furnishings that should have been buried long ago. Phil tried to imagine himself standing inside this mausoleum, welcoming mourners, grabbing armfuls of leatherette-shrouded menus, and asking a party of local shit-kickers in cowboy hats if they wanted their usual dim sum and pork balls. Jesus H. Christ, how the hell would a guy like Phil ever—

Hey. What's that? Did something just move in there?

Naa, must be Phil's lousy night vision. Or a trick the street lights are playing on the warped floor-to-ceiling window glass.

Oh, shit. There it is again. A pinpoint of light. Flitting. Like a firefly. But fireflies blink on and off, don't they? This light is burning steady, floating like a ghost, bobbing and weaving around the tables and chairs. It must be a reflection from something outside here. But what? No cars are passing by. And no wind is animating the tree branches in front of the street lights.

Phil backed away to glance up and down the street and make sure he was still alone out here. And that distraction was all it took for the tiny spark to blossom into a small flame. He watched the flame grow. And as it brightened it carved sharper relief of the furnishings. Of the tables. Of the chairs.

And of the silhouette of a man.

Holy shit. Phil is watching someone set fire to a restaurant. *His* restaurant. *Carol's big fucking dream of retirement* restaurant.

Phil grabbed the door knob and pulled. It wouldn't budge. He spun around and yelled into the empty street, "Help! Fire!" He stepped backwards, out onto the road, so he could see up to the second-story windows. He knew the apartment over his Chinese place was vacant, but maybe there were people above the other stores.

Yes, he saw lights in the windows. "Hey! Up there! Help! Fire! Hey, you guys! Call the fire department! Call the cops. Call nine-one-one!"

Phil turned his eyes back to the restaurant window again. The flames had grown larger. Hungrier. He could see the shadow of the arsonist moving around toward the back of the room. The guy must be leaving, probably going out the same way he got in — through the back door.

Phil heard a siren. Good. Somebody heard his yells. Nothing to do now but watch the perp make his escape. No point in trying to catch the guy. He's probably got a car waiting back there. But no, hold on. The firebug isn't finished yet. Despite the flames now spread out in rivers and pools across the carpeting, the perp seems to be walking around looking for something. He's interested in something mounted on the wall. A decoration of some sort.

Phil stepped closer and watched the man try to remove the item from the wall. But the thing won't budge. He pulls hard on it. Suddenly the decoration comes loose, or maybe he has just lost his grip. Either way, the guy falls backwards to the floor. Knocks a table over on his way down. Now Phil can see the man's feet sticking out from behind the fallen table. The perp isn't getting up. Isn't moving at all. He's just lying on his back, toes up. The guy must have hit his head on that table and knocked himself out.

The flames crept along the floor in a giant spider web pattern. The idiot must have poured out gasoline. And now the man is lying unconscious in the middle of it, moments away from melting in flames like the Wicked Witch of the West. Only this witch is being quiet about it.

The siren was growing louder, but not loud enough and not fast enough to do this man any good. Phil kicked at the front window — not with the toe of his silly Top-Sider boat shoe but with the heel. Trouble is, the heel was no harder than the toe. The glass didn't give. He needed something hard. Something heavy. He looked around.

The closest thing out here was a wrought iron bench. He tried to pick the thing up. But it wouldn't budge. Must be bolted to the concrete.

Phil could now feel the heat radiating out through the glass. He checked on the lifeless body. The hungry flames hadn't quite got round to tasting it yet, but they would any second now. Phil threw his shoulder against the glass. No luck. This was damn good glass.

Phil had noticed cast iron litter baskets screwed onto the street's lamp posts. Didn't those baskets usually have loose trash bins inside? Some sort of canisters? Phil ran to the closest one.

Yes. He pulled out the aluminum container. He hurled it hard at the window. The glass shattered, raining down onto the sidewalk like fallen ice in a Chicago winter.

Phil's Top-Siders crunched over the shards as he stepped up and over the restaurant's tiled window sill. He headed straight into the flames, and when he reached the body he slipped his hand under the man's neck. He looked closely at the man's face. "It's *you*," Phil said.

The young man didn't answer. He was out cold.

Phil tried to carry the teenage boy, but the dead weight of a young footballer was too much for Phil's fifty-year-old back. So he hooked his forearms under the kid's armpits and half-lifted, half-dragged the limp body up and over what remained of the front window sill and out onto the sidewalk. Once outside, Phil tried to lug the kid farther along the concrete to a bare spot, free of the carpet of broken glass. But Phil's old worn-out knee cartilage just wasn't up to the task. So, he kicked some glass shards out of the way and, as gently as possible, lowered the boy's head onto the pavement.

The kid opened his eyes and looked up at Phil.

Phil smiled. "Remember me?"

The boy blinked up at him, "Oh, yeah." Then the kid thanked his rescuer by puking on Phil's brand new Top-Siders.

Phil hadn't noticed the fireman running up to him. "You okay, sir?"

"I think so," Phil indicated the kid retching at his feet. "You might want to see to him, though."

Phil stepped out of the way and sat down on the curb to get his breath. He now noticed that his left hand hurt like hell. He'd burned it. Phil stayed seated and watched the fire fighters unroll their hose. The firefighter who seemed to be in charge sauntered casually over to the young fire bug who'd started all this and asked, "Isaac. Who authorized this?" Phil didn't understand this comment at all.

A woman firefighter hurried over to Phil. She was carrying a tube of something which she promptly started rubbing onto Phil's burned fingers. Meanwhile, two firemen picked up the young arsonist and loaded him onto a stretcher.

"Go easy on him, boys," Phil said. "He just got shot down for a date." Phil looked up at his burning restaurant. "And he seems to be holding a grudge."

CHAPTER TWELVE

Carol didn't bother to look up from her book. She just mumbled from the bed, "The pub open?"

"Nope." Phil used his good, unbandaged hand to close the door.

"So what'd you do?" She flipped a page. "Go for a walk?"

Phil headed straight to the mini-fridge. "Hear the sirens?"

Too engrossed in her paperback, Carol didn't answer him. But Taylor did. She actually stopped texting for a moment and looked up. "Daddy! What did you do to your hand?"

Now Carol looked at him. "Oh, my god!"

"Good news and bad," Phil announced as he opened the door of the fridge with his good hand. "The bad news is, I'm afraid our real estate interest in this town has become less an asset and more a liability." He bent down to lift out a can of beer, and with his butt now aimed toward the ladies like a confetti cannon, fired off the rest of his bulletin, "The good news is, you are now looking into the eye of the town hero."

"Your hand," Carol said. "You got into a fight."

Normally, Phil would have gone along with this accusation and proudly ridden it to its logical tough-guy conclusion. But for once he had an even better choice — the truth. He gingerly lowered his painful, slightly scorched ass into one of the room's two upholstered chairs. "Should be quite a ceremony. Mayor says you ladies might want to dress up nice, put on your Sunday best." Phil was enjoying this.

"Dad, what are you talking about?"

"Most of the town is expected to be there. Lots of press. A free lunch." Phil held up his can of beer. "Somebody want to get Daddy a glass? Heroes shouldn't drink from cans."

Taylor got up to fetch a drinking glass from the bathroom.

As his daughter poured the beer for him — gently, down the side of the tumbler so there'd be no head — Phil said to his loving, considerate young server, "Honey, next time you shoot some kid down in flames I want you to remember this story."

And then he told her the whole flaming tale.

• • •

Town meetings in Perpetuity, Wyoming, used to be held in the town church. But that was long ago, back when people feared God. Nowadays, both the fear and the church are overgrown with weeds. And the roof leaks. And the pews have splintered. People find the upholstered seats of the Opera House much more comfortable. Plus, the Wi-Fi is better.

Mayor Sam Beckwith called today's town meeting for nine in the morning. As he expected, the turnout was small — barely fifty citizens. Nine o'clock was far too early. But this was fine with Mayor Beckwith. He wasn't looking for any large group discussions. He was here to officially announce his plan, not to debate it.

Sam kicked things off by telling everyone in the Opera House about the fire at Shangri-La Gardens last night and about how this outsider, Phil Hodworth, saved the life of Sam's son, Isaac. Mayor Sam then went on to explain that he thought the town should honor this hero with the key to the city. Or more correctly, the key to the town.

Caleb Norquist was the first to whine. "Geez, Sam, I don't know. That's quite a fuss. We never done nothing like that before."

"Cal," Sam struggled to keep things as simple as they indeed were. "The man saved my son's life."

"You say that like it's a *good* thing," said Rachel Minton from her usual spot in the front row.

Sam wasn't surprised at the woman's snarky attitude. Like many middle—aged gals in Perpetuity, Rachel endured a love-hate relationship with Isaac. She loved the boy for sharing her bed whenever she was fortunate enough to draw his name at the monthly pot luck dinner. But she hated him for burning down her gazebo after her cat killed a couple of Isaac's precious racing pigeons.

"Rachel," Sam said. "I know my boy has pulled some dumb stunts over the years. And I know last night he was rather impetuous..."

Bob Gilchrist said, "Sam, he coulda burned down the whole town."

"I know. I know. I warned him. But you gotta understand." Sam rested his forearms on the podium and leaned forward as a gesture of sincerity. "Isaac loves this town. He loves the whole magical valley. And he wants to keep it magical. He wants to keep everything just like it is. And that's just what he was doing last night. He was fighting. Fighting to maintain the status quo. Things just got a little out of hand, that's all. Could have happened to anybody."

"Heard he was pissed out of his gourd," said Clay Dawson. Clay was a few years younger than Isaac and Sam believes he has always been jealous of Isaac. Young Clay is at that awkward age — fifteen. He begrudges the older boys' popularity with the womenfolk. He also resents not being able to be seen driving an automobile in public. Same for drinking alcohol out in the open. Fifteen's a tough age to be locked into.

Sam straightened himself up to his full six-feet-three-inches. "Isaac was not drunk. Doc Milburn believes the boy was just overcome by the gasoline fumes."

"Doc Milburn believes leeches will cure the clap," Bob Gilchrist said. "For three weeks that quack had me walking around with a pant-load of live bait."

"Which never would've happened to us if Isaac would learn to leave the tourist girls alone," added Melanie Bochner. "The boy's a menace, Sam. He really ought to be locked up."

"Sure, but where?" Yance Knowles said. "I told you — we should never have converted the jail to daycare."

"Had no choice," Cora Thatcher said. "Where else we supposed to put our kids for the day?"

"How about leaving 'em at home?" Yance Knowles said. "Let their mothers take care of 'em for a change."

"Easy for you, Yance," snapped Cora. "You ain't had a three-year-old tugging at the hem of your skirts for a hundred and eighty years."

"Skirts?" Bob Gilchrist spat into the spittoon which he was considerate enough to sit beside. "Who the hell wears skirts anymore? All's I ever see you ladyfolk sashayin' around town in is pants."

"Just keepin' up with the times, Bob. Just keepin' up with the times."

"Yeah?" Caleb Norquist got back into the fight. "Well, maybe some of us don't think the times is worth keeping up with no more, you ever think of that? Maybe some of us would like to let *the times* go rollin' on ahead without us for a change."

As the meeting coasted downhill, totally out of control, Sam leaned on the podium and let it roll. As mayor and wagon master, he could step on the brake, of course. But sometimes it's best to let the momentum die of its own friction.

As he waited, Sam recalled a similar town meeting — one he had organized almost two centuries ago, back in 1846. That meeting, too, had been sparked by the rash behavior of Sam's son, Isaac. The purpose of that gathering, however, was not to decide whether the young man should be scolded for arson, but to decide whether he should be hanged for murder.

At the time, most of the waggoneers said it wasn't murder at all. How could it be? The dead victim was a runaway slave, and everybody knew you could no more murder a slave than you could murder a dog or a rabbit. It was not an indictable offence. You could be charged with stealing or poaching a slave, but you couldn't be charged with murdering one. Seems crazy now, but in those days that's what a lot of folks believed, especially folks from below the Mason-Dixon line, which was where many in the Beckwith wagon train had come from. But there were also some Northerners travelling with the train, and these people held a different view. They thought killing a negro could, in certain cases, be classified as a crime. That's why Sam decided a trial was in order.

It was Sam's decision and Sam's alone. He was more or less captain of the ship. Back in 1846 no formal judicial system existed in these western territories. So Sam held his own court. He asked the men of the party to decide right then and there if what Isaac had done was indeed wrong — that is, whether the boy had moral justification for shooting that slave dead. Sam argued that Isaac was simply defending Becky Thatcher's honor, and several eyewitnesses agreed. They saw for themselves how the half-naked slave was trying to force himself on Becky and how Isaac had come to Becky's rescue. Curiously, the only person to dispute this story was Becky herself, but that didn't matter much since Becky was only seventeen years old at the time — *really* seventeen years old — and at such a tender age a young girl couldn't possibly know if a man's ultimate intent was to defile her or dance a jig with her.

The day the attack happened the Beckwith train was passing through this valley on their way to Oregon. Nobody knew where the runaway slave had suddenly come from — he'd just showed up. Alone. No master. No wagon. No horse. According to Becky, she was riding the ridge by the river when her horse bolted at the sound of a prairie rattler. The horse threw her, and she rolled down hill into the water where she hit her head on a rock. That was the last thing she remembered until she woke up in the slave's arms with his lips firmly pressed against hers.

Luckily, at that very moment, young Isaac came riding over the hill. He saw the negro leaning over his best gal's body. He did what any decent white man would do. He pulled his Springfield 1840 musket out of his saddle sling and shot the black devil dead.

In hindsight, it was a shame white folk back then didn't know about, nor recognize, mouth-to-mouth artificial respiration. That was probably what the black fellow was doing to her. Giving her the kiss of life. CPR. Cardiopulmonary resuscitation. A real shame. Well, you live and learn.

So that night back in 1846, Sam Beckwith hastily assembled a court of Isaac's peers. If the waggoneers decided the killing of the slave was justified, then Sam wanted the issue dropped and never spoken of again. Sam didn't want the weight of this unfortunate incident hanging heavy in Isaac's saddle bags for the rest of the journey. The upcoming trek over the Rockies was going to be difficult enough without toting something like that along. Of course, if the waggoneers' tribunal decided the shooting was not morally justified, then the guilty party, Sam's very own son, would be delivered to the territorial marshal at Whitman Mission, the nearest settlement on the other side of the mountains. Sam promised he would hold to his fellow waggoneers' verdict on the indictment.

And then something happened.

A cold rain was falling. The men of the jury were anxious to wrap things up fast, declare Isaac innocent of the slave's death, and crawl into their warm, dry bedrolls inside or under their wagons. So Sam expected their verdict to come in quick. But the whole matter was settled even before the jury was sequestered. That'll happen when, in the middle of the trial, the dead victim walks into your court room.

They thought he was a ghost. Had to be. Sam himself had seen this negro lying dead on the river bank with a bullet hole through his chest. Doc Milburn himself had pronounced the man dead. And if there's one medical condition a man of Doc Milburn's skills knows real well it is *dead*.

Luckily for the runaway, the waggoneers hadn't buried him yet. They would have if he were white. But being colored and all... Well, the ground was pretty rocky in that particular spot where the man had fallen. Crazy thing was — if anything could get crazier than a walking corpse — it seemed the black fella didn't feel any particular resentment about what Isaac had done to him. The slave just casually strode into the camp that night ginning, whistling a happy tune, and apologizing to everyone for causing so much fuss and commotion. Sam was impressed. This boy was one damn good sport.

Sam offered the slave some coffee and beans, but the black fellow just tipped his Stetson hat and said no thanks, baked beans didn't agree with him. He did, however, accept some johnnycake which he seemed to enjoy immensely. He even asked for a second helping, which Sam thought was pushing his luck a bit far. Kind of uppity.

That next morning, when Sam woke up, the runaway had run away again, never to be seen. Curiously, Sam always wondered if the man was actually a runaway or not. His voice bore no southern accent, no Yankee accent, no accent at all. And he spoke with proper book-learned grammar like Sam had rarely heard from his sort.

And one other thing. Because the black fellow's recovery from that bullet wound was so miraculous, a mythology has grown around him. Folks started to link his voodoo magic to the magic of this valley. To this day they can't help but think he is somehow responsible for nobody here ever dying unless they fall into a harvester or try to charge up their laptops while taking a bath. Folks call it *the gift*. Or just the *magic*. Or the *status quo*.

Sam tapped the microphone on his podium to get the attention of the assembled Opera House audience, "Enough talk, pilgrims. Before I dismiss this morning's meeting, I have one more thing to tell you. This afternoon, after I hand over the ceremonial key to the city to Mr. Hodworth, I'm going to take the man aside, speak to him privately. I am going to tell him what has been going on, *exactly* what has been going on. Why we've been so unpleasant. Why we've been so rude to him and to his kin." Sam quickly corrected his antiquated reference, "His *family*. I'm going to explain why we're so afraid of new folk moving into our little valley. I'm going to do this because I think we owe it to him. *I* certainly do, anyway."

Sam stopped and waited for his heavy wagon-load of words to ford the narrow stream between the theater's stage and the first row of seats. He worried that the weight might be too much for the well-worn wheels and axles, so he listened carefully for any signs of trouble. Any groans of strain.

The first creak came from Angus Murphy. It was just a small creak. He spoke only a few words, and he spoke them softly, "You gonna tell 'em about the *magic?*"

"Yes, Angus, I am going to tell them about the magic." Sam was afraid to utter any more words for fear of shifting the load. He remembered how once, when he was working as mule skinner for a mining company in Utah, he had to transport a wagonload of the newly invented explosive, nitroglycerine, over sixteen miles of rough road. He'd listened for creaks that day, too.

The next creak came from Bob Gilchrist. It was a little louder. "Hodworth won't believe you."

Sam answered truthfully, "Probably not."

"Are you going to try hard to make him?" Roy Frith asked.

Sam was gaining some confidence now — the springs and axles seemed to be holding. So, he asked the questioner, "You think I should try hard, Roy?"

When Roy didn't answer him, Sam's eyes searched the rest of the crowd. He took time to examine each and every face. It wasn't hard to do — he knew these faces well. They were the luckiest damned faces on Earth, and what he was proposing threatened to change that luck. And those faces. This could be the beginning of the end.

No outsider had been allowed to settle permanently into the valley since nineteen hundred and seven, and that was a different time. A slower time. Secrets were safer then. No radio. No television. No internet. And lots more secrets.

Sam searched the eyes before him for any sparks of unrest. He noticed an occasional glimmer here and there but saw nothing that could actually combust. He was a little surprised. Granted, he hadn't expected a lot of heat from his neighbors. Not anymore. But geez, he'd expected *some* sort of reaction.

As the small empty seconds stretched into giant hollow minutes, Sam could only conclude that, while folks in this valley may be living forever, their spirits certainly seem to have suffered a limited lifespan. Sam wasn't complaining, mind you. He hasn't come to this meeting looking for a fight.

And it looks like nobody else has either.

• • •

The ceremony on the steps of city hall was scheduled for eleven in the morning which was peachy-fine with Phil Hodworth because it gave him time to pack his bags and settle up his motel bill before accepting this silly award. Sure, it might seem a tad rude to receive a ceremonial key to the city and then immediately leave town, but what else could Phil do? Hang around Toontown another day? No way. Besides, most folk in this itchy crack in the Big Horn Mountains have been plenty rude to him and his family. He doesn't owe them anything. So let the good citizens of Perpetuity, Wyoming, erect a statue of Phil Hodworth if they so desire. Before the first pigeon gets to take a dump on it, Phil Hodworth plans to be a thousand miles away. That was the plan, anyway. And at first things went according to that plan.

The ceremony started with a quick speech from the mayor, who just happened to be the father of the young idiot whom Phil had rescued from the flames. The mayor then presented Phil with a wooden key which some local shop teacher had cut out on his jig saw and spray-painted gold. Phil made a joke about hoping the gold key was filled with chocolate, but nobody laughed except Isaac Beckwith who has obviously taken a lot of fast balls to the head. Seated stage-side in a wheel chair, the young firebug's hands were wrapped in bandages and, what appeared to be, leeches.

At the end of the ceremony a few people gathered at the top of the steps of the town hall for pictures. Phil's burned fingers felt pretty good, and seeing as how he was having his photo taken for the newspapers and social media, he had removed his bandages earlier. After all, a guy doesn't look very heroic wearing a giant white oven mitt. This morning when Phil removed those bandages he was surprised to see how well his burns were healing. That salve the firemen had used must be amazing stuff. Phil made a note to get the name of it before he leaves town.

Phil closed the show with a brief speech and told a few bald-faced lies about what a wonderful place this rat hole was. He left out any complaints about getting marooned on a chair lift for three hours. What would be the point now that the family is leaving. Besides, Carol's sunburn was already feeling a lot better just like Phil's burned fingers.

Phil introduced Carol to the crowd, and she added a few sweet words of her own, once again proving that a woman can shovel the shit as well as a man can. The ceremony ended with an invitation from the mayor for the big hero and his family to enjoy a free lunch with some of the townsfolk at the Shamrock pub. But Phil declined, explaining that he and his family had to hit the road. He had some pressing business back home. But thanks anyway, folks. Really. You've been great. And I really mean that.

When Phil was finished lying, Mayor Sam Beckwith — a rugged, square-jawed fellow — put his big muscular arm around Phil's shoulders and asked if he could please have a few words with him. Right now. Privately. Upstairs. In the mayor's office. The fellow promised not to take up too much of Phil's time. "We need to talk,

Mr. Hodworth. Just you and me. Alone. Man to man. This is too important to trust to the womenfolk."

Wow, bare naked male chauvinism like that gets a fella's attention. It's like from a whole different era. This guy is talking the way Phil's grandfather used to talk. But only when Grandma wasn't around. Hell, maybe Phil can spare this guy a few minutes. Should be worth a few laughs for the ride home.

CHAPTER THIRTEEN

Phil didn't know whether to laugh, cry, or shit his cargo shorts. Seeing as how his shorts were dry-clean-only, he laughed.

"Let me get this straight." Phil said while Mayor Samuel Beckwith poured another shot of bourbon into Phil's coffee. It was a little early in the day for hard liquor, but after what the mayor had just told him, Phil gladly accepted the booze. "You're telling me that you... you and every person I've met in this town... the guy who checked me into the motel, the mechanic who fixed my car, that real estate lady who showed us the restaurant, that hot Irish waitress who spills breakfast in my lap every morning, all you people... you are all actually... in reality..." Phil just couldn't bring himself to complete this crazy sentence. The mayor, however, had no such hesitations.

"Over a hundred and seventy years old and counting." Sam Beckwith sat the bottle of bourbon down on the desk and took the seat across from Phil. The mayor's insane words had been delivered in a monotone as dull and lifeless as the ho-hum drone that wheezed from the creaky old air conditioner clinging to life in the window behind the mayor's ergonomic computer chair. With little emotion other than maybe a slight bemusement, the mayor continued his ridiculous tale, "I was born in 1805. Arrived here at the age of forty-two, which makes me... well, you do the math."

Phil didn't bother doing this or any other math. He just lifted up his cup of fortified coffee and said, "You do realize there isn't enough bourbon in the whole fucking state of Wyoming to wash down the load of buffalo shit you're trying to feed me." Phil was free to swear. He and the mayor were alone. None o' them pesky womenfolk around.

The mayor didn't argue with Phil. He just nodded and said, "You're absolutely right, Mr. Hodworth. A man would have to be feeble-minded to swallow such a tall tale. And you, sir, are clearly not feeble-minded. Nor are you feeble-bodied. That was a strong, brave thing you did last night. My son is no light-weight." Mayor Sam Beckwith raised his coffee cup in a toast. "To your continued good health, sir."

"And to yours," Phil answered.

"Kind of you, but hardly necessary." Sam Beckwith slurped his coffee. "Mr. Hodworth, I'm not asking you to believe our story — no sane man would. It's just something I had to get off my chest, that's all. After what you've done for me, for my son, I couldn't let you leave our little community without knowing exactly what it is you are saying goodbye to. I just want you to know that, if you should decide to keep the restaurant and move your family into the valley permanently, you will be getting considerably more than you asked for. Maybe more than you want. But I assure you, contrary to what you've experienced so far, you will be welcomed with open arms. No more shenanigans. If on the other hand you'd rather sell the property, I have been authorized by the council to pay you fair market value plus ten percent for your trouble. I'm told there was very little damage from last night's, uh, incident."

"Mostly water damage," Phil said.

"I do apologize. The boy meant well. He was just trying to protect our status quo. Our little secret."

Phil leaned back. He was stumped. He just couldn't figure this guy's angle. Why would anyone make up such an insane, over-the-top fairytale? What was this man's game? Did he really want Phil to stay? If so, it was one hell of a way to promote local real estate. *Relocate to our town and you'll never grow old.* It sure beats hell out of, *If you lived here, you'd be home by now.*

Phil looked around the office for the hidden camera. The ceiling fan wasn't turning even though the room was hot. Could there be a camera lens it?

Meanwhile, Sam Beckwith switched gears. "On your way to Denver, huh? I hear it's a nice town. Lots to do. Shows. Museums. Attractions for the young folk. Never been there myself, of course."

"Because you can't leave town." Phil smiled at the ceiling fan to show he could be a sport and go along with a joke.

"Can't roam beyond the foothills."

"'Cause you'd shrivel up and die." Phil winked at the ceiling fan.

"That's the usual order."

"Like Zachariah did." Phil was still smiling. Sam Beckwith was not.

"I'll miss young Zack," Sam said, looking deep into his coffee. "It was me who originally hired him. The lad wanted to get away from home. From his old man. Back then, parents were different. Less understanding. A sensitive boy like Zachariah had it rough. So I got Lee Wong to take him on as cook's boy. Worked out well for all concerned. When we started out, that kid didn't know how to boil water. By the time we got here Zachariah made better egg drop soup than Lee Wong did. Smart kid."

"*Kid.*" Phil quoted.

"Five years younger than my boy, Isaac."

"He sure didn't look like a kid when I last saw him."

Sam leaned forward, resting his elbows on his desk. "Tell me, Mr. Hodworth—"

"*Phil.*" When getting screwed, Phil preferred to get screwed on a first-name basis.

"That first time you met him, that very first night in the park, how old did you think Zachariah was?"

"I don't know. Pretty old."

"Like eighty? Ninety?"

"More like late sixty."

"And the next morning, when you and your wife found him?"

Phil got the idea. He had witnessed Zack's metamorphosis with his own eyes. But there had to be a more rational explanation than the baloney this man was feeding him.

While Phil's mind was struggling to find that explanation Mayor Sam Beckwith addressed what might logically be Phil's next concern. "Don't worry," the mayor reassured Phil. "If you do decide to stay but then change your mind after a short while and want to leave, you and your family will be fine. The deterioration happens only if you've remained here in the valley for an extended period of time. Takes years. Decades. The clock just plays catch up. But when it does, it does so very quickly. Our metabolisms go into overdrive. Like when any patient stops a medication."

"Is that what it is? A medication?" Phil couldn't believe he was taking this story seriously. He wasn't. Not really. He was just playing along, being polite.

Sam Beckwith didn't answer right away. So Phil tried again. "Something in the water?"

Mayor Beckwith seemed reluctant to get into details, probably because he didn't want to stretch Phil's gullibility to the breaking point. Finally, the mayor spoke. But quietly, with no conviction. "Our water supply does seem to be the source. Or part of it. I suspect there's more to it than that."

"More?" Phil prodded.

"Early on, a few walkers — that's what we call citizens who leave town — a few tried taking a supply of our water with them. A good month's supply. Straight from the lake. But it didn't help."

"The lake up on the ski hill?"

The mayor corrected him. "The *mountain*."

"The hot spring."

"Right."

"You drink it."

"Don't have to. It seems to work externally. Topically. Just have to bathe in it."

"Like the waters of Lourdes."

"Sort of."

"Or the hot baths of Budapest."

"I wouldn't know, I don't travel. And neither does the magic."

"The *magic?*"

"We tried piping the water down the mountain and into town. Didn't work. Folk started aging again. But those of us who kept going up the mountain to the source, we stayed young. That was back in the fifties."

"*Nineteen* fifties?"

"*Eighteen* fifties. Back then, pipe was hard to come by, especially out here in the territories. So we had to make do with a sluice, a homemade millrace."

Phil understood. "The water slide."

"Like I say, it didn't work. The old millrace sat idle for a hundred years or so. Then somebody got the idea of lining it with plastic, make a few bucks from the tourists." Sam Beckwith then anticipated another unasked question. "And no, we have no idea what's in the water."

"You've never had it tested? Sent it to a lab somewhere?" Phil thought he had the mayor nailed with this obvious question.

"How could we do that without giving the secret away?"

Good point, thought Phil. If some scientist came across a magic elixir that kept his mice from getting old, the valley would soon be over-ridden with middle-aged mice looking to outlive the cat.

Woops. Phil caught himself. He was taking this story seriously. So he started doing what he usually does at times like this. He started mocking the idea.

Phil waved jazz hands in the air as if he were wearing white gloves in a minstrel show. "Must be some sort of voodoo. Some sort of black magic." He knew he was acting like a dork. But geez, this was getting insulting.

"Funny you should say *black* magic" Sam said. "When the magic was first discovered — back when Emma Langtree and Stella Scheuller noticed their young 'uns weren't coming along as they naturally should — folks used those very words. *Black Magic*. Tried to blame it on the runaway slave."

"Slave?" Then Phil remembered. "Oh, geez. Eighteen fifties. Before Lincoln."

The mayor swiveled his chair around so he could fiddle with the air conditioner's thermostat as he explained, "We'd come across this colored fellow on the trail. There was a misunderstanding. One thing led to another, and well, the fellow sorta got himself shot. Doc Milburn did all he could, but I'm afraid Doc is really just a barber with a strong stomach. Even if he were a real surgeon, there was nothing he or anyone else could do for a gut wound like that. The poor African-American kid didn't have a hope in Hades of ever seeing another sunrise. But then low and behold, within a couple of hours of getting himself blasted to Kingdom Come the deceased slave comes bouncing into our camp full of piss and vinegar like he was ready for a Saturday night hoedown. Barely a scar on him. We couldn't believe our eyes."

"I'll bet you couldn't." Phil was playing along again so he could politely draw this meeting to a close. Sure, every little tourist outpost needs a legend. Loch Ness has it's monster. Roswell has its space alien. Branson used to have Kenny Rogers. This town has a magic runaway slave. So Phil played along, "And what's this ex-slave doing today? Still in town? Got a faith healing booth set up at the county fair?"

"No idea. Never saw Kip again."

"Kip?" That name rang a bell in Phil's swirling noggin.

"That's what he called himself. Never found out his last name. Or if he even had one. Most slaves didn't. He left us that very night — autumn of forty-six."

"*Eighteen* forty-six."

"He was just a little guy. Must have been *house*, not *field*. We offered to pack him a few day's vitals, but he said he was okay — he had plenty of supplies back in his ship. All he wanted from us was some johnnycake."

"His *ship*?"

"His wagon. Back then folks referred to covered wagons as *prairie schooners. Ships of the plains.* Freshen your coffee?" Sam Beckwith reached for the bottle of bourbon.

Phil let him pour. And as the mayor fortified Phil's black, fresh-brewed cup of coffee Phil tried to recall. *Kip... Kip... Kip...* Where had he heard that name before?

• • •

Taylor hit the *enter* button and sent the video clip flying high on digital wings across three states to land on all her friends' screens back home in Chicago. This was the video she'd just shot. The one of her father receiving that town hero award. She would never admit it to him, of course, but she was proud of her dad.

Taylor was sitting on a park bench, the noon-day sun high above. In the bright light she was having trouble seeing the screen of her phone. Happily, a shadow passed over her. It wasn't a cloud. Someone was standing behind her. A man. His voice didn't startle her. It should have. But it didn't.

"You must be very proud."

She turned around. The man was staring down at her.

"Pardon me?" Taylor said.

"Your father... You must be bustin' your buttons."

"Uh, yes. They're bustin', all right."

The man was in silhouette, but from what she could see of his features he looked kind of familiar. Or maybe it was his voice. "Do I, like, know you?"

"You, like, should. We spent a delightful seventy-nine minutes hanging together yesterday."

Right. Now she remembered. The African American hippie on the chair lift. Taylor hadn't had a chance to take a close look at this man yesterday — his chair was parked farther up the lift, dangling next to Mom and Dad. But she recognized his voice. And his hippie outfit — the bell-bottom jeans and fringe vest. Taylor liked retro clothes. If she recalled correctly, the guy was close to her own age.

The young man looked around the little town park area. "So, where is the big town hero?"

"Over there." Taylor pointed to a bronze statue of one of the town's founding fathers.

"I mean your father."

"Oh. He's in the town hall. Talking with the mayor. My mother is off giving an interview to the lady from the newspaper."

"The New York Times?"

"Yeah, right." Taylor laughed although she wasn't sure whether the man was joking or not.

"Mind if I share the bench with you?"

"Hey, knock yourself out. There's no charge." Taylor hoped that didn't sound too snarky. She was always saying the wrong thing. Especially to boys. She moved her bag to make room for him, although he didn't need much room — he was rather slight.

Taylor wasn't sure if this guy was coming on to her or not, but as there were still plenty of people milling about on the street, she saw no risk in being friendly. Besides, he was kind of nice looking. Lovely voice. *Well-modulated*, her media arts teacher would call it. The man, or kid, was younger than she'd remembered. But of course, she hadn't had a real good chance to check him out dangling on that ski lift.

As soon as the young man sat down, he proceeded to take off one of his platform shoes and massage his bare foot. "Gravity's a bitch, don't you agree?"

"A bitch," Taylor agreed, going along with the silliness. "But what're ya gonna do. Can't live with it, can't live without it."

"Funny you should say that." The guy turned toward her and rested one elbow on the back of the bench as if settling in for a good long chat. "There are ways around it."

"You don't say."

"I do say." The young man smiled. It was a lovely smile. Very peaceful. He was a bit older than Taylor but not a lot older. Just a year or two. Maybe three. He looked at her closely, a little too closely for Taylor's comfort — like a cosmetic surgeon assessing for areas of improvement. Finally, he said, "If I remember correctly, you aren't from around here. Not this immediate vicinity."

"Chicago."

"I've heard of that. Is it very far away?"

"From this town? Only, like, a million miles."

"Good. Then you must be okay." He turned his attention back to rubbing his foot.

"Yeah, I'm okay, I guess."

"It hasn't affected you."

Taylor chuckled. "That's always good to hear."

The man looked around at the few people who were walking by on the street. He seemed nervous. Finally he said, "I really shouldn't be talking to you."

"No?" Taylor was a little offended. "Why not?"

The man swiveled himself around on the bench to check out the bushes and trees behind him. Then he said, "Last time I did this with one of you people I got into trouble."

"Trouble? Why? You mean... because I'm...?" Taylor didn't want to say *white*, but that's what it sounded like he was getting at.

He asked, "How old are you?"

Oh, now she got it. Now she understood. This guy was afraid he might be seen as a pervert, trying to pick up a hot under-aged girl in the park. Taylor laughed. "You don't have to worry." And then she lied, "I'm eighteen."

"Really? Really and truly eighteen?"

He must have caught her in the lie. "Don't I look eighteen?"

"Of course you do." He winked. "But that doesn't mean a lot nowadays, does it. Especially around here."

"I know what you mean. They say we grow up much faster than our parents' generation. My Dad blames the internet."

"Naw, that's not it," said the boy. "It's more likely the water."

"Okay," Taylor laughed. "Whatever you say." Will she ever know if this guy is joking or not?

The boy went back to massaging his foot. "I really must score myself an ATV. Or a horse. Something I can take off-road."

"First you should score some decent shoes." She picked up his discarded sandal. "What are you wearing these stupid things for?"

"I was misinformed."

"I hear ya. Shoe salesmen. Total douches."

"Ah, *Vous parlez Francais, oui?*"

Taylor laughed. "*Mais oui, monsieur.*" Taylor had made up her mind. This guy was fun. And cute. Maybe this trip won't be so bad after all.

• • •

Carol couldn't believe this old gal was knocking back her third vodka screwdriver and it wasn't even noon yet. No wonder Violet Snelling was talking nonsense — the crazy real estate agent was smashed.

Carol slid her can of diet cola around on the desk top as if she were contemplating her next chess move with it. Finally, she summed up the game so far, "And you say right this very minute, Mayor Beckwith is giving this same orientation lecture to my husband."

"Sam and I thought we should tag-team this one. Man-to-man, woman-to-woman. Might have more credibility that way. When someone tells you at a big cocktail party that pigs can fly, you simply write that person off as nuts. But when one person tell you privately, face-to-face, you might look up before you wash your car."

Carol was sitting alone with Violet Snelling in the dusty second-floor offices of the Perpetuity Banner newspaper, alone that is, except for Nate. He was seated at another desk, playing on a computer.

"You must admit," Carol said, "this story of yours is a little hard to swallow."

"A *little?* Are you kidding? Christ, Carol, it's fucking *impossible* to swallow. But Sam figures we owe you guys. Especially your husband, Bill."

"Phil."

"Whatever. The guy risked his life last night. So Sam Beckwith insisted we treat you guys like homeboys, 'fess up so our conscience will be free and clear and you can either stick around and join the party or go on your merry way back to Detroit."

"Chicago."

"Even better." Violet Snelling then turned toward the back of the room and called out, "You anxious to get back home, Blake?"

"Not really," said Nate. He hit a few keys on the computer then he called back to Violet, "You know a girl named Eunice?"

"Eunice Cartwright?"

"Thank you." Nate turned back to the computer and resumed typing.

Violet Snelling frowned. She seemed concerned over Nate's query about this Eunice girl. Violet leaned toward Carol and said, confidentially, "Uh, if he hasn't done so already, you may want your husband to have a little talk with the boy." Violet's voice now fell to a whisper. "Eunice has been keeping her sweets bottled up longer than *Mrs. Butterworth.*"

That's it. Carol has had enough of this idiocy. She stood up and called, "Come on, Nate. Time to go." Then she turned back to the crazy reporter/real estate agent, "I don't know what your game is, Violet, but you don't have to worry. You people can keep your restaurant and your town to yourselves. We won't be bothering you anymore." Carol started for the door.

"I understand." Violet stood up and followed her. "That sounds best for all concerned. You'll be getting a good price for the place, I promise. We want to be fair."

Carol had nothing more to say to this woman. "Let's go, Nate."

But Nate was busy studying the computer screen. "There sure are a lot of Cartwrights in this town."

"Now!" Carol marched over and grabbed Nate's hand. She added to Violet, "And here's a tip: Next time you want to keep new folk from moving in, just be honest. Tell them you don't want them. Treat us with some respect. Big city people aren't idiots. We don't want to live where we're not wanted. You don't have to insult us with silly stories."

With that said, Carol dragged her son away from the desk and down the narrow stairs.

Behind her, Violet was still talking, but Carol was no longer listening. Her ears were full, her head was full, and her stomach was full, all overflowing with new-age garbage, tales of hot springs blessed with healing powers, a magical valley, a modern-day Lost Horizon, a Shangri-La of the old west. Utter craziness. Phil had been right all along. Small towns mean small minds. Carol was longing to get back to the city. Back to civilization. Back to reality.

Carol stepped out from the dark hallway and into the bright sunshine. She shielded her eyes from the high, noon-day sun and looked around for Taylor. Or for Phil. Or for any other familiar adult face that would slap her out of this bad dream.

Nate yanked his hand free from hers. She understood. The boy was getting to that age where he was embarrassed to be seen holding his mother's hand. He was probably afraid that the little girl named Eunice might see him. Well, screw that. And screw her.

She grabbed her son's hand back again. And she held it tight.

She needed it.

• • •

Phil stood up to leave the mayor's office. "You're a smart man, Sam. You know that if you're going to tell a lie, best make it a whopper. The big lie is always easier to sell than the little one. This has been fun. If you ever want to leave politics, come see me. I think you'd do well in the marketing and public relations racket."

The mayor stood and escorted Phil to the door. "Sorry your stay with us was so unpleasant, Mr. Hodworth. But at least now you know why we've been so dog-gone rude to you and to yours."

"Apology accepted, Mister Mayor. And don't worry — your town's little secret is safe with me." Phil put his hand on Sam's shoulder and said, "But now that I'm in on the deal, isn't it a little selfish to keep something like this to myself? You don't mind if I tell one or two close friends about this, do you? Back home. I'm sure they'll keep it to themselves." Phil couldn't wait to get back to the city and tell his pals about this nonsense. Should be good for a laugh or two.

The mayor winced slightly as if the dentist had just found the bad tooth. "That's a bit of a sore point. We've wrestled with going public for many a year. But think about it, Phil. Our little valley here is barely five miles long, maybe two to three miles wide. All in all, we figure we got us ten to fifteen square miles to work with. You know how big ten square miles is?"

"I think you just told me." Phil said.

"Ten square miles is roughly half the size of Manhattan Island. And you know what the population of Manhattan Island is?"

This time Phil had the answer. "Seven million."

"*Greater* New York City, yes. But Manhattan Island itself embraces just one and a half million souls. All squeezed in tight on top of each other. If we folks in Perpetuity could, or wanted, to live like that, we could squeeze in maybe seven hundred and fifty thousand, tops. Seven hundred and fifty thousand *never-aging* individuals. In the meantime, Phil — do you think the other six billion, nine hundred million, three-hundred-and-fifty thousand slowly decaying bodies presently on this planet would be happy being locked out?"

Wow. Phil was impressed. This guy may be crazy as a shit-house rat, but he's a shit-house rat who's done his homework. Phil had to take this to its logical conclusion. "Okay. So you have to keep it under your ten-gallon Stetsons — I get that. What I don't get is how you've kept your secret. What about the government? The tax people, social security, census bureau, the military, all that giant bureaucracy out there. How the hell do you keep your secret from them? Are you trying to tell me the government donkeys in Washington — or in whatever the capital city of Wyoming is — you're telling me those agencies haven't checked their records and noticed that the good folk down the road are a smidge past their expiry dates?"

"Records? What records? We were all born the early 1800s. Some came from back east, some from down south. This was long before Wyoming was even a state. State records? Federal records? Most of us were born at home. Unannounced. Undocumented."

"And since then?"

"It hasn't been easy. The key is, never ever ask for a penny from any government agency."

Wow, Phil was impressed. This guy has truly thought this through. Phil had to finish this. "Okay. What about outsiders? Surely some tourist has passed through this nice little valley and said, 'You know, I think I'd like to move here. Retire. Work from home selling carved dinosaur turds on the internet. I think I'll buy me some property.'"

"A property buyer needs a property seller, and that's not allowed. Not anymore. Sure, at the very beginning we welcomed some new blood. But once we realized what was going on — or *not* going on — we put a halt to all property transfers. No real estate in this town has changed hands for well-over a hundred years."

Phil said, "And then Zachariah threw a monkey wrench into your system."

"Had to happen one day. Kinda surprised it took this long." At this point the mayor decided it was time to conclude this meeting. "Sure you won't stick around for lunch?"

"Really do have to run."

"Colleen will be disappointed."

"Colleen?"

"Waitress. The Irish girl."

"Oh, right." Phil tried to play down his interest in this particular line of thought. Nonchalantly, he asked, "She, uh, usually serve lunch?"

"She will today — her husband says she's taken quite a hankering to you."

"Her *husband*?" Phil didn't like the sound of this.

"Don't worry, he's cool with it."

"Cool with it?" Phil couldn't believe his ears. Or his luck.

The mayor put a hand on Phil's shoulder. "When a fine healthy young woman in her sexual prime has had the same handful of men under her quilt, night in, night out, for almost two hundred years, a handsome new face in town can be quite welcome."

Phil feigned humility. "Well, I wouldn't exactly call myself handsome."

"Two hundred years. The same, uh... faces."

Phil reconsidered the situation. "I guess standards might drop a bit."

"It's a small town, Phil. Very small."

Phil added, "With a big secret."

Sam smiled. "The biggest."

CHAPTER FOURTEEN

Phil Hodworth stepped out the double doors at the top of the steps of the Perpetuity town hall, took a deep breath of clear, fresh mountain air, and almost passed out.

He grabbed the iron railing. Wow, this thin, dry Wyoming air is really getting to him. Or maybe it's the high, noonday sun that has hit him like a brick to the forehead. Could it be that spiked Kentucky coffee that the mayor has been pouring into him? Whatever the reason, Phil's knees had turned to rubber. He was not yet ready to tackle the wide flight of steps down to the street. So he didn't.

Yeah, it must be the booze. Whiskey before noon is not a good idea for anyone over forty. Or over fifty. Phil paused to get his breath.

From up here at the top of the steps he had a good view of the business section of town, both blocks of it. Not much business going on today. Just a half-dozen pedestrians sauntering along casually. Aimlessly. As if they have all the time in the world. But do they? Really? Like the mayor claimed? Of course not. They just have nothing better to do, that's all. Their pace is the pace of all small towns. Slow. Languid. Pointless. In a place like this nothing needs to be done today. Everything can wait until tomorrow.

On the other hand…

What if Mayor Sam Beckwith is telling the truth. What if nobody in this valley has gotten older. What if all these people actually are the original settlers. What if this town truly is guarding the biggest secret in the history of humankind. No, this is insane. No wonder Phil feels dizzy. He has to bring himself back to reality. Back to ground level. Back to Carol. Yes, that's it. He's got to share this with Carol. Wait 'til she hears this. She'll love it. She always enjoys a good laugh.

Phil fished his phone out of the pocket of his shorts, shielded the screen from the sunlight, and checked for messages. Carol is supposed to text him and let him know when she is finished meeting with the woman at the newspaper. But there's no message. She must still be yapping away. Carol likes to talk.

He put his phone away, grabbed hold of the iron railing, and started down the steps. He was starting to feel better now.

He slid his hand along the cast iron bannister and noticed that the festive ribbons and helium-filled balloons were still tied to the handrail. It was on these steps, just an hour ago, that Mayor Sam and the town's Fire Chief had presented Phil with their *Local Hero* Award, a nice scroll tied with a blue ribbon. Phil had passed the scroll along to Taylor to stow away in the car. Wonder where she is now. He looked up and down the street for her but saw no sign of her. She must be waiting in the car.

Phil paused to untie one of the balloons from the railing, and with his gas-filled prize held high and proud like a kid coming home from the circus, Phil continued down the steps to the street. He turned right onto the town square, a little dried up patch of grass, shade trees, and benches that served as refuge for downtown shoppers to relax, sit, and try to figure out why they didn't stay home and shop online. Carol is supposed to meet him here in this little park. No sign of her yet, though. Poor kid. That lady reporter/real estate agent must be talking poor Carol's ear off.

With nothing better to do, Phil wandered over to have a look at the park's pride and joy — its statue of the town's founder. Earlier this morning, while on his way to the big ceremony, Phil had walked past this thing without granting it much attention. That was when Phil was the center of attention. But now that he's just another bored tourist killing time...

The statue was your standard small town stuff — a slightly larger-than-life bronze figure placed here for the pigeons and the tourists to either poop on or take their photo with — visitor's choice. The figure portrayed a sturdy male pioneer valiantly standing proud despite the bird shit dripping from his cowboy hat. The figure wore what appeared to be a thick sheepskin coat much like the coat Phil had admired hanging from a peg in the mayor's office.

The handsome bronze dude on the concrete pedestal held a rifle in one hand and a pocket watch in the other as if he had an appointment to kill something. A green-tinged copper plaque screwed onto the front of the concrete base identified the figure as Joshua Samuel Beckwith, the wagon master who, according to the raised block lettering, had guided the first wagon train of pioneers to this mountain pass in November of 1846.

Phil cast his eyes up to the bronze face. The statue didn't return his glance but instead continued staring off to some lost horizon, or maybe to infinity, whichever came first. Phil studied the face. Hard. From several angles.

Okay. Yeah. Sure. The chiseled puss did kinda look like Mayor Sam Beckwith. But seriously, don't most statues of founding fathers look like Mayor Sam Beckwith? A big rugged adventurer with a square jaw, strong hands, and a cowboy hat glazed with bird poop? After all, who's going to erect a statue to a chinless dink in a derby? This guy is probably Mayor Sam's great, great grandfather or something.

Yet... actually... on closer inspection... the face does look a hell of lot like the guy Phil just shared coffee with. A whole lot. Right down to that mole on the statue's neck. Phil had noticed that mole when Sam had leaned over him with the whisky to fortify Phil's coffee. Phil had almost suggested to Sam that he might want to have the mole looked at, but then he thought better of it. After all, who needs medical advice from a man who still refuses to have the colonoscopy his doctor, his wife, and even his hair stylist keep pestering him about.

Phil couldn't take his eyes off the statue. Seriously, that's a pretty distinctive mole. Hey, maybe the mayor's mole was phony. Maybe the guy has tattooed a fake mole on his thick, muscular neck just to perpetuate the town's story of perpetual youth. *Perpetual... Perpetuity...* Phil wondered which came first — the mayor's tall tale or this town's screwy name. Phil lowered his gaze to check out the rest of the bronze form.

The statue was actually a pretty impressive piece of work. Besides neck moles, the artist had included fine details of the wagon master's clothing and accoutrements. Phil noticed one detail, however, conspicuously absent — no hour or minute hands on the man's pocket watch. The numbers were there. And the tiny winding stem was there. But no hands. Nice touch. A little on the nose, a little Rod Serling, but nice touch just the—

"Anyone you know?"

Phil nearly jumped out of his cargo shorts at her voice. He had no idea Carol had snuck up behind him. She must have crept up quietly just to startle him. She does that sometimes. Tries to blame his hearing loss.

Carol was holding Nate's hand. The boy looked up at the statue. "That's Mayor Sam."

"No, it isn't," said Carol a little too quickly and too firmly.

"You know, Nate might be right, honey." Phil handed Nate the balloon he's been carrying, then chuckled out his next news bulletin, "You aren't going to believe what I just heard. It seems—"

"Don't tell me," Carol interrupted. "You were just fed the biggest load of buffalo shit served to a tourist in these here parts since General Custer was a private."

Phil was surprised at his wife's words. She always gave him hell for swearing in front of Nate.

And then Carol topped herself. She put her hands over Nate's ears and said, "I suggest we get the fuck out of this insane asylum while the inmates are distracted."

Wow. That lady reporter/real estate agent must have served Carol the same spiked coffee that the mayor had poured for Phil.

Nate pulled his mother's hands off his ears and said, "I don't think that's a good idea. There's a cold front moving in." He then turned his head skyward and shaded his eyes. "Gonna get some heavy precip. Maybe a storm. I strongly suggest we stay here for one more night."

Carol explained to Phil. "Got the hots for a little girl."

Phil ruffled his son's hair.

Carol looked around the park. "Where's Taylor?"

Nate answered, "Over there." He pointed to a bench on the far side of the grass.

Sure enough, she was sitting there, talking to a man. Phil squinted to see better. "Don't we know that guy?"

"It's Kip," Carol said matter-of-factly.

"Kip?" Phil repeated.

"The man from the ski lift."

"Oh, yeah, right. Name's Kip, huh?"

"Phil, I really think you should have your hearing checked."

"I'm not good with names."

Nate smiled at his father, "I bet you remember the name of our waitress from breakfast."

Phil would have shushed his smart-ass son, but Phil's mind was on other matters: *Kip... Didn't Mayor Sam mention someone named Kip?*

Carol instructed Phil, "Tell Taylor we're going." And she ushered Nate towards the sidewalk.

"What about lunch?" Nate pleaded. "They're waiting for us."

"Let 'em wait," Carol said. "People in this town are good at waiting. Apparently they've been doing it for two hundred years."

Aha! Phil remembered it now. Kip was the name of that runaway slave that the Mayor's son Isaac had supposedly shot two hundred years ago.

Phil took a closer look at the young man sitting beside his daughter on the bench. African-American? Yes. A runaway slave from pre-Civil War? No. For one thing, he didn't look big enough. Or old enough. Or long-since dead enough.

Carol yelled across the lawn to her daughter, "Taylor. We're leaving."

The runaway black zombie slave flashed Carol and Phil a big smile and gave them a big wave. Phil waved back and called again to his daughter, "Getting' late, Tay. Time to return to our home planet."

The black guy gave Phil a big thumbs up on that one.

• • •

Isaac Beckwith stood in the bushes at the edge of the parkette licking his cell phone. Well, *licking* isn't quite the right word. What Isaac was doing was tapping the touch screen with his tongue. Felt like licking, though.

The boy would rather have used his fingers, of course, but Doc Milburn had wrapped Isaac's scorched hands in so much gauze that the two giant mitts were now the size of canned hams, and the only way Isaac could hold his phone was to sandwich it between his two clumsy lobster mitts. This made it enormously difficult to aim the phone's camera. Adding to his digital difficulties was the awkward stance that Isaac had adopted in order to stay hidden from his subjects — crouched down low between a buffaloberry bush and a cottonwood tree.

Isaac licked the zoom button, but his tongue overshot and closed the phone's movie app. This was a bad time of season for licking phones. Damn hay fever made Isaac's tongue slippery as catfish shit. After suffering through a couple hundred allergy seasons you'd think a guy's autoimmune system would develop some tolerance for wheatgrass pollen. But Isaac's mucous membranes still ran like maple sap every spring.

Isaac poked his phone's movie button with his nose and then poked the zoom function. He wanted a good close shot of the slave's face, and he feared the boy's smooth, dark skin might underexpose in this bright light and appear featureless and unidentifiable, and that would not be good for Isaac's plan. Of course, for a closer shot Isaac could simply step out of the bushes and approach his subject head-on, but that might scare the Hodworth girl. She would surely recognize him from his performance last night playing waiter at the Shamrock pub and think he was some sort of stalker.

So Isaac just stayed hidden and shot his video of the happy couple. Isaac thought about how the last time he'd shot this fellow wasn't with a camera — it was with a Springfield musket. In fact, it was the exact same Springfield his father had posed with for that bronze statue over yonder fifty yards away. Back then, the slave's black magic had saved his skinny ass. But that won't be the case this time. Not if Isaac Beckwith has any say in the matter.

Isaac was just about finished shooting his video when he heard the girl's father call out, "Gettin' late, honey. Time to return to our home planet."

Then Isaac heard the slave say to the girl, "Home planet? I thought you said you were from Earth?"

"I lied." The Hodworth girl laughed. The slave did not.

Instead, the black fellow studied her face. "You look very much like these people. Same skeletal structure. Same coloring. Your eyes are particularly lovely."

What a load, thought Isaac. He could tell a con when he heard one, and evidently, so could this girl. She turned away from the slave. "I bet you say that to all the Earth women."

"You decorate your eyes well. Much better than the other ladies around here do."

The Hodworth gal turned toward him again. "You noticed that, too, huh? It's like they're allergic to good makeup."

"Your eyebrows are particularly well defined."

"Country women don't tweeze enough."

"The entire effect is very pleasing aesthetically."

"Thank you."

Shit, she seemed to be buying this crap. Isaac had heard enough. He licked the phone to turn off the movie function. But his tongue pressed the screen too hard and knocked the device out of his giant bandaged mitts. Isaac bent down to fish through the grass for his digital gadget, and as he searched he heard the Hodworth girl bid goodbye to the black man.

She didn't sound terribly happy to be leaving him. In fact, she even gave him her phone number, said he should text her. The young girl's wistful tones of departure reminded Isaac of Becky Thatcher's mournful voice that night by the campfire when she had bid goodbye to this very same negro fella back in eighteen hundred and forty-six. Isaac wondered if Becky would feel the same way about this boy if she ran into him today, two hundred years later. Isaac's guess is that she probably would.

To Isaac's knowledge, Becky doesn't know this fella is back in town. Isaac hates to be the one to tell her. But he has to.

He has to tell everyone.

• • •

Phil didn't usually drive this slowly. He seemed distracted. Was he concerned about the bad weather that Nate had warned about? The clouds were indeed growing dark, but Phil isn't normally afraid of a little rain. He didn't look terribly worried. No white knuckles. In fact he was holding the steering wheel quite loosely, with just his fingertips. Normally Phil grabs hold of the wheel like it owes him money.

"You okay?" Carol asked.

Phil traded her question for one of his own: "Why do you think they split us up like that?"

"Probably to keep us from giggling like school kids. If you had an insane story to tell, wouldn't you prefer pitching it one-on-one?"

Phil shifted in his seat. Yes, he was uneasy. "You gotta admit," he said, "they've sure gone to a lot of trouble. Erecting that fake statue in the park, vandalizing our car, sabotaging the ski lift, setting fire to Shangri-La Gardens." Phil suddenly realized, "Shangri-La... that's the name of the place in that show, *Lost Horizon*. The place in the Alps where nobody gets old."

Carol was not impressed. "I think it's the Himalayas. And for all I care he could have called his restaurant *Moulin Rouge*. Doesn't make this place Paris."

"But think about it. The way Zachariah died — all shriveled up like that." Phil slowed the car to an even gentler crawl. "That was the way the young girl died in the TV show when she left Shangri-La."

"A movie, honey. First a book. Then a movie. But always fiction."

"But still," Phil eased the car over to the curb and shifted it into park so he could turn and face Carol. He said, "One minute Zack was a vibrant, healthy seventy-year-old. The next, a sun-dried tomato. You saw it yourself. Exactly like in the TV show."

"Movie," Nate corrected.

Carol tilted her head back and closed her eyes. She'd been expecting this. She had seen the look on Phil's face this afternoon when he was staring up at that statue in the park. It was the look of a leper staring up at Jesus.

She had to get this caravan back on the road. "Would you like me to drive?"

Phil looked up into his rear view mirror. "Taylor, what did Kip say he was doing here?"

"Oh, Dad." Taylor was as fed up with this as her mother was.

"You said he was here on *a mission*. What kind of mission?"

"Supposed to, like, clean up pollution or something,"

"Pollution?"

Taylor kept her eyes on her phone as she spoke. "He'd left some stuff behind on his last trip. Said he was here now as a cylindrical garbage man."

"*Celestial*," Nate corrected her. He, too, had heard this story from Taylor already. "A *celestial* garbage man."

Phil turned back to Carol. "That could very well have something to do with all this."

"All this what?" Carol asked, knowing the answer but forcing her husband to say it aloud so he would hear how silly it sounded.

Phil dodged the ploy with a slight change in direction. "The guy says he left something behind. Maybe he's like, like a..."

Carol led the witness, "Like a space alien?" She said it as if she were talking to an over-excited child, which indeed she was. Carol turned toward the back seat and asked her daughter, "Did your hippie friend mention anything about being from another planet?"

Taylor didn't look up from her phone. "He was joking."

"May I make one simple suggestion?" Phil spoke his next words gently. He obviously knew he was treading on eggshells. "May I suggest we don't leave quite yet."

"You want to stay," Carol said. "Here. In Never Never Land."

"Just for lunch. A few hours. Until the storm passes by."

"I concur with Dad," said Nate, removing his ear buds.

"We're staying?" Taylor asked, showing a sudden renewed interest, as if this was good news to her as well. She even looked up from her phone.

Carol's heart sank. Suddenly, her whole family seemed to be in love with this crazy town — a town they all hated a few hours ago.

"What could it hurt?" Phil said, "It's a free lunch. We don't want to be rude. You've got to admit, those burgers at the pub were good."

"The Shamrock Pub!" Nate announced, punching his fist into the air as a victory celebration. "Where Eunice works."

Carol never felt more alone. Her son has the hots for an eight-year-old kitchen helper who smokes cigarettes and walks like a stripper. Her daughter has the hots for a hippie drifter she met on a ski lift. And her husband is buying into an insane story of eternal youth.

Phil grabbed Carol's knee and gave it a playful squeeze. "Just one more night. C'mon. It'll be fun."

"Fun?" repeated Carol. "Suddenly you think this town is *fun*? Are you out of your fu—" She was going to say *fucking mind*, but she was interrupted by a sudden bright flash of lightning.

Nate counted down the seconds, "One, two, three, four, five..." And then the crack of thunder arrived and slapped the sleeping Toyota awake. "Six!" Nate said. "That means the storm is just over one mile away."

But of course Carol knew the storm was much closer than that.

CHAPTER FIFTEEN

"I don't know, son. The picture is awful small." Mayor Sam Beckwith squinted hard at the miniature figures displayed on the tiny screen of Isaac's phone. The ex-wagon master's eyes worked well when spotting trouble waiting on a distant ridge, but they've never been good close up.

"I tell you, it's him." Isaac fumbled with his bandaged hand trying to zoom in on the man's thin dark form. "I'd recognize that little devil anywhere. Skin the color of caramel pudding. Pale blue eyes, always darting this way and that so as not to miss anything. And that foreign accent." Isaac held the phone up to his father's ear. "Hear it, Pop? Kinda English? Kinda homo?"

Sam scanned the restaurant to make sure no outsiders had heard his son's bigoted slur. But then he remembered that today's lunch was strictly *Townees Only*. No outsiders allowed. Except for the Hodworth family, of course. Too bad they were so intent on hurrying back home to Chicago.

Sam tried to listen to the video Isaac had recorded in the park this afternoon, but he couldn't hear anything over the noisy crowd in this pub.

Isaac persisted. "That voice is the exact same voice we heard shouting 'cross the river at us." Isaac slapped the screen with the back of his bandaged hand. "That's him, I tell you. That's the runaway slave. The runaway we shot."

"The runaway *you* shot," Frieda Bjorquist corrected him.

Sam held the phone up to his ear. And after a moment's assessment, he gave his verdict, "Canadian."

Isaac laughed. "That's exactly the same thing you said the first time. You figured the boy had come down from north of the border."

Frieda Bjorquist corrected him, "Never had slaves up in Canada. They had to pay Chinamen."

"Asians," Sam corrected her.

"No, I'm pretty sure they were Chinamen." Frieda pointed across the table. "Could ya pass the mustard, please, Sammy. That's a dear."

He handed the condiment caddy to her and handed the phone back to Isaac. "Might be the ex-slave, might not. I can't tell. That was a long time ago."

Frieda held her burger bun agape so the elk patty could receive a long juicy fart of mustard from the squeeze bottle. She tapped the photo on the phone. "If that *schwarz* is our *schwarz*, you know who'll know?"

Sam understood what she was getting at. "You're right."

Isaac understood too. And he didn't like it. "Oh, gee whiz," He whined, "Do we have to bring Becky into this?"

"Why not?" Sam said. "She's the one got the closest look at the fella."

Frieda added, "That fella was the first man to ever kiss Becky. Probably the *only* one."

"He wasn't *kissing* her," Isaac protested. "He was *attacking* her."

"Tomato, tomahto," Frieda said as she put the top bun back onto her meat patty. "I don't get it, Sam. Who's Becky think she's saving it up for, anyway?" She took a bite from her elk burger.

Sam Beckwith picked out a French fry and bit it in half. He waved the remaining stub of fry at the video picture now paused on Isaac's phone. "Maybe she's saving it up for this fellow right here."

"Him? Are you kidding? No way," Isaac snapped back.

Looking again at the photo of the African American gentleman Sam thought of an issue that hadn't yet been addressed. "You say he looks *exactly* the same?"

"Exactly. Hasn't lost a hair nor added a wrinkle."

"If that's true, that means he must never have left this valley," Sam offered.

"Here all this time?" Frieda said with her mouth full of burger. "Impossible We'da seen him."

"So where's he been then?" Sam asked.

Isaac shrugged. "Who cares? He's here now. That's all I'm worried 'bout."

Sam turned to Frieda. "See?" He waved his French fry at Isaac. "Not a curious bone in his body."

"Curiosity killed the cat," Isaac announced with pride.

Frieda added, "Didn't do young Zack Mossip much good neither."

She had a good point, and Sam was just about to acknowledge her perspicacity when he heard a fuss cooking up at the front of the restaurant.

"Hey! Look who's here!" someone shouted.

"They've come back!" said someone else.

Sam Beckwith stood up. Now it was his turn to be curious.

· · ·

The applause started on a low simmer and quickly heated up to a rolling boil. Finally it exploded into bubbling cheers, laughter, and slaps on backs.

Carol felt like a bit of a coward letting Phil and the kids enter the room ahead of her, but this was their idea not hers — she was here as an observer, not a participant. At least, that was her plan.

The happy faces advanced on the family like an incoming tide. Young Nate was the first to get his feet wet and therefore the first to get attacked, not by a shark but by an eight-year-old girl. Little Eunice came cruising out of the pub's kitchen doors, her white apron flowing round her pink knees like a billowing sail. She threw her arms around Nate's neck and planted a fat juicy smooch on his rosy cheek. "This is so cool," she gushed. "We are going to have such fun together."

Nate smiled.

Carol grabbed her little boy's hand, tugged him close to her side, and watched the sea of joy rise. This was weird. Sure, it's nice to feel welcomed, but this is *too* welcomed. Seems like the eyes of every man in the restaurant were on her. And on Taylor.

Taylor didn't like the vibes either. "What's going on?"

Phil dismissed his daughter's concern, "They're just happy to have new neighbors."

A man laughed and patted Phil on the back. "You can say that again, brother Phil."

A man grabbed Carol's hand and started pumping it like her dispenser was out of soap. "Welcome home, Mrs. Hodworth. Welcome home to Perpetuity."

Taylor picked up on the man's words. "*Home?* What are you talking about?"

Carol said, "Nothing to worry about, Taylor." Carol spoke loudly to make sure as many ears as possible could hear her. "We're just here for lunch. That's all. A quick bite and we're on our way."

"Of course, you are, dear," said Violet Snelling as she wrapped her arm around Carol's waist. "Over here. I've saved you a seat."

As Violet guided Carol, Phil and the kids across the room to a table, every townperson they passed seemed to have a question that needed answering immediately.

"You play bridge?" a rather stout woman asked.

"Not really," Carol answered.

"Hearts?" someone else asked.

"'Fraid not."

"Backgammon?"

"Used to, back in college, but—"

"Crokinole?"

"Crokin-what?"

"How about golf?" a man in his forties asked.

"You bet," Phil volunteered.

"Curl?" a young man asked. "Please tell us you curl."

Taylor fielded this one, "Are you friggin' retarded?"

"Don't suppose any of you play bass?" This one came from a man in his sixties.

Phil answered with some pride, "I play guitar."

The man turned away. "Who doesn't."

They reached a table where Carol recognized Mayor Sam Beckwith and his son, Isaac. Sam, quite a handsome fellow, stood as Carol approached. Very gallant, she thought. He nudged his son to do the same forgetting that the boy was injured and in a wheel chair. Still, the polite kid struggled to his feet anyway.

Someone added four empty chairs to the table so the Hodworths could sit. Mayor Sam Beckwith addressed the huddled crowd, "Pilgrims, there'll be plenty of time to offer your own personal *howdy-dos* later. For now let's leave our guests to eat in peace."

Carol assured Sam and the rest of the room, "But we really are leaving right after lunch."

The crowd, still a-grinnin' and a-mumblin', backed away and returned to their tables. Meanwhile, Violet Snelling had pulled another table over to join up with the one at which the Hodworth family was now seated. Sam extended his arm and invited several more people from the crowd to join the expanded party. He introduce them to the Hodworths, "Olive Gorely, Pastor Gorely, Doc Milburn, Enoch Dagleish, Lee Wong—"

"Lee Wong?" Carol recognized that one. "Isn't that the name of the original owner of the restaurant? Of Shangri-La Gardens?"

The Asian man, who seemed to be in his early thirties, said in a thick Chinese accent, "Yes, Missy. Me Lee Wong, humble first ownah and propritah of honorable Shangri-La Gahden. Good Chinee-Amelican food. Vely, vely clean kitchen. You likee."

"You can drop the Chinky shit, Lee," Violet said. "They're hip to you. Hip to us all."

"Awesome." Lee's accent slid into mid-western neutral. "Nice t'meet cha. You guys need a hand at the Gardens, you give me a ring. okay? Unless it's the plumbing or electrics. That shit's now your problem. But for food — I'm your dude."

Mayor Sam Beckwith explained further, "Lee Wong was our chuck wagon master on the trail. He took on young Zachariah Mossip as cook's boy. Later on they opened their own restaurant together."

Lee Wong continued the story. "Unloaded The Shangri-La on young Zack back in 1995 so I could open a video store. Man, I took a royal reeming on that fucker." Lee suddenly realized Taylor and Nate were listening. "Sorry, kids. Excuse my Chinese."

"I don't get it, Mr. Wong." Taylor said, justifiably perplexed. "Did you say you were with the original wagon train?"

Carol hadn't yet had a chance to tell Taylor the details about the crazy story she and Phil had been fed this morning. But there's no time like the present. "You'll get a big kick out of this, Tay," Carol said. "You see, according to local legend, every single person in this room is over two hundred years old. They all came here by horse and wagon in 1846. Have I got that date right, Mr. Wong?"

"Call me Lee." He smiled.

Taylor's eyes slowly surveyed the crowd of townsfolk that were gathered round, smiling like absolute dolts. Then she asked her mother, "Is, like, weed legal in this state or something?"

Now it was Phil's turn to run with the ball. Or pick up the shovel. He addressed both of his children with gravity, as if he were holding them by the shoulders and asking them to accept a new stepmother. "Taylor, Nate, because of some special magic in the valley, nobody in this town has ever gotten any older than they were when they first stepped foot here. Not one year. Not one week. Not one day. They just don't age."

"Like Peter Pan?" Nate suggested.

An elderly man spoke up, "Not quite, kid. In Never-Never Land only children stay young. Here, the young stay young, the middle-aged stay middle-aged, and us toothless old farts just keep on gummin' and fartin'."

"Truly a miracle," said a man wearing a blue suit who had been introduced to Phil as Pastor Gorely. "A blessing from the Lord."

A man wearing sweat pants and a t-shirt chuckled at the pastor's comment and said to Nate, "Most of us believe it's from a slightly more palpable source. Maybe a meteor. Or maybe something left behind by a more advanced civilization."

Taylor, who was sitting with her mouth hanging open, turned to her mother and asked, "And we're supposed to buy this?"

"Don't be silly. Of course not." Carol didn't care who heard her, least of all her husband. So she looked straight at him and put him on the spot. "Right, Phil?"

Phil leaned close to his daughter and said in a low whisper, "Just play along. The lunch is free."

All the townsfolk sitting around the table laughed at this one. So did Phil.

"May I take your orders?" a male voice boomed.

Carol almost jumped out of her skin. She hadn't seen the waiter come up behind her.

"Something from the bar, darlin'?" the waiter asked in an Irish brogue.

Carol noticed poor Phil's face fall as he realized that his server for this lunch was not going to be the buxom Irish lass from breakfast, but instead was this handsome Irish fellow, Angus —the Irish woman's husband.

Angus flashed Carol a big smile and a crisp nod of his curly black hair. His Irish brogue rolled thick as mulligatawny as he poured it on Carol, "Nice to see that ya changed yer travel plans, m'darlin'. Ye'll be wantin' the same rooms this eve?"

"Well, we weren't really planning on—"

Mayor Sam Beckwith interrupted, "This time the rooms will be 'comped, courtesy of the town."

Phil squeezed her hand, "Isn't that generous, honey? The rest of our vacation — free." Phil looked like he was about to lick Carol's hand. "How about it?"

Carol always was a sucker for puppies, even when they begged at the table. "Maybe one night," she said.

Angus and the mayor started applauding, and the rest of the table joined in. Then Angus finished asking Carol, "May I get you a wee dram from the bar, m'darling?"

Carol thought two in the afternoon was rather early in the day for hard liquor. But what the hell. She was on vacation. And the waiter had such a pleasant smile. So warm and genuine. The sort of smile that inspired trust.

"An Irish whiskey, might be nice," she said.

Phil ordered a drink, too, but Carol didn't notice exactly what it was. She was busy watching the waiter walk away.

CHAPTER SIXTEEN

Isaac fiddled the focus wheel on his binoculars with no problem at all. His fingers felt just fine. It has been eight days since the fire at the restaurant, and Isaac's hands have heeled up good as new. Doc Milburn credits his willow bark, witch hazel, and leeches for the cure, but Isaac knows better. He knows it was the hydrocortisone cream he'd ordered on the internet. But he won't tell the Doc about this. No point in hurting the old guy's feelings.

Isaac heard a metallic click, so he focused his field glasses on the side door of the vehicle. This rusty old van, a Volkswagen camper, was the same kind of mini-bus the hippies used to drive through these mountains back in the sixties. Isaac liked hippies. Especially the girl hippies. He used to sell pot to them. But Police Chief Dagleish got antsy and made everybody in the valley stop growing the stuff. The town council was worried it was drawing too much attention from outside the valley.

This Volkswagen bus Isaac has had his eye on was just like those old sixties buses except for two things: First, instead of a radio antenna, this vehicle has a small satellite dish mounted on the roof.

And second, instead of a long-haired white kid inside, this vehicle has a short-haired black kid squatting in it.

He calls himself Kip, and he's the ex-slave Isaac had photographed in the park last week, sitting on the bench talking to that Hodworth girl. Isaac followed him here. And every morning since then Isaac has watched the little guy go through the same routine, the routine he was about to go through right now.

From Isaac's hiding place under a staghorn sumac high atop the ridge overlooking the river, he watched the caramel-colored fella hop out of his psychedelic-colored vehicle, climb up onto the roof, and remove a gizmo from the center of the satellite dish. After slipping the little electronic do-hickey into his pocket Kip then proceeded to wade across the river to the stand of cherry trees, the Montmorency cherries Becky Thatcher had planted during World War One as part of her victory garden. Kip then followed the berry trail down the river valley. And as always he sang to himself. Always the same song. It's a ditty Isaac recognizes as a pop hit originally recorded in the sixties by a cowboy singer named Glen Campbell.

I am a lineman for the county. And I drive the main road...

Odd tune to choose. Certainly not the sort of music Isaac was used to hearing from black folk. Perpetuity valley has never had any negroes of its own, of course — nobody in the wagon train was rich enough to own one. But back when Isaac was a boy, back in Mississippi, he used to listen to the darkies sing their spirituals as they worked the bean and cotton fields. Later, long after Ma died and Isaac and his pa moved here to the valley, Isaac noticed how the freed slaves passing through town favored the new blues music over the old traditional hymns. Next came the ragtime and the jazz music. Isaac didn't like that junk at all. Nowadays, the blacks mostly favor the hip-hop style, which is just fine with Isaac. Lots of rhythm and words, and not too much of anything else going on to confuse matters.

Yes, indeed, this Kip fellow certainly has a nice voice. God has kindly blessed these folk with some fine musical talents. Isaac wished he could sing, but the only gifts the good Lord has bestowed upon Isaac are a sharp eye for aiming a rifle, quick legs for running away from a fire, and a good-sized pecker for making due amends. Oh, and of course there's this never-getting-old thing. That surely must be a gift from the Lord.

Everything considered, Isaac doesn't mind not being able to carry a tune.

Isaac stayed hidden and watched Kip walk down the berry trail dressed in his usual outfit — bell-bottom jeans and fringed buckskin vest. Lately, Kip has been leaving the trail to follow one of the spring freshets or dry creek beds that snakes down from the hills and joins up with the Perpetuity River. And as he walks, the ex-slave will search for something, but Isaac can't figure out what that thing might be. Can't be gold — the fellow never totes a pan or a screen. Whatever it is, the stuff must smell strong on account of Kip often stops and sniffs the air as he walks, much like a black bear smelling for honey. Occasionally, he even stops to pick up a leaf, examine it, sniff it, taste it. Like he's never seen the leaf before. Of course, Kip could be looking for marijuana leaves, but Isaac doesn't think the ex-slave would come all the way back here after all this time just to look for weed, especially since it's so easy nowadays to get off the internet. No, this Kip guy must have something else up his puffy paisley sleeve. And Isaac thinks he knows just what that something else might be.

Isaac suspects Kip has come here to mess with the valley's magic. After all, if this runaway slave was the one who brought this black magic here — and some people in town think he very well might be — then it figures that he's the one who might take it away.

Of course, there's one other possible explanation for why Kip might be here. The boy might have returned because he misses his girlfriend, Becky Thatcher. Last time he was here, the little fella took quite a shine to Becky. Maybe that's why he's come back. Maybe he plans to carry her off with him. Whether she wants to go along or not.

Either way, Isaac is sure this weird little fella is up to no good, and Isaac has no intention of letting him get away with it.

Isaac snapped the lens caps back onto his binoculars and slowly got to his feet. Very slowly. His legs were stiff from lying up here on this ridge all night.

Guarding the magic of this valley is hard work. But Isaac seems to be the only person willing to do it. The only person who still cares.

So once again, Isaac started after the ex-runaway-slave. Isaac didn't want to lose his quarry in the dense switchgrass, dogwood, and mountain ash. Of course, even if he did, this fellow was pretty darn easy to track. All Isaac needs to do is follow the singing.

I am a lineman for the county.

And I drive the main road.

Searchin' in the sun for another overload.

Gotta admit, the little fella sure has a nice voice.

• • •

Carol didn't have much to work with. No balloons. No ribbons. No banners. The local Dollar Store had used them all up for that celebration last week to honor Phil at town hall. This left Carol with nothing to add zip to tonight's party but some cheesy candle holders that Zachariah Mossip had stored away, holders that were actually just old Mason jars wrapped in plastic netting. Of course, Carol could buy some proper candle holders from the internet, but she couldn't see making a capital investment in Shangri-La Gardens, a business that will soon be up for sale. So she continued scraping out the old wax and dropping new tea candles into the jars.

Tonight's party will be Carol and Phil's way of saying thanks and goodbye to the generous citizens of Perpetuity. Tomorrow the Hodworths will head back to Chicago. The family has been here for a whole week now, free food and lodging, and it's time for Carol to drag Phil back to his job.

And back to reality.

Phil still pretends not to swallow this never-aging baloney. He claims he's just been playing along and enjoying the free vacation the town has so generously awarded him and his family. And Carol must admit, once the locals stopped being rude and started treating the Hodworths as friends, the family has enjoyed a fun week. Carol has found some lovely trails to hike and some interesting historical sites to explore. The kids have even learned how to horseback ride. And Phil... Well, Carol has never seen her husband so happy. Happy all day, happy all night. He even whistles. He whistles while he works, he whistles while he plays, he whistles while he whistles. And that is why Carol is concerned about him. Concerned about his sanity. No middle-aged man should be this happy unless he's on drugs or he's lost his mind. And sadly, Phil has never been one to use drugs.

But Phil isn't the only member of the Hodworth clan Carol is watching with a butterfly net handy. For the past week, young Nate has a had a constant grin pasted on his freckled face — the grin of a horny little boy who is smitten with a pretty little girl. A pretty but *weird* little girl.

Her name is Eunice, and Carol must admit, if any evidence points to these people really being older than they look, this little Eunice chick is Exhibit Number One. The pig-tailed scamp is beyond precocious. She's unsettling. There's something frightening going on behind those big brown cow eyes, something Carol finds deeply disturbing. Of course, Carol feels guilty about disliking a nine-year-old child like this, especially after Carol learned the poor kid's backstory.

Apparently, Eunice is an orphan who has been adopted by an aunt here in town. Carol hasn't met the adoptive aunt yet, but she assumes the little girl is having trouble dealing with the situation. To compensate, the little thing has made up some fantastic tale about her birth parents dying in a train on their way here. Apparently, the girl's parents had taken a different train than the one Eunice and her aunt had taken. The parents' train was called the

Donner Party train. Yes, like the Donner Party wagon train from the 1800s. This girl has quite the imagination.

And then there's Taylor. She, too, seems to be in an unusually good mood these days, which makes no sense at all. A seventeen-year-old girl stuck with her parents in a backwater town with no malls, no dance clubs, very few restaurants, and even fewer young people her own age? A girl in that situation should be miserable. But it takes only one special person to change an equation like this, and it looks like Taylor has found that one special person. His name is Kip, and he's the young man the family met when they were stuck up on that chair lift.

Taylor has been spending quite a lot of time with Kip. Well, not actually *with* him. Not physically, that is. Like most hookups in Taylor's life, this relationship is mainly digital. She and Kip have been communicating strictly by texts and video calls. But tonight that's supposed to change. Apparently, Kip is coming to this party tonight. Taylor is looking forward to seeing him again, and so is Carol. As with Nate's little girlfriend, Carol wonders if this boy is all that he appears to be. She would like to know more about him, and she hopes Phil can help her assess the situation. But considering Phil's mental state lately she isn't sure she can trust his judgement.

"You want me to light these things yet?" Phil asked. He was holding a candle in one hand and a long-handled butane lighter in the other.

"No, better wait for a while. Candles burn oxygen, and something tells me a lot of your friends in this town are running low."

Phil laughed at her little joke. "Honey, you're a pistol." He aimed the lighter at her and triggered it as if it were a gun. "No wonder all the men have their sights on you." Then he slapped her butt.

Yup, this is one happy family, all right.

● ▪ ● ▪ ●

The festivities weren't scheduled to kick off until eight, but by seven-thirty the Shangri-La Gardens restaurant was jam-packed with joyful revelers. Phil noticed that everybody had a drink in his or her hand — a drink Phil was paying for. But he didn't mind. These people have been generous to him.

Phil stood at the service bar and pointed out the obvious to Mayor Sam Beckwith, "People round here like to party, huh?"

"This bunch does."

"*This* bunch?"

The mayor rested his elbow on the bar as if he was readying himself for a long chat. "Phil, have you noticed yet that most of these faces always look particularly familiar?"

"Of course they do. It's a small town."

"Small, but not this small." Sam turned to the bartender. "My usual, please, Josiah." He then turned back to Phil, "You're looking here at a very small portion of the population of Perpetuity, but it's the only portion you're ever likely to see at a gathering after dark."

Phil nodded. He thought he understood. "Farmers have to go to sleep with the chickens."

"True, but we don't have many farmers."

Phil tried again, "Young parents have to stay home with their children."

"Not many parents either. Young or old."

Phil tried once more, "You probably have a lot of religious types, church-goers who don't believe in drinking or dancing."

"Used to," Sam said. "But not anymore."

"I get it." Phil thought he had it this time, "The internet. Social media. Streaming TV... Nobody leaves the couch anymore. Yeah, we have the same problem in the city. All our neighborhood pubs are dead."

The bartender, Josiah, butted in, "I'm afraid there's a little more to it than that." He placed Sam Beckwith's beer on a cardboard coaster and then left for a customer farther down the bar.

Sam picked up his glass and took a good big slug of beer. He wiped the foam from his lips with the back of his big, sun-tanned hand. Then he leaned close to Phil and said, quietly for Phil's ears only, "Nice of you to keep Josiah on."

The mayor had a good point. It truly was nice of Phil to hire this young man. Apparently, Josiah had tended bar here for Zachariah, but Phil had been reluctant to re-hire him. The problem was optics. Phil didn't want to be cruel, but he feared this guy might put people off their food. Who wants to eat their egg roll while looking at a toupee that resembles something the plumber has yanked out of a clogged sink. When Phil heard the story behind, or under, the young man's mangy rug, however, he knew he had to give the poor fellow a gig if for no other reason than to have a good story for the gang back in the golf club. To buy the story a person has to go along with the valley's living-forever premise, which Phil doesn't mind doing. For laughs.

Seems back in 1868, this very bartender, Josiah McGee, was employed as a scout for Mayor Beckwith's wagon train. One day, while riding ahead, Josiah was attacked by a band of *Shoshones*. He received several bad injuries, including an arrow through his hand and a couple more in his chest. He fell unconscious, and he looked rather dead. So the natives scalped him. Shortly afterwards, the wagon train caught up with him and found he was still alive. Doc Milburn went to work with his sewing needle, herbal medicines, and leeches, and Josiah recovered from his terrible wounds.

For a while, poor Josiah hid his badly scarred skull under a coonskin cap. But eventually the local womenfolk, who were already good with quilts, fashioned him a wig from a grizzly hide or a prairie dog pelt or something equally tonsorial. Trouble today is, for sentimental reasons Josiah has refused to trade the ear-to-ear taxidermy for a modern piece. Shame, actually, because the guy is a darn good-looking young man who'd certainly make much better tips if he'd invest in a decent rug. As for Josiah's other injuries, the poor guy has never regained the use of his right hand, but he seems to do a pretty good job of mixing drinks with his left. Unless, of course, a native American Indian wanders into the bar, in which case Josiah gets rather nervous and spills more than he serves.

Sam Beckwith grabbed a handful of pretzel sticks from a hand-painted oriental candy bowl and used one of the sticks to point out someone in the crowd. "Stella Logan asked your daughter to babysit for her yet?"

"Not that I know of."

"She will." Sam popped the pretzel into his mouth. "Stella's young 'uns can be a handful."

Phil had to set the mayor straight. "Even if Carol and I should decide to move here, I'm afraid Taylor wouldn't be coming with us. She's off to college in the fall."

"That's okay. Maybe your wife would like to earn the extra money. Stella and Clement have twins. Two-year-olds."

Phil winced. "Two-year-old twins. That's gotta be rough."

"For a hundred and sixty-six years it is."

Phil looked at the mother more closely and decided to go along with the joke. "It's a wonder mommy and daddy haven't climbed the clock tower with an Uzi."

"We keep the clock tower locked," the mayor winked.

A rather attractive middle-aged woman, maybe late fifties, stepped up to the bar. Assuming she'd come to order a drink, Phil stepped aside to make space for her. She smiled, grabbed Phil's right butt cheek, and said, "Good party, Phil." She left her hand clamped to his ass.

"Uh, thanks."

"You like to dance?" Now she was massaging his ass.

"Gee, I, uh..." Phil was taken aback, her hand was moving down to his upper thigh. Inner upper.

Sam stepped in. "Put it on simmer, Rachel. The guy just got here. He's still perfectly happy with what he's got. Right, Phil?"

Phil laughed. "You betcha. I'm happy. Real happy. We, uh, we both are."

"Of course, you are," Rachel said. "Tell me Phil, you curl?" Her hand skated up his butt to the small of his back.

"No, but I might give it a try some day."

One more pat to the ass. "See you on the rink. I'll look forward to sweeping with you." She laughed at her joke, winked, and walked away.

In amazement, Phil turned to Sam and said, "These women... they're all horny as jack rabbits."

"Horny. Bored. You'll find there's a fine line between the two." Sam toasted Phil with his glass of beer. "Excuse me while I mingle." And with that, Sam walked off.

Phil stood and took a good look at the crowd. Especially at the men. He wondered if Carol would ever get so bored with life that she'd want to sleep with any of them. Right now she has her Sudoku. But someday...

Phil watched Sam Beckwith walk to the front of the restaurant. For some reason, the man proceeded to close the vertical blinds. In city bars this usually means the strippers are coming on. But Shangri-La Gardens has no strippers. Is something about to happen here that shouldn't be witnessed by children?

Phil pondered the erotic inferences to Sam's closed window coverings. Meanwhile, a teenage boy strolled up to the bar. Phil had seen this kid around town and had already taken a disliking to him.

The kid, no more than fourteen years old, was of a familiar type — short hair with lots of gel, over-sized jeans falling off his under-sized ass, assorted metal rings and posts piercing his ears, nose, and eyebrows, and a tattoo of a winged lizard crawling up his neck. What sort of parents would allow their teenager to do this to his young healthy body?

The over-indulged twerp patted out a quick paradiddle on the bar's countertop with his pale hands and shouted to the bartender, "I do believe it's martini time, my good man." The kid then shot Phil a belligerent grin.

Phil waited for Josiah to tell the brat to beat it, but to Phil's amazement, the bartender went ahead and poured a generous shot of gin into a martini glass. He then dripped in some vermouth, plunked in an olive, and placed the high-proof assemblage in front of the kid. The boy reached for it but didn't quite get it all the way to his waiting lips before Phil gently grabbed the glass from his hand.

"Hold on, there, flash." Phil's fingers lifted the rim of the glass away like a claw machine picking up a plush toy. "You're not drinking that here."

The kid watched Phil place the glass down on the bar. Then the boy glanced towards the front of the restaurant. Satisfied with what he saw, he turned back to Phil, "What's your prob, dude?"

"My *prob* is my liquor license." Phil picked up a paper napkin and wiped the gin from his fingers. Meanwhile, a little girl approach the bar. Phil recognized her as Eunice, the little eight-year-old who's been playing with Nate.

The little tyke first addressed the teenage boy, "How they hangin', Clay?" Then she addressed the bartender, "Hey, Josiah. What imports you poisoning us with these days?"

"Usual, Eunice — Corona, Heineken, Moretti, Molson's."

Phil couldn't believe his ears. Was Josiah about to serve this eight-year-old girl a beer?

"Molson's sounds good." She smiled up at Phil. "Always like to support our neighbors to the north."

And sure enough, the bartender yanked a bottle of beer from the fridge and popped the cap for her.

"Josiah," Phil exclaimed to the bartender, "What the hell you doing?"

The horrible hairpiece turned this way and said, "Don't worry, Mr. Hodworth, she ain't driving."

But the little girl understood Phil's problem. She indicated the front window and assured him, "It's cool — the blinds are closed."

So that's why Mayor Sam had shut the blinds. He didn't want any tourists seeing the local kids knocking back booze. Phil turned to the young male tattooed punk who, by now, had picked up his martini. Phil said to him, "So you can drink but only behind closed doors."

"Cheers." The kid toasted Phil with a sip of the dry martini.

"And how about other adult activities?"

"Whatcha got in mind?" the boy asked.

"I don't know... I presume you can't be seen sitting behind the wheel of a car, right?"

Eunice fielded this one, "Not anymore."

The boy explained to Phil, "Nineteen-forty-seven, Wyoming decided it was time to license drivers. I should have been good to go — the state didn't have any record of my birth. But town council said we shouldn't take a chance on some state cop seeing me tooling around in my Pontiac Streamliner. So that was the end of that. Great ride, that Streamliner." The boy gazed into his drink as if his martini glass were a crystal ball, and he didn't like what he saw. "I gotta tell ya, man, eternal youth ain't all it's cracked up to be."

"Amen to that." The little girl held up her beer bottle and toasted her friend's words. "I'll never be legal to drive. I'll never be legal to drink. And I'll never have children — legally, illegally, or any other freakin' way."

The teenage boy chuckled, "You say that like it's a bad thing."

"Don't play the hard ass, Clay. I've known you too long." Eunice turned to Phil and explained. "There's nothing more this guy would rather do than be a father — teach his son how to rope a calf, how to slap a puck, how to Top Gun a skateboard. But he never will."

"Never?" Phil didn't understand. He could see that, while the boy is young, he certainly looks like he has passed the age of puberty.

Eunice explained, "Nothing ages around here, including fertilized eggs."

Phil didn't know whether to cry or laugh. If these kids are making this up as they go along, they are damn good. They should be on stage. Or on TV. At least a podcast. They were fast on their feet. And very convincing.

This unreal talk was making an unreal situation seem very real. Very true to life. Phil felt odd. This whole exchange had set a flock of butterflies free in Phil's stomach, the same fluttering flock that had taken wing when he'd looked up at that historic statue of the town's founding father and realized he was looking into the eyes of Mayor Sam Beckwith. This whole phenomenal tale was starting to look less like a dream and more like... like...

"You okay, Mr. Hodworth?" little Eunice asked.

"Dude, you look kind of pale," the boy named Clay added.

Phil lowered himself down onto a bar stool. "I, uh, I'm fine. It's just, well, it's been a long day."

"They all are," said little Eunice.

Clay sipped his martini. "Almost as long as the nights."

Phil sat and watched the two little kids drinking — an eight-year-old girl knocking back a bottle of beer and a fourteen-year-old punk sipping a dry martini. It was an appalling picture. A disturbing picture. A shocking picture. And yet, in this whole room full of adults, Phil Hodworth seemed to be the only one who found it odd.

CHAPTER SEVENTEEN

She has to face it — he's not coming.

Taylor checked the clock on the wall behind the cash register. It was almost eleven. The party's been rolling for three hours now, and Kip hasn't showed. He obviously isn't interested. Well, too bad. His loss. She and her family leave early tomorrow morning. He'll never know what he missed.

Taylor straightened her back in defiance and walked to the front door of the restaurant for one last look. If he's not out there, fine. She'll just dance with someone else, maybe one of these old perverts who've been gawking at her all evening. Geez, you'd think these guys had never seen a hot young woman before. Or any woman. Poor Mom. She hasn't stopped dancing since the party started, and it looks like she has no plans on quitting anytime soon. Same for Dad. And he hates dancing. Yet he's danced at least once with every woman at this party. Young, old, thin, large. Hell, he's even *boogied on down* with that little girl, Eunice — the weird little kid who has the hots for Nate. What's a little girl that age even doing up this late? Nate isn't here, of course. He's in bed at the motel with his babysitter. Well, not in bed *with* his baby sitter. Although in this crazy town, anything is possible.

The window in the front door was the only window that wasn't covered up. The shuttered room felt weird, like she was in an illegal booze can like the one she sometimes visits back in Chicago after cheerleading practice. Tonight, with Mom and Dad around, Taylor hasn't had anything to drink. Well, not much. The young bartender spiked her first diet soda with a shot of vodka. But he says he can't do it again. Not until she moves here permanently. Fat chance. This town is a nice place to visit — most zoos are. And talking about zoos, what was that thing on top of the bartender's head? He'd actually be quite nice looking if he lost that insane wig.

Taylor gazed out the door's window, into the night. The street was dead. No people. No cars. No action at all except for a gang of dizzy moths bashing themselves stupid against a street lamp across the street. Taylor's eyes slid down the lamp pole like a dancer finishing her act. And that's when she saw it. The bicycle.

It was leaning against the lamp post as if it were waiting for someone to ride it away to a more exciting town. Taylor has been keeping watch, and she could swear that, a few minutes ago, that bike wasn't there. She was sure of it. She would have remembered that buckskin leather vest with the fringe that lay draped over the bike's crossbar.

Taylor opened the door and stepped out onto the sidewalk. To her right, about a block and a half up the street, she could see the town hall where her father had received his award. And just beside that was the little park, the grassy knoll with the statue and the bench where she'd sat and talked with Kip. He had been wearing that buckskin vest with the fringe.

Taylor walked a little farther up the street. She wasn't going to go far — the road was deserted and kind of spooky — she'd go just far enough to see into the shadows of that park.

The shadows were darker than she'd expected. Or the street lamps were weaker. She walked a little farther.

"Hey, Taylor! What's happening?" He hadn't frightened her. His voice was too gentle for that. He stood up from the bench and walked toward her. It was a distinct walk. A cool, easy walk. But not a long stride. His legs were too short for that.

Taylor stood still, making him come to her. He owed her that much.

The street lamp backlighted his narrow hips and slim, bell-bottomed legs. "How's the family?" he asked.

She pointed to the restaurant. "Come on inside and see for yourself."

He ignored her invitation. "You look exceptionally groovy this fine eve."

She tried again, "Why are you sitting out here?"

"Been on my feet all day."

"I'm sure I can find you a seat."

"I believe it is healthier for all concerned if I stay out here, away from your friends."

"My friends? Why?" Taylor backed away from him. "What have you got?"

"No, no, it's nothing like that. I'm in perfect health. It's just that, if there's any gunplay I'd prefer it take place out here. Away from bystanders."

Taylor's eyes flashed to the line of his corduroy pants. "You're carrying a gun?"

"No, not me. Never. We're not allowed."

Taylor was getting more than a little fed up with this nonsense. "Kip, what are you talking about?"

"Him. Over yonder. The dude in the bushes." Kip pointed to the line of trees at the edge of the park.

Taylor squinted into the black mass of foliage, but it was too dark to see details. "Who? I don't see anyone."

"He keeps himself hidden. But he's there. Follows me around every day. All day. Like a... like a..."

"Like a body guard?"

"A bad smell."

Taylor squinted into the dark wall of bushes. "Do you know who he is?"

"I believe his name is Isaac."

"Isaac?" Taylor recognized the name. "The boy my father pulled out of the fire?"

"Wouldn't know 'bout that. He's your wagon master's son."

"Wagon master? I thought Isaac was the mayor's kid."

"I know him as the wagon master. Sam Beckwith."

"And you say Isaac Beckwith has been following you."

"And I'd rather he didn't follow me into any crowded rooms. Could be collateral damage."

Taylor now understood what Kip meant. Isaac was indeed dangerous. He took it pretty badly after Taylor shot him down for that dessert date. And now if he sees her with Kip, who knows what he'll do. "And you're worried he might harm someone at the party?" she asked.

"He has a history. The fellow has already shot me once."

"Shot you? Like, with a gun?" This was news to Taylor.

"No hassle. I was cool, I had my meds with me. I was soon fit as a fiddle and back truckin'. But if he should start shooting again and I'm in a crowded room, or near you..." Kip backed a few feet away from Taylor. "I shouldn't even be here with you. Last time I was seen close to a woman some of your local men-folk got pretty bent out of shape."

"You can't still be worried about the racial thing." Taylor stepped closer. "That's so yesterday."

But Kip backed away, saying. "I've been digging our digital communications." He took a cell phone out of his pocket. "I'm sorry my replies have been so brief, but I can't use these devices for very long. The radio frequencies you people have chosen have strange effects on me. They cause my epidermis to—"

"That's bullshit." Taylor waved his concerns away like she was swatting at a mosquito. "My science teacher says cell phones are perfectly safe."

"Maybe for you they are, but for us..." He pointed to the back of his hand. "Can you see the glow?"

Taylor laughed. She enjoyed Kip's sense of humor. She stepped closer. He, in turn, stepped backwards. She stepped again. He backed again.

This was dumb. Taylor had had enough. She turned towards the trees and called out to the shadows, "Isaac, you can come out now. We know you're in there."

Kip didn't like this at all. "No, no, no," he whispered. "Leave him alone. I didn't come here to make trouble."

"*He's* the one making trouble." Taylor turned to the bushes again, "Isaac, take off your hood and white sheet and stop bothering this man. Get a hobby. Find a restaurant to burn. Or maybe a cross."

She heard rustling in the trees. Twigs breaking. The idiot was finally leaving. She turned back to Kip, "You gotta know how to talk to these people."

"Oh, I do," Kip said. "I learned from your television broadcasts on my way here — same way I learned about your current fashions of dress." Kip tugged at the puffy sleeves of his paisley rayon blouse. "You dig my far-out threads?"

Taylor stepped back to take in the full splendor of his outfit. "Vintage duds suit you."

"Thank you. I scored them at a second-hand store. Traded them for the costume I wore last time I was here."

Taylor took his hand and started walking him toward the restaurant. Heck, somebody had to take the initiative.

Kip continued, "Scored my wheels from a second-hand vehicle dealer in Casper. Honest Otto's Honest Autos. You must have seen his TV ads."

"I don't watch much television."

"No? You should. Excellent for research. Keeps me up to date when I'm on the road. And entertained. Glen Campbell certainly makes the time go fast."

"Who?"

"The Good Time Hour. I also dig *Laugh In*. 'Sock it to me.'"

Taylor had no idea what Kip was talking about, but she enjoyed his goofy enthusiasm. Most guys her age try to play everything too cool. But this guy was real. Totally in the moment. Totally honest. Totally sincere. Totally sweet. "Any idea yet how long you're going to be in town?"

"As long as it takes," Kip said. "Like I told you, I'm here to clean up my mess."

"Yeah, you mentioned something about that."

"It was my own fault. And I take full responsibility."

"Your fault?" His words were setting off a small tinkle bell of alarm.

"I couldn't explain fully on the phone, but..." Kip seemed embarrassed with this confession. "Last time I passed this way, it seems I may have left a little something behind."

"A little something?" Taylor's alarm rang louder.

"It was an accident, mind you, but it was *my* accident. I failed to take proper precautions. So I figure it's up to me to do the right thing about it."

The right thing. The alarm bell clanged high and Taylor's heart fell low. Shit. Sounds like her cute new friend here has knocked up a local girl.

Taylor loosened her grip on Kip's hand. Man, she really can pick 'em.

• • •

Isaac Beckwith had it all figured out. The black fellow never was a slave. Not unless they have slaves on Mars.

After following Kip around the valley for almost two weeks, Isaac has come to one and only one conclusion. The little guy is a space alien. Nothing else explains the fella's peculiar ways and habits. Like the way he's always smelling everything he sees on the ground — rocks, plants, dirt. Heck, no Earthling would pick up a handful of deer shit and smell it like he was fixin' to put it in a casserole.

And then there's the way the little guy chirps into his cell phone like a dolphin talking to a fax machine. That's certainly no Earthbound lingo he's speaking. The guy is on a direct line to his home planet.

And finally, there's the fella's crazy skin color. Most of the time it's just plain milk chocolate. But when the little guy holds that phone up to his head, his smooth brown skin actually sparkles with bright electric flashes of glitter like he's just had a lap dance from a clumsy stripper. No, something extra-terrestrial is going on with this boy.

Luckily, for everybody involved, Isaac knows all about space aliens. He's seen them on the internet. He finds the whole subject fascinating. In fact, if Isaac were ever able to leave this valley, the first place he'd head for would be Roswell, New Mexico. That's where the Air Force has a space critter locked up in an Amana Freezer. But of course, Isaac isn't dumb enough to ever do something like that. He doesn't have to. He's got the internet. And The History Channel.

Pa says Isaac doesn't have a curious bone in his head. But that's just not true. Isaac has more curious bones in his head than most people do. Especially the people in this town. Folks in Perpetuity just don't care anymore. They're content to sleep their way through eternity. Well, it's high time somebody woke them up. There's something going on with this Kip guy, and it could be threatening the whole valley. This man is not simply a danger to the womenfolk as Isaac first expected, he's a threat to the town's very existence, the town's magical *status quo*. After all, everybody knows that when a space alien starts probing you, he usually has something more in mind than just dinner and a movie.

It's up to Isaac to sound the alarm, and there's no better time to do it than right now while Kip is busy out there courting that

Hodworth gal in the park. Happily, the mayor and most of the movers and shakers of this valley are conveniently gathered together tonight at the big wing-ding Mr. and Mrs. Hodworth are throwing.

The windows of Shangri-La Gardens were shuttered tight — that meant the party was in full swing. Isaac opened the door and stepped inside.

And then he stopped.

Jumpin' Jehoshaphat. What a sight. Isaac couldn't help but smile. He hadn't seen this many folks having this much fun for many, many years. The room was full to bursting with happy faces. Giggles and laughter floated atop a sea of joyful drinkers and spritely disco dancers. Squeals of gaiety bounced off the walls and ceiling like ping-pong balls blowing around in a church bingo machine.

Isaac scanned the crowd for Olive Gorely, the preacher's wife. Only six years older than Isaac, Olive is the best dance partner in town. And Isaac loves to dance. Olive used to be one of the best sex partners, too, but lately the gal has been a bit cold in the sack. Isaac doesn't take it personally, of course. Every gal has her ups and downs. Every gal except Becky Thatcher, that is. She has only downs. No use looking for Becky in here. She hasn't been to a party in fifty, maybe sixty years. Nowadays, Becky leaves the house only for Sunday worship. Or to go marketing. Or occasionally to babysit tourist children at the motel. Becky loves kids. Too bad, considering.

Isaac stepped farther into the room. He has to warn these good folk about this ex-runaway-slave who's really a Martian come to destroy the valley.

He stepped into the party like he was stepping into a warm bath. He eased himself onto the dance floor. All his friends and neighbors were gathered tight, rocking and swaying to the steady familiar rhythm. This felt nice. It would be good to dance again. And disco music is Isaac's favorite.

• • •

Becky Thatcher sat on the side of the bed and tried not to think impure thoughts. But it wasn't easy. Motel rooms and impure thoughts walk hand in hand. Especially in rooms with free Wi-Fi and satellite TV.

Becky knew just what she needed to fortify her resolve. She rolled herself across the chenille bedspread and reached into the top drawer of the nightstand. Good, it's still there. Even looks like one of the originals. Becky remembered when these Bibles were first handed out by that nice travelling drummer from The Gideons in the spring of 1910. It was a welcome gift back then, and it's a welcome gift tonight. A few verses from the Good Book will surely distract her from Satan's visual temptations on the satellite television screen. Of course, she could just seek her comfort and strength from the King James app on her phone, but snatching the Lord's bits and bytes from out of the ether is a poor substitute for clutching an actual leatherette-bound hard copy close to your heart. But before she starts browsing her favorite chapters, Becky must check on her young charge.

She rolled herself off the bed and tip-toed her stockinged feet to the entrance of the adjoining room. Gingerly, she cracked open the door a few inches until the thin wedge of light stretched its golden ray across the little boy's face. Good, her charge seems to be sleeping soundly. Young Nate Hodworth seems like a nice child. A tad foul-mouthed, but nowadays aren't they all?

Becky eased the door shut, her hand cradling the smooth round knob taking extra care not to let the long, hard bolt scrape or click as it prodded itself into the hole that waited eagerly to receive—

Darn.

Becky snatched the Bible from atop the quilt and carried it with her to the room's single easy chair. As she passed the flat-screen television, she recalled how one of the featured titles on the pay-per-view channel was an old comedy movie called *The 40-Year-Old Virgin*. According to the advertising blurb, the film recounted the hilarious trials and tribulations of a man who had held onto his virginity for forty years.

Big deal, thought Becky. *Try holding onto it for a hundred and forty years — then you'll have something worth making a movie about.*

Of course, Becky could have eased her hormonal burden many years ago if she had done what all the other young post-pubescent teenagers in town have done and started living as the adult that she truly is. But Pastor Gorely says that would be a sin. No matter what her age is biologically or chronologically, in the eyes of the Lord she is still an unmarried woman.

Pastor Gorely is the one man in town who still encourages Rebecca to remain chaste. He and Becky's father, of course. It hasn't been easy, but with the help of the Lord, Becky has had no sex, no courting, no close dancing, no suggestive party games, and absolutely no kissing. Well, except for that one kiss. But that kiss saved her life.

Becky has never forgotten that kiss. Nowadays they would call it The Kiss Of Life. She has also never forgotten the man who gave it to her. He was a kind man. A gentle man. A man of good humor. Becky often thinks of that lovely man who saved her life and how, if circumstances were different and he were here today...

Well, there's no need to worry about that particular temptation. Nobody has seen that fellow since the night of November 3, 1846. That was the night Becky witnessed the miracle.

While lying there dying from the bullet wound to his chest, the slave used his last breath to whisper to her: *Please fetch my medicine from my campsite.* To get it Becky knew she would have to walk a good half-mile through Indian territory in the dark of night. But she owed it to him. So she went and got it. It was inside his bedroll, some sort of small crystalline rock.

When she got back, he asked her to hold the rock to his wound and keep holding it there even if he screamed. She did. He squirmed a bit, but he didn't scream. Meanwhile, Becky did the only sane thing — she prayed for his good health. And sure enough, within moments, that runaway slave jumped to his feet good as new. Becky's prayers had been answered. The Lord had listened.

Boy, did He listen.

Little did Becky know, that when the Lord granted her wish and blessed that nice slave with a few extra years of good health that He was also blessing Rebecca's entire wagon train with extra years. Many, many extra years. Too many, some say.

Since then, Becky has been careful what she prays for.

Becky Thatcher reached to the table beside her chair and switched on the goose-neck reading lamp. She opened the tattered leatherette-bound Gideon Bible and started reading. And as she did, she thought about another person who had lived for many, many extra years.

The Good Book says Methuselah lived for nine hundred and sixty-nine years. And according to Pastor Gorely, during all those years Methusalah managed to resist all temptations of the flesh and remain in grace with the Lord.

Of course, Methuselah wasn't sitting in a motel room with free Wi-Fi and satellite TV.

• • •

Olive Gorely placed her dirty highball glass in the dishwasher and slid a clean sherry glass out of the cupboard beside her sink. After all, cleanliness is next to Godliness, and God certainly wouldn't want her sullying the taste of her dry sherry with the sweet pearl onion that had been pickling her Gibson martini.

She poured herself a shot of Spanish sherry and carried the cut crystal glass down the hall to her bedroom. As she passed the Pastor's office, she noticed his monitor screen was burning bright. "You still working?" she asked, purely out of politeness.

The Pastor didn't bother to look up from his keyboard. "Just a few more minutes, snookums. Almost done."

"That's what you said two hours ago." Olive took a sip of sherry. "For once, why don't you break down and give them a repeat performance. Look on it as a '*Best Of.*'"

The Pastor turned his head to look at his wife standing in the doorway. "Nine thousand, seven hundred and thirty-six."

"What?"

"That's how many sermons I've written. This one will be number nine thousand, seven hundred and thirty-seven."

"Well, why not give 'em number six thousand nine hundred and twenty-two again. That was a doozy. That one had 'em repenting in the aisles."

He went back to his typing. "Snooks, you know I never repeat a sermon."

Yes, she certainly did know. After one hundred and you-do-the-fucking-math years of holy matrimony a wife knows everything about her husband. Every hair. Every freckle. Every blessed thing. Of course, it wasn't always like this.

When Olive first met Hadwin Gorely, back in Louisville, she didn't know a thing about him other than what she had been told by her mother. Mom said Hadwin Gorely was a man who could be trusted to give a young lady a buggy ride home from a picnic without expecting payment with a kiss. Plus, Hadwin approved of Manifest Destiny, which was important to Olive's Mother. The picnic was a political rally for President James Polk who was running against Henry Clay. Pastor Hadwin Gorely apparently supported the President because he believed the United States had a God-given right to extend its domain from sea to sea. It didn't matter what Olive herself believed, of course — women back then didn't have the right to think, let alone vote. Olive and her mother were in attendance at the rally just to serve lemonade.

Pastor Hadwin Gorely, who was then twenty-three, was a freshly ordained, but still unassigned, lay preacher in the Methodist church. At that time, Olive had just turned twenty-five, but she lied and told Hadwin she was twenty-two. After a whirlwind courtship they got themselves hitched. A few weeks later they set out for Wyoming Territory.

To this day, Olive Gorely has never told her dear husband the truth about her age. He's proud of his hot young twenty-two-year-old wife, so why spoil things by telling him that, for over a century, he's been married to an older woman? He would surely wonder what other secrets she might have tucked away under her petticoats, poodle skirt, bell-bottom slacks, and now yoga pants. Of course, living with a lie for a hundred and who-the-fuck-knows years hasn't been easy, which is why Olive Gorely drinks. Well, it's one of the reasons.

Olive took a sip, then said, "I'll leave the bed lamp on."

"No need, snooks. I'll find my way to your side. The Lord will guide me."

"Yeah, right. Last night He guided you straight into the fucking laundry hamper. How's your toe?"

"Nail's broken. I do wish you would ease up on the F-bombs a mite."

"Afraid I'll embarrass you?"

He laughed but kept typing. "You know I don't embarrass that easily."

That's certainly true. Olive leaned on the door frame and watched her husband work. As usual at this time of year, he was wearing pajama bottoms but no top. Amazing how, after all this time, Hadwin's body still didn't carry an ounce of fat. The man looked, quite literally, like the twenty-six-year-old boy she had married, the only change being in his posture. Years of toting a heavy burden of professional failure has rounded his shoulders and bowed his spine.

Olive remembered when her husband walked tall, back when he was a man with a mission. As the only clergyman on the trail, Hadwin served as the train's spiritual scout, guiding the flock along the path of righteousness as surely and as boldly as Sam Beckwith guided them along the Oregon Trail. But of course, back in those days the preaching gig was easy. Most every wandering soul believed. Very few pioneers would think of doing battle with the rough land, the harsh elements, and the heathen savages without having a Bible shielding his heart and the firm hand of God steadying his rifle.

But that's all done with now. Few people in this valley need Divine help anymore. Times are far too safe and easy. Seems when folk lose their fears they lose their need for God. The Pastor has discovered that, just as there are no atheists in fox holes, there are very few believers in Utopia.

Olive watched her husband for a few moments more. Eventually, she felt she had to say it. "You know I love you, don't you."

"Yes, sunshine," he answered without looking up from his computer monitor.

"Do you really?" she asked. "Do you really know that I love you?"

He stopped typing. "Darling, is something wrong?"

"No, just... Please don't ever forget it."

"I won't, dear." He went back to his work and added, "I love you, too."

Yes, she knew he loved her. He loved her with all his heart. Trouble is, she no longer cared. And this was the great tragedy of Olive's ridiculously long life. She no longer cared if anyone loved her.

She continued walking down the hallway to the bedroom where she plopped herself down on the side of the king-sized bed. And as always, she placed her glass of sherry on her nightstand. This nightcap would usually be her last drink for ten or twelve hours, but tonight it will be her last drink ever. Period. Full stop. That's all, folks. Tomorrow morning Olive Gorely is going to skip her usual shot of gin in her orange juice. Tomorrow she is going for a long drive. And for once she plans to be sober for it.

Olive opened the drawer of her nightstand and took out her hand mirror. The lovely antique, with its pewter edging and tortoise shell back, was a keepsake from her mother and one of the few personal items Hadwin had allowed her to pack for the wagon trip west. Tonight Olive will leave the mirror out on her nightstand so she won't forget to take it with her in the morning. It will lend a sense of unity to this, her final journey.

"Sweet dreams, darling." Hadwin was standing at the bedroom door. He looked happy. Of course.

"I love you," Olive said.

Sure, it was a lie. But it will be the last lie she will ever tell. So why not make it a doozy.

CHAPTER EIGHTEEN

Phil hefted a cooler full of ice and pop into the back seat. He paused to catch his breath. Last night's party had left him a little the worse for wear. Too much dancing.

Carol folded a rain jacket and tucked it into the car's open trunk. "Want me to drive?"

"Thanks." He tossed his car keys to her. His head was a little sore from that the locally brewed beer.

Nate came out of the motel room carrying a pile of wet towels. He threw them into the trunk. Phil turned to him and said, "You never told us how you liked your babysitter, what's-her-name."

"Becky." Nate spoke the name with distaste, the same way he says Brussel sprouts. "Rhymes with *blechy*."

"Not good?" Carol asked.

"She wouldn't let me watch anything but The Shopping Channel. Says it's the only channel that is suitable for young Christian eyes to behold."

Phil stated the obvious. "Religious."

"Or she just likes cheap jewelry," Carol reasoned.

Nate said, "I don't see why Eunice couldn't have stayed with me."

Carol obviously didn't like this idea. "Now, what would be the point of that — an eight-year-old taking care of an eight-year-old?"

"She says she's older," Nate countered. "A *lot* older."

"Nonsense." Carol led the way back into the motel room with Phil and Nate following behind. As they entered the room, she said, "That little girl is exactly as old as she looks. Just like everyone else in this town."

Taylor, who was standing just inside the front door checking out a pimple in a wall mirror, added her two-cents worth, "I don't think Kip believes I'm as old as I say I am."

"He doesn't?" Phil was interested in anything Kip might have to say.

"He wanted to know if I was really seventeen or was I one of the pioneers."

Phil understood Kip's comment. Possibly. Because if this mythology about the town were actually true, Kip could be wondering if Taylor has been here long enough to be preserved like everyone else. So Phil pressed on, "Did you tell him you're not from here? Not one of the locals?"

"That was another weird thing..." Taylor squeezed her pimple as she spoke. "When I told him I was from Chicago, he didn't seem to know what I was talking about. Like, he never even heard of Chicago before."

"Of course he hasn't," Carol looked pointedly at Phil. "He's from outer space."

"Huh?" Taylor was only half listening, her attention on her newfound zit. "Outer-*who*?"

Carol explained, "According to some people at the party last night, your friend is an alien." Carol looked at Phil again. She was goading him for a reaction. He didn't take the bait.

"You mean, like, from Mexico?"

Carol said, "They mean, like, from another planet." She checked through the dresser drawers for any accidental leave-behinds.

Phil faked looking through a clothes closet. He wanted to hear this, but he didn't want to seem too interested.

"A space alien?" Taylor asked. She finally looked away from the mirror. "Who said that?"

"The mayor's boy," Carol said. "He told me when we were dancing."

"Oh, him." Taylor dismissed the issue and went back to examining her zit. "Isaac's an idiot."

Phil tried to sound casual as he asked, "So did Kip happen to say any more about where he was from?" Phil watched his daughter's face carefully on this one.

"I dunno, some place. Says I never heard of it."

Phil pushed a little more, "How about what he's doing? Did Kip say why he's here?"

Taylor, who was still more interested in her pimple than in this conversation, said, "Some sort of mission."

This got young Nate's attention. "Mission? Oh, oh. Sounds like my babysitter."

"Not a *religious* mission, dum-dum," Taylor said. "More like an ecological mission. Says he's come back to clean up a mess, like pollution or something."

Phil no longer tried to disguise his interest. "Like a chemical spill?"

"Something like that." Taylor picked up a tube of ointment from a table top and started dabbing it on her pimple. "Whatever it is, he says it's his own fault. Says last time he was here he got careless. Left something behind."

"Left something behind?" Now Carol was suddenly concerned. "Sounds like—" She didn't finish her thought. So Taylor finished it for her.

"Yeah, that's what I thought," Taylor said. "But no, he didn't get anyone into trouble. Turns out he just spilled something. Something he says might, like, hurt the town's water."

"The drinking water?" Phil asked.

Taylor finally turned her full attention to both her father and her mother and said "You know, Kip is very responsible. I think you guys would like him."

"I'm sure we would," Carol said.

Phil could feel his heart rate picking up as he asked, "This pollution... did he say what it was? Any clues about what he spilled?"

"Not really. Could be something to do with work. I think he's in pharmaceutical sales."

"Is that what he spilled?" Phil asked, his blood pressure rising. "Pharmaceuticals?"

"Or maybe he just takes them for his own health, I don't know." Taylor used a tissue to wipe the excess ointment from her finger. "Sorry, Dad, I don't usually swap medical histories until the second date." She put the zit ointment down on the table and picked up her cell phone.

Phil kept pushing her, "And he didn't say what the drugs were for. No hint what they might do to the town's water."

"I wouldn't worry about it."

"Why not?"

Taylor's fingers danced a jig across her phone's touch screen. "Because he's almost got it cleaned up. Says pretty soon everything will be back to normal again."

"Normal?" Phil truly didn't like the sound of this. "Is that what he said? *Back to normal?*"

Suddenly Taylor cried out. "Oh, no!" Her eyes were glued to the screen of her phone. "Oh, my God!"

"What?" Phil snapped. "What is it?"

Taylor laughed. "Guess who's missed her period again."

Carol who was now checking the drawers in the bathroom fielded this one. "Madison."

Taylor nodded without looking up from her phone. "Geez, would someone please tell this girl there are other ways of keeping a guy on the hook other than by..." Taylor glanced sideways to see if her little brother was listening. He was.

"Don't worry about me," Nate said. "I'm only allowed to watch The Shopping Channel."

Phil, who didn't care about Madison's accidents as much as he did about the town's, pressed forward. "You say Kip *almost* has this toxic spill cleaned up?"

But Taylor kept her eyes on her phone. "Sometimes I wonder if Madison ever attended sex-ed classes."

"Sounds like she was too busy," said Nate.

Phil struggled to push the train back on track, "Your friend Kip... you say that once he finds this thing everything will return to *normal* again?"

Carol came out of the bathroom carrying two small shampoo bottles. As usual, she could read Phil's mind. "Phil, he's not a space alien." She tossed the bottles into Taylor's gym bag.

Phil remembered how Mayor Beckwith had mentioned that some folks believe the valley's charmed status is the result of black magic, a voodoo curse brought here by a runaway slave back in the 1800s. A runaway slave named Kip. And now a man named Kip has mysteriously shown up saying he's come to make the place *normal* again.

Phil didn't need to hear any more. He started unpacking his folded socks and underwear.

Carol saw him. "Phil, what are you doing?" She looked suspicious.

"Uh, nothing." Phil reconsidered what he was about to do. He decided there was a better way. Not an honest way. But a better way. "Excuse me, honey, I have to go out to the car for a minute. Gotta check the, uh, the fluid levels. We have a long trip ahead of us." He grabbed a single sock from his pile of laundry and stuffed it into his pocket. "You guys, just keep packing. See if there's anything else you can steal."

As he walked out of the room, he heard Carol explain to the kids, "It's not stealing. The shampoos are complimentary."

Phil didn't have far to go — the car was parked directly in front of the room. He popped open the hood. Then he opened trunk, took out his tool box, and removed a wrench. With tool in hand he hurried to the car's open engine compartment. After checking to make sure nobody was watching, especially Carol, he fitted the wrench around the negative battery terminal. He gave the little nut a sharp twist and removed the cable from the battery post. He then slipped the single cotton sock out of his pocket and tied it round the naked end of the cable so it wouldn't short out when he hid the loose end under the battery.

"Whacha doin', Dad?"

Phil nearly jumped out of his skin. He hadn't heard Nate come out of the room. "Nothing, son. Just trying to fix something." Phil clanged the hood shut. "Go tell the ladies we aren't going anywhere. Not today, okay?"

"We're staying here?" Nate seemed happy with this idea.

"Something's wrong with the car. Won't start."

Nate smiled. "We're stuck again?"

"Looks like it. Go tell your mom."

"Yippee." Nate ran off to spread the good news.

Phil felt bad about deceiving Carol this way, but if he's right about this, she will live to thank him. The whole town will live to thank him. Hell, maybe the entire world will thank him. And if he's wrong, well, it will just be one more day spent in Perpetuity, Wyoming.

And how bad could that be?

• • •

The mid-morning sun shone directly into the VW van's windows revealing that no person or persons of interest were hiding inside. Nevertheless, just to do things proper-like, Chief Dagleish rapped on the side door and announced, "Marshal's office."

"*Police*," Deputy Isaac corrected him. "*Police* Department."

Old habits die hard. Enoch Dagleish had been calling himself Town Marshal long before the council had modernized his job description.

He tried the handle of the van's side door. It opened. No surprise to that. These transients rarely have anything worth locking a vehicle for.

Isaac tapped Dagleish's utility belt, "You forgot your cuffs. I'll go get them."

"We're not here to arrest anybody."

"But he's been camped here for at least nine days. That's two days over the limit."

"Municipal violations mean fines, not jail."

Chief Dagleish opened the vehicle's side door wide and leaned his shoulders into the Volkswagen bus.

"Uhh, aren't we supposed to have a warrant?" Isaac said

With his head still inside the van, the Chief pulled a folded piece of paper from his shirt pocket and handed it backwards to his deputy. The signature on the document was phony, of course. So was the entire document. No judges resided in Perpetuity. No lawyers either, which, if the town weren't magical enough, would certainly qualify it as the best little town on Earth. Dagleish carried the document just in case an out-of-valley perp got his or her shorts in a knot.

Dagleish quickly cast his eyes around the interior of the vehicle. Contrary to the loud, colorful graffiti and peace signs that shouted from the exterior of the minibus, the interior of the van barely whispered. No litter. No fast food containers. No comic books. No bongs, no rolling papers, no crack pipes. Just a neatly folded pile of clothes lying atop a sleeping bag which, in turn, lounged upon a slab of foam rubber. The only materials that approached clutter were the road maps, folded and lying on the bed and the floor. Lots and lots of road maps. Some of them, local. Some state. There was even a national chart that covered the entire U. S. A. plus the lower regions of Canada.

Finally, Dagleish discovered the oddest map of all. This chart seemed to illustrate the entire globe. No roads or highways — the scale was much too large for that. But some sorts of routes had been hand-drawn across it. Probably airline routes. Chief Dagleish sat down with his feet out the door and studied the chart's penciled curves and parabolas.

Meanwhile, up front, Deputy Isaac was leaning over the seats to examine the dash. He called back, "Here she is, Chief. Here's what we want." The boy lifted a small black laptop computer from between the driver's seat and the passenger seat. Isaac held the device up high with pride as if he were accepting the Academy Award for best performance by a town deputy.

Chief Dagleish noticed that the laptop had a USB cord connecting it to a small metal box which was mounted on the vehicle's dashboard. He warned his deputy, "Careful of that cable."

Isaac ran his finger along that cord, following it up to a hole drilled in the vehicle's ceiling. "Looks like she's hooked up to that dish on the roof."

"Wouldn't be surprised."

Isaac opened the laptop and asked his boss with a sly smirk, "Your warrant allow us to search this baby?"

"Let me check." Chief Dagleish did absolutely nothing. "Looks like it does."

Isaac hopped onto the passenger seat and started fiddling with his newfound treasure while Dagleish went back to examining the map of the world he was now spreading open on the bed.

First thing he noticed was that the projection was a modern Gall-Peters type rather than the old standard Mercator. Dagleish knew a lot about maps. To him, maps and travel brochures were like Playboy magazines were to a school boy. Except more frustrating. After all, a horny school boy always has hope. He can dream of growing up one day and actually touching one of those wonders in the flesh. Not so for Dagleish and his maps and travel brochures. He knows he will never see, taste, or smell the exotic lands he has been drooling over.

"Glen Campbell!" Isaac exclaimed as he studied the screen of the open laptop. "This thing is full of music by Glen Campbell."

"Do say." Dagleish started humming *Rhinestone Cowboy* as he continued to study the hand-drawn pencil curves that swept graceful parabolas across the seas and continents of the map. There were dozens of them. And whenever one of them passed over the Wyoming area, as they all did, a time of day had been jotted down. Military time. Being an astronomy buff, Dagleish recognized the parabolas as possible tracks of orbiting satellites. Judging by the times marked, and the infrequency of their passing over Wyoming, these orbits were pretty high.

"No porn," announced Isaac from his seated position with the computer on his lap. "Maybe the guy's gay."

"Then wouldn't he have gay porn?"

Isaac, who had the attention span of a fruit fly, noted something else on the computer. "Hey! Here's his email account. Let's see if I can..." He paused. Then he laughed. "Aha! The moron has stored his passwords on his machine." Isaac shook his head in delighted wonderment. "And they think *we're* dumb."

While Isaac happily diddled further with the computer, Dagleish opened the double doors of a small cabinet that stood at the foot end of the sleeping bag. Inside he found a stash of food, mostly tin cans of French onion soup. Dagleish bent down and slowly slid open a drawer from the bottom of the cabinet. As he did so, it rattled with the laughing clinks of small glass bottles.

The size of prescription drug bottles, they seemed to be filled with powders and pills. Dagleish removed one and studied the label. He leaned forward and held it out for Isaac to see. "You recognize this language?"

Isaac snatched the bottle from Dagleish's hand. After a quick glance he handed it back. "Arab."

"Don't think so. It's cursive, true, but it's neither Abjadi nor Aramaic. Not really any script I've read before."

"That's 'cause you've never read Martian before. I wouldn't open it. Who knows what shit's in there."

The boy had a point. Dagleish put the jar back in the drawer.

"I can tell you one thing,' Isaac stated, "The guy's from outer space. I'd bet my left nut on it. Keep your eye open for medical instruments. Scalpels. Tweezers. Rubber gloves. These guys love to poke and prod."

"You watch too much television."

"What's wrong with that? How else are we supposed to learn?" He clicked a couple of buttons on the laptop's keyboard then said, "Looks like he's been emailing that new gal."

"The Hodworth girl?"

"I wonder if she's sent him any videos." Isaac typed faster.

"If you find any, don't open them."

"Why not?" Isaac said. "We catch him taking liberties with her, we got him. We can nail him for, uh…" Isaac had to think about this one.

Dagleish helped him. "For having sex with a consenting adult? She's seventeen. She's legal."

"Yeah, but she's white."

"Jesus, man, when are you going to join the twenty-first century? Nobody cares about that nonsense anymore. That thinking went out with buggy whips and taffy pulls."

"Taffy pulls." In bemused contemplation, Isaac looked up toward the heavens, or at least toward the tattered ceiling of the bus. "You know, when I think of all the fine old traditions that have gone by the wayside over the years —taffy pulls, barn raisings, lynchings — I almost think maybe I've lived too long."

"You're not the first one to say that, Isaac." Dagleish replied, confident his deputy would not get the insult. He didn't.

Chief Dagleish went back to snooping around the van. He had noticed a cookie tin on top of the cupboard. The lid of the circular container was printed in a red and white Scottish tartan and was labelled *McTamney's Shortbreads*. Dagleish pried the lid open a crack. The contents certainly didn't smell like cookies. They smelled acidic. Dagleish carefully removed the lid.

Inside sat two small rocks, each about the size of a small bar of soap. Hotel size. But they didn't look like soap. They looked like low grade gem stones. Maybe amber. With a crystalline structure, like quartz. But with pinkish flecks, like feldspar. And the color changed depending on how he looked at them.

Dagleish reached his hand in to lift one of the rocks out, but as soon as he touched it...

"Oww!" He dropped the rock back into the cookie tin

"Y'okay?" Isaac asked.

Dagleish checked his fingertips. They seemed fine. No burns. No blisters. With his other hand he felt the underside of the tin box. It was cool. He then cupped his hand close over top of the rocks. Again, no heat radiated up from the mysterious mineral.

Isaac abandoned his seat up front to come get a closer look. He crouched down next to the Chief to peer inside the tin. "Weird looking cookies." The deputy started to reach for one of the rocks, but Dagleish yanked the tin away from him.

"They're hot," he explained. Dagleish touched the cool underside of the tin container again and added, "Or at least, they *feel* hot."

Isaac immediately backed away. "Know what you got there? What you got there is moon rocks."

"It doesn't feel like rock." Dagleish hefted the weight of the cookie tin. "Too light. And they're kind of waxy. Sort of like rosin. You ever felt rosin? Violinists use it."

"Makes sense. The boy's musical. Likes to sing." Isaac glanced around the van. "Don't see any violin, though." Then he got an idea, "You know what we should have brought along?"

"Taffy?"

"A Geiger counter." Isaac pointed to the mysterious rocks. "Cause I'll bet my left nut that shit's plutonium."

"You already bet your left nut this guy is a space alien. How many left nuts you got?"

"None if we hang around those moon rocks any longer." Isaac backed away from the tin.

Police Chief Dagleish pressed the lid onto the cookie tin and placed it back in the cupboard. "Any idea where this Kip fella might be at this hour of the day?"

"Can't say for sure. I wasn't here to watch him last night. All that dancing at the party kinda knocked me out." Isaac paused to think. "By now I'd say our boy has finished his morning swim. It's a bit early for lunch. So my guess is he's somewhere down canyon, nosing along the river."

"And you say he carries a cell phone."

"That's what it looks like."

"Don't suppose you have the number."

"No. But you know who might?"

Dagleish understood. "The Hodworth girl." He eased himself out the side door of the van and started back to his patrol car.

Isaac jumped out of the van and tagged along. "But aren't they supposed to be on their way back to the city?"

"The Hodworths don't strike me as early risers."

"You're right. But then who is nowadays." Isaac walked fast to keep up with his boss. "Ever since we closed the mine have you noticed how folks been sleeping in late? Not me, though. I'm still up with the cows. Early bird, that's me. Hell, I'd bet my left nut I'm still the earliest riser in town."

Chief Dagleish didn't bother commenting about his deputy's seemingly endless supply of gonads — the Chief's mind was on something else.

He was thinking about those amber hunks of crystal rosin in that cookie tin. He has seen them before. But he can't remember where. Or when. But he's seen them somewhere. A long time ago.

A very, very long time ago.

• • •

Normally, Becky Thatcher doesn't pay much heed to rumors blowing over the fence from her neighbors' garden. She is happy to tend her own flower bed with little thought to the weeds popping up on the other side of the hedge. But lately, one seed of gossip has managed to take root in the fertile soil of Becky's imagination. And she doesn't like what it has brought to mind.

It's this talk about the mysterious stranger who has been seen wandering the river banks. They say that he's young and that he's colored — *African-American* is the current preferred term — and for several weeks now he has been roaming the pine forests and larkspur meadows that border the river. Apparently, the young fellow always walks alone, which is odd considering most young visitors travel with their families or friends. Also, they say he wears funny, miss-matched clothes, which isn't so odd considering he's young. But these details aren't what is worrying Becky. What worries Becky is the reaction her friends and neighbors are having to this mystery man.

They think he's from outer space. Perhaps Mars.

Such a preposterous conclusion deeply troubles Becky. It indicates that what Rebecca has long feared has at last come true — her neighbors are finally losing their minds as well as their faith.

This troubling news comes as no surprise to Becky. She's been waiting for it. Sure, the shelf-life of human flesh, muscle, and bones might be extended, but what about the shelf-life of her neighbor's souls, their mental and emotional health? For what length of time can clear-thinking, God-fearing Christians remain clear-thinking and God-fearing? Or even Christian?

Rebecca has seen evidence of this coming on for years. She knows that many of her friends have lost their fear of the Lord. And now it seems they've replaced it with this nonsense, a fear of space aliens. Rebecca must do something. She must speak with Reverend Gorely. And she will. Today. Right after she eats lunch.

Rebecca bowed her head over her daily luncheon oatmeal and closed her eye. It's not easy thanking the Lord for porridge. Especially buckwheat porridge. At the best of times, porridge is not a dish to get excited about, but after a hundred years it can get downright boring. But she gives thanks anyway.

When Rebecca opened her eyes again, she noticed a memo posted on the LED screen of her new smart fridge. It reminded her that the berry patch down by the river is ripe to bursting with juicy sweet strawberries. Lovely! That's just what she needs.

Becky placed her freshly blessed bowl of porridge back into the microwave so it will be ready when she gets back. She then grabbed an empty wicker basket from atop the fridge and headed out the door.

The noon sun had risen high over Perpetuity Mountain, but it had not yet had a chance to burn the morning dew off the grass. That's the problem with living in a mountain's shadow. Becky hurried through her yard and across the meadow, all the while wishing she had worn proper cross-trainers instead of these silly old moccasin slippers — the moisture was soaking right through. Happily, the berry patch isn't too far away.

She followed the old Indian trail through the tall prairie junegrass down to the river. This well-worn path had originally been trod by the Arapahos before the government had moved them out of the valley and onto a reservation. People thought it strange when this one small group of natives from this valley started aging more quickly than others of their tribe. At the time, people blamed the band's sudden demise on diseases brought to them by Sam Beckwith's wagon train. Folks in Perpetuity knew better, but they kept this secret to themselves.

By the time Becky reached the river bank her feet were soaked. Her own fault. The moccasins were very old.

Beck followed the bank of the river, and that's where she ran into him. Actually, he saw her before she saw him. He wasn't surprised. She certainly was.

He had been kneeling down low, half-hidden under a Rocky Mountain sumac at the water's edge. He must have heard her footsteps. Or maybe he heard her unconsciously humming. Becky occasionally hums without realizing it. A lot of folks in the valley hum. Doesn't mean they're crazy. Just not a lot else to do. After all, every conceivable subject has been pretty much mulled, chewed, and swallowed, usually without taste. Much like buckwheat porridge. Anyway, whatever sound it was gave her away, the young man popped up with a cheerful, "Good morning."

Startled is too gentle a word for how Becky felt. Her heart near stopped. She clasped her hand to her chest and took a moment to get her breath. It wasn't the shock of seeing a colored man alone in the woods that had struck her so hard. It was the shock of seeing this particular colored man. In these particular woods. By this particular river. Again.

He smiled. But not for long. He looked carefully at Becky's face. Studied it. Then he said, "Oh, it's you." No traces of that smile now remained.

Becky didn't answer his greeting. She couldn't. She'd forgotten how to speak. Or maybe she was afraid to. A dream can be like that. She had recognized him immediately, of course. How could she not? She'd been seeing his face for a very long time. Often in her dreams. She wondered if this was just another one of those dreams. Was she losing touch with reality? Like her neighbors?

The young black man seemed nervous. He took a couple of steps back, away from her. His pale blue eyes turned away and scanned the forest. His sharp gaze carved through the underbrush behind her, sliced upwards along the slope on this side of the river, then cut across the edges of the steep cliff face on the far side. Finally, those steel-blue eyes returned to rest on Becky's own eyes. And they softened. He asked her, "Your friends around?"

All Becky could manage to say was, "You've come back."

The poor man still seemed nervous. Still distracted. "Your father with you?" His eyes flitted back to the woods behind her. "Or your friend with the gun?"

"I'm alone." Becky made this confession mostly to herself. After all, being without an escort was not something she would normally admit to a stranger in the woods like this. But of course, this man was no stranger.

"Rebecca, right?"

"Friends call me Becky." It was a silly thing to say. Or maybe it wasn't.

"You may not remember me." Kip extended his hand. "Name's Kip."

"I know." And she did. Just as she knew she was safe. Perfectly safe.

Safer than she'd been in almost two hundred years.

• • •

The grandfather clock in the front hall struck twelve noon, and yet Pastor Hadwin Gorely was still seated at his morning breakfast table.

The table setting which sat before him included a juice glass, a dinner plate, and a fruit bowl. All still clean. All still empty. She must have set the table before she left. Typical.

Hadwin Gorely picked up the note and read it once again hoping that somehow the words had magically changed since the last reading. It was a silly thing to hope for, but Pastor Hadwin Gorely was skilled at hoping for silly things.

Her message was short and signed with love. She had tucked it under his fruit bowl. Must have written it hours ago. Olive is an early riser. Hadwin, not so much. He prefers to work late into the night and then sleep until eight, sometimes nine.

By the time Hadwin had found the letter this morning, Olive was long gone, so he knew there was no use in chasing after her, no point in having Chief Dagleish set up a road block. Regardless of which direction Olive might had chosen to drive, she would have been out of the valley within a half-hour.

Hadwin wasn't surprised by her message. He knew his darling was unhappy. Everybody knew it. A woman of Olive's spiritual strength doesn't turn to drink without a damned good reason — the operative word now being *damned*. That's the most disturbing part of this. The eternal damnation. Olive has not just run away from this valley — she has run away from the Lord. She knows full well that by leaving this valley she is inviting a quick and certain death. She knows that suicide is the one unforgiveable sin. Hadwin has preached this many times.

Seems all Olive has done now is traded one eternity for another. And all Pastor Hadwin Gorely could do now was to place his elbows on the abandoned breakfast table, lower his face into his steepled fingers, and pray for her soul just as he had recently prayed for the soul of young Zachariah Mossip. And before that, Laura Lee Anders. And before that... well, there have been many. And yet Pastor Hadwin Gorely keeps praying. He knows his prayers are pointless — a hundred and eighty-odd years of unanswered prayers have taught him that. But Pastor Hadwin Gorely keeps praying anyway because faith is not about results. It's about hope.

CHAPTER NINETEEN

Becky Thatcher hoped the excitement didn't show in her trembling voice. "It's good to see you again," she said, her galloping heart finally slowing to a canter. "Last time you visited us you left rather quickly."

"I kinda felt I wasn't welcome," Kip said.

"Yes, I suppose a bullet through the chest will do that." Becky didn't mean to sound flippant. She was referring to the first and last time she saw this man. It was the third of November, 1846. "Your wound healed, I presume?"

Kip tapped his chest. "Fit as a fiddle, thank you. And may I say you are looking fine your own self. A tad older, but then I guess you must—"

"Pardon me?" Becky had never heard those words before. "*Older?* You say I look older?"

"Must be the way you're wearing your hair. You've cut it, right? Used to be long, almost to your mid-section."

"Well, yes I did wear it longer at one time maybe, like, a hundred years ago."

"Well, you shouldn't wait so long between trims. Suits you. Very sophisticated. Mature. Adds five years. A very *pretty* five years."

"Thank you, I guess." Becky allowed herself to look closer at Kip's face, at his lovely smooth milk chocolate skin. "You haven't changed at all. Not one bit. Except maybe for—"

"The do." He ran a hand over his short, but straight, salt-and-pepper hair. Don't worry, by tonight the grey will be gone. My own fault. I missed a dose at dinner yesterday."

"Dose?"

"My meds. Completely forgot. Too busy tearing into the ol' Johnnycake." He patted his stomach. "Probably added a few pounds since last time you saw me." He stepped back for a better look at Becky's figure. "I see you've added a pound or two, yourself."

"What?"

"It works. I dig it. I always thought you were a little too skinny."

"Oh, you did, did you." In a failed pose of defiance, Becky put her right hand on her hip while still holding the basket of strawberries with her left. But try as she might, she couldn't take real offense at his comment. She was just happy this young man had noticed her figure at all.

Kip started to stroll along the path. Becky followed along. Invited or not, she wasn't going to let this man escape so easily this time. She had too many questions. Like, where is he from. And where has he been all this time? And why has he come back? And why, like her, has he not aged? And is he single or is he married? A million such questions. But of course, she can't just start grilling him right away. Such a cross examination might be misinterpreted as idle curiosity rather than true concern. So for the time being she will try to keep her questions tucked away, buried at the bottom of her wicker basket.

As they walked, Kip regarded Rebecca's basket of berries and commented, "You seem to have a purpose planned for those."

"The berries? Oh, nothing special. I like to sprinkle them on my oatmeal. They're also nice on ice cream."

"So those things are edible."

"Of course, they're edible — they're strawberries. They grow wild along the river." She laughed. "You city boys. I'll bet you've only seen them on shelves or in jars."

"No, I've seen them right here, on the ground. But I was afraid to eat them." Kip patted his stomach. "Dodgy colon. Gotta be careful. Especially when I'm on the road."

Becky took advantage of the opening. "On the road? The road from...?"

"Oh, you wouldn't know the place. Just a fly speck on your radar screen. Blink and you miss it." He picked a strawberry from her basket. "Seeds scare me." He examined the little fruit. Then he licked it.

Rebecca tried another approach, "This place you're from, it must be similar to our valley then." By *similar*, she was thinking of magical, ageless. After all, another hidden valley like Perpetuity could exist somewhere out there, somewhere beyond the mountains. No reason to think Perpetuity is the only place on Earth the Lord hath this way blessed.

Kip popped the strawberry into his mouth and chewed. "Nice. A little tart. But nice."

"You don't have strawberries back where you come from?" Now Becky was getting suspicious. Was Kip being deliberately evasive? What was he hiding? Could he really be from outer space like people say? Obviously, the idea was absurd. But it would certainly explain a lot.

"We have berries. Just not this variety. Most of ours have very small seeds. It's the small ones that cause the grief. How's your colon?"

Becky couldn't help but chuckle. "Fine, thank you for asking."

"So, the rosin hasn't messed with your gut yet?"

"Rosin?"

"That was your name for it, not mine. Big fella named Dagleish. He saw you bring it to me. Remember? That clear amber stone I had you fetch from my camp site?"

"The magic crystal that healed your wound."

"It's not crystal. Not magic either. Just a simple topical ointment, but in a hard, plasticized form. Gives it a shelf-life of centuries. The chemical name is... Well, let's just call it rosin."

"You had me hold it on your chest, over your heart."

"It's handy stuff. Trouble is, like most miracle medications it has a few downsides — small print warnings the sales rep keeps covered with his thumb. If he still has thumbs."

Becky said, "I'm not sure if I understand."

"It fiddles with your DNA, which is good, but it plays havoc with your bowels, which is not so good. I won't bore you with the details — let's just say you don't want to take any long hikes. Or balloon rides. Hey, how about your lungs? They fully recover?"

"Yes, they have, thank you."

"Cool." Kip stopped to look at the wide bend of the river where they were presently standing. "Happened right about here, as I recall."

Becky gazed out at the water and into the distant past. The top of that cliff across the river was where Crusader had thrown her. He was a strong horse but skittish. He must have seen a prairie dog. She'd tumbled down the hillside and ended up in the water. Unconscious. Face down. She surely would have drowned if not for the young negro man who happened to be bathing nearby. People saw him drag her unconscious body up onto the shore and kiss her. Of course, back then folks never heard of the kiss of life. They thought he was trying to take liberties with her. But Becky knew better. She knew by the fullness in her heart when she woke up in his arms. And she knew by the emptiness in her soul when she saw Isaac Beckwith's .69 caliber musket ball rip a hole through the man's naked brown chest.

Becky turned away from the horrid memories and turned instead to the hero of her tale. "And you?" she asked. "No lasting effects from the wound?"

"Tickety-boo, thanks to you." Kip snapped his long fingers and pointed one of them at Becky. "You, my lady, saved my life."

"Don't be silly. All I did was fetch your medicine. Your rosin."

"True. But you had to walk a long way to fetch it. In the dark. Against the wishes of your friends." Kip looked deep into her eyes and said, "I owe you one."

Rebecca tried to be off-hand. "You saved my life — I saved yours. Tit for tat."

Kip's eyes immediately went down to her chest. She wasn't sure if he had misunderstood her words or not, but she was happy when his eyes returned to hers and he said, "I've thought about you many times during my journeys. Especially when I was awake."

Becky chuckled nervously, "I do some of my best thinking when I'm awake." Becky always joked at times when she was uneasy.

Kip clasped her shoulders, and Becky was fine with that. She looked up into his pale blue eyes. Oddly, the man was no taller than Becky was, yet somehow she felt he towered above her. With his hands holding her shoulders like this, she felt as if he was about to pull her close. Maybe kiss her. And she was fine with that, too. Unlike the last time, this kiss won't be for recuperative purposes. And she was especially fine with that.

Becky closed her eyes. She puckered up. Then she heard music. Not bells. Not violins. But a guitar. Was this what true romance sounded like? A guitar picking out a familiar tune? Becky recognized the melody as a song from the 1970s called *Wichita Lineman*.

Kip must have heard the music too because he quickly let go of her shoulders. When Becky opened her eyes, he was pulling a cell phone from the pocket of his leather vest. Turns out the guitar music was just a ringtone.

Before answering it, Kip read the caller display aloud, "Beckwith."

"*Sam* Beckwith?" Becky asked.

Kip angled the phone away from the high-noon sun and cupped his hand over the screen so he could read the display. "Nope, Isaac. Isaac Beckwith."

"Don't answer it!" Becky snapped.

"Why not?"

"Just don't."

"But isn't that kinda like, rude?"

"It could be a trick."

"You mean, he'll ask if my fridge is running and then he'll tell me it just ran past his house?" Kip laughed. "Sock it to me." Then he swept the icon on his phone to answer the call.

Becky had no choice. She swung her berry basket hard and knocked the phone from his hand. But she must have swung too hard. The device went flying out over the river.

Poor Kip stood with his mouth agape, and together he and she watched the phone skim the water's surface. Like a flat, silver stone it bounced leaving a ragged zipper of splashes before it finally slowed to a stop, rested to get its breath, and sank.

Kip didn't lose his temper. He didn't even yell. He just stared out at the water and watched the ripples blossom out from the phone's watery grave. "Why?" He finally asked. "Why would you do that?"

Becky pointed to the phone, or at least to the spot in the middle of the river where the phone was last seen alive. "That's the man who shot you — the man with the buffalo gun. Remember?"

But Kip's attention was still on the expanding ripples. "I needed that device. I still need that device. A lot. It's my main means of communication with my drone."

"But that was Isaac." Becky repeated. "He was the man who—"

"I know who Isaac is," Kip finally turned his face to Rebecca. "I see him every day. Ever since I arrived here he's been on my ass."

"Following you?"

"Like the tail of a comet."

"Has he tried to shoot you again?"

"Not yet. I believe he's just curious."

"Isaac? Curious?" Becky scoffed. "I hardly think so."

"He's trying to figure me out. Wants to know why I've come back. What I'm doing here."

"And has he?"

"Has he what?"

"Figured you out?"

"Maybe. If he hasn't, he soon will. The fellow strikes me as pretty bright."

"Isaac?" Becky wasn't sure if she was hearing right. "Isaac Beckwith?"

"The dude doesn't miss much. He seems to have a keen eye. I've been thinking about asking him to join up with me. Help me with my search."

"Search for what?"

"The rosin. The piece I left behind.."

"I'm sorry, I don't know what—"

"Yes, you do." Kip sat himself down on a large outcropping of rock much the same way Rebecca used to take a seat at the church when she was about to start story time for the children. "Two hundred years ago," he said. "The thing you brought to me that night, remember? About the size of a bar of soap? hand-sized, not bath-sized."

"Your crystal medicine."

"Let's stick with *rosin*. Crystal is so new-age." Kip glanced toward the river. "I got a bit careless. In my haste to split the scene as quickly as possible I got clumsy."

"People were shooting at you."

"Yeah, well, try to explain that to my boss."

Rebecca was starting to understand. "You dropped it here, in the river."

"That'd be my guess."

"The medicine that brought you back to life."

"Yes. More or less. I mean, it can't really help someone if they've gone completely tits-up, but—"

"The miracle drug from your bedroll," Rebecca was realizing the enormous implications of what she was about to say. "You dropped it here. Into our town's water supply."

Kip looked truly ashamed. "Call me butter fingers."

It was like the clouds had parted and the noonday sun had suddenly flared a million times brighter. In this brief instant Becky understood it all. Everything. The mystery. The magic. The science. The craziness. The truth.

She looked to the river. An oak leaf sat motionless on the glassy surface. It had fallen behind a log where it was sheltered from the current. The leaf just rested there. Not drifting. Not doing anything. While on the other side of the log, the other leaves flowed by.

"So they were right," Rebecca said, speaking more to herself than to her companion. "It really is just something in the water."

"I feel terrible. I can't apologize enough."

Rebecca turned away from him and announced to the birds and the squirrels and the chipmunks and the frogs, "It isn't my fault. It never was."

"*Your* fault?"

She turned back to him. "The magic. The blessing. Our people not getting older. It isn't my fault. Never was."

"Of course not. What do you mean?"

"I mean, I didn't cause this. It wasn't an answer to my prayer — the prayer I made over you that night."

"Not unless you prayed for me to go hiking with a hole in my pocket."

Rebecca closed her eyes and took a deep breath of relief. "All this time, it has simply been something in the water."

"You know, I've been thinking about that." Kip got to his feet and strolled down to the water's edge. "Sure, it could have been lying down there at the bottom all this time. But I honestly don't think so. Because whenever I bathe I'm super careful. I always leave my meds safe on shore, inside my knapsack, or tucked into my shoe."

Becky joined him by the water's edge. "Are you sure you had it with you at all?"

"Oh, I had it. First rule of interstellar sales — *Never board your rocket without a spare in your pocket.* Boy, did I catch hell from head office."

"*Interstellar.*" Becky said. "So it's true. You're not from here. You're from outer space."

Kip looked down and shuffled his feet like a child who had just got caught with his hand in the cookie tin. "It was the threads, wasn't it." Kip opened his fringed leather vest to reveal more of his tie-dyed cotton t-shirt. "I knew it! I told them this outfit was probably out of date. Your television signals take forever to reach us."

Rebecca restated, "You're a space alien." But saying it again didn't help her accept it.

"*Alien* sounds kinda harsh, don't you think? A bit racist."

"An extra-terrestrial."

Kip gazed out at the water. "And now an extra-terrestrial without his phone. I guess I could wade out there. But it'll be murder to find. Water's full of sediment."

"You say you came a long way."

"Very long way. That's why we use the rosin."

"It keeps you from aging during your trip."

"Great stuff. Slows metabolism to a crawl. Puts the brakes to cellular deterioration. Without it a simple sales trip would be impossible." Kip looked out once again at the river. "But without that device I'm toast. That's was my only way to call my drone. Unless..." He turned to Rebecca. "Unless I can adapt one of yours. Can you help me score something?"

"A phone?"

"Anything with your current GPS technology will do."

"Sure. No problem."

"I'll need to download some apps. I think I put some backups on the laptop I purchased when I first got here." Kip turned and resumed walking.

Once again, Rebecca followed close behind him. "This rosin... does everybody on your planet use it?"

"Used to. But not anymore. We learned our lesson. Nowadays the stuff is strictly prescription. For long-distance travel only. Wasn't always like that, though. At first it was over-the-counter. At the checkout next to the breath mints. We thought it was the greatest thing since individually wrapped cheese slices. The rosin seemed to cure everything. But then things went sideways. We noticed side effects. Bad ones. I'm not talking just what it did to your gut. These ones were behavioral."

Although Becky was walking behind him, she felt she was ahead of him on this subject. "Sloth," she said. "Lethargy. A lack of interest in anything but watching life pass you by."

"Throw in goat yoga and you got it. Our entire society almost disappeared up our own ever-young, ever-healthy, ever-pointless butts."

Becky laughed. "You seem to have picked up our language and idioms rather well."

"Like I said, I watch your television."

"I'm afraid our television has deteriorated considerably. The rough language and the overt sexuality—"

Kip held his hand up like a traffic cop signaling Becky to stop talking. She felt terrible. What must he think of her talking about overt sexuality like this. Alone. In the middle of the woods.

"That him?" Kip was looking at something farther along the path. Something through the trees. "That his?"

Becky stepped up close beside him to see what had caught his eye. At this point the trail paralleled a dirt road. Becky could see sunlight glinting off the metal hood of a pickup truck parked in a grove of sumacs.

"Your friend's vehicle?" he asked her.

"Isaac's truck?" Becky squinted. "Could be."

Kip seemed impatient. "This dude is starting to get on my wires. I bet if I tried to kiss you now he'd just shoot me again. Like last time."

"You... you want to kiss me?"

"Thanks, but not right now. Maybe later." And with that said, Kip started toward the vehicle.

Becky tagged along. She knew every vehicle in the valley, and she could now see that this truck did not belong to Isaac Beckwith. No, this truck belonged to Pastor Gorely. But what in heaven's name would the pastor be doing down here by the river? Especially at this time of day? Everybody knows the pastor sleeps late. Didn't used to, but he does now.

As Rebecca got closer to the truck, she could make out a figure sitting in the driver's seat. But it was not Pastor Gorely. It was Olive Gorely, the pastor's wife. And she was slumped forward, leaning against the steering wheel.

Poor Olive. Drunk again.

Olive has developed quite a drinking problem. So sad. Looks like she's passed out. Probably been here all night. Alone. Just her and a bottle. Usually sherry. Maybe Rebecca should let her sleep it off.

But wait.

What's that on the side of the truck? Is it a crack in the paint? No. It's a garden hose. One end is stuffed into the truck's tailpipe where it was sealed up with a rag.

"Oh, my Lord!" Rebecca pushed Kip aside and ran to the truck. The truck was still running. She flung the door open. Olive Gorely's limp body tumbled out like a sack of potatoes. The woman fell onto Rebecca, knocking her backwards and into the dirt.

Olive was not a big woman, but she was muscular. Kip lifted her off Becky. Gently, he carried Olive clear of the truck and placed her onto a soft ridge of sand. Kip then proceeded to unfasten the top buttons of Olive's blouse. He put his ear to her chest.

"Still alive," he said. He then instructed Rebecca, "Check the woods, please."

"The woods? For what?" Rebecca was just getting to her feet.

"Gun barrels."

Rebecca understood. She ran her eyes through the trees and bushes surrounding the parking site before announcing. "You're safe."

Kip placed both his hands, palms down, on Olive's chest and started pumping. After a series of quick, hard pumps Kip paused to listen to Olive's heart. "We may be too late." He resumed pumping some more.

"Your rock," Becky said.

"Pardon me?"

In her panic Rebecca couldn't remember the name he used for his piece of crystal medicine. Finally she recalled, "The rosin. Use that."

"Sorry. No can do." And he continued pumping Olive's chest.

"But won't it will help — you know, the way it helped you?"

"Not allowed. Against regs. Besides, I don't carry it with me anymore." Kip talked in rhythm with his steady pumping. "Learned my lesson. No footprints. In the sand. Remember?" He stopped and put his ear to Olive's chest. He glanced around at the surrounding woods. "You're sure nobody is watching?"

Becky scanned the trees again. "Don't see anyone."

Kip called out to the forest, to the birds, chipmunks, and squirrels: "Hold your fire. I'm going to oxygenate this woman's lungs." He then pinched Olive's nose with one hand, placed his mouth to her lips, and started blowing.

Becky watched Olive's chest heave. Once. Twice. Three times. And that's when the Lord stepped in and reassured Becky that He was listening, that some prayers are still answered. Olive coughed. Then she groaned. Finally, she opened her eyes.

Kip, ever the gentleman, quickly started buttoning up her blouse. But he wasn't quick enough. Olive Gorely was a strong young woman and Kip was a small man — her right-hook easily knocked him off his knees and into the sand.

"It's okay, Olive," Beck said. "He's just trying to help."

Kip climbed to his feet, rubbing his sore jaw. He held a hand out, palm facing her. "I come in peace."

Olive squinted up at the young black man in the hippie clothes. "Hey! Don't I know you?"

"Probably not." Kip smiled. "I have one of those faces."

Rebecca handled the introductions. "Olive, meet Kip, an old friend who drops by every two hundred years to save a woman's life."

Olive turned her head to look back at the pickup truck. The engine was still running, and the hose was still stuck in the exhaust pipe.

She said to Kip, "Excuse me if I don't thank you."

CHAPTER TWENTY

Phil Hodworth stood behind the back row of seats in the Opera House and watched the audience members slowly trickle in. Sure, the turnout was pretty thin, but Phil had faith in these people. They have successfully fought for and guarded their incredible secret for two centuries — surely they'll have the strength to fight a few days more for it. It shouldn't take long to overcome this new threat. If he really is a threat. A hippy in a VW bus? A space alien? That sounds like bit of a stretch. But Phil will keep an open mind.

Standing next to Phil and his open mind were Police Chief Enoch Dagleish, Mayor Sam Beckwith, and the mayor's son, Isaac Beckwith.

Isaac looked to Phil and smiled. The kid still seemed a little sheepish, but that's understandable. Phil gave him a thumbs-up to let him know all was forgiven. Sure, the kid tried to burn down Phil's restaurant, but Phil wasn't the type to hold a grudge. After all, the kid was just trying to defend his hometown's big secret. And now Phil is here to do the same thing.

Today's meeting had been called by Mayor Beckwith to discuss this hippie who's been hanging around the valley. There are several theories as to who the fellow might be, ranging from a space alien to a very, very old runaway slave — the runaway who, Phil has been told, passed this way back in 1846. Could this man have been hiding out here in the valley all this time? Seems far-fetched that somebody in town wouldn't have run into him before now. But people in town say his description fits that slave. Phil has been invited here because his daughter, Taylor, has been in communication with this mysterious stranger, and that makes Phil the expert witness. Phil has told them that the man's name is Kip, but that is about all he knows for certain.

Mayor Sam Beckwith checked the time on his cell phone. "Ten past. No point in waiting any longer. Let's get these wagons rolling." He started down the aisle toward the stage.

Phil grabbed him by his sleeve. "Let's just give them a few minutes more."

"We do and we'll lose the precious few bodies we got." Mayor Sam Beckwith pulled away and walked down the center aisle, periodically stopping to pat a shoulder and say howdy.

Phil turned to the mayor's son, Isaac, "I thought you said you'd contacted everybody in town."

"I did."

"By phone?"

"Landline and cell."

"Text?"

"SMS, personal messaging, and email."

Phil said, "So where is everybody?"

"Where they always are," said Isaac. "Sitting at home not giving a flying fuck." And with that, the young man followed his father down the center aisle to the stage. This left Phil alone with the Chief of Police.

Chief Dagleish put a hand on Phil's shoulder and escorted him over to the side aisle and down to the stage. They walked slowly, neither man in a hurry. "Mr. Hodworth, there's something you ought to know."

"Call me Phil." Phil liked Dagleish. The guy seemed to be more hip than many of the citizens of this town.

"Phil, you are about to learn a valuable lesson about life here in Perpetuity."

"Uh, huh?" This was good. Phil was anxious to learn everything he could about this incredible place, these incredible people.

"You, my friend, are about to join a very exclusive club."

Phil chuckled at the understatement, "I know." And he did know. Sort of. Phil was pretty-well convinced that these people were what they claimed to be. And now Phil is joining their ever-loving, ever-living, ever-humping club, a club that hasn't had a new member for a hundred years. *Exclusive?* Yes, this club is exclusive.

Chief Dagleish continued, "You, sir, are about to join up with the laziest bunch of slack-asses that have ever wasted time, oxygen, and space on God's green Earth."

Phil stopped walking. But he kept smiling. "Say again?"

"See, Phil, here's the problem..." The two men had reached the front corner of the auditorium and were about to ascend the steps up onto the stage. Dagleish continued, "It's a simple problem, really. We've discovered that when you have all the time in the world, nothing needs to be done today."

Phil thought this over. "Makes sense."

"Want gum?" Dagleish held out a stick of chewing gum.

"No, thanks. It plays havoc with my caps." This thought sparked Phil to realize that he may never need dental work again. After all, if a person's teeth don't get older... Shit, this town just gets better and better.

"You see, there's a good side and a bad side to this never-aging deal." Dagleish popped a stick of gum into his own mouth and chewed out a few sentences of homespun wisdom. "Sure, getting old is no bed of roses. Losing your hair, losing your sex drive, losing your mental faculties... old age has its down side, I'll grant you."

Phil nodded. What else could he do to such a moronic statement.

"But mortality has its upside, too," Chief Enoch Dagleish's words were still dumb, but thanks to the gum they now smelled minty fresh.

Phil had to challenge this guy. "An upside? To mortality?"

"Sure." Dagleish explained, "Knowing that your time on Earth is limited — that's a powerful motivator. It's what gets you out of bed in the morning. It's what gifts you with dreams when you close your eyes. It's what awards you with hope when you open them. Nothing inspires human achievement like that good ol' ticking clock of biological decay and impending death. Sure you don't want some gum?"

"Enoch," Phil ignored the kind offer and put his hand on the Police Chief's substantial shoulder. "I know what you're getting at. But come on... I mean, seriously..." Phil didn't know how to argue this, but he sure wasn't ready to accept that getting old and decrepit was better than staying young and healthy. That's just pure bullshit.

Dagleish said. "You probably think this is pure bullshit."

"Well, I don't want to be harsh, but..."

Dagleish continued, "Some say that all human intellectual, artistic, and spiritual pursuits stem from the knowledge that we aren't going to be around forever, that someday we are going to die. If you think about it, knowledge of our own mortality is what separates us from the other animals. *That* and the ability to get a reverse mortgage."

Phil chuckled. He asked, "Is this your standard orientation lecture?"

"Hardly standard when I've never given it before. I just wanted to let you know what you were getting yourself into, that's all." And with that, Chief Dagleish climbed the steps to the stage.

Phil followed him up and across the stage to a row of five folding chairs where Mayor Beckwith and Isaac Beckwith were already seated. Phil glanced out at the audience. Good thing Carol had decided to stay back at the motel this evening. Otherwise, she would take one look at this lame excuse for a crowd and agree with Dagleish about the town's lack of spirit. Carol is very community-minded, always volunteering for this or that or stirring things up for a local cause. She would not be impressed by this bunch.

Phil took his seat on the stage. Beside him sat Enoch Dagleish, Sam Beckwith and Beckwith's son, Isaac, who was busy with his cell phone. As Phil sat down, Isaac turned to Police Chief Dagleish and told him, "The spaceman's still not answering texts."

Dagleish said, "We don't know he's a spaceman."

"*Some* of us do," Isaac then elbowed Phil and winked knowingly.

Huh? Phil didn't get it. Was he missing something here? Phil had given Isaac the number to Kip's cell phone, but Taylor said she wasn't sure the guy's phone was turned on — she hadn't gotten through to him all day.

While Mayor Beckwith got up and approached the podium, Phil looked around at the room's architecture. He liked this old theater with all its big square wooden beams that arched high to support the vaulted ceiling. It made Phil feel as if he were in church, an impression strengthened by the posture of the audience, all of whom had their heads bowed in prayer. On closer examination Phil could see they were just working their cell phones.

Mayor Samuel Beckwith adjusted the gooseneck microphone and said, "Evening, pilgrims." The mike squealed back with ear-piercing feedback. The mayor shut the device down. He stepped away from the lectern and continued, "Looks like we got ourselves a problem. Could be a big one."

Phil watched the crowd and was struck by how modern and up-to-date the historic assemblage of original settlers and hardy pioneers behaved as they heard the mayor's dire announcement of doom this fateful summer evening.

Not a single one of them looked up from their cell phones.

• • • •

Olive Gorely ran up the front steps of the Opera House two at a time. The evening sun was riding the horizon — it was just past seven-thirty — she hoped that the meeting wasn't finished yet. Sam Beckwith had called this gathering to discuss the new stranger in town, and Olive had news about that stranger. Wonderful news.

When she reached the top step, Olive had to pause and take a breath. Her head was still swimming from those exhaust fumes in the truck. Kip, the young African-American fellow, had brought her back to consciousness. After that he told her his whole fantastic story. It was a doozy.

Becky Thatcher wants Olive to keep the story to herself, at least for a while. But that's Becky. She's very good at waiting. Olive is not. Olive thinks most people in town will welcome the news. Who in their right mind wouldn't want to start aging again? Especially if, as Kip promises, everybody will age at a safe, normal rate. Kip says he's brought along an antidote or some sort of concoction that will ease the citizens back into the waters of mortality gently. The river of life will then once again flow as it should. How can Olive keep great news like this to herself. Olive crossed the creaky wooden floor of the theater lobby, and entered the double doors of the auditorium.

She emerged at the back row. And when she saw that half the seats were empty she knew that her decision to come here this evening was the right decision. This town needs a kick in the pants.

Up on the stage Violet Snelling was speaking from the podium. Four men were seated behind her, listening. No surprise that Violet was at the helm — the seventy-year-old newspaper reporter likes to take charge. She still carries a chip on her shoulder about the fuddy-duddy menfolk refusing to vote a woman as mayor.

"I'm not suggesting shooting the boy again," Violet said to the house. "We just want to talk to the boy, find out his intentions."

"Ain't supposed to call 'em *boys* no more," Zeke Spivak called out from his usual seat in the fifth row. "Gets up their noses. Makes 'em uppity as shit."

"I didn't call him *boy* because he is black," Violet explained. "I called him *boy* because he appears to be young, a teenager." Violet added, "Although with these people, it can be hard to judge their exact age."

"*These* people?" someone else questioned.

"I mean people from outer space."

"How many people from outer space you know?"

"Why are we wastin' time here?" asked somebody with his face turned away from Olive but who sounded like Roy Frith. "Why ain't we tossing him back into his space ship and sending him home to Mars?"

"Can't find his space ship," Isaac answered. "Just his VW bus. Been watching it all day. No sign of the little squirt. I think he's gone to ground."

"Gone to town?" yelled Lorelei Grundig at the top of her lungs.

"Would somebody please order Lorelei a new battery," Garth Meeker pleaded.

"No, thank you," said Lorelei. "Just finished dinner."

"Tell us more about this crystal rock you found, Chief," Violet Snelling prompted from the podium. "You believe it might fuel the boy's, I mean *the fella's* ship?"

Before Chief Dagleish could answer that question, Olive spoke up, "It's not a rock."

All heads turned her way.

Olive started down the aisle. "And it's not a fuel."

"Darling!" Pastor Hadwin Gorely called out. "I thought you'd left."

As she passed him by, Olive squeezed her husband's hand. "I'll explain." Then she turned to the rest of the house. "I'll explain to all of you."

Olive continued down to the stage, saying as she ran, "Wait till you hear this, gang. You're gonna love it."

Or at least, she hoped they would love it.

• • •

Becky Thatcher carried the serving tray across the chicken yard towards the barn. Happily, she didn't have to worry about her mother or her father following her — both of them were firmly planted in front of the television screen eating their usual dinners off their usual TV trays.

Once safely inside the barn, Becky placed the serving tray on the tack bench and lifted the inverted mixing bowl that had been keeping the flies off the plate. "I hope the smell in here hasn't killed your appetite."

Kip examined the meal. ""Looks yummy. Nothing here with seeds, I trust."

"No. Just some asparagus fresh out of the garden — it was a little late coming this year. Plus some carrots, roast potatoes, Yankee meatloaf with gravy." A thought suddenly occurred to Rebecca. "You're not a vegetarian, are you?"

Kip pulled his stool closer to the bench. "Not at home. But when I'm on the road like this..."

"Oh, I'm sorry. I should have asked."

"That's okay." He examined the meatloaf. "Consuming unfamiliar flesh can be iffy. I never know whether I'm chewing on a farm animal or a possible business associate."

Rebecca wanted to ask him what business he was referring to, but she didn't want to appear nosy. He'll tell her when he's ready. All things come to those who wait.

He stabbed a chunk of potato with his fork and popped the piece into his mouth. "Mmm, garden fresh and mouth-watering delicious. Did you prepare all this yourself?"

"I do all the cooking, also the cleaning, the laundry."

"You're a busy girl."

"Father runs the farm and the auto shop. And mother, well, she's not good for much. Not anymore."

"She not well?" Kip stabbed a piece of buttered carrot with dill.

Becky was proud of her dilled carrots. They were always a favorite at church suppers. "Mother's in perfect health. But like so many here in the valley—"

Kip nodded. "Bored, depressed, and ridden with guilt for outliving the rest of the planet."

"Happily, she has her *Sudoku*."

"Well, don't you worry your pretty head. We'll have her up and off the couch in no time."

Becky knew what he meant, but she still had her concerns about the process. "You're sure it will be okay? I mean, she'll age gracefully? We all will?"

"As gracefully as your inbred DNA will allow."

"Inbred?"

"You know you people would be a lot healthier if you mixed up your breeding practices a bit more. Let natural selection take precedence over color and design preferences." Kip waggled his fork at the carrots. "You know what these could use?"

"Salt. I'm sorry, but I didn't know if you—"

"Chocolate chips."

"Pardon me?"

"Had some yesterday. Sprinkled on ice cream. Very tasty." Kip stabbed a spear of asparagus and popped it into his mouth. He started chewing.

Becky watched him chew. And chew. He seemed to be chewing a long time. Finally she asked, "The asparagus to your liking?"

"I been thinking." Kip kept chewing. "Maybe I should go back to my van."

"I overcooked it, didn't I."

"I wouldn't know." He continued chewing. Finally, "Hey, I just remembered — do you like French onion soup? I got lots in my bus. It's not far." He stood up. "I'll just go and—"

"No, no. You can't go back there." Rebecca urged him back down onto the stool. "Isaac is watching your camp site. Tell me..." Becky pulled a stool up to the bench for herself. She sat down, rested her hand on Kip's wrist, and asked, "Do you think you'll be here with us long?"

"Hard to tell. I'm already running behind. I thought I'd have that missing bar of rosin by now. I thought I knew exactly where it was. It has to be in that water somewhere."

"Are you sure you dropped it in the river? Not up in the lake on top of the mountain?"

"Already checked there. No idea how it would get up there, but I checked anyway. No sign of it. At least..." Kip tapped a small electronic fob that hung from a lanyard around his neck. "Not unless this thing's on the fritz."

The instrument reminded Becky of one of those beepers that elderly people wear so they can call for help when they fall. "That some sort of Geiger counter?" she asked.

"Sort of. Works more like the nose of a, uh," Kip searched for the right word. "That dog... the one on *The Beverly Hillbillies*."

"A bloodhound?"

"Yes, like a bloodhound. Very sensitive. I just sample any scent — in this case the scent of my rosin — and this gizmo will indicate any subsequent phonon increase in those particular air-borne odorant molecules as I walk along. For instance..." Kip held up a spear of Becky's asparagus. "I could sample this vegetable matter, and it would warn me if I ever got near it again."

"I'm sorry. I did overcook it."

"Oh, no, it's quite good." He popped more asparagus in his mouth. "Tasty." He chewed. Smiled. Seemed to wince a little.

Rebecca got back to the vital subject at hand. "I really think maybe you should check the lake again. We noticed a long time ago that we have to bathe in that water for the magic to work. Doesn't that mean the rosin is up there, in that lake?"

"Not necessarily. I'm no chemist, but I'm told that the medicine's active ingredient is bound in something closely related to silica. That means it dissolves best in warm alkaline water."

"Alkaline? Our hot springs are alkaline."

"Yes. And warm. Added to that, my research tells me that your river bed, especially the area where I went bathing, is largely limestone, a porous rock."

"Which means the water seeps into the aquafer."

Kip smiled his approval at her deduction. "It recycles, goes back to where it started. It then reheats and bubbles up through volcanic fissures that take it up to that mountain pond where the cycle starts over again."

"Like a coffee percolator."

"And we all know what happens to coffee if you keep percolating it," Kip said.

"It gets stronger."

"And it keeps you awake too long."

Rebecca added, "Or alive too long."

Kip waggled his fork at her. "You, my lady, are as intelligent as you are beautiful."

Becky had to look away. She didn't know what to say to this. She hoped it was a compliment.

Kip looked quizzically at her face. "How do you do that?"

"Do what?"

"Change your color, go red like that."

"You've never seen a young lady blush before?"

"No. Most of the TV shows I've been watching are in black and white." He then reached out and touched the back of his hand to Becky's cheek. "And your body temperature... it's risen by a good one degree Celsius. Almost two degrees, Fahrenheit."

"You're embarrassing me."

"No need — it's not your fault your country hasn't gone metric yet." He touched her face again.

His touch was soft. Gentle. And surprisingly familiar. Exactly as she'd remembered it from that night by the campfire when he'd held her face and kissed her goodbye. She'd never told anyone about that kiss. How could she? Her father and the others would have strung him up from the nearest cottonwood.

Becky repeated the advice she'd given Kip earlier. "They're watching your bus. You'd best stay here in the barn tonight."

"If you insist." Then he smiled. "Do you ever sleep in the barn?"

Becky felt her face blush again.

• • •

Phil Hodworth couldn't believe his ears. Were these people saying what he thought they were saying? Are these lucky souls walking away from the glorious all-you-can-eat buffet that is eternal life. Are they patting their full stomachs and saying *thanks but no thanks* to more helpings of the everlasting main course? Are these spoiled fools so bored with the endless dessert trolley that they're ready to snap their fingers for the server to come bring them their checks?

Certainly looks that way.

A few minutes ago, Olive Gorely took to the stage of the Opera House and told the town about her run-in with the mysterious stranger, the man who calls himself Kip. She says the encounter was a real eye-opener.

First of all, she learned that Kip is the runaway slave whom she and the waggoneers met back in the autumn of 1846. Except he's not a runaway slave. He says he's a space alien. And if that little news flash isn't enough, he also claims to be the one responsible for the valley's magic, the ageless *status quo*.

Apparently, on his last visit here, this Kip fellow left something behind. He wasn't too clear on the details, but it sounds to Olive like the guy accidentally dropped a medical device or a bottle of prescription medicine from his shaving kit. It fell into the river. Kip figures, it soon polluted the town's water supply.

Being the responsible extraterrestrial that he is, Kip feels terrible about this, so he has come back to clean up his mess. Doing this, he says, will restore the natural order of life to the valley and start everyone's biological clocks spinning again. But don't worry. Kip has assured Olive that he has brought along some special pills that will keep everybody's DNA from deteriorating too quickly. In other words, no instant apple dolls.

Olive ended her speech with the recommendation that the town cooperate with Kip, the clumsy space alien, maybe even help the little guy locate his lost crystal, or rosin, or whatever he calls this drug delivery device he has lost. Finished with her report, Olive handed the podium back to Mayor Sam Beckwith so that he and the townsfolk can discuss how they want to handle this situation.

And thus the debate began.

The first person to step to the microphone was Isaac Beckwith, and to Phil's relief, the kid appeared to be on the side of reason. Isaac tried his best to rally the crowd to action, saying they should send the space man packing pronto thereby saving the valley's wonderful status quo.

"I like being nineteen," Isaac announced from the podium. "Always have, always will."

"Wouldn't you like to be twenty?" asked a young teenage punk sitting in the third row whom Phil recognized as the martini drinker from last night's party.

"Of course I would, Clay," Isaac said. "And I'm sure you would, too. Nothing wrong with turning twenty, except for one thing — twenty will lead to twenty-one. And twenty-one will lead to twenty-two. And twenty-two will lead to twenty-three. And twenty-three will lead to—"

"I think we see where you're going," said Violet Snelling as she elbowed Isaac away from the microphone. "Never thought I would say this, gang, but I agree with numb-nuts, here. I think we should tell this Kip fellow to hop the next rocket ship back to Mars."

"Of course you do, Vi," said a middle-aged lady seated in the second row. "What do you care — you're coasting at a nice comfortable seventy-two. I'm forty-eight and menopausal. Do you know what it's like to have hot flashes for over a hundred-and-fifty years? No, of course you don't. Well, I'll tell you. It sucks. In winter, tourists stop and ask why my house has the only roof in town without snow."

"I'm Seventy-*one*, Cora," Violet said indignantly. "And yes, I admit to enjoying the autumn of my years. Why wouldn't I? Autumn is a glorious time of year. Mild days, cool nights, and no bugs. I don't know about you, but I'm in no hurry to rush headlong into the short, dark days of winter."

"But the fellow says we'll age at a normal rate," said someone who Phil didn't recognize.

"Sure he says that, now," Isaac Beckwith offered. "But can we trust him? Does anybody here know if Martians are good for their word? 'Cause I sure don't." Isaac pounded the podium with his fist. "I say we send this feller packing. Send him off the same way we sent him off last time. A couple of warning shots from my Henry should do the trick."

A man in the audience said. "Your warning shots tend to be fatal, Isaac."

"Then give the gun to me," Violet Snelling suggested. "You all know I can nip off an ear lobe from the church steeple with one eye tied behind my back."

To this, Isaac stuck a couple of fingers in his mouth and whistled his enthusiastic approval.

Phil joined in, shouting out a phrase that he couldn't believe would ever cross his lips: "You go, girl!" Phil whistled and applauded and waited for the thunder and cheers of support to roll down the aisles.

But the thunder never rolled. Nor did the cheers. Not one voice joined the Hallelujah chorus. So Phil rested his hands quietly in his lap and watched the dusty silence settle over the room, draping itself over the small theater like a shroud. After the dead moments rotted out to empty minutes, Phil decided there was only one thing left to do — he must step up to that microphone and make a pitch. After all, as a marketing maven Phil Hodworth is no stranger to selling a hot idea to a cold room.

Phil got to his feet and approached the dais. But as he reached the front of the stage he heard a commotion bubbling up at the back of the auditorium. A man was crab-walking along between the last two rows of seats, stepping on toes as he worked his way toward the center aisle.

"Wanna know what I think?" the man asked nobody in particular as he stepped into the aisle. "You probably don't, but I'm gonna tell you anyways." Using a cane for support, the man clicked and clacked his way down the aisle in quick small steps. Considering this gentleman was about sixty years old, Phil figured the guy was likely coming to speak in favor of keeping the magical status quo. After all, without the life extension, this guy would not have a lot of years left on his odometer. So Phil returned to his chair beside the others on stage to let this man speak.

As the man worked his way down the aisle, Phil turned to Isaac, "You know this guy?"

Isaac dismissed any concerns, "It's just Crazy Lucas."

"Prospector," Mayor Sam added. "Runs the gold mine."

Gold mine? Phil took a good look at the old fellow who was now about halfway down the aisle. The man sported a diverse wardrobe that comprised over-sized work boots, stained chinos, an ill-fitting button-down flannel shirt, and a black bowler hat with a frayed brim. His scruffy beard was free range, and so was his ear hair. Phil turned to his associates on stage and commented, "This guy owns a gold mine?"

"We *all* do," said Isaac. "He just runs it for us."

Oh, so that's it, thought Phil. That explains the nice cars and well-kept homes. This little town owns a co-op gold mine.

Mayor Sam clarified his son's words, "*Green* gold. Nephrite. A kind of jade. Ours is the best in the state. Gem quality. Crazy Lucas discovered it back in nineteen-aught-seven."

Chief Dagleish added, "If by *discovered* you mean tripped over a canyon full of the stuff."

"Jade, huh..." Phil mulled this news over. "Funny I haven't seen any of it around town. You know... jewelry, knick-knacks, tourist souvenirs."

"Oh, we don't sell locally," Dagleish said. "Can't afford the attention. If word ever got out about our rich deposit we'd be up to our necks in rock hounds."

Mayor Sam finished the story, "We ship it all to the Orient. The Far East. Asia. We have some people who know some people, people who know how to keep their mouths shut."

"Gotcha." Phil turned his attention back to Crazy Lucas, who was now climbing the steps to the stage. The prospector's limp was slowing him down quite a bit. Phil asked, "He hurt himself in a mining accident?"

Isaac fielded this one, "Shot his foot off to avoid the draft."

"The draft?" Phil said. "Which war?"

"Eighteen-twelve," Mayor Sam answered. "Didn't want to go to Canada."

Phil was impressed. "So the guy shot his foot off?"

Dagleish explained, "Niagara Falls militia was tough. A missing toe? We'll give you a crutch. Two missing toes? We'll give you a horse. But a whole foot? Put your musket away and go home."

"Crazy is a very peaceable man," Violet Snelling said. "Never would carry a gun. Not even out here in grizzly country."

"That why they call him Crazy?" Phil asked.

"That, plus he married his mule," Isaac said.

Phil had to laugh. "Now *that* is crazy."

Isaac nodded. "Especially if you saw his mule."

Crazy Lucas hung his cane on the lip of the speaker's stand and took hold of the podium with both hands. "You folks know me. You know I ain't one to waste words, breath, or soap. So I ain't going to run on 'bout all the moronic crap I've seen go down over the past one hundred-and-who-the-fuck-cares years. We all been riding the same buckboard — a buckboard that, two hundred years ago, got stuck in the mud up to its axels. And what did we do about it? Not a damn thing. We just sat on our confused asses and watched the circus roll by. We watched the clowns in Washington declare war after war. Hell, most of them wars weren't even declared. The Indian wars. The Mexican War. The War Between the States. The Spanish-American war. The War To End All Wars. The Second War-To-End-All-Wars. Korea. Vietnam. Afghanistan. Ukraine. Shit, we've watched them all."

"You left out the Gulf War," said somebody

"And the Iraq war," somebody else added.

"I thought they were the same war," a woman in the front row said.

"No, whole different wars."

"They're all different," Crazy Lucas said. "And they're all the same. But hey, what does it matter to us? We're tucked away safe and cozy here in our little valley. We can just look the other way, pretended nothing's happening out there. So we did. We shut our eyes, plugged out ears and raised denial to a high art. Hell, we had to. Otherwise, we'd have gone nuts decades ago. Nobody can watch that much stupidity for that many years without it leaving a mark. So we turned a blind eye. But you see, friends, here's the thing..."

Crazy Lucas leaned forward and rested his forearms on the podium. He tented his hands together, not toward heaven but toward the audience because that was where his words were aimed.

"Seems we can't stay blind any longer. Can't turn our eyes or our ears away from the madness anymore. And I'll show you the reason why..." Crazy Lucas slid a hand into the breast pocket of his flannel shirt and pulled out a smart phone. He held the device up as if he were a school kid at show-and-tell. He looked down at a man in the fifth row. "You listening to me, Otis?"

Otis, who was busy thumbing his own phone, looked up, "Huh?"

A few people chuckled. But Phil Hodworth did not. He could feel a change in wind direction. This old prospector's words were rustling some leaves. He was getting through to these people. A few of them had actually put down their phones.

The man at the podium continued his sermon, "The internet, the World Wide Web — this devil has changed everything. This digital magician has turned every idiot with at least one opposable thumb into a broadcaster, a film maker, a news reporter, a television producer, and a network executive all rolled up into one, but with one important difference: This network has no standards. No standards of integrity. No standards of decency. No standards of truth. No way to tell genuine gold facts from the pyrite bullshit. And the worst thing about this bluetoothed monster?" Crazy Lucas waved his phone like he was trying to rattle some sense into it. "There's no escape. It's everywhere. You can't get away from it."

Violet Snelling interjected, rather quietly, "You could always turn it off, Lucas."

"Yes, Vi, that's true. I can indeed turn it off. But do I? Does anybody in this room ever turn it off? No. We're all hooked on what it feeds us. Like the black bears behind the donut shop we'll stick our snouts into any garbage this thing dumps out. Why, just this morning I ate my bran flakes and yogurt while watching a naked lady in Saskatchewan tune her piano."

"You're welcome," said a man a few rows back. "I reposted that."

Crazy Lucas continued, "And right after that, I went out to the shithouse and took a dump while watching some religious zealot halfway round the world chop some fella's head off. With an axe. In color. High def. Live. While I'm sitting on the crapper."

"Nice to see the bran is working," said a woman in the front row.

Crazy Lucas slipped his phone back into his pocket. "My point is, fellow pilgrims, I have seen enough. Heard enough. Felt enough. I'm finished. I'm full up. It's time to move along. I'm not saying I want to die. Hell, if I wanted to do that I'd go for a walk the way young Zack did. No, I want to live, just like all of you. But part of living is aging, changing, moving on and seeing what's around the next bend. Friends, it's time we freed our wheels from the mud. I say give this alien fella from... from wherever... give this man all the help he needs to carry out his mission. Good on him for coming back to clean up his mess and set our wagons to rolling again. It's about time. It's just... about time."

The prospector took a handkerchief from his pocket and wiped his mouth. Then he did something that surprised Phil. The man turned around and addressed Phil directly, "Sorry to burst your bubble, kid. But take it from me — eternal life ain't all it's cracked up to be. My advice to you is, keep your wheels rolling, enjoy the ride, hang on to your hat, and never send anything back to the kitchen."

And with that, the man picked up his cane, turned, and limped toward the steps. Nobody hurried to help him. They all knew he could handle the steps just fine on his own. They've been watching him limp along for almost two hundred years.

Phil waited for the audience reaction to the man's speech. But there wasn't any. Just silence. They all just sat. Like they were stunned. Or bored. The only sounds were the tapping and scraping of the prospector's cane along the planked wooden floor.

But then it started. Someone clapped. Just the one pair of hands at first. But others soon joined in. The applause grew. Not to thunderous proportions, of course — the theater was barely a third full — but the slaps of approval gradually built as more and more hands put down their phones to make noise in support of this man's words.

By the time the draft-dodging prospector reached his seat the flow of support was splashing down the aisles like water gushing from an open hydrant.

Up on stage, Mayor Sam Beckwith turned to Violet Snelling. "There's your headline for next week's edition, Vi — *Town Votes To End The Status Quo.*"

Violet didn't look happy. "I'm afraid you're right Sammy." She stretched out her hand to outline an imaginary banner headline floating in mid-air, "*Waggoneers Vote To Hitch Up The Horses Again.*"

Mayor Sam patted her knee. "That's why you're the journalist and I'm just the mule skinner."

As the waves of applause continued to roll down the aisles and break over the stage, young Isaac Beckwith turned to Phil, "Well, Mr. Hodworth, looks like we're sunk. Sorry you never got a chance to sail with us. You would have enjoyed the ride. But there's nothing we can do about it now."

"Don't bet on it," Phil answered.

"No?" Isaac's eyes started to twinkle. "Whatcha got in mind, Skipper?"

Phil said, "We'll have to use your truck."

Isaac's sly grin blossomed. "No problem."

"I want to leave my car at the motel in case my wife needs it. I've already reconnected the battery." Phil thought of one more question for his young friend, "You got lots of gasoline?"

"In my tank?"

"In your jerry can."

The young man's smile flamed bright. "Always."

CHAPTER TWENTY-ONE

The door opened easily.

"Told you so. He never locks it." Isaac Beckwith was turning out to be a bit of a know-it-all.

Phil leaned inside the Volkswagen van and swept the darkness away with the flashlight app of his phone.

From behind, Isaac warned him, "Careful of the uranium."

"We don't know it's uranium."

"Whatever it is, it burns," said Isaac, "Chief Dagleish says you don't want to touch it."

Phil stepped back from the vehicle. Isaac immediately took advantage of the vacated doorway and started to climb in for a look. But Phil stuck out an arm and blocked his way. "Just stay out here and watch those trees."

The woods were dark but noisy. Lots of witnesses, but they were all crickets. High overhead, an eyelash of crescent moon winked down at the crime scene that was about to play out on the sandbar.

Phil grabbed the gas can from the back of the pickup. He'd have asked Isaac to do this, but he wanted the kid to keep his eyes, and his rifle, trained on the surrounding forest. Phil hadn't been crazy about bringing the firearm along, but the kid had mentioned something about grizzly bears.

Phil rested the metal gas can on the ground and unscrewed the cap.

Isaac asked, "Figure he's got his space ship hidden hereabouts?"

"Uh, huh." Phil didn't want to talk. The fresh gasoline fumes were stinging his lungs.

Isaac patted the side of the VW bus. "It's a cinch he didn't fly here in this thing."

"Uh, huh." Phil splashed gasoline into the open door of the vehicle. He tried not to inhale. His throat was already chocking from this dry Wyoming air.

"Mmmm," Isaac purred. "Don't you just love the smell of gasoline."

Phil finished dousing the interior. Then he splashed gasoline over the outside of the vehicle.

Isaac continued his babble, "I can't understand why girls stink themselves up with flowery perfume when all us guys really want is a whiff of good ol' high octane."

Phil shook the last drops out of the jerry can.

"Or popcorn," Isaac said. "Hell, I'd hump just about any gal in town if she smelled like the floor of a multiplex."

Okay, Phil just had to say something. "You can't possibly know what a multiplex smells like."

"I got a good imagination."

Phil laid the empty can on the sand. Then he extended his open palm to his young assistant and said, like a surgeon addressing his nurse, "Lighter."

Isaac switched his rifle to his left hand so he could slide his right hand into the pocket of his jeans. But his hand came out empty, so he switched his rifle to the other hand and tried the left pocket. "Damn," was all he said. He patted the breast pocket of his denim jacket. "Double damn."

Phil grabbed the rifle from the boy. The weapon was old and heavy, something called a Henry repeater. Apparently it dated back to the civil war. Phil stuck the muzzle of the gun into the gasoline-soaked weeds beside the tires and tried to squeeze off a shot. But the trigger wouldn't budge.

Isaac reached over and slid back a little button on the side. "Didn't come with a safety. Dad added it after we lost Puss Puss."

Phil hoped that was the name of a cat and not of a grandmother.

Phil pulled the trigger. The muzzle's blast sparked an ember which immediately blossomed into a flame. Together, Phil and Isaac watched the line of flame snake through the weeds and jump up onto the van. When the fiery reptile reached the open door, it slithered inside the vehicle where it soon swallowed the seats whole.

Isaac yanked at the sleeve of Phil's sweatshirt to urge him farther back from the vehicle, cautioning, "Who knows what'll happen to that radioactive shit."

Phil reassured the boy, "Just because that rock felt hot doesn't mean it was radioactive. It could just contain some skin irritant. Like capsaicin."

"What's that?"

"The chemical that makes a pepper hot."

Isaac was impressed. "You a college graduate?"

Phil smiled. "Don't like to brag, but yes, I'm a college graduate. How about you?"

"No colleges anywhere near where I grew up, not in eighteen and forty-three."

Phil grinned. "You actually went to school in eighteen-forty-three." It was not a question, just a statement. Phil enjoyed talking about it. The very idea set butterflies flitting in Phil's stomach.

"I'd like to have had more schooling, but when a war between the states looked like a sure thing, Pa, I mean *Dad*, decided we should head west. He wanted no part of the killing. Dad was a lot like Crazy Lucas that way. A lot of folks out here are. They came to the territories to farm, not to fight. Heck, most of the towns in the old west didn't allow a man to carry a gun in public. Certainly not into a saloon." Isaac turned his face away from the flames to look straight into Phil's eyes. "So, what do you think? You believe our story yet?"

Phil took a moment. He wanted to answer truthfully. "I do. And I don't."

Isaac turned his face back to the fire. He watched the hungry flames devour the little bus and rise twenty feet high, spearing bright holes into the black heavens. "I'm thinkin' you do," Isaac said.

Okay. Maybe the kid wasn't as dumb as he looked.

• • •

An early summer morning in the high country should smell of many things — blue columbine, poppy mallow, purple prairie clover — but not of this.

Rebecca and Kip had been strolling along the river bank — she, trying to learn about his life back home, and he, avoiding the topic by asking about her life in the valley — when Rebecca noticed traces of an acrid fragrance souring the air. "Something's burning." She sniffed again. "Rubber. And maybe gasoline."

Kip didn't act concerned. He seemed familiar with the smell. "Most every place on this planet smells like this. I didn't think you people noticed it anymore."

Becky picked up her walking pace to lead the way forward. She had a pretty good idea what she was smelling and she didn't like it. Sure enough, when they reached Kip's campsite on the sandbar she saw it — the charred, blistered aluminum corpse that was once Kip's Volkswagen bus.

Kip threw up his arms and said, "Aw, geez. My fault, I guess. Must have left the soup on."

He continued to walk to the pathetic, blackened hippie cadaver, but Becky grabbed his arm and stopped him. "No. Hold on." She scanned the cliff across the river. Then she turned her eyes to the woods behind her. Finally, she whispered, "They might still be here."

"They?"

"This is why I didn't want you to sleep here last night."

"The only reason?"

She didn't answer him. Her attention was on the woods.

Kip looked at what remained of his burned-out home. "You think somebody did this on purpose?"

Becky had to smile. "You're terribly naïve, you know that?"

"Really? Back home I'm considered a bit of a hard ass."

"Well, many of my neighbors don't want your ass here. Hard or soft." This was language Rebecca didn't normally use, but these were special circumstances.

Kip's eyes were still on his bus. "I have to see what's left. There's some things I need."

He tried to pull away from her, but Becky held his sleeve tight. "We have to get you out of here. Right now." And she started to pull him toward the cover of the trees and bushes. But she didn't get that far. A spray of bark exploded from a maple branch just inches above Kip's head. It was followed by the crack of a rifle.

Becky threw an arm around Kip's neck and yanked him to the ground with her. It wasn't difficult, the man was no taller than she was and a bit slimmer. And not much of a fighter.

Together, they scrambled to the cover of a large fallen log where Kip placed himself on top of her as a shield. He certainly didn't weigh much. She could easily have pushed him off. But he seemed to want to protect her, and how could she discourage such gallantry? So she didn't. She just lay still. And together they waited for the next shot.

And waited.

Nothing. The woods were quiet. No sounds except the buzz of a nest of angry ground wasps and the scolds of an offended squirrel.

Rebecca asked, "You're not allergic to wasp stings, are you?"

"How would I know?"

"Then don't swat."

Pretty soon a chickadee added a happy chirp to the mix. And from across the river a robin started whistling his *cheerily, cheerily*. The birds' songs reminded Becky of a young Union cavalry soldier she had met towards the end of the War Between The States. The young soldier told her that once, during a horrific massacre in Virginia, while he was awaiting certain death on a blood-drenched battlefield, he had heard a lark singing. He expected the lark's song to be the last sound he ever heard, and that thought comforted him. How much better, he thought, to die hearing the birds songs rather than to die in the antiseptic silence of an army hospital.

Needless to say, that soldier survived that battle, and as soon as he could he deserted the army and scooted up north. He ended up here in Perpetuity where he changed his name, married a local gal, opened a barber shop, and learned to play chromatic harmonica. Today he gives music lessons that enjoy immense popularity on the internet.

Funny, the things that come to a girl's mind when she's stuck behind a log with a space alien on her back.

And then Becky recalled another story — an event more relevant to her immediate plight. She remembered how Kip's miraculous crystal rock had healed him when he'd been shot in 1846. Would it work like that again if he were shot here today? More important, did he presently have the thing with him or had he left it back in that burned-out VW bus?

Rebecca lifted her face out of the sand just far enough to mumble, "Where's your magic crystal?"

"The rosin?"

"Where is it?"

"In my cookie tin."

"And that is...?"

"In my bus." Kip announced this news with little emotion. He obviously wasn't worried about it. But Becky was.

"Could it have survived the fire?" she asked.

"Hmm," He thought this one over before answering, "Probably not."

"No? But won't you need it to get home? To survive the long voyage?"

"No problem. I'll have my spare. You know, the one I accidentally left here."

"But you don't have that one. You don't even know where it is. And if you never find it won't you be stuck here?" Becky was worried about this, but not as worried as she felt she should have been.

"Don't worry, I'll find it. I know it's here someplace. It must be — it's still doing its job on you people. Right?"

Rebecca then thought of another important pharmaceutical Kip had mentioned. "The serum? The antidote you told me about. Where's that?" She was referring to the medicine that would prevent her and her friends from aging overnight.

"The serum is safe."

"Where?"

"Your barn."

"You brought the serum to my barn?"

"It's tucked under your work bench. In my back pack."

"All of it?"

"All of it." Kip smiled with self-satisfaction. "They don't give these jobs to chimps."

Rebecca breathed a sigh of relief. Kip was a smart man. A funny man. A clever man. A man she could trust with her life. And the lives of her friends. She wished she could tell him this to his face. But she was in no position to do that.

"I think the shooting has stopped," Kip said, his gentle breath caressing the nape of her neck. "Shall we get up now?"

"Best wait a little longer. Be safe." Rebecca wished Kip were a little less naïve. She wished he were a little more cautious.

"Aren't I heavy?" Kip's warm breath sent a cool shiver down Rebecca's spine.

"Oh, no, not at all." Rebecca was ashamed of what she was wishing for now.

She wished she were lying face-up.

• • • •

Phil grabbed the rifle from his idiot partner's hands. "Are you crazy? You might have hit the girl." Phil laid the rifle down in the tall grass.

The two men were lying prone on a cliff overlooking the river. Isaac looked insulted. "I'm a better shot than that," he said. "I would never risk hurting Becky. Coulda nailed her boyfriend easy, though. If I wanted to."

"We're not trying to *nail* anyone. We're just trying to *scare* them." Phil got to his feet and stretched his stiff muscles. He and Isaac had been lying up here all night watching that burned-out VW bus. No sign of Kip until a few minutes ago.

"I'm going down," Phil said.

"I'll cover you." Isaac reached for the rifle.

But Phil grabbed the rifle from the dirt. "No you won't."

Isaac looked up at him, shielded his eyes from the early morning sun, and said, "If they see you coming with that in your hands, won't they just run off again?"

Phil hated to admit it, but the kid had a point. Reluctantly, Phil handed the rifle to Isaac but with a firm warning, "Under no circumstances are you to shoot at anyone or anything. Understand?"

"What if he's got, like, a ray gun or something?"

Phil turned around and started down the hill, saying without looking back, "Have you seen him with a ray gun?"

"Well, no."

Phil continued walking. The loose gravel and shale made for slippery footing, so he zigzagged his way down, all the while keeping an eye on that large fallen log at the bottom where Kip and the girl had taken cover.

When he reached the river's flood plain and was about fifty yards from the log, Phil called out in a casual tone of voice, "Sorry about that. My friend is what you might call a shoot-first-think-later sort of guy."

Phil watched the log. No heads popped up. He kept walking. As he closed the gap, he started to regret not bringing that rifle with him. Is this Kip guy really as peaceful and non-violent as Olive Gorely seems to think he is? We'll soon find out. Phil called out again, "Hey, Kip, you remember me. Phil Hodworth. We met on the ski lift. I think you know my daughter, Taylor."

Kip answered without revealing himself, "Taylor? She with you?"

"I just talked to her. On the phone. Says she's worried about you. Says you haven't been answering her texts."

"Couldn't." Kip popped his head up over the log. "I, uh, sort of dropped my phone into the river." Kip then proceeded to get to his feet. He stepped out from behind the log. He asked, with a naïve sincerity that Phil found endearing, "Hey, man, did you see who torched my crib?"

"Well, I, uh... to tell the truth..."

Now the girl stood up. "He did." She was talking to Kip, but she was looking straight at Phil. "He set fire to your van."

She was pretty, blonde, and had a nice figure. Phil knew her name was Rebecca and that she was a year or two older than Taylor. Taylor would be jealous if she knew this girl was hanging with Kip.

"That right?" Kip said to Phil. "You set fire to my bus?"

Phil hesitated. This called for tact. Best to appear warm and caring. Chummy would be nice. "Look, buddy," Phil said. "We all know why you're here. You've got a job to do. And I'm sure you mean us no harm. But we just can't let you carry out your mission. We can't allow you to take the stuff away. I'm sorry, pal, but you have to leave the crystal here." Phil was happy with his performance. He sounded sincere but authoritative.

"Crystals..." Kip spread his arms wide like he was dumping a heavy load. "What's this thing you people have about crystals? It's nothing like a crystal. A rosin, maybe. A heavy, waxy polyethylene plastic, sure. But it's not a crystal."

"Whatever it is, we can't let you take it," Phil said.

"And you figure that, with my wheels char-broiled, I can't go home?"

"I set fire to your vehicle for the same reason that a similarly concerned citizen once set fire to my restaurant. It's a message. We just want to let you know you aren't welcome. We want you to pack up your things and go back where you came from." Phil scanned the surrounding hills. "So where'd you park your, uh, your craft?" For some reason Phil thought the words *flying saucer* or *spaceship* might offend this guy.

"She's circling. High orbit. I'll dial her up when I'm ready."

"You'll *dial her up?*"

"She's unmanned. A drone. When I'm ready I enter my PIN number, bang in a few co-ordinates, and I'm out of your hair. Me and my meds."

Phil wanted to be sure he understood. "The meds that keep us all from aging."

"The stuff kinda works differently on different beings, different races. For my folk it's purely topical. Gotta have direct skin-to-skin contact to get any real oomph. But you guys... whoa, Nelly! Bang, zoom! A few molecules in your bath water and you're singin' *Rubber Ducky* for a couple of centuries." Kip then added. "But don't sweat it. I'll get things moving along normal lickety-split, just as soon as I locate the chunk I fumbled."

"Which you haven't found yet."

"No, but..." Kip turned to the young woman. "Becky, here, has a theory. She thinks it's been moved, and she has a pretty good idea where they took it. We're on our way up there now. "

"Up there?"

"Not looking forward to riding that rickety old chairlift thing again, but—"

"Kip!" The young woman interrupted. She flashed him a *shut-the-fuck-up-darling* look. It was a familiar look to Phil. But not to Kip. He was on a roll.

"Hey, man," Kip said. "Maybe you can give us a lift. Did you bring your wheels?"

The girl spoke up again, "I don't think that's a very good idea."

"Don't worry, Becks, he's cool." Kip turned back to Phil. "You don't mind, do you, Mr. Hodworth?"

"I'd be happy to help." Phil saw this as a good opportunity.

"Cool." Kip stepped closer gave Phil a big, hardy slap on the back. "It'll give us a chance to rap."

"You got it. And please, call me—" Phil's invitation to familiarity was interrupted by the ricochet of a bullet. With a bang, a small chunk of rock exploded just inches from his foot, sending up a spray of shale shards.

Phil hit the ground. Kip and the girl did not. She grabbed Kip's hand and yanked him straight off into the woods.

Phil stayed still. Didn't move a muscle. He remained where he was, lying face-down on the sandy rock. He didn't look up. Soon he heard two large, size-twelve boots scraping over the loose shale.

"You okay?" Isaac asked.

Phil slowly lifted his head off the rock. The few moments of lying quietly had helped him corral his anger. He looked at the big rifle dangling from his partner's hand and simply said, "I told you not to use that."

"But he punched you. In the back. I saw it." Isaac extended his hand to help Phil to his feet. Phil accepted the assistance. He was tired and sore. Especially his knee.

Phil gently felt his knee to make sure it wasn't broken. "We'll take your truck," he said.

"But they ran down there," Isaac pointed along the path that ran along the river. "Towards town."

Phil brushed the grit off the scraped flesh of his knee. He flexed the joint a couple of times, then started walking. "I have a good idea where they're headed. And it's not towards town."

CHAPTER
TWENTY-TWO

"You don't think your husband will do anything stupid, do you?"

"Well..." Carol hated to insult Phil when he wasn't around, but she had to answer the nice policeman truthfully. "The idea of staying young means a great deal to my husband."

Chief Dagleish drummed his fingers on his desk in thought. "And he gave no indication of where he was calling you from?"

"Not really. Outdoors. He complained about the cold. Said he should have brought his cardigan."

The police chief looked up at the one other person in the room. "You figure Isaac is with him."

"Didn't come home last night," Mayor Sam Beckwith answered.

The police chief stood up and grabbed his cap from a peg by the door. "Your husband carry a gun?"

"Of course not."

"My Henry repeater is missing," Sam offered.

Chief Dagleish clearly didn't like that news bulletin. The policeman opened a desk drawer and lifted out a revolver. A very large revolver.

• | • • • • • | •

"Can't you see the change? Doesn't it look different?" Rebecca gave Kip a moment to study the shoreline and call forth his visual memories of this part of the river. It will be difficult. It's been a very long time.

According to Kip, this part of the stream was where had bathed that final morning back in 1846 after he had left Rebecca's campfire and just before he left for home. The spot would therefore be the last place he had the misplaced piece of rosin with him.

"I suppose some of the trees are different. A little bigger."

"I'm not talking about the trees. I'm talking about the river bed."

This bend in the river is called Wilson's Falls, but it is more a set of rapids than an actual waterfall. Kip studied the rolling froth churned up by the tilted slabs of bedrock and the shallow whirlpool that swirled at the bottom. "I remember wading in to wash up. My wound was closing up nicely — thanks to you — but I was afraid of infection. My pilot was scheduled to pick me up at dawn."

"Your company provides you with a pilot?"

"Back then they did." Kip shook his head with sadness. "Another government gig lost to robots."

"Government? I thought you worked for a pharmaceutical manufacturer."

"We socialized our drug industry long ago. All advanced civilizations have." He looked at Rebecca pointedly.

Rebecca understood. "We'll talk politics later. Right now, let's concentrate on what you did here."

Kip regarded the banks of the river. "I remember hanging my jeans from one of those." He pointed up to a couple of huge cottonwoods whose branches spread out over the water. "'Course, they were a lot smaller back then. The trees, that is, not my jeans."

"So your medicine could have dropped out of your pocket, straight into the river."

"Could have. Denim was a lot stiffer back then. Not like this stuff you've got now." Kip bent a leg and rubbed his backside. "I dig how it stretches. In some ways you've made some great advancements. But in others..."

Rebecca struggled to keep him on track. "And you've searched this part of the river."

"First place I looked." With the toe of his sandal, Kip kicked a small stone into the water. "No luck, though. Not a sniff. The needle on my gizmo never budged." Kip looked into the shallow water where he'd just kicked the stone. After a moment of consideration he said, "You know, I think I do see the difference now."

"If I had a photograph from when you were last here, you'd definitely see a difference." Although Rebecca knew every inch of the river, she was particularly familiar with this section — she used to pan for gold here with her father. At this point in the river's journey the water drops about three feet from a shelf of shale, phyllite, and gneiss onto a table of sandstone. The small gneiss rocks contain veins of quartz and feldspar — minerals that make the stones look particularly pretty.

"Yes," Kip said with some confidence. "Now I can see it — fewer rocks."

"A lot fewer." Rebecca confirmed.

"Why did you remove them?"

"River rocks are smooth. They're attractive. Ornamental. We use them to decorate walls, pathways, gardens, fireplaces."

Kip didn't seem thrilled with this news. "So you're telling me my rosin could be anywhere in the valley — bordering a driveway, sprucing up a chimney, pimping out somebody's backyard barbecue."

"Yes, but," Rebecca raised a finger of hope as she suggested, "the rosin must still be in contact with water, correct?"

"Of course. Otherwise, you and your friends would be... Well, you wouldn't be. Not anymore."

Rebecca grabbed Kip's hand. "Follow me." She led him along the trail that led from the river and up toward her and her parents' farm and her father's garage. In about fifteen minutes she and Kip emerged from the hills of low scrub pine and into a field of wheatgrass that bordered her family's property. She and Kip then wound their way through the rusty graveyard of vehicles that her father cannibalizes for parts. When they reached the chicken yard outside the barn, Becky instructed Kip, "Wait here. I'll fetch the keys." She continued on alone up to the main house.

From behind her she heard Kip say, "What's happenin', ladies. These people treating you gals with the respect such hard working women are due?"

She looked back. Sure enough, he was talking to the chickens. Did this man from another world not know what a chicken was?

Kip looked at Becky for a moment. Then he broke out into a sly grin. "Just yanking your chain."

Becky had to smile. Young Zachary Mossip used to tease her like that. She misses Zack. Everybody does. The boy had such a positive, good-humored outlook, much like Kip has. Kip would certainly be a welcome addition to this valley. But of course, that's not possible. Once Kip finds his special piece of rosin he's leaving for home.

On the other hand, if he is unable to find that rosin...

Once again, Rebecca couldn't help but feel ashamed of what she was thinking.

• • •

Isaac Beckwith lifted his hand from the steering wheel to point out an old square-timbered farmhouse up ahead. "That's hers on the left. You reckon that boy spent the night here?"

"We know he didn't come home to his bus," Phil offered.

"I'll bet she made him bunk in the barn."

"The barn? Why not the house?"

"Becky lives with her parents. If her old man ever found out she was keeping company with a fella like this, he'd have a conniption."

"Her father a racist? Or does he just have something against his daughter dating space aliens?"

"Her father has something against her dating anything. Rupert Thatcher insists his little princess remain pure as the mountain snow."

Phil wasn't sure he understood correctly. "You mean, Rebecca is a virgin?"

"The virginest."

Phil repeated the word for his own unbelieving ears. "A virgin... for two hundred fucking years..."

"I wouldn't call them *fucking* years."

Just as they neared the house a classic two-door muscle car came racing out of the driveway. It spun out onto the dirt road and sped off in the opposite direction, away from Isaac's truck. Through the cloud of dust Phil had caught a glimpse of Rebecca behind the wheel with Kip seated beside her.

"Sweet, huh?" Isaac purred.

"What?"

"Her old man's Road Runner Hemi. Fastest wheels in the valley. No way we can keep up with that baby."

"Can I presume she recognized your truck?"

"Looks that way. I'm not her favorite guy in town." Isaac added, "Folks 'round here tend to hold grudges."

"Don't you worry," Phil assured his young driver. "After today this town will build a statue to you. You'll be famous."

"Famous?" Isaac turned his head to look straight at Phil. "Famous for what?"

"For preserving the greatest medical marvel mankind has ever known."

"Mankind? That's a lot of people. How do you figure that?"

Phil took a moment to consider his next words. Can Isaac handle some honest talk? If so, it would make Phil's job a lot easier. Phil took a chance and tested the waters, "You do realize we can't keep a discovery like this to ourselves, don't you? It just wouldn't be right."

"That's your plan? You plan to, like, tell the world?"

Phil noticed Isaac had lifted his foot off the gas pedal. The car was slowing down. So Phil pulled back on the honesty a bit. "I'm not talking right away, of course. I mean someday in the far, distant future. Now that we know what's causing this we'll be able to locate it ourselves and, one day, present it for scientific study."

The look on Isaac's face told Phil he was making a mistake, that this was no time for a lesson in ethics. Phil needed this boy's help, and he needed it now.

Isaac's foot was now hovering over the brake. Phil sped up his lying, "But I'm talking a long way in the future. Not now. Hell, maybe never." Phil watched Isaac carefully. The truck was still slowing, so Phil hastily added, "Right now we should concentrate our efforts on getting rid of this little black dude who's trying to run off with your girlfriend."

Isaac put his foot back on the gas pedal and said, "She's not my girlfriend."

"No? Well, she should be. Make a lot more sense than her being *his* girlfriend."

That did the trick. The truck sped up again.

There's a time for honesty and a time for bullshit. Even if it's racist bullshit.

• • •

Carol stayed inside the patrol car while Chief Dagleish went to inspect the burned-out minibus. If there is a dead body inside that thing, she certainly doesn't want to see it.

Of course, she knew it couldn't be Phil's body in there — she had talked to Phil on the phone early this morning and according to an old prospector named Crazy Lucas who lives down the road, this bus was set ablaze sometime around eleven last night.

Chief Dagleish suspects the arsonist was Isaac Beckwith, the neighborhood firebug who had attempted to burn down Shangri-La Gardens. The big question for Carol now is, was Isaac alone when he did this or was Phil with him at the time? Several people saw Phil and Isaac leave the meeting at the Opera House together last evening, and nobody has seen either of them since.

Carol opened the car window. Thinking of Phil going over the top like this was actually making her a little dizzy. It's like she was losing him, not to another woman but to a crazy cult. This isn't like Phil at all. He's usually so sensible. He can't possibly believe this baloney about people here never aging.

Carol needed some fresh air. She opened the door and stepped out into the mid-morning sunlight. She proceeded toward the river bank, but in the opposite direction, away from the charred corpse of that VW bus. She was seeking a more hopeful tableau. And she soon found it.

A couple of ducks, a handsome iridescent drake and whatever a female duck is called, were leading a line of little downy ducklings along the water. The river's flow must have been fairly strong because the family of adorable waterfowl was paddling like crazy but barely making any headway against the current. Carol knew the feeling well. She thought of her own brood of paddling quackers.

Nate and Taylor were currently splashing around at the Perpetuity Water Park. After breakfast, Carol had dropped them both off with instructions for Taylor to watch over her brother so Mom could help Chief Dagleish go hunt for their duck-brained father.

Thinking of her children brought to mind Taylor's new boyfriend, the owner of this burned out VW bus. Taylor seems to be somewhat smitten with the guy, which doesn't thrill Carol at all. Oh, he seems nice enough, but nobody in town really knows anything about him, just some ridiculous rumors. Carol is not worried about his being a space alien, of course — that's just the silliness of small voices made large by social media. No, what Carol is worried about is the way Kip avoids talking specifically about what he's doing here — what precisely it is he's come to *clean up*. Who knows what Taylor could be getting herself involved with. Of course, if there's a dead body up there in that burned-out bus and it turns out to be Kip's, well, that would certainly take care of that problem. Carol was not proud of this line of thought, but it didn't stop her from thinking it.

Carol watched the ducks fighting their way against the current and wished she could yell at the mother duck, *tell your family to turn their little feathered asses around and paddle the other way, downstream with the current*. But ducks, kids, and husbands have to learn for themselves. Yelling rarely helps.

From behind her she heard a voice call out, "It's okay." It was Chief Dagleish returning from the minibus. "Nobody inside."

Carol shouted back, "Great." And she meant it. Carol climbed the river bank to meet the police chief.

He held up an empty gas can. "Isaac's. I know it well."

A cell phone rang. The Chief placed the gas can down on the sand so he could pull his phone from his pocket. After checking the caller I.D. he answered, "Morning, Rupe."

After a few moments of *Uh huhs*, *yeahs*, and *thank you*, Dagleish signed off. He proceeded to fill Carol in, "Seems Rupert Thatcher was driving home for lunch when he was almost run off the road by his daughter." The Chief picked up his gas can and proceeded to lead Carol back to the squad car. "Says she was in his Road Runner. Going like a bat out of hades. Very strange. Becky's a quiet sort. Doesn't usually drive like that."

"Uh, huh?" Carol didn't know what else to say to this seemingly minor news bulletin. She felt there was more to it. And there was.

"Becky had a passenger with her. Young. Male. Black."

Carol knew what to say to this. "Kip."

"Don't get many fellas like that 'round here. Rupert figures it must be a carjacking."

Carol certainly knew what to say to this. "That's a bit racist, isn't it?"

"Welcome to Perpetuity." Chief Dagleish still had one more point to make, one final detail from Rupert's report. "Becky's car was being followed by a truck. A truck I know as well as I know this gas can."

"Isaac Beckwith's truck?"

The Chief nodded, yes.

Carol was afraid to ask this next question, but the cop seemed to be waiting for it, "Was Isaac alone in the truck?"

Dagleish shook his head a silent, *no, ma'am.*

By the look on the police chief's face Carol didn't have to ask who the passenger was. She simply asked, "Any idea where they were going?"

"Yes, I believe so." With that said, Chief Dagleish started dialing his phone. "And we'll need backup."

• • •

Taylor Hodworth cinched up the belt of her chiffon caftan so it covered more of her one-piece bathing suit. No point in giving those pervs at the snack bar a free show. She placed her plastic cup of diet soda on the table and sat down on the plastic chair across from her idiot brother who was using a plastic spoon to pick little red berries, one by one, off the top of his ice cream. After a moment or two of watching this nonsense she finally had to say something, "Why did you order them if you didn't know what they were?"

"'Cause they're called buffalo berries."

"So, what... you thought they'd taste like buffalo?"

He picked out another berry with surgical precision and deposited it onto the pile with the others. "No, but I sure didn't think they'd taste like buffalo shit."

"Shhh!" Taylor glanced around the snack bar patio to see if anybody had heard her foul-mouthed brother. "Watch your language, toad. We're in public."

"Not *very* public." Nate said, continuing with his picking.

The little squirt was right. This so-called amusement park was beyond grim. Apart from the two old perverts seated at the snack bar and a sprinkling of middle-aged women standing in the wave pool like zombies waiting for the noon tide to bring them more brains to eat, this place was empty. Sure, occasionally one or two kids around Nate's age will come shooting down the giant slide and into the pool, but the kids always arrive silently with no screams of joy like you'd hear at a normal water park. And as for older teenagers, well forget it. Taylor hasn't seen any kids her own age anywhere, not even working as staff which is odd considering that seasonal places like this usually employ college students for the summer. God, this place is so freaky.

And so boring. Taylor spent the entire morning doing nothing but watching her little brother splash around in the wave pool and mess around on the children's slide. He wanted to use the big slide, but Mom instructed Taylor not to take him on the chair lift, which made getting to the top of the slide impossible. Just an hour ago, Mom texted to say she wouldn't be coming until at least one o'clock, so they should go ahead and eat something. That's why Taylor is here at the snack bar keeping an eye on the parking area below, hoping Mom shows early. No sign of her car yet, though. There is, however, some action happening down there on the road.

An old muscle car, like from the stone age or something, was racing along the road in a cloud of dust. When it reached the entrance to the park, it pulled a sharp left into the parking lot. What an idiot. The moron shouldn't be driving that fast, not with kids around. Okay, there were no kids around, but he couldn't be sure of that.

The driver zipped past the designated parking spots and straight up to the ticket booth where he skidded to a stop. The car door flew open. The driver jumped out. Holy crap, it was a woman. A young woman. Maybe even a teenager. From this distance Taylor couldn't tell.

Nate, who was ignoring the fuss that was going on below, said, "You know, once you get the berries out, this ice cream isn't half bad."

Taylor looked at her brother. "You're dripping it on your shorts." She turned her attention back to the action that was playing out down at the bottom of the hill.

The girl driver was standing by the side of her car, waiting while her passenger stepped out of the other side. Unlike the crazy driver, the passenger was in no hurry. He moved cool. Kind of graceful. He was slender. Not too tall. African-American. And he was wearing oddly colored—

Taylor stood up. She squinted to make sure her eyes weren't playing tricks on her. Unfortunately, they were not. The male passenger was indeed wearing a paisley shirt, a brown leather vest with fringes, and bell-bottomed pants. So this was why Kip hadn't answered her texts. He already has a girlfriend. A hot blonde with a sports car.

"Wanna try some?" Nate held his spoon out to Taylor. When Taylor didn't answer him back, Nate looked at her with some concern. "You okay?"

Taylor used the sleeve of her chiffon caftan to wipe away a tear as she said to her brother, "Who would want your stupid ice cream after you've had your grubby little fingers in it?"

She now noticed two more cars pull into the parking lot. And then a pickup truck. And then another car. Taylor's eyes tracked up along that dirt road that led into the park. Lots of dust. Lots more cars. It was like a parade, and it seems Kip and his hot girlfriend were the grand marshals.

Taylor pressed her stomach against the cold stone wall and leaned over it to get a better look straight down at the pedestrian walkway that snakes into the park. No sign of Kip and his blonde girlfriend anymore. They must have entered the grounds and were now covered by the tree tops. Taylor turned her eyes up towards the road and noticed a police car racing along the two-lane blacktop. The car's cherry lights were flashing, but the siren was silent.

Could Kip and the over-weight blonde be in trouble? Well. Maybe she wasn't over weight, but she certainly had a few pounds on Taylor.

Taylor now turned around toward the patio tables again but looked beyond them, beyond Nate, beyond the snack bar, beyond the pervs at the counter. She gazed across the lawn to the boarding platform for the chair lift. No winter skiers there today, of course. Just two people walking toward the lift — Kip and his girlfriend. No, they weren't walking. They were running. Hand in hand. Like eloping lovers.

Taylor tucked herself under the shade of an awning so Kip wouldn't see her. From the shadows she watched the happy couple wait for the next bench seat to arrive. They didn't look lovey-dovey or anything, but Kip certainly looked relaxed and comfortable with her.

The girl, however, didn't look so relaxed. And she certainly didn't look comfortable.

As a matter of fact, she looked downright terrified.

CHAPTER TWENTY-THREE

Suspended high over the rocky hillside, Rebecca Thatcher twisted round in the ski lift's bench seat to look down at the line of benches trailing behind her. She and Kip were now about halfway up the mountain, and so far all the benches following were still empty. Thank the Lord.

She turned back to Kip, "We'll have to work fast."

"But you say these rocks are set in concrete."

"All you have to do is locate your stone, make note of where it is, then come back later. Tonight. After dark. We can bring whatever tools we need. A pick axe should suffice." Rebecca twisted around once again to check the line of chairs following below.

Two figures were just about to board a bench. They appeared to be two men, probably Isaac and his new friend, Mr. Hodworth, but they were too far away to say for certain.

"Upsy daisy. Here we are," Kip said as the chair approached the loading platform at the top of the mountain. He fiddled with the chair's safety bar. "So, what do I do with this doo-hickey?"

Rebecca lifted the bar for him and pushed it out of the way. She then jumped off so she could help him step away from the swaying bench seat. For a physically graceful man, Kip seemed rather uncomfortable with machinery. Rebecca couldn't help but tease him, "I'll bet you're not crazy about riding escalators either."

"Don't know. Never ridden one."

"Neither have I," Becky said. She kept tight hold of Kip's hand. "We mustn't dawdle." She tried her best to hurry him along, across the grassy knoll, but Kip just didn't get it. The poor man simply had no idea what danger he was facing now that the townsfolk know who he is and why he is here. Rebecca wanted to tell him that Isaac Beckwith is not alone in his thinking that violence, especially gun violence, was the key to preventing change and conserving the status quo. There are plenty more men and women in town just like him — good people but frightened people who shoot first and ask questions later, questions they think they already know the answers to. A good man like Kip could never understand this. Luckily, Kip has Rebecca's hand to guide him. Just as Rebecca has the Lord's.

So hand-in-hand-in-hand she and the Lord led Kip across the grass-topped mountain dome toward the far side of the park. That's where the brick, ranch-style clubhouse of The Perpetuity Ski Club sits gazing out at God's beautiful Perpetuity Valley by the shore of God's equally lovely Perpetuity Lake. The mountain's summit park wasn't terribly busy today. Rebecca noted only a half-dozen or so unfamiliar faces strolling the paths. Tourists were always easy to spot up here — they were the ones who still showed awe and wonder in their appreciation of the heavenly view.

As quickly as ever she could, Rebecca led Kip along the flagstone walkway to the front of the clubhouse. She didn't, however, take him into the building. Instead, she led him around the side and down the hill to the back, to the lake side.

The clubhouse, a split-level affair, had been wedged into the hillside close beside the lake. The main floor of the clubhouse sat level with the upper, grassy dome of the park. Becky's interest lay round back where the building's bottom floor sits level with the lake. This backyard is popular in winter when members of the ski club, which is everyone in the valley, get together for their Saturday night swim and steam parties. It's an invigorating event. While the snow falls and the cold winds blow, the party-goers run out from the change rooms and jump into the hot spring waters of Perpetuity Lake. After bathing in the warm, soothing mineral waters, they then dash back through the snow and finish off their evening in the steam room. Becky generally finds the hot swim and subsequent sprint through the snow quite revitalizing. Unlike her neighbors, though, Becky does not take the plunge au naturel. And she skips the following co-ed steam bath entirely. Any Christian girl would.

Becky and Kip hurried down the gentle slope and circled around the rear of the building. Here, she finally let go of his hand and paused to rest. Becky was out of breath from the excitement, so she just pointed to the wall and let him have a look.

Kip understood. "These from the river?"

She nodded. "Mostly from Wilson's Falls."

The foundation wall was constructed of plain concrete blocks. To spruce them up, the town had faced them with decorative, fist-sized river rocks. Kip ran his hand slowly over the rocks. "The water wears them smooth like this?"

Rebecca didn't answer. She heard voices. Someone was coming. She said to Kip, "Please, hurry."

Kip reached down the front of his paisley shirt and lifted out the chain necklace with the little Geiger gadget thing attached. He switched the device on, and proceeded to walk along the wall, carefully watching the screen of the little gizmo. Meanwhile, Becky stayed right where she was, at the bottom corner of the building with her eye focused on the hillside beside the clubhouse.

No sign of Isaac. Nor his friend, Mr. Hodworth. But somebody was coming. She turned her eyes back to Kip. Heavens, can he not go any faster? He's working at a snail's pace. Impatience is a sin, but she had to ask, "Anything?"

Kip answered by not answering. He just crept along that wall, inch-by-inch, his eyes glued to his little electronic gadget. Becky turned her eyes back to the top of the hill.

Two figures came into view. They stopped, stood in shaded profile, a man and a woman, backlit by the sun. The couple looked out toward the lake for a moment. Then they joined hands. She couldn't make out their faces, but they were obviously tourists. Few couples in Perpetuity held hands anymore.

When Rebecca looked back at Kip, he was walking this way.

"Nada," He reported. He slipped his gadget back under his shirt. "To be honest, I didn't really expect anything. That wall is too far away from the water. If the rosin was cemented into that thing, how could it affect your water supply?"

"I thought maybe... I don't know, maybe rain and snow might wash over it and run down into the lake or something."

"No way. Far too dry. I've checked your climate charts. This area is almost a desert. No, to still be working this well the rosin has to be routinely in touch with your ground water."

"And you've searched in the lake."

"First place I looked after I finished at the river. If it's in the deep center part, of course, I'm out of luck — my gizmo works only to about eight feet. But really, how would the rosin ever get in that lake? I never came up here. Would one of your people have thrown it into the lake?"

"I don't see why."

Ever positive, Kip bounced past Rebecca. "Oh, well, at least we tried." He continued up the hill.

Rebecca followed him, but slowly. She was so down and discouraged she was almost ready to use the Lord's name in vain. She was sure Kip's rock had been transported up here with the other rocks to be placed in that wall. The town had cannibalized that part of the river the way her father cannibalizes old cars for parts.

Kip was well ahead of her now, cresting the top of the rise. And as he did, he called out to someone unseen, "Howdy, gang. Glad you could join us."

Rebecca ran to catch up. She could see them now — a group of people was headed this way. A large group. Ten maybe a dozen townspeople. Walking side-by-side. In a line. Like an advancing army.

The army's ranks included Chief Dagleish, Mayor Beckwith, Violet Snelling, Pastor Gorely, Clay Dawson, Angus Murphy, his wife Colleen, plus a couple of visitors Becky recognized by face but not by name. And finally, over on the far right flank stood Becky's father. And what's that on his hip? Oh Lord, it's a holster. Daddy's wearing his gun. Becky hadn't seen her father carry his six-shooter for at least a hundred years. She noticed Chief Dagleish was toting a handgun as well.

Becky looked around for an escape route. But there wasn't one. With the lake behind her and the building beside her and the citizens advancing, she and Kip were boxed in.

Mayor Sam Beckwith called out, "It's okay, Becky. We mean your friend no harm. Just want to talk to the boy. That's all."

Kip smiled at the mob. He even waved a big hello to one person, a young woman whom Becky did not know. "Hey, Taylor," he called out. "How's tricks?" He then started toward her. "Saw your dad this morning. He says you—"

And that's all he got out before the rifle shot rang out.

Everybody froze. Everybody, that is, except Rebecca. She immediately turned to check on Kip.

He seemed fine, thank God. She turned back toward the group to see who had fired the shot. It had to be Isaac Beckwith. But she didn't see him anywhere around. And nobody in the group was holding a gun. In fact, they all seemed as surprised and as puzzled by the rifle's crack as Becky had been.

Becky had to get Kip out of here. She went to grab his hand.

"Don't move, miss," someone yelled at her, "or I'll shoot your friend."

It was a man's voice. And she thought she recognized it. And this time she could tell what direction it came from. So could everybody else.

One by one, the faces turned toward the small, single-story outbuilding about twenty yards away, the brick building that housed the public restrooms and maintenance equipment. And up top, high up on the flat roof, to absolutely nobody's surprise, stood Isaac Beckwith.

"Oh, for Christ's sake, son." Mayor Sam was never hesitant to speak the Lord's name in vain.

"Wasn't me, Pop." Isaac held out his empty arms to show he was indeed unarmed.

Then the voice of a woman cried out, "Phil!"

The woman who had shouted was standing beside Chief Dagleish, and she, too, was looking at the maintenance building. But her eyes were not fixed on the roof. Her attention was on the bottom corner of the structure, specifically the door to the men's room. That's where Mr. Hodworth was standing. With a rifle.

He stepped out from the shadows and into the sunlight, all the while keeping Isaac's buffalo rifle pointed this way.

"Daddy!" yelled the young woman whom Kip had addressed as Taylor. "What the fuck are you doing?"

Rebecca took full advantage of the young woman's profane distraction. Rebecca grabbed Kip's hand and yanked him along with her, down the hill. And as she ran, she heard the buffalo gun fire again. The shot was immediately followed by the voice of Rebecca's own father screaming out, "Don't shoot, you fool. You'll hit my daughter."

Rebecca's father had an excellent point. In fact, it was an inspiring point. Rebecca pulled Kip close to her to act as his shield. Together they rounded the bottom corner of the building. They continued along the back wall to the rear entrance. This back door was made of thick wooden boards and had a small window in it.

She tried the knob. Locked, of course. It always is in summer. But that's okay. She quickly dialed the four-number security code into the jam's electronic keypad. The latch clicked open. She pushed Kip in ahead of her and shut the door tight behind her. She threw the heavy bolt that overruled the electronic latch.

She and Kip were now standing in the ski club's mud room, the vestibule where skiers kick off boots and bathers grab towels. A dark hallway led to the locker rooms, steam room, and showers. But Becky didn't come here for a steam or a shower. She posted herself right here at the door where she could keep watch out the little window.

She watched the group of citizens come round the corner of the building. They didn't hug the wall the way Rebecca and Kip had done — they fanned out, dispersing themselves randomly between the building and the shore of the lake. They obviously weren't sure which way Rebecca had taken Kip. Had she come to this door or had she followed the paths out around the lake where she could hide him in the underbrush? Rebecca saw no sign of Mr. Hodworth or his rifle out there.

She glanced around behind her to check on what Kip was up to. He was wandering down the dark hallway. "Keep away from the windows," she warned. She knew there was a window in the change room.

Kip found a light switch and flipped it on. "Hey! Steam baths. Man, I love these things. Too bad we're pressed for time."

Becky had nothing to say to that. She just kept her attention on the crowd outside. As usual, the citizens of Perpetuity were proving themselves a disorganized lot. Some were strolling along the lake shore, as if their quarry might be hiding in the shallows. A few had continued across the property in case Rebecca had led Kip up around the far side of the building. Clay Dawson, however, was talking with Violet Snelling and pointing this way, toward this very door. Rebecca eased her head back from the window, hoping the light was too dark in here for them to have seen her.

Meanwhile, Kip called out from the steam room down the hall, "Wish this thing was turned on. I could really go for a spritz right about—" Kip's voice trailed off. Then, "Hey, what's this? These things kinda look like—"

Rebecca called to him, "We're going upstairs. I doubt they've posted anyone at the front door yet."

Kip called from down the hall. "You might want to come see this."

Becky was normally a patient woman. But this was too much. "Would you please stop fooling about. I'm trying to save your life. If you're not going to take this seriously..."

"Honest, you really ought to come see this."

Rebecca hurried to grab Kip and drag him upstairs with her. Drag him by the ears if need be.

When she found him, he was standing in the middle of the steam room. He was holding his Geiger counter gadget. "Look!" he said. "It's going ballistic."

Kip had his gadget pointed at the wooden bin of rocks — the pile of rocks which, when heated, produce the steam. And suddenly, like a flash of that steam, Rebecca understood. "Those rocks," she said. "They're from the river."

Kip slipped his Geiger gadget back into his shirt and started pulling out stones from the bin one-by-one and placing them onto the floor. He did this achingly slowly. But after a dozen or so discards he held up one particular rock that caught his interest. This one was smaller than the others. It was amber colored, smooth as soap, and sparkling with flecks of pink crystals. Feldspar, Rebecca would have guessed.

Kip tossed it into the air. He caught it. He turned to Becky. And he smiled.

"Your rosin?" she asked.

"It ain't chopped liver."

"May I?" She reached out to touch the magic rock.

"No, no." Kip pulled the stone away from her. "It might burn."

"But you're touching it."

"Like I told you, it affects everybody differently." Kip then pointed to the pile of rocks in the crib. "Your friends wear gloves when they built this?"

"Could have. Probably leather. Maybe cotton."

Kip turned his attention to a galvanized pipe that hung down over the wooden bin. The pipe ended at a shower nozzle, and that nozzle had a drip of water hanging from it. The drip didn't hang for long. It released and fell, landing right where Kip's magic rock had been sitting. And another drip took its place.

Kip ran a finger along a length of chain that hung from a lever on the nozzle. "You pull this to release water onto the heated rocks."

"Yes."

He continued, "And that water turns to steam."

"Yes."

"But not all of it." Kip looked down at the slatted cedar floor. "Some of it continues down through the cracks in the flooring and into a central drain."

Becky finished this thought. "Which empties into the lake." She understood his point but still had to ask, "And that little bit will do it?"

"Doesn't take much. Not for some genetically flawed beings." Kip clutched the rock and breathed a big sigh of relief. "I gotta tell you, Becks, I was getting a little freaked. I mean, I like your planet and all, but like Dorothy says..."

Rebecca finished the quote for him. "There's no place like home."

"And without this baby..."

"You'd never get home. You'd be stuck here. With me. Forever and ever. How awful." Rebecca smiled, tried to sound like she was joking.

"Oh, no, no, no." Kip could see that he had insulted her. "I didn't mean it that way. Hey, I'd be quite happy to be stuck here with you.

What man wouldn't?" Kip grabbed her by her shoulders. "You're quite the looker. A real dish. Geez, Becky, I gotta tell you, I've—"

"Stop it," Becky whispered placing her hand over his lips. She wanted him to be silent. She had heard wood cracking. Splintering. The front door was being forced open.

But Kip was on a roll. He pushed her hand away. "Rebecca, ever since I first fished you out of that river, I've gotta tell you, I haven't been able to forget you. But you see, my company has this rule. We're not allowed to fraternize with the—"

"Shhh!" she demanded. She heard footsteps. Someone was coming down the hall. Sounded like a man. A large man.

She indicated Kip's crystal rock. "Put that away."

"But—"

"Hide it!" She pushed his hand, the one clutching the crystal, down toward his pants. He got the message and pocketed the rock. Rebecca then let her hand continue its travel, slipping around Kip's hips. As she cupped his rear end, she whispered, "You never found that rock. We came in here to make love." She hooked her other hand round the back of his neck and pulled his face to hers. She kissed him.

He seemed to like this plan. He certainly got right into it. His mouth even opened slightly. She wasn't sure what to do next. But she had a pretty good idea. She opened hers. Then, just as her tongue started exploring his alien dental work, Rebecca heard a voice. And it was the last voice she wanted to hear in this position.

"Step back," her father bellowed.

She turned to see his dark form in the doorway. He was holding his six-shooter. Becky intentionally left her hand on Kip's rear end and kept him close to her. "Daddy, you remember Kip, the gentleman who saved me from drowning?"

Kip smiled. Her father didn't smile back. Undiscouraged, Kip extended his hand. "Pleased to meet you, sir."

Becky's father waved his Colt .45 at Kip. "Outside."

Becky kept Kip close as she marched him down the hallway with her father following. When they neared the front doorway, Becky noticed the splintered wooden bolt housing and a broken chunk of wood lying on the floor.

Before stepping outside, she called out through the open entranceway, "Don't shoot. We're coming out." Rebecca grasped Kip's hand and stepped out into the bright sunshine.

The town posse had swelled to include at least twenty or thirty townspeople. Somebody must have posted about this on line. The townsfolk were keeping well back from the doorway, none of them brave enough nor concerned enough to have accompanied Rebecca's father inside the building.

Over to the side, Chief Dagleish came striding down the hill. His deputy, Isaac Beckwith, was trailing along with him, but that was okay — the trigger-happy young man was not carrying a gun.

Chief Dagleish reported to the townsfolk that he couldn't locate Mr. Hodworth, the man with Isaac's buffalo rifle. The only people in the crowd who seemed upset by this news was the middle-aged woman named Carol and the young woman, Taylor, whom Becky assumed were Mr. Hodworth's wife and daughter.

Mayor Sam Beckwith seemed friendly towards Kip. The mayor stepped forward and invited him to attend a special meeting tonight, a meeting at which the citizens of Perpetuity will vote on whether they wish to pitch in and help Kip complete his mission or send the space man packing. This plan seemed fine with everybody in the crowd. Everyone, that is, except Isaac Beckwith.

"Why wait," Isaac suggested. "No time like the present, I always say. Let's go upstairs right now, up to the dining room. We can talk this over, see exactly what this space man has in mind for us." Isaac turned to the crowd and added, "I happen to know the fridges have been left running. Lots of cold beer."

The crowd thought this was a fine idea. So did Mayor Beckwith and Chief Dagleish. But Rebecca didn't like it one bit. First, she didn't trust Isaac. And second, she didn't trust this particular bunch of townsfolk gathered here. She knew that the valley's truly reasonable citizens were home relaxing, watching television, playing video games, or posting inspirational thoughts on social media. Who knows what this group of fired-up activists and reactionaries, will decide to do with Kip. No, a hasty meeting will be wrong. A discussion of this importance requires an assemblage of cool, rational citizens.

But alas, it was too late — the crowd had heard about the cold beer. They were already filing through the basement door to take the stairs up to the dining room. On the plus side, Rebecca has noticed that her father has put his old handgun away.

She and Kip marched along with the others down the narrow hallway to the stairs. As they walked, the clip-clops of their flip-flops and the click-clacks of Chief Dagleish's leather police boots reverberating off the concrete walls. When she had a chance, Becky leaned close to Kip and whispered, "Don't forget — you haven't located your magic rock. You are still searching for it. Okay?"

"It's not magic," he corrected her.

"Whatever it is, these people must not know you've found it."

"I enjoyed our kiss."

Rebecca pressed on. "Do you understand?"

"Mind if I stay in your barn another night?"

"First things first," Becky said.

"Is that a *yes*?"

Becky could only smile.

The group reached the top of the stairs and started walking across the club's main foyer toward the dining room. Up here, the floor was carpeted, so the footsteps were silent. Plus, any reverberation was muffled by the draperies and the flocked velvet wallpaper. All this was probably why, when Rebecca and her neighbors had been climbing the stairs, nobody had heard the window glass breaking up here.

Clay Dawson was first to discover the mess. "Holy shit," he said as he entered the main dining room. "What the fuck happened here?"

The double French doors on the far wall were spread wide open, and one of those doors was missing several panes of glass. A sparkling wedge of sunlight painted the parquet floor in broken crystal shards. A sheer, white, floor-length curtain swayed in the gentle breeze like the nightgown of a grand lady who had just left her boudoir to come see what the fuss was all about. But of course, every person in this room knew what the fuss was all about. They knew somebody had broken into the dining room. And they knew who that person must be. What they did not know was where that person was hiding. Not until he stepped out from the kitchen.

Phil Hodworth was clutching the buffalo gun. His lethal weapon wasn't aimed at anyone in particular, but his lethal words were. "That's far enough, Kip. You're coming with me."

Becky immediately looked across the room at Isaac. Yes, he was smiling. This was why he had suggested coming in here. He and Mr. Hodworth had cooked this up together. Becky touched Kip's arm. "Don't move. Stay right where you are."

Carol Hodworth stepped forth and addressed her husband as if he were a belligerent child, "Phil, what the hell do you think you're doing?"

"You'll live to thank me, Carol. You all will. You people don't know what you have here. You never did. You thought it was some sort of magic voodoo or some such nonsense. A miracle from heaven. A blessing from God. Sent just for you. But you were wrong. It's not God. And it's not meant just for you. It's science. Cold hard science. And it belongs to everyone. You can't keep science to yourselves. It has to be shared. For Christ's sake, the world has to know about this miracle drug."

Rebecca had to say something or she would burst. "Sir, I can't let you blaspheme. I can't let you take the Lord's name in vain."

Clay Dawson jumped on the bandwagon. "And don't hand us bullshit about wanting to save the world. We know why you're here. You just want to save your own wrinkled ass."

Taylor Hodworth came to her father's defense. ""That's not true. You don't know Daddy. He pulls shit like this all the time. He's a very principled man."

A young boy, probably Mr. Hodworth's son, added, "And his ass isn't wrinkled."

Carol Hodworth stepped forward to try and settle her husband down. "Honey, I know you think you're doing the right thing. I know you mean well. But this isn't the way." Carol's voice sounded sweet. Soothing. Like a psychiatrist trying to talk an emotionally fragile patient off a window ledge. "Just put down the gun. Okay? I'm sure these good people will do the right thing. I'm sure they'll agree to keep the medicine and send Kip on his way."

"Sorry, Carol." Phil Hodworth stayed frozen to his spot. "You don't know these people. They're not going to fight this man. They *can't* fight him. There's no fight left in them. They're just going to sit back and let what happens happen. I'm sorry. Somebody has to do something."

"I understand." Carol took a step closer to her husband. "You're right. We have to find out what's going on here. And that's just what we'll do. Just put down the gun, darling. Okay? Please? For me?"

Rebecca was touched by this sight. This brave woman was walking straight into the barrel of a loaded weapon, and yet she showed no fear. This was trust. This was faith. This was true love. Becky hadn't seen devotion like this in a long, long time. That's why Rebecca couldn't believe what she saw next.

Phil Hodworth raised the rifle and pointed it straight at his wife. At her chest. The heart of his true love. He then slipped his finger from off the guard and onto the trigger. Rebecca knew this gun. She knew how Isaac had bragged about shaving the action down to a hair trigger. One involuntary twitch from Mr. Hodworth and his wife would be dead.

The look on Carol Hodworth's face was... well, Rebecca had never seen anything quite like it before. It wasn't shock. And it wasn't fear. It was far worse. It was the look of a woman seeing her entire universe crumble before her very eyes.

The picture was so painful Becky had to look away. And as she did so she heard Phil Hodworth ask Kip, "So have you found it? Have you found the crystal?"

Rebecca jumped in, "No, he hasn't."

"I wasn't asking you." Mr. Hodworth turned back to Kip. "Have you? Have you got it?"

All eyes went to Kip. And what they saw was the tortured face of a good, strong man wrestling with a moral dilemma. Truth obviously meant a great deal to Kip. Bearing false witness does not come easily. Rebecca suspected it will not come at all.

Mr. Hodworth pressed further, "Was it where you thought? In that wall?"

"Wall? What wall?" This question came from Mayor Beckwith.

Isaac Beckwith explained to his father, "I told Mr. Hodworth about the wall, the one we faced with river rock. I figured if the space guy had dropped his crystal stone in the river by Wilson's Falls, it might have ended up here."

The mayor smiled. He was impressed, "And you figured that out yourself?"

"Yes, sir. I did."

The mayor grinned like a father who has just watched his son hit one out of the park.

Meanwhile, Becky noticed Kip's face brightening, a twinkle coming to Kip's eyes as if he were seeing a new dawn breaking, a clear blue sky with no lies, fibs, or prevarications on the horizon.

Kip turned to Mr. Hodworth and said, "Actually, I had just begun searching the wall for my... my crystal thingy when you folks showed up. I hadn't found it, though. Then you folks came along and, at Becky's suggestion, we booted it. But hey, if you'd like to follow me I'll be happy to show you where I last left off. We can resume the search together. Come along. Always good to have an extra pair of eyes. And a nose. I promise you, if I find my crystal there it's yours. Follow me." And with that said, Kip proceeded to walk through the open French doors and outside onto the patio.

Phil Hodworth paused for a moment to weigh his choices. Then he took his finger off the trigger, but he kept the gun in hand, and followed Kip outside.

Becky had no idea what Kip had up his sleeve, but one look at his tight pants told her he still had that rock of rosin safely tucked away in his pocket.

The assembled crowd, keeping a safe distance from the crazy man with the gun, proceeded to trickle out the door and onto the front lawn. But Becky hung back. She was waiting for someone. Becky didn't want to seem too familiar with the woman, but she just had to say something.

When Carol trailed the parade out the doorway, Becky stepped close and placed a gentle hand on the woman's forearm. "I'm sure your husband would never have harmed you."

Carol said nothing. She just smiled at Becky's kind words.

Becky continued, "I'm sure it was all a bluff. He was just trying to show everybody in that room that he means business."

Carol accepted the words gracefully. She patted Becky's hand. "Thank you. I'm sure you're right." Carol and Becky stepped out into the sunshine together.

Becky just wished that Kip could lie as well as Carol Hodworth just did.

• • •

With the heavy buffalo rifle still clutched in his hands, Phil followed the little space guy around the side of the clubhouse and down the grassy slope to the rear of the building. When they reached the bottom corner, Phil paused to look back up the hill for any sign of the townsfolk. Nobody there yet, so he turned his attention back to Kip.

The space alien was strolling along beside the wall, sweeping his hand slowly over the decorative stones. His slender brown finger tips massaged the smooth rocks with a gentle, tentative touch like a jeweler's hand assessing a diamond for the first cut.

Phil stuck his hand in his pants pocket and nervously jingled the bullets that he'd removed from the gun. Of course, he'd never have pulled that stunt back there with a loaded weapon. A warning shot from up top of the hill was one thing, but Phil wasn't dumb enough to take a loaded gun into a crowded room.

As Kip examined the stones, the young man explained to Phil, "Since these were removed from the river, their colors have deteriorated significantly. Your planet's precipitation is highly corrosive."

"Probably the acid rain. We made a lot of it back in the sixties." Phil was starting to relax. This guy wasn't a bad sort, really.

"Ahh, the swingin' sixties." Kip said. "Glen Campbell ever tour these parts?"

"I'm afraid Glen's touring days are over." Phil couldn't believe this man's short attention span. "Any sign of the crystal?"

"No more Glen Campbell. Gee, that's a drag. Lovely voice. Underrated guitarist. Did you know he played on some of the Beach Boys tracks?"

Phil was starting to think about loading the rifle again. This guy had the attention span of fruit fly.

But then Kip suddenly exclaimed, "Whoa, Nelly! Here's something." He tapped and scratched a stone. "Hear that?"

Phil stepped closer to the wall to listen. And while Kip tapped some more and scratched some more, Phil pondered his next move. Of course, he never planned to actually shoot this little guy, but Kip doesn't know that. He probably thinks all Earthlings are as trigger-happy as that Isaac Beckwith kid. Kip can't possibly know what a pussy cat Phil really is. Carol does, of course. She knew Phil wasn't serious back there. She knows he would never pull a loaded gun on her. Not in a million years. But she certainly played her part well. Geez, that look on her face... utter shock. Phil never realized Carol was such a good actor. Or was she? Geez, could she actually have thought—

"You've been an idiot!" Kip shouted.

"Huh?"

"Idiot, idiot, idiot."

"But she had to know I was just bluff—"

"Not you — me." Kip scratched at the rock. "I should have seen it. I must have walked right past this thing a dozen times. This baby, right here." Kip tapped a fingernail on the rock. "Hear it? Different mass. Different specific gravity. It produces a higher pitch from the others. Hear it ping? Twenty-two hundred hertz — what you people call a double-high D flat. Here, have a listen." Kip stepped aside, so Phil could get closer.

The rock in question lay imbedded at the bottom of the wall, so Phil had to bend down to listen as Kip tapped. "Yes, yes," Phil said. "I hear it. A higher pitch." Feeling almost giddy with delight, Phil crouched lower to get his ear closer. And then lower. And lower. Too low, actually.

It was Phil's own fault. With his knees folded under him like this and his weight forward on his toes, his center of gravity was off. Kip had no trouble pushing Phil back with one hand while snatching the rifle away with the other.

With his empty arms flailing, trying to clutch handfuls of the thin mountain air, Phil tumbled backwards onto the flagstone path. Happily, his shoulders hit first, easing the bounce for his head. Still, his world spun. He shut his eyes tight. And when he opened them again Phil was surprised at the picture that greeted him.

Phil expected to see Kip towering over him, pointing the rifle's huge muzzle inches away from his face. But no, that wasn't the scene at all. Instead, he saw Kip, the supposedly superior being from another planet, doing something quite dumb. Rather than use his newly gained weapon to his advantage, Kip was running away with the thing. Sure, he clutched the rifle tight as he sprinted, but he didn't try to use it. Did he know the weapon wasn't loaded? Phil watched Kip skid around the far side of the building and disappear up the far hill. Meanwhile, the townsfolk were now arriving from around this near corner of the building.

Phil struggled to get to his feet, but he couldn't do it — the wind had been knocked out of him. The best he could do was lean on one sore elbow and watch the action unfold. He'll just have to lie here and watch the horde of angry villagers chase the monster, watch them stop the thief who was threatening to steal away their magic, their youth, their eternal life. But of course that's not what Phil saw at all. What he saw was a gaggle of kind, caring simpletons amble toward him to check on their newest neighbor's welfare.

Police Chief Dagleish was the first to enquire. "You okay?"

"I... I'm fine," Phil wheezed. He pointed to the far corner. "He's down there."

The cop extended an arm to help. Phil gladly accepted the offer and got to his feet. As he fought to draw air back into his lungs, he again pointed to the far side of the clubhouse, "He's... he's getting away. Hurry. Get him!"

But the lawman didn't get much of anything, including Phil's desperation. The cop didn't chase after the alien. He didn't fire a warning shot at the alien. Shit, the guy didn't even draw his big ol' forty-five revolver. All he did was point to Phil's leg and say, "We better wash that off."

Phil looked down at his pants to see what the cop was talking about. He'd torn them and apparently scraped his knee on a flagstone. It was bleeding. But not much. He turned back to the cop. "He's getting away!" Phil repeated.

"Ever heard of lock jaw? Tetanus? Tell me, Phil, have you had your shots?"

"For Christ sakes," Phil's cried. "If you don't stop him, I will." And with that, Phil yanked the cop's pistol out of its holster. It was easy — the clasp on the old cracked leather was broken.

"Aww, geez, Phil." The cop raised his hands in the air even though Phil wasn't pointing the gun at him. "Cool down, fella."

But Phil had no intention of cooling down. Clutching the cop's revolver tight, Phil took off. He jogged around the corner of the clubhouse and up the hill. It wasn't easy. Phil's lungs were still struggling with the thin mountain air, but that didn't matter. One way or another, Phil is going to stop this guy. Sure, Kip may not have the magic crystal with him yet — not if it's the one he just found stuck in this wall — but what if that was all just a ruse. What if Kip was the one who was bluffing. Sure, the space guy dresses like a moron, acts like a moron, but seriously — any creature from a civilization that is smart enough to beat genetics at its own game should have no trouble outwitting an Earthling marketing executive who sells ginseng memory supplements, ginseng boner pills, and ginseng car wax.

As Phil reached the top of the hill, his heart was pounding like he'd just downed a case of his ginseng energy drink. Kip was a good hundred yards ahead. Phil took a deep breath and poured on more speed. But before he got halfway across the park's dome of grass Phil had to pause to catch his breath again. He glanced back to check on the policeman and the crowd of townsfolk that were chasing after him.

Yup, they were following him, all right. But they weren't exactly in a hurry about it. The group seemed to have expanded. Most of them, maybe a couple dozen or so, were sauntering along casually, like a tour group returning to their bus after a particularly filling lunch. The police chief whose pistol Phil had stolen was ambling casually beside a man whom Phil recognized to be the local preacher, Pastor Gorely. Close behind them walked young Isaac, Phil's partner in crime who had helped orchestrate this whole scheme. Isaac looked at Phil and waved, but he didn't rush over to join the chase. He just waved.

The Irish motel manager, Angus Murphy, and his hot wife Colleen also walked with the parade. When Colleen saw Phil, she flashed her big juicy smile. Then she blew him a kiss as if this was all some sort of party game.

At seventy-something, the newspaper woman, Violet Snelling, was striding at a pretty good clip. She was too old to sprint, of course, but at least she was trying. Clay, the skateboarding teenager in the flat bill baseball cap, was certainly young enough to run if he wanted to, but he was too cool and too hip to risk breaking a sweat.

A dozen more locals whom Phil recognized but didn't know by name had joined the meandering herd. Unfortunately, not a single one of them seemed terribly excited about the idea of initiating a stampede to save themselves, their eternal youth, or their magical valley.

In other words, it looks like Phil is alone. It's all up to him. He just hopes he has the lungs for it. Or the stomach for it. Kip was now a good hundred yards away, and even if Phil did have the guts to shoot, his target was far out of range for a pistol. Maybe a warning shot will do it.

Phil couldn't tell if the safety was on or off, so he just pointed the handgun straight up at the blue sky and pulled the trigger.

An innocent white cumulonimbus took the bullet without flinching, but the explosion almost deafened Phil. And the kick-back just about broke his wrist. Meanwhile, Kip just kept on scurrying along. The warning shot hadn't slowed the alien down one bit. Phil stuck the heavy revolver into the waistband of his chino pants and resumed the chase. After a few steps, he stopped, reconsidered his weapon storage, and switched the gun to the relative safety of his pants pocket. No point in living forever if you've blown your balls off.

Phil followed Kip past the water slide tower and along the gravel path that led farther up the hill to the chair lift boarding platform.

Looks like Kip is planning to catch the next passing bench down to the bottom.

But no. The space alien scooted right past the chair lift and over the crest of the dome to a patch of rough ground on the far side where the cliff dropped sharply off the mountain. Here, perched on the lip of the precipice, Kip started swinging the buffalo rifle in a wide circle like an Olympic hammer thrower winding up for a toss. He let the weapon fly, and the big-bore gun sailed out over the treetops and tumbled down into the canopy to be swallowed up by the pine forest far below.

Phil took advantage of the moment to turn and see what the parade of townsfolk behind him was up to. Had they organized themselves into a serious posse yet? Had Phil's gunshot sparked them to action?

Of course not. In fact, what they were doing now made Phil's jaw drop.

The whole herd of locals had jammed to a stop at the bottom of the wooden tower of the water slide where, one by one, the ageless and carefree twits were climbing the steps to the launch platform. Once at the top, each participant then plopped his or her useless bum onto the fiberglass chute and then let themselves go. "Yippee!" they yelled as they threw their hands over their empty heads with glee and slipped into the warm flow of tumbling waters gliding down the mountainside.

Phil searched the crowd for any sign of Carol. But no luck. She must have decided to stay back at the clubhouse building with Taylor and Nate. Smart woman.

Phil turned his attention back to Kip and saw that, after throwing that rifle away, the alien had circled round, back to the chair lift.

Phil broke out in a sprint, but the run didn't last long — his injured knee was killing him. He limped along watching as a bench seat arrived at the lift platform.

Kip assumed the standard crouch position in preparation to mount the moving seat, but his first attempt failed. The seat passed him by, vacant of alien butt. The little guy seemed to be having trouble coordinating his skinny rear end with the moving target. Phil yanked the heavy revolver out of his pocket.

Using both hands to steady it, he aimed the weapon at the spaceman. But of course, Phil couldn't shoot the guy. He wanted to, but he just couldn't. So he tilted the barrel toward the sky and injured another perfectly innocent cloud.

Once again, the noise had no effect on the alien. Kip was busy concentrating all his attention on planting his bell-bottom jeans firmly onto this next bench seat.

Phil shoved the gun back into his pocket and took off again, each step causing the heavy revolver to clank like a bell clapper against Phil's fifty-year-old scrotum.

The chair arrived, and this time the space alien succeeded in boarding it. But that's okay. Phil was now within easy reach. He should be able to yank the little guy off that bench before it gets very high off the ground.

At least, that's what Phil told himself as he hurled himself like Superman into the thin air and across the widening void that now stretched between the swinging chair and the swiftly departing granite mountainside.

CHAPTER TWENTY-FOUR

The ground dropped away. By the time Phil had his hands firmly planted onto the back of the seat, the chair was a good five feet off the ground.

By the time Phil had swung his right leg up and over the back of the bench, the chair was a good twelve feet above the ground.

And by the time Phil realized he had screwed up and was not going to make it all the way up into the seat, the chair was twenty feet high and Phil's fifty-year-old ass was dangling helplessly in mid-air, high over a mountainside of solid rock, swaying in the gusty breeze like a hairy pink wind chime.

Phil struggled to pull himself farther up onto the bench, but he simply couldn't do it. His arms were just too weak. He'd made a big mistake. Probably a fatal one. His two hands and one leg might hold him dangling in this position for a minute or two, but they will not hold all the way to the end of this ride.

Phil didn't look down. There was no need to. He knew he'd never survive the fall, especially if he fell backwards like this. Upside down. Head first. Onto solid granite.

He grunted and twisted and pulled for all he was worth, but now his hands were slippery with sweat. He was losing his grip.

"Here, Phil," Kip said. "You look like you could use a hand." And with that, Kip bent over and grabbed the back of Phil's waistband. With one good yank, and a wedgie that brought tears to Phil's eyes, the space alien pulled him up, over, and into the seat. Man, this little guy was stronger than he looked.

Phil wanted to say thank you, but he couldn't — he was too busy gasping for breath. He could only look down through the slats of the bench and watch the mountainside fall away, thirty feet below. Maybe forty.

Meanwhile, Kip apologized, "Sorry, man."

"Huh?" Phil struggled to fill his lungs. "What?"

Kip thumbed back toward the top of the mountain. "The physical violence back there. Shoving you over like that. I don't like pulling that heavy stuff. But geez, man, that rifle... your planet's firearms freak me out."

Phil checked to make sure the pistol was still safe in his pocket. It was. But he didn't pull it out. He had a more important matter to take care of. "The crystal rock," he asked. "You've got it on you, right?"

Kip seemed genuinely contrite. "Sorry I had to mislead you. Yeah, I got it."

"And you're taking it away."

"No choice."

"You don't care about your friends? About Rebecca? About my daughter?"

"Sure, I do. I care about all of you." Kip looked at Phil's bloodied knee and asked. "Did I do that?"

"It's okay. I'll live."

"That's true, you will. You all will. I promise." Kip looked out across the green valley, the brown hills and the far purple mountains. "This is a nice place. Now your friends will be able to get out and enjoy it. That'll be cool. Hell, I'd like to see a few spots around here, myself. Mount Rushmore is near here, isn't it?"

"Yes. Matter of fact, I was planning on taking the kids there on my way home." Phil suddenly got a brain wave. "You can come along with us if you'd like."

Kip's eyes narrowed in suspicion. "You wouldn't still be trying to get ahold of my medicine would you?"

"No, of course not," Phil lied.

Kip bought it. He said, "Sorry, but I gotta run. Been a long trip. I miss home. Sure, road gigs can be a laugh when you're young, but I'm ready to fly a desk. Settle down. Get married." Kip regarded Phil and said. "You've done okay for yourself. A nice wife who loves you. Couple of nice kids who don't hate you. You're doing fine. What kind of car you drive?"

"Car? I drove the Toyota here. Back home got a 'Vette."

"Ooh, sweet. I've seen photos. I think Glen Campbell drives one."

"Not anymore he doesn't."

"Oh, yeah. He's passed. I forgot. But hey, what're ya gonna do. Life goes on, right?"

"Some of us would prefer it goes on a little longer."

"I hear you. Some things never last long enough. The fiberglass helps."

"Huh?"

"Corvettes. No rust. Body lasts forever."

"Oh, yeah. But they're lousy in snow."

"That why you got the Toyota?"

"It's my wife's."

"Nice gal. Taylor tells me she's very smart."

"Smart enough not to drive a "Vette."

"You know, first time I came here Mount Rushmore was just a plain old untouched mountain. A virgin. Wasn't even called Mount Rushmore then."

Phil let Kip continue this nonsense for a couple of minutes — what else could he do suspended fifty feet above the ground? But as soon as they reached the bottom of the mountain Phil got back to business. He had a plan.

Phil stepped off the ride first. Then he offered Kip a helping hand.

"Thanks, man." Kip slid out of the moving chair. Then he noticed something across the way. "Hey, snack bar's open. You got any cash on you? I left my wallet in my other—" Kip stopped talking when he saw Phil's pistol pointed at him.

Phil said, "Sorry, but I'm afraid I must insist."

"Huh?"

"The crystal." Phil pointed to the bulge in Kip's pant pocket. If that's not a wallet, I think I know what it is.

Kip's shoulders dropped as he realized he'd been caught. Giving up, he said, "Take my word for it, Phil, you don't want this."

"You came here to save lives, right?"

"Yes," Kip looked puzzled. He obviously had no idea what Phil was getting at.

"And I imagine you'd be in big trouble if you were responsible for the death of a local, right?"

"You bet. I'd feel just awful."

Phil stepped back, several yards back, away from Kip and up a slight slope. He then put the pistol to his own head. The metal barrel felt cold against his temple.

"Holy cow!" Kip's jaw fell open. "What are you doing, Phil?"

"Just remember. You could have saved my life, but you refused to give me the crystal."

"Aw, geez, man."

"Tell my wife I loved her very much."

"No, no, no," Kip was apoplectic. He'd clearly never seen a being do anything like this before. "You can't do this. It's wrong. It's not worth it."

"And tell Taylor and Nate that their daddy loved them very, very much."

"Don't. You're making a big mistake."

"I'm going to count to three. One…"

"Okay, okay." Kip reached into his pants pocket. "But there's something you should know."

"Two…"

Kip pulled the rock out of his pocket. "Some beings have different reactions. Especially pale beings with low melanin levels."

Phil reached for the rock. But the moment his fingers wrapped around it, "Shit!" And he dropped the thing like the hot potato it felt like. "Motherfu—"

"I tried to warn you, man." Kip stepped up close to examine the redness on the palm of Phil's left hand. "Wow, I've never seen that happen before. Your epidermis must be super sensitive. You'll want an ointment. Maybe an unguent. Something greasy. Hey, that snack bar smells like it will have something."

But Phil was not listening. His attention was on the ground where he had dropped both the pistol and the crystal rock. Somehow, Phil had to pick up that rock, but how? Maybe if he wrapped his t-shirt around his hands…

Phil started to peel off his t-shirt. Meanwhile, Kip walked over to retrieve the rock. Phil yelled, "No, no, no, you don't. Just leave the stone where it is."

Kip pointed at the pistol that was lying in the nearby grass. "And what are you going to do to me if I don't? Shoot me?"

And that's when a deep, dark voice called out, "If he doesn't, I will."

The man was standing about ten yards away. Phil recognized him as the tow truck driver who had fixed the Toyota's flats. His name was Rupert Thatcher.

The man was dripping wet. He must have just come down the water slide. In his right hand he clutched a big revolver much like the one Phil had just dropped. Unlike with Phil, Thatcher looked like he would use his weapon. He cocked the hammer back and addressed Kip, "I don't know where your spaceship is parked, fella, but you're getting into it right now."

"Fine." Kip pointed to his medicinal rock lying in the grass. "But I'm not going anywhere without that."

Rupert Thatcher seemed unfazed by this stipulation. "Take it. I don't care. Just as long as I'm rid of you."

Phil was as speechless as he was helpless. He watched Kip pick up the magic rock.

Phil turned to Thatcher, "You idiot! You're letting him take the crystal?"

"Feller can take the towels and ash trays for all's I care, just as long as he doesn't take my Becky's honor."

Phil got it now. He said to the man, "You're that girl's father. Rebecca. You're afraid she'll sleep with him."

"She's been waiting," Thatcher waved the gun at Kip. "Waiting for this here fella. I'm here to make sure she keeps on waiting."

"And I must say I was flattered." Kip, smiled, his teeth shining bright as the white Wyoming clouds. "Lovely girl. Excellent cook. We spent a beautiful evening together."

"Uh... that's enough, Kip." Phil was trying to save the poor sap.

But Kip was on a roll, "We had quite a groovy time. Just the two of us. Alone in the barn. She made a comfy bed in the straw. Brought me dinner. A few glasses of cider. Potatoes with chives. Carrots with dill. But the best part came when she let me taste her pie."

That was all Rupert Thatcher needed to hear. The knuckles of his fingers turned white as he tightened them around the pistol's bone handle and squeezed the trigger.

Phil dove. He didn't understand why he dove. He just dove. It was a dumb thing to do. If he'd had time to think about it, he'd have let the outraged father shoot the space alien and solve everybody's problem. But no, Phil did the honorable thing. He dove at Rupert Thatcher's gun hand. Why? Habit, most likely. Or maybe he'd seen too many action movies. Whatever the reason, Phil succeeded in knocking the big man's thick forearm aside and throw off his aim. Just a smidge. But it was enough. The bullet missed its intended target.

And it hit Phil.

Phil fell to the ground. No pain at first. Then a whole lot of pain. So much pain Phil had to shut his eyes tight. His chest was on fire. He heard somebody's feet run up beside him.

"Hurts, huh?"

Phil opened his eyes to see Kip kneeling over him.

Kip continued, "I remember the feeling. Don't move. It just makes it worse."

Phil tried to speak. He wanted to shout, *Look out*. Because standing behind Kip Rupert Thatcher was raising his pistol for a second shot at the space alien. The man who, in his thoughts, had so obviously deflowered his daughter.

"Don't shoot," someone screamed. This time it was a woman's voice.

Phil turned his head to see Taylor, his very own darling daughter, running this way from the water slide. Aw, this was cute. She obviously wanted to save her friend, Kip, the young space alien she's been hanging with.

"You'll hit Daddy," she screamed.

Phil smiled. He watched his little girl, the bravest young woman in the universe, run up behind the big fat auto mechanic and swing her little size-eight sandal-clad right foot like an NFL place kicker square between Rupert Thatcher's tree-stump legs. She didn't knock the big guy off his feet, of course, but she certainly ruined his day. And his aim.

The bullet missed its intended target, Kip, and chipped a small divot out of the lawn just a few inches from Phil's head.

Rupert Thatcher never got off a third shot. While he was bent over holding his aching crotch the town cop, Dagleish, came leaping out of nowhere and grabbed him. Apparently, choke holds are still legal in this little town. Maybe small towns aren't so bad after all.

Phil felt safe now. He felt at peace. The pain in his chest was easing. He could probably go to sleep now. So, he closed his eyes.

But he didn't go to sleep. He felt someone's hot breath on his neck. It didn't feel like Taylor. Nor did it smell like her. Didn't smell like Carol either. She was probably too pissed at him to bother kissing him goodnight. Or goodbye. But someone was about to kiss him.

Kip whispered, "I'm not supposed to do this. Don't tell anyone, okay?"

Huh? What did this goofy space alien have in mind? The space guy couldn't be gay, could he? If he is, the joke will certainly be on Taylor and Becky. And on Rupert Thatcher.

Phil managed to force one eye open in time to see Kip place his magical crystal rock lightly against his chest.

Once again, the thing burned like hell. And once again Phil cried out in pain. His cries included a word — he didn't know what word. Then he heard a familiar voice from the crowd call out.

"*Motherfucker*," Nate yelled. "Dad said *motherfucker*. He's gonna be all right." Nate's happy, jubilant announcement was the last sound Phil heard before he passed out.

CHAPTER TWENTY-FIVE

The four American Presidents gazed down from their granite mantelpiece atop Mount Rushmore as if to say, *Check us out, pal. Here's the closest thing anyone's ever going to get to immortality.*

Phil turned to his son, "Amazing how thousands of years of wind erosion could do something like this."

Nate laughed. "Good one, Dad."

Phil tousled his boy's head and thought about how his own father had fed him this old line, and now he's telling it to Nate. And one day Nate will pass it along to his children. And so on and so on. Etcetera, etcetera. For ever and ever, amen. Now, that's immortality. A good joke never dies.

Phil turned away from the stone faces. "Better head back. Don't want to miss the bus."

"Don't worry," said Nate. "It's not going anywhere without you."

Nate was right. The passengers will have to wait for Phil — he's their driver.

For the past week Phil has been using the town's old yellow school bus to take his friends and neighbors out on day trips like this one. On their first outing, he drove of bunch to the Little Bighorn

River up in Montana to see where General Custer lost his final argument with the Indians. That excursion was going along just fine until a park ranger referred to Custer's fight as The Battle of the Little Bighorn. Upon hearing this, Jasper Teasdale got himself all in a tizzy and corrected the ranger, insisting that the fight was actually called The Battle of the Greasy Grass. Jasper went on to explain that he knew this for a fact because his younger brother, Theodore, had served in the 7th Cavalry with Custer and had subsequently lost his life right here on these very hallowed battle grounds of Greasy Grass.

Your brother? the confused ranger's raised eyebrows asked silently.

Phil quickly stepped in and explained to the puzzled ranger that Jasper's brother was a re-enactor, a military buff who takes part in famous battle re-enactments including the Custer re-enactment held here every summer. The ranger bought Phil's story, but it was a close call. Phil has since warned his tour passengers that, unless they want to be considered clinically insane, they must think twice about what they say in public.

Of course, Phil has no right to lecture anyone about thinking twice. If he'd put a little more thought into his own words and actions, Carol would be with him today. But she isn't. And maybe she never will be with him again.

Yes, she finally left him. This morning. After breakfast. Knowing that Phil now has this school bus for his own use, she felt free to toss her bags into the Toyota and drive it home to Chicago.

She claims she just wants some time to herself, time to think things over. Of course, the main thing she wants to think over is, Does she really want to stay hooked up to an idiot who would point a loaded rifle at her. Phil has explained over and over that the buffalo gun wasn't loaded, it was just a bluff, a ploy to show everybody that he meant business. But Carol won't buy it. She says he went too far. And as usual, she's right.

Taylor went along with her mom to help with the drive. Nate voted to stay back with his old man, not so much out of any misplaced loyalty but because the boy really wanted to see Mount Rushmore. And now Phil is walking down the national monument's Avenue of Flags with the flags of every state waving a colorful *so long idiot* to him on Carol's behalf.

Phil sighed a big lungful of hot, dry South Dakota air and thought about how healthy his chest felt. No pain at all. And almost no scar, Yet it's been only a week since Rupert Thatcher's bullet had passed through it, narrowly missing his heart. Amazing stuff, that medicine Kip had rubbed on him — easily the greatest pharmaceutical discovery in the history of humankind. It's a crying shame humankind will never hear a word about it. Granted, Kip hasn't taken the miracle rosin away yet, but he will any day now. And there's nothing Phil can do about it. Or nothing Phil *is willing* to do. Not to a nice space alien like Kip.

And that's another reason Carol has taken off — she doesn't believe Kip is an extra-terrestrial. And she thinks anyone who does believe in extra-terrestrials is crazy. Same goes for anyone who believes that these townsfolk are two hundred years old. It's got to be a scam. And as for Phil's amazing recovery from the bullet wound, Carol puts that down to Doc Milburn and the curative power of auto-suggestion. For true believers, a mind can be a powerful healer. Even a mind like Phil's.

Ironically enough, Carol's skeptical outlook on life was one of the things that first attracted him to her. That and her great shape. And her beautiful face. And her quick wit. Her sweetness and honesty. Her capacity for forgiveness...

Aw, shit. Phil turned around to the huge chiseled stone faces looking down on him from the granite mountainside and made a pledge to the rock-jawed sour pusses: *For once in my life I, Phil Hodworth, am going to succeed at selling something besides ginseng car wax and ginseng-flavored toilet bowl cleaner. One way or another I am going to sell my wife on the idea that she is making a huge mistake, that her dumb husband is truly sorry and worth granting a second chance.*

"She won't buy it," a familiar male voice said.

Phil turned to see Kip walking toward him. A few yards beyond Kip, Rebecca Thatcher was walking away, on her way back to the town bus.

"She won't buy what?" Phil asked.

"That I'm gay."

Phil had to laugh. "Let me get this straight — Rebecca will buy that you are from another planet, but she won't buy that you are gay."

"I guess some things are harder to sell than others."

Young Nate looked up at Kip and asked, "So are you?"

"Am I what?"

"Gay."

"Not so I've noticed. But what else could I do — tell her she's not my type? That would be terrible. She'd feel awful. So I told her I prefer dudes."

Phil noticed a glaring contradiction here. "I thought you people didn't know how to lie."

"Yeah, well... you folks have taught me a lot."

"You're welcome," said Nate.

Kip smiled a big, sly grin as a second thought occurred to him, "But you know who *is* my type?"

Phil was ahead of him on this one. "My daughter."

Kip nodded a big, bold *yes*. "Smart. Pretty. Assertive. Not afraid to speak her mind. You know, if circumstances were different and I was able to stick around..." He mulled this delightful thought over for a moment before finishing with, "But no. Gotta run."

Nate asked, "When's your ride coming?"

"Soon, little man, very soon. No muss, no fuss. I shall simply disappear. Ride off into the sunset."

Phil added, "Who was that masked man?"

Kip caught the reference. "*A cloud of dust and a hardy Hi Ho Silver!* Don't ya love that show."

"Hey, Nate!" A little girl came running out from the washroom area. It was Nate's young friend Eunice. She grabbed Nate's hand. "Just heard someone talking. There's a trail. Goes all the way up the mountain. We can get a closer look, see right up their noses. C'mon."

Nate looked to his father for permission to run off. Phil understood his son's plea — she was a pretty little thing — but Phil knew the little girl just wanted to get away from the crowd so she could light up a cigarette. Or a joint. "Sorry, kids, the bus is leaving."

Phil turned to march everybody back to the main gate. But he soon noticed Kip was not joining the parade — the space alien was hanging back, staring up at the mountain sculpture. "You coming along?" Phil urged.

"You know..." Kip kept his eyes fixed on the stone faces. "Back where I come from, we would never do something like this."

Phil understood. "Too much respect for the beauty of the natural landscape?"

"Too little respect for politicians. Sure, we might carve someone's face up there. A great scientist. A philanthropist. Maybe an artist or a musician or..." Kip suddenly got an inspiration. "Hey, you know who would be great up there?"

Phil was ahead of him. "Glen Campbell?"

Kip started singing, *"I am a lineman for the county."*

Phil chuckled. "I think I'd like your planet. How about taking me and Nate back with you?"

But Nate saw a flaw in this idea. "What about Mom and Taylor?"

"You never know, son — the ladies might have other plans." For Nate's sake Phil tried to sound like he was joking.

But Kip understood. He put a reassuring hand on Phil's shoulder. "Don't worry, man. She's coming back."

"I'm sure you're right." Phil tried to sound optimistic. "A couple days to think things over and she'll see the light."

"No, I mean *now*." Kip pointed to the roadway out front. "Isn't that her car?"

Phil had to shield his eyes from the sun to see it, but yes — a red four-door sedan had pulled off the main highway and was coming this way down the entrance drive. But was it Carol's car? At this distance he couldn't tell.

"Go ahead," Kip said. "I'll watch the young 'uns."

Phil took off. He ran past the café, past the gift shop, and across the mall. He scooted out the main gate, flew down the steps, and weaved a saw-toothed path through the tourists on the sidewalk.

Ignoring the nods and smiles of his friends waiting for him by the town's yellow school bus, Phil continued out onto the roadway. He jogged along the hot asphalt toward the entrance to the parking garage. And as he ran he begged. And he bargained. And he conjectured. *Has she changed her mind? Has a few hours away from her idiot husband been enough? Has she convinced herself to give the moron a second chance? Hey, maybe Taylor has put in a good word for her dad. Why not? Taylor always thought well of her old man. Hell, she kicked a guy in the nuts for him.*

By the time Phil reached the entrance to the garage he was close enough to the red Toyota to see the dealer sticker. It was from Chicago, the dealership where the salesman's toupee was so obvious Carol said it could be spotted by Google Earth. That line made Phil laugh then, and it made him laugh now. Especially now.

A hand extended out the driver's side window and pushed the button for the lift-gate ticket. It was a woman's hand, but it wasn't Carol's hand — it had fake nails. Carol never wears fake anything. Must be Taylor's hand. Yeah, that made sense. The kid's been trying to log some practice time behind the wheel, and Carol is a patient instructor. Much more patient than Phil is. He finds his daughter's driving style too aggressive. Her foot is heavy on the gas pedal. Like she's kicking a guy in the nuts.

Phil reached out to tap the rear bumper. But he was too late. The car leapt forward through the open gate and into the garage. Yes, that was Taylor at the wheel, all right.

He chased the vehicle into the cool darkness of the multi-level garage. "Hey! Taylor! Stop! It's me!" Phil's words bounced off the concrete walls and clattered along the cement floor like bowling balls careening down an alley. But they hit their target. The car stopped. Taylor stuck her head out the window. "It's Dad," she announced.

Phil yanked the rear door open and spilled his sweaty self across the back seat, soaking into the upholstery like a bad stain. He'd made up his mind. This vehicle was not leaving this garage without him.

From her seat up front Carol wasted no time with *Missed ya, handsome.* "Taylor wants to say goodbye to Kip," she said.

"Bullshit," Taylor suggested from the driver's seat.

Carol corrected her daughter. "You said you regretted not bidding him a proper goodbye. You thought you'd offended him."

"That's not why we're here, Mom, and you know it." Taylor looked up at the rearview mirror to catch her father's eye. "Believe me, Dad, I'm not worried about Kip. She's welcome to him."

"*She?*" Phil asked.

"Becky Thatcher," Carol answered for her daughter.

"I didn't mind playing along with the *Mork and Mindy* bit for a while," Taylor said. "I thought the whole space alien routine was kind of cute. But geez, poor Becky, I think that chick actually believes him."

Phil looked at the two strong, no-nonsense women sitting side-by-side up front, and he had to laugh. "You two... two peas in a pod."

Taylor pointed to her mother with a hitchhiker's thumb. "Well, this pea has no intention of leaving the pod, believe me. She just wants to teach the daddy pea a lesson. But she won't admit it."

Phil pulled himself up close behind his wife's creamy vanilla neck and kissed it. "I'm sorry, honey. I lost my head. That was a dumb move. I never should have pointed that gun at you, loaded or unloaded. I was a jerk. But I've always been a jerk — shouldn't I get points for consistency?" He kissed her neck again. "It's good to be dependable. I love you, and I'll always love you. You can depend on it." He went in for one more smooch, this time a big wet kiss on her ear, but he never made it. His soppy passion was blown to dry dust by the blast of an automobile horn.

Phil turned around to see a pickup truck sitting behind him. A big diesel brute. The driver raised both his hands off his steering wheel to signal his immense frustration with this silly little family sedan that was blocking his way.

Phil gave the guy a cheery thumbs-up and flashed him a we'll-get-right-on-it-pardner smile.

Phil was in a gentle, loving mood. The truck driver was not. He honked again. This time longer and somehow louder.

Taylor stuck her head out her window. "Hold your bladder, cowboy. The stone presidents aren't going anywhere." She shifted her car into gear. But before her wheels had a chance to follow her orders, the truck driver pulled out and around her.

As he passed by, the guy flipped Taylor his finger.

Without missing a beat, the three Hodworths flipped him back, their middle fingers extending in perfect unison like three little pink legs of a rude synchronized swimming team.

"This is what family is all about," Phil said, his finger still raised at full attention. "Doing stuff together."

Taylor laughed. And Carol laughed. And that was all Phil needed to hear.

Taylor never did park the car that afternoon. Instead, she and her mom continued on back to the Shamrock Motor Court to wait for Phil and Nate.

Next morning, while the Irish waitress was spilling breakfast, the Hodworth family had a visit from Becky Thatcher. The young woman dropped by the Shamrock Pub to tell them that Kip had finally left town. Apparently, he had disappeared from her barn sometime during the night. He had been staying in the barn, this time, with the full approval of Becky's father, the only person in town who seems to have bought the story about Kip being gay.

After breakfast Phil and Carol had a quick visit with Mayor Sam Beckwith to say goodbye. Then the Hodworth family headed back to Chicago.

At the end of the summer Phil and Carol received a check from Mayor Sam for the town's purchase of Shangri-La Gardens. Phil tried to donate the funds back to the town, but Mayor Sam wouldn't have it. He said the community was soon going to be wealthy thanks to the valley's sizeable deposits of rare earth, a mineral lode which Crazy Lucas had discovered a hundred years ago but had always thought was worthless. Crazy has since learned that the stuff is a valuable component in smart phones. He learned this, of course, from his hated internet.

Phil and Carol still wanted to do something meaningful with their inheritance money. So they chartered a plane and took a load of the townsfolk on their very first airplane ride. Carol called the excursion The Zachariah Mossip Memorial Tour. For a destination she chose Disneyland.

Everyone agreed it was darn shame young Zack wasn't around to join the fun. If that impetuous kid had hung on just a little bit longer he would have lived to enjoy Adventureland, Fantasyland, and Frontierland.

And most important, Tomorrowland.

THE END

ABOUT THE AUTHOR

Richard Adamson has worked as a scriptwriter/story editor on several U.S./Canadian TV series, a script doctor for film and Broadway productions, and a contracted freelancer for such diverse talents as David Letterman and Yakov Smirnoff. Previous to writing professionally, Adamson earned his living in Toronto as a jazz pianist.

NOTE FROM
THE AUTHOR

Word-of-mouth is crucial for any author to succeed. If you enjoyed *Wake the Neighbors*, please leave a review online—anywhere you are able. Even if it's just a sentence or two. It would make all the difference and would be very much appreciated.

Thanks!
Richard Adamson

We hope you enjoyed reading this title from:

www.blackrosewriting.com

Subscribe to our mailing list – *The Rosevine* – and receive **FREE** books, daily deals, and stay current with news about upcoming releases and our hottest authors.
Scan the QR code below to sign up.

Already a subscriber? Please accept a sincere thank you for being a fan of Black Rose Writing authors.

View other Black Rose Writing titles at
www.blackrosewriting.com/books and use promo code
PRINT to receive a **20% discount** when purchasing.

www.ingramcontent.com/pod-product-compliance
Lightning Source LLC
Chambersburg PA
CBHW02134513 0726
47899CB00019B/3248